MW01225262

ROGUE
HARVEST

DANITA MASLAN
introduction by ROBERT J. SAWYER

Robert J.
SAWYER
BOOKS

Copyright © 2005 Danita Maslankowski
Published in the United States in 2006
5 4 3 2 1

All rights reserved. No part of this publication may be reproduced, stored in a retrieval system or transmitted, in any form or by any means, without the prior written permission of Red Deer Press or, in case of photocopying or other reprographic copying, a licence from Access Copyright (Canadian Copyright Licensing Agency), 1 Yonge Street, Suite 1900, Toronto, ON M5E 1E5, fax (416) 868-1621.

ROBERT J. SAWYER BOOKS ARE PUBLISHED BY
Red Deer Press
Trailer C
2500 University Drive N.W.
Calgary Alberta Canada T2N 1N4
www.reddeerpress.com

CREDITS
Edited for the Press by Robert J. Sawyer
Cover and text design by Erin Woodward
Cover images courtesy Corbis and iStock
Printed and bound in Canada by Friesens for Red Deer Press

ACKNOWLEDGMENTS
Financial support provided by the Canada Council, the Government of Canada through the Book Publishing Industry Development Program (BPIDP), the Alberta Foundation for the Arts, a beneficiary of the Lottery Fund of the Government of Alberta, and the University of Calgary.

THE CANADA COUNCIL | LE CONSEIL DES ARTS
FOR THE ARTS | DU CANADA
SINCE 1957 | DEPUIS 1957

NATIONAL LIBRARY OF CANADA CATALOGUING IN PUBLICATION
Maslan, Danita
Rogue harvest / Danita Maslan ; introduction by Robert J. Sawyer.
ISBN 0-88995-329-5
I. Title.
PS8626.A7985R69 2005   C813'.6   C2005-903918-3

★ ★ D E D I C A T I O N ★ ★

This novel is dedicated to the memory of Robyn Herrington. She would have been my biggest fan and remains my biggest inspiration.

∗ ∗ A C K N O W L E D G M E N T S ∗ ∗

In some cultures it takes a whole village to raise a child. In this case it took a whole writing community to raise a first novel. My deepest gratitude goes to the members of IFWA (the Imaginative Fiction Writers' Association), its satellite group, Seven of Forty, and the marathon critiquers: Robyn Herrington, Randy McCharles, Sandy Fitzpatrick, Tannis Ewing, Tony King and Katie Harse.

Thanks also to the many writers I've met over the years who, either through lengthy and intense discussion or short words of encouragement, have made this journey less fraught with terror.

My thanks must go to Robert J. Sawyer in particular for his astute advice and constant encouragement as a writer and as an editor who hasn't let me get away with anything, well at least not much.

My willingness to tackle writing a novel, I owe in large part to my parents: my father who showed by example that you should follow your dreams and my mother for passing on her love of the written word and for her constant support and friendship.

Descriptions of the rain forest are based on my own travels to the tropics as well as on the works of two pioneers of the rainforest canopy, Mark W. Moffett's *The High Frontier* and Donald Perry's *Life Above the Jungle Floor*. The writings of Adrian Forsyth and Ken Miyata, Tropical *Nature: Life and Death in the Rain Forests of Central and South America*, have also helped to flesh out the novel.

If after reading this novel, the setting fascinates you at all, put this book down and get out there. The present-day world is full of wonders as enthralling as any fiction. Happy travels.

✶ ✶ F O R E W O R D ✶ ✶

by Robert J. Sawyer

In February 2004, Danita Maslankowski—that's her full name, by the way—was in the audience for a keynote address I gave at Mount Royal College in Calgary, where she lives. The conference, organized by Dr. Randy Schroeder, was about "Science Fiction and Social Change." In my speech, I fretted that science fiction perhaps pulled in opposite directions so much that any message one author had was canceled out by what another said.

I didn't use the following example in my talk because neither book had yet been published, but later that year two of SF's heaviest hitters came up to the plate to confront the state of our environment. First was Kim Stanley Robinson—definitely a southpaw on the political spectrum—who hit one out of the park with *Forty Signs of Rain,* a spirited warning about rising temperatures.

Michael Crichton countered with *State of Fear,* telling us that the evidence for global warming was trumped-up, and that the whole environmental movement was way off track. (Fittingly, Robinson's book was a June title, arriving on the shelves at the beginning of summer, while Crichton's offering was a December title, coming out in the midst of one of the coldest winters in recent memory.)

The existence of these two blockbusters underscores that the environment is at the front of a lot of people's minds these days—but, sadly, taken together, *Forty Signs of Rain* and *State of Fear* cancel each other out: a pair of bestsellers carrying equal but opposite charges, resulting, I suspect, in no net societal change.

But maybe that's where this book, *Rogue Harvest,* comes in. It's a passionate ecological thriller, providing a third perspective—not a neutral middle ground, but one that shears away at right angles from the current polarized debate, taking our thinking in new directions by predicting both environmental collapse *and* environmental salvation.

Certainly, as a small-press title, *Rogue Harvest* will likely never have the sales of either Robinson's or Crichton's book (although I'd argue vociferously that it's as good as the former in literary terms and infinitely better than the latter). But I dearly hope it *does* have an impact; despite what I said in Calgary, perhaps when the big guys cancel each other out, maybe there *is* room for a smaller player to get an important message through.

I first met Danita on July 17, 1996—and, on that same day, I also first met the characters in this novel. I'd been invited to Calgary by a group called the Imaginative Fiction Writers' Association to facilitate an intensive two-day writing workshop. Danita was one of ten participants in that workshop, and, with this book, becomes the sixth to subsequently be professionally published. The piece Danita was workshopping, "The Invisible City," was a portion of this novel, a work that she developed slowly and carefully over the next seven years, aided by members of IFWA.

When Dennis Johnson, the publisher of Red Deer Press, asked me to create an SF line for him, I immediately knew that I'd end up publishing some of the writers I'd worked with back in 1996 under our new imprint; Danita is the first, but I doubt she'll be the last. I told Dennis up front that I wanted to publish novels that are *about* something, that are thematically important, that turn our preconceptions upside down, that change the way we look at the world. I firmly believe *Rogue Harvest* does all those things.

But *Rogue Harvest* also does what all good fiction must: it tells an engaging, moving story about memorable characters we care deeply about. So, yes, read it and enjoy—but also *think* . . . for it's not just this book that's in your hands. It's the future, too.

* * O N E * *

It was panic that killed Martin Yit.

He had very nearly gotten away from them when he bolted into a blind alley rather than along a street.

Jasmine knew every blind alley in the Core. She'd grown up on these streets. She would have died there if she hadn't run into a man who took her in, who let her anger and self-disgust wash over him till it spilled out of her entirely. He'd filled the void with hope and with laughter. That was all gone.

The man who ran from her had shattered her life for the sake of a political struggle Jasmine hadn't known about and didn't care about.

Jasmine and Mane ducked off the lit city sidewalk to follow him. Her eyes stayed on her target. Months of preparation for this day now cleared her mind of any thoughts other than catching the man who had killed her father.

She lifted her feet higher as she ran to avoid stumbling over the debris littering the narrow trench between buildings. Their shadows were long black fingers reaching in front of Jasmine and Mane in the near darkness. Mane, with his long legs, drew ahead of her. He was close enough to fire his tripline. As Yit went down, his legs in a tangle of thin cable, Mane stopped and stood aside to let Jasmine pass by. Yit rose to his feet again in seconds and worked to free himself. He started to run.

It had taken too long to identify him—too long to get this close to him. Jasmine sprinted after him and when she was close enough, leapt onto him, flattening him to the ground. She let go just enough to let him turn to face her. Yit stopped struggling when he felt the spiker at his throat. He moved his hands slowly to a position behind his head and tried to appear as harmless as he could. He didn't recognize her in her Core Rat clothes.

"If you want money . . . " he gasped.

Jasmine grimly whispered, "No."

His face showed confusion as, still straddling him, she moved the spiker to a spot just below his sternum and angled it up. She paused for a moment to catch her breath, then Jasmine spoke the words she'd so carefully chosen.

"Martin Yit, the courts have held you and found you blameless. I judge you now and I won't be bought. For the murder of Owen Lamberin, I, Jasmine Melanie Rochelle, find you guilty."

Yit's recognition turned to panic. Jasmine's thumb found the firing button and before he could squirm out from under her, the spiker jolted in her hands. Ten centimeters of sharpened metal cut through his heart. Jasmine stood and took a stumbling step back because he wasn't dead— he was staring at her. Had she missed? She'd practiced with the spiker until her arms were numb. A spike in the heart was supposed to—

"He'll be gone in a minute," Mane's quiet voice rumbled as she turned away.

Jasmine shook out her arms and looked at her gloved hands, realizing she'd probably left her mark on him. Hair, a few flakes of dandruff, spit from her little speech. It would be enough. She hadn't thought this through—evidence remained.

When she looked back, Mane splashed Yit with an acrid-smelling fluid and put his hand out for the spiker handle. She gave it to him. Mane placed it on the dead man's chest and set flame to him. Jasmine turned away once more. Yellow light flickered on the walls. The fire wouldn't destroy the body but it would destroy any trace of her.

Mane took her by the arm and led her out of the alley. They walked for several blocks down the night street. Jasmine hadn't thought beyond the death of Martin Yit. The outrage and hatred had nothing to focus on now and time spread out before her like an open pit, Jasmine standing frozen on the edge. She finally gave in to the dizziness and made for the alcove of a storefront doorway to sit on the step. She put her head on her knees, hugged her legs, and deep breaths became sobs without tears. She struggled to control her emotions.

"Hey." Mane crouched in front of her.

Jasmine looked up into his eyes for a moment. She spoke through the constriction in her throat. "The bastard deserved it. Why am I fractured over this?"

"Don't know, Doll." Mane stood and surveyed the street. He leaned against the edge of the storefront window and just waited. Jasmine had an urge to run and catch the next rail out of the city but that wasn't the plan. She couldn't afford to be seen as avoiding the investigation that would follow. She had to stick to the plan. Jasmine looked up at him.

"I thought you were only in this for the hunt, not the kill," she said, accusing him, she didn't know of what.

He shrugged without looking at her.

"I appreciate the help," she added and stood, "but I'm not paying you extra for it."

Mane's burst of laughter caught her by surprise because it was the first time she'd made him laugh and he sounded like he really meant it.

"Back to the den?" he asked as she stepped beside him. "No, need to be around people," he said when she didn't answer. "Let's go to the virtual dome. This time of night there's so many people there you can't move but go with the crowd." His eyes twinkled but she just stared at him. "Not that many people. We could use a drink," he said for her. "Say no more, come with me."

After walking a few more blocks, Jasmine followed him into a small bar. It had a long counter, eight battered tables and lots of dark corners. It was the kind of place where people came in the door looking for trade as much as for drink.

Half a dozen people sat at tables and leaned against the bar and, as Jasmine and Mane walked in, everyone's attention focused on Mane, the tall young man with the flowing hair. No one noticed the small dark-haired woman behind him. Jasmine enjoyed the anonymity. Mane left her at the table and went to get drinks. She pretended to look around but let her mind wander.

It took a physical effort to stay in her chair. Shouldn't they be running? That had always been the best part when she really had been a Core Rat. The running was a physical release after hours of planning and doing the actual job, whether it was stealing, running street scams, or dealing in illegals.

The clunk of glasses startled her and she glanced up. Mane took a seat beside her by lifting a leg over the back of the chair. Jasmine just looked at her glass. Mane held his up.

"To Owen Lamberin?" he suggested.

"To Owen Lamberin," she agreed and raised her glass. They each took a sip.

"What now, boss?" he asked.

"Now we get drunk."

"Hmm," he grunted and gave her a sidelong glance.

He was right. Jasmine never got drunk. She shrugged. Mane glanced at her once more, got no response, and sat back in his chair, turning it a bit to get a better view of the room.

Jasmine let the beer linger, savoring it before she swallowed. Little by little she let herself remember the chase. When she remembered the recognition in Yit's eyes she waited for a sense of satisfaction.

Nothing.

It would come. Once the adrenalin was gone there would be peace and her life would be the way . . . no. How could it ever be the way it was? Then she felt a dread so fierce she drained her glass to bring herself back to the table she sat at, to Mane who sat beside her. She tried to concentrate on what Mane was saying. The best she could do was to stop thinking altogether while he chatted to her about things she didn't hear until she could at last focus her thoughts on him; on that friendly face framed by a thick mass of red-gold hair.

The more time she spent with him, the more he baffled her. When Jasmine had decided to go back to the streets to find her father's killer, she'd been away for eight years. She knew she needed help. She spent most of what her father had left her on bribes and to hire Mane. He was a mercenary who pretended, very well, to be an investigator. Yet she couldn't help liking him. He was charming, supportive, and extremely competent at dealing with Core street games. She felt safe with him.

"Mane?"

"Mmm?"

"Why'd you help with the . . . at the end?"

He looked at her, then, seemed offended. "Think you're the only person on the planet who thinks what that guy did deserves punishment?" He turned back to his perusal of the room. "Besides, somebody had to bring the lighter."

"Thanks."

He shrugged. After a moment he turned to her. "What are you going to do now?"

She stared at him. A hired investigator wasn't supposed to care about his clients after the job. "Dunno." She looked at her glass and felt like she was falling. There was nothing to catch her. Owen Lamberin was gone— her adopted brother hated her for going back to the Core. If she told her school friends what she'd been doing while she'd walked out on her classes. . . . She had nothing left. Martin Yit had left her with nothing and she could only kill him once.

"'Kay?" Mane asked.

"No. Are you?" she snapped.

He shrugged and let his gaze wander to the door. Mane took a sip from his glass, his eyes following a woman who'd just walked in. She sauntered to the counter, ordered a drink and looked around. Her eyes rested on Mane and he smiled at her.

"There's Manda. Be right back," he said, rising and taking his drink with him.

Of course he knew every street trader in the Core. Jasmine knew from experience it made sense to know all the players. As she expected, Mane had the woman laughing in six seconds. Jasmine had taken to timing him. His height and big build scared most people, until he opened his mouth. He could get people laughing more quickly than anyone she knew. She'd miss him.

Jasmine saw him hook his thumb in her direction. Manda glanced at her and shook her head. They continued their conversation and Jasmine tried not to stare at Manda. She was a patch job; patching or popping too many of the chemicals she traded. That was one trap of Core life Jasmine had never fallen into. No matter how self-destructive she got, she never liked the loss of emotional control that came with patching.

It seemed Mane had finally convinced Manda to join them. Jasmine gave her a bow of the head as Manda took up a position opposite her. Jasmine could tell she was being purposely kept in Manda's direct line of sight. A lot of Core Rats loved the paranoia—went with the image.

Mane's voice grew low and quiet. "Manda's got some Green. Thought we might like to sow it."

"What have you got?" Jasmine asked, stalling while she tried to think what the benefits might be from peddling illegal natural drugs.

"All the most potent recs." Manda sniffed deeply and took a swallow from her glass. "Then there's this Green called veejix—a spec buy. As a euphoric it's power of zero but the guy told me it was endangered and would grow me rich beyond—"

"You mean VJX?" Jasmine asked. She'd heard Adrien talk about it with regret that it was illegal Green, but it sounded like he had a use for it. Eventually, she'd have to tell him she'd gone after their father's killer. She could use a peace offering.

"Know what it is?" Manda asked.

"A mild euphoric but mostly they use it for some kind of medical research."

"Aw, frass, did I go extinction on that one. Medical shit. That's all I need."

"How much you got?"

Manda squinted with concentration. "Point three k, far as I remember." Her expression brightened. "Want it?"

"How much?"

"Six hundred dollars."

Jasmine prepared to haggle the price down when Mane said, "She'll take it," and looked at Jasmine as if he'd done her a favor. She had to admit she had no idea what it was really worth and for some reason she trusted Mane.

Manda turned her attention to Mane. "H'bout you? Need anything?"

"No thanks."

"Got some—"

His raised hands stopped her. Manda shrugged, then a potential customer caught her eye. "Crown the trade tomorrow at twenty." She rose and left without another word.

"Why'd you make it so easy for her?" Jasmine whispered.

"Know what she paid for it. She's giving it to you at cost."

"Oh." She didn't know what else to say. The world was tossing her wherever it wanted. "I assume she's got a trading spot?"

"Yeah, I'll take you out there."

⋆ ⋆ T W O ⋆ ⋆

The rail car stopped and the door latch clicked open. Mane unfolded himself from the two-passenger pod to stand on the platform. Jasmine followed. She'd been surprised when Mane assumed he was invited to come with her to see Adrien. Then she imagined walking the halls of Adrien's immaculate clinic with her large, street trading companion. The shocked stares of Adrien's co-workers would be worth it. She felt a little betrayed when Mane met her dressed in cotton shirt and pants with a hemp jacket, rather than the false fur and leathers she usually saw him in. She couldn't imagine what use he'd normally have for the clothes he wore now. In her fur bolero and false leather balloon pants, Jasmine looked more the street trader than he did. She wasn't even sure Adrien would see her, and if she embarrassed him by looking like a Core Rat, it could only make her feel better.

The clinic was part of a larger building shorn off at the eighth floor the way so many outside the city Core were. The shortening of old buildings let the sun in while the removal of others had made room for green patches.

Once inside, Jasmine stopped at the end of the hall and stared at the reception panel. It greeted her and asked who she was there to see five times before Jasmine finally took a breath and answered.

"Adrien Lamberin," she said.

"Who may I say is calling?" the mechanical voice enquired.

"It's a surprise."

"No one by that name is on the admittance list. You do not have an appointment. Would you like to speak with Dr. Lamberin?"

"Yes."

The screen wavered and a laboratory came into view. She heard Adrien's voice. She froze.

"It's the dosage that's going to be the key factor," he was saying. "Hold on. I have to get this."

As Adrien turned to her, his eyes widened. "My God, Jas." He paused as he took her in and noticed Mane behind her. "Why didn't you say it was you? Have Linda send you through." He showed no sign of anger.

Adrien reached for the entry release and the screen faded while a door unlatched beside the reception panel. Jasmine and Mane walked through to an office area that was a hub for the activity generated behind the doors that led from it. The woman who kept it all running smoothly sat behind a semi-circular desk. Linda looked up and smiled with cautious recognition.

"Jasmine." She took in the street clothes. "We haven't seen you for a while."

Jasmine winced a smile and said, "Been pretty busy."

"Adrien is in the process of extricating himself from a meeting. He'll be right with you." Her eyes hesitated on Mane and she seemed unsure whether to ask about him.

Mane took that as a cue and leaned over to talk to her in a loud whisper. "Unexpected guests are such a bother, aren't they?"

Linda laughed. "Not at all."

Jasmine tried not to stare as Mane smiled back at Linda. Did she really hear him say 'such a bother'? Mane? She noticed now he not only spoke differently, but he'd lost his street swagger. She watched him, uneasy. Where would a twenty-some-odd Core Rat pick up manners?

"Adrien's in his office now." Linda's voice intruded into Jasmine's speculations.

"Thanks," Jasmine mumbled and led Mane through a maze of doors and halls to find Adrien's office.

The door was already open and the first thing she saw was Adrien pacing. He looked over as soon as he heard footsteps, focused on Jasmine, ignoring Mane. There was so much pain and betrayal in his eyes, she wanted to turn away.

He choked out, "Jas?" and invited her into his arms. He held on to her with such intensity she had to fight back tears.

"I thought I'd lost you too," he said in a voice thick with pain. He finally released her to look into her face as if to be sure she was actually standing in front of him. Jasmine found herself speechless with relief.

"You could have called." His voice hardened. "I've really needed a friend since Dad died."

Jasmine took a step back. "The last words you said to me were 'get the hell out of here.'"

He glared for a moment. "That's just an excuse." Then, more softly, he said, "There's still all of Dad's things to go through and you just disappear. Isn't this kind of disaster supposed to bring family together? Why did ours fall apart?"

"You left before I did. You just called it going to work."

"You can't blame me for getting tired of your constant angry outbursts. I was trying to grieve and all you could think about was your own anger and telling the police how to do their jobs."

"This the same conversation that ended last time with the two of you not seeing each other for four months?" Mane asked cheerfully. For someone of his size it was amazing how he could disappear from a room when he wanted to. Jasmine had forgotten he was there. Now he stepped forward and stood in front of Adrien.

"Mane Silverstar," he said and bowed slightly.

"Adrien Lamberin," Adrien replied stiffly and bowed just enough to avoid being rude. "You've been taking care of her."

Mane glanced at Jasmine then regarded Adrien with a smirk. "I don't think she lets anybody take care of her."

Adrien smiled a bit, and when Jasmine gave no further explanation for Mane, Adrien turned back to her and sighed. "I was angry and I was afraid for you. I'm glad you came."

Jasmine hesitated, not trusting the gentle words. "Me, too," she finally answered.

He motioned to a small conference area that usually served as a corner where he could sit with a colleague or two and discuss their latest theories or just share clinic gossip. Three of his most recently acquired box puzzles cluttered the table top. Mane sat down, took out the package he'd been carrying for Jasmine and placed it on the table in front of him. Adrien looked at it but didn't comment.

"We . . . found some VJX," Jasmine said. "Thought you might have a use for it."

Adrien didn't move. After a few moments he sat beside Mane and picked the package up, weighing it in his hands.

"Where did you get this?" Adrien asked, his voice hoarse. "There's enough here to start trials."

"For what?" Mane asked.

"Frontal Sclerosis, Lightning Madness."

That's what it was. Jasmine remembered now. A long time ago, Adrien had described it as the only disease whose diagnosis came with a prescription for tranquilizers. Those diagnosed often chose suicide or a sealed room so friends and relatives couldn't watch the rapid mental deterioration. Most lost their entire personalities within eighteen months while the brain centers that controlled vital functions kept the body going.

"I thought diseases like that were no problem, once they came up with that drug that breaks down the cysts so the bugs inside can be killed." Mane was leaning forward now.

"Most were, but as soon as you win a battle against one disease, a new one appears or an old one mutates so we can't fight it with the same weapons. That's what happened with frontal sclerosis. We can't break through the capsule that holds the organism because the capsule coat is constantly changing—we've got nothing to target so the capsules divide and spread, destroying brain tissue as they go."

"What's this veejix do?" Mane asked.

"It prevents changes in a small portion of the capsule wall so we can get through it with drugs that kill the organism."

"You know that for sure?" Mane asked.

Adrien smiled. "Not yet."

"Why can't you just grow the stuff?"

"We don't have a legal supply of the plants or the mold. There was a botanist who tried but the growing conditions were so complex—"

Jasmine moved aside as the door slid open to reveal Linda with a tray. She took in their expressions as she placed the tray brimming with pastries encircling a thermos decanter, on the table in the corner. Coffee aroma flowed into the room

"Since you've probably gotten him to sit still for more than a few minutes, I thought some refreshments were in order." She glared at Adrien playfully. "Eat something."

Linda smiled at Jasmine and put a reassuring hand on her shoulder as she passed on her way out. Since it seemed Adrien had made peace with Jasmine, Linda would too. There was no question at all where her loyalty lay.

Adrien absently poured out coffee as he continued his explanations to Mane. Jasmine felt like the odd person in the room and with the realization, some of the pressure lifted. She squeezed between them to sit down and sipped from her coffee cup, surprised at how comfortable Mane was with what she had always jokingly called Adrien's techno-speak. She sat back and enjoyed the calm.

Adrien seemed himself, but his usual haggard look had deepened and the hollows around his eyes had become more pronounced. Out of everyone in his family, he carried his great-great-grandmother's Chinese features most strongly. A slender build and high cheekbones gave him a beautiful androgyny heightened by thick, black, shoulder-length hair that he left loose to frame his face. His delicate look and quiet confidence had sent most of her female classmates into swooning fits whenever they got together on campus. Jasmine was often mistaken for his real sister because of her coloring and small build. Adrien looked more like Jasmine than he did his father.

Adrien's great-great-grandmother had been a Tiananmen Square baby, left by her parents who wanted to try again, but have a boy next time. She joined the thousands of other girl children adopted by North Americans, and Jasmine suspected she was part of the reason Owen Lamberin had taken a Core Rat into his home eight years ago.

"—so the first trials actually showed some response," Adrien was saying as Jasmine reached past him for one of the pastries the two men had apparently forgotten were there.

"What trials are being done now?" Mane asked.

"None that I know of," Adrien answered. "Using natural VJX is illegal. EcoTech won't acknowledge that it even exists, so we can't get permits to harvest it."

Adrien scrutinized them both. "Where did this come from? It's Green, isn't it?"

"You said yourself veejix hasn't been synthesized. Where do you think it came from?" Jasmine answered.

"Damn it, Jas. Isn't one criminal in the family enough for you? I can't work with this."

"Because it's from a preserve?" Jasmine sniffed with disgust. She couldn't help but think what their father used to say on the subject.

How can the Emerald coalition still get away with keeping people out of the preserves? Whose money do they think they've been spending to build them? Green drugs are illegal because the Emerald Coalition and the Emerald Warriors want it that way. It's their whole power base. Don't think for a minute they've got your best interest in mind.

Owen Lamberin's politics hadn't died with him. She shook the memory out of her head and stared at Adrien, perplexed. "It's Green so nobody is researching it?"

"It's also extremely hard to come by. I'm sure if they could get it, somebody would be working on it."

"We can get it."

"No. It's illegal."

"Illegal." Jasmine laughed. "I spent five years watching the law in action in the Core. There are petty criminals being wasted by the so-called justice system while the Core Kings who set it all up and have all the money use it to keep themselves out of jail. How do you think Martin Yit avoided being investigated for murder? It only took Mane and me four months to collect evidence and track him. Why couldn't the police do that?" Jasmine glared at him. "Sometimes you sound like you've been living in a bubble."

Adrien's expression hadn't changed.

Jasmine continued. "The only laws worth keeping are in here." She put her fist over her heart.

Each law must have a seat in the hearts and minds of the people they serve. If they don't, they are invalid.

"What happens when we get caught?" Adrien said softly. "I have my staff to think about. This could cost the careers of everyone involved, not to mention destroy the legitimate parts of the clinic."

"You're on the wrong track already," Jasmine replied. "You have to assume you'll get away with it, not that you'll get caught. The law wants you to believe it's all-knowing and all-seeing but it's not. People get away with breaking the law all the time. Some are just lucky—most think their way around the system. You just have to find a way to set it all up."

"Use an out-of-the-way lab. Skim money from other projects. Invent several fictional staff members and use their salaries to keep it running," Adrien said, barely audible.

"You've thought about this before?" Jasmine was surprised.

He looked at her sheepishly. "It's an old fantasy of mine. Who knew you would challenge me to go through with it? You make it sound so easy." Adrien picked up the package of VJX and leaned back in his chair. "Every year, 80 people in North America die from frontal sclerosis and it's spreading. It's the most feared disease we've got."

Eighty people, she pondered. That didn't seem like many but then few diseases could compare with the ravages of the plague years.

"It doesn't kill so much as bleeds a person away, right out of their body." Adrien took a deep, shuddering breath. "My mother was bled away."

Esther Lamberin had died a year before Jasmine came into the household. Jasmine had no idea it was from Lightning Madness. She couldn't imagine what Esther's death was like to witness. It would have been devastating. Jasmine found no words to express her sorrow for Adrien.

"Death of the mind," he said softly, mesmerized by the plastic-covered treasure in his hands. "This could be the answer." Then he looked up at Jasmine, contemplating her. "I won't let you do this," he finally said.

"Adrien—"

"I won't be an excuse for you to become a criminal again."

She stared at him for a moment until she was convinced he wasn't going to budge. The three of them studied their cups.

"When are you going back to school?" Adrien asked. "Term starts in two months."

Back to school. She hadn't even thought about it. The freedom and challenge of the last four months working the Core were the best time she'd had in years. The tedium of her mech eng labs—the constant moaning from her music instructors to stick to the composer's vision to refine the rawness she played with. She could quite easily leave it all behind.

"Dunno," she replied, not ready for more criticism.

Silence descended again.

Finally, Mane stood and shook out his legs. "Mind if I take a look around before we go?"

"No. Go ahead." Adrien stood as well. "Ask Linda to set a tour up for you." This time Adrien was the first to bow.

Mane returned the bow, then waved a hand at Jasmine and said, "Soon."

Jasmine waved back and watched him leave.

"Where did you find him?" Adrien asked with a tone of admiration.

"I'm beginning to think he found me," she grumbled.

"Is it serious between you?"

"What? Oh. No. I just hired him to . . . his contact was the one with the veejix so he came along today."

"He knows a lot about you for a contractor."

"Yeah, I know." She thought a moment. "I've trusted him from the first time I met him. I think he feels the same." She shrugged. "It just happens sometimes. You meet somebody who syncs you."

"He could be dangerous."

"Not everybody in the Core is dangerous." She smirked. "And I thought being a *Core Rat* was supposed to make you cynical."

Jasmine picked up her cup and put her feet on the table, leaned back in her chair and let the cup warm her hands. Adrien sat with his elbows on his knees.

"What exactly did you hire him for?"

"You remember Martin Yit? He was a witness during the trial. Mane and I did a lot of digging and found out he's the one who actually did it. Trouble is we still don't know who ordered the murder. It just doesn't sync that it was Green Splinter's idea."

"Did you report what you found to the police?"

"Why should I? They probably know. They did more investigating than we did. Besides, I took care of it. Martin Yit died yesterday."

"What?" Adrien searched her face as if looking for a sign of the person who could take such drastic measures.

"Mane tracked him," she said. "I killed him."

"So now you're a fugitive and a murderer." Adrien stood. "I knew something like this would happen when you left. How could you do this? Do you think Dad would have approved of you for breaking the law and killing someone to avenge him?" He paced a few steps. "You've turned your back on everything he ever wanted for you. Do you think he would have liked to see you in street clothes again? He gave you a chance to do something with your life and as soon as he's gone you fall back into old habits. You're always going to be a Core Rat," he stated, anguish clear in his eyes. Why couldn't he understand?

"I went back to the Core to find out what happened to him."

"That's what the police and the courts are for."

She shook her head at his naivety. "The courts are there to play with the laws. They've got nothing to do with justice. Don't you care what happened to him? Don't you want to know?" Somehow Adrien wouldn't understand that it was the last thing they could do for their father.

Adrien shook his head and leaned on the desk with his hands. "I've lost my father," he said to the desk and then turned to Jasmine. "Don't you get it? Anything else doesn't matter. He's gone. That's all."

"You can say that because you had something to do after he was gone. Tell me you haven't been putting in twenty-hour days for the past six months."

Adrien didn't answer.

"I had nothing until the trial crashed. Then I knew exactly what I could do and I did it."

"You killed a man."

"I killed the man who murdered our father."

"Our father gave you a live education—"

"He's dead." Jasmine stood. "At least I—"

"And you react by turning into the same vicious little Core Rat my father took in eight years ago." Adrien's lips pressed together and his cheeks pulled in. He turned away. "I hate it when you do this."

"What, disagree with you?"

"I've got work to do." Adrien left without another word.

Don't let her rattle you, son. Just walk away and she can't hurt you.

As if having an honest fight with somebody would kill him.

Jasmine stared at the door and her breathing slowly calmed. She was falling again. Adrien was gone.

Jasmine made her way back to Linda's desk.

"Mane still here?" Jasmine asked.

"He's still at it and will probably be a while. I've never met a lay person who's so curious about our research."

"My luck. I get stuck with a partner who's a closet intellectual."

"Would you like me to call him?"

"No. Let him be. I'll wait, at least for a while." Jasmine sat in the waiting nook and picked up the screen pad that lay there. She tapped her fingers across the pad without paying attention and found she had asked it to display the most recent international news.

The new leader of the Emerald Coalition was making speeches. His Mayan heritage stood out clearly on his features: straight black hair, smooth brown skin. He was repeating the same election promises that had swept the election for the E.C. He wanted to clean up the party. Owen Lamberin had had opinions on that and every other political question.

Of course they have outlived their purpose! What possible good can come of having the same government in power for over a hundred years, even if they are only half of a coalition.

Her adopted father had wanted to change things and that fight had cost him his life. Though the Green Splinter had taken the credit, Jasmine had no doubt they were working for the same Emerald Coalition who had outlawed the terrorists, saying they represented the kind of intolerance that could only work against the goals of a peace loving population. As helpful as Mane had been in finding evidence against Yit, they hadn't been able to figure the real motive or why it was Owen Lamberin and not one of his political friends who'd been killed.

The police didn't have any reason to suspect her of killing Yit, although the Green Splinter did. She hoped they'd rather forget Martin Yit and not risk drawing more attention to their part in Owen Lamberin's murder by coming after her.

Jasmine switched to entertainment news, then sat staring at the screen, not seeing the read-out. She was too busy trying to bury her disappointment.

*   *   *   *   *

The flower-head of the grass tickled Jasmine's hand as the breeze kept it in motion. Mane just sat cross-legged and took in the grass and flowers that stood around him, almost perfectly camoflaged by his copper hair and pale green and yellow clothes.

From the beginning, Mane had reminded her of the whisky her father sometimes drank, golden in the glass cupped in his hands. She'd tried it once and had winced at the bitterness but she understood that to her father, it was a warm, soothing, comfort.

Mane had suggested they stop in the little meadow before going back. There were no green patches in The Core. He'd followed as Jasmine led him off the manicured path, away from the benches, to sit in the middle of the largest section of meadow. They had spent the last ten minutes just taking in the earthy smells despite glares from passers-by who didn't step off the path.

"You know there were once a hundred times more trees than people?"

Jasmine nodded. And there would be again if people kept working towards reclamation the way they had for the past hundred years.

"Guess he didn't sync it."

It took a moment for Jasmine to realize he was talking about VJX.

"No."

"Said that EcoTech botanist who discovered the stuff disappeared." He shook his head. "For true—in the ground with Green Splinter's signature."

Like her father. He was gone and she had to make a life without him, without Adrien. Jasmine looked up to see Mane studying her. "Think we can set up a veejix artery?" she asked.

"Without Adrien?"

"He's not the only one who'd like to get his hands on the stuff. I know these people. They care about doing the research, not about why the drug they're testing is illegal. If Adrien won't do it, someone else will. They just haven't considered the Core as a source."

"Got some people I can ask."

Jasmine felt like she was finding her footing again—connecting to something familiar. "So, are we going to be partners or what?"

He shrugged and smiled at her. "Fine by me."

She smiled back. "I figured. How about we make this at least a little bit formal?"

"Sure, Doll. What did you have in mind?"

Jasmine couldn't help feeling he was laughing at her for taking their partnership so seriously. "Can't you stop calling me that?"

He just smiled.

She went on. "How about we do a fifty-fifty split of all profits including anything other than veejix we decide to trade?"

He nodded.

"No business secrets," she continued. "If we run a deal on the side we still share."

He nodded again.

"And you tell me how you know so much."

"About what?"

"About everything."

He laughed. "Tell you if I can still call you 'Doll'."

Jasmine frowned and didn't answer.

"Get a lot of time on my hands. Done about twenty remote courses. Mostly historical geography, some electronics."

"Why?"

That surprised him. "A man can't rise to greatness without an education." He smirked then put both his hands out, palms up, towards her. "We got a deal, Doll?"

Jasmine couldn't hide a smile. "Yeah. We got a deal." She placed her hands in his.

Mane still hadn't explained why he'd spent all his money on remote courses rather than on jewelry and whatever status symbols were in fashion with Core Rats.

"Hey!" Mane said with delight and pointed to her knee. A tiny iridescent gem with six legs was making its way across the folds of her pants. They watched the beetle negotiate the relative mountains, then it dropped out of sight in the grass beside Jasmine.

"Going to take a while to set up a veejix artery and I don't have any security contracts right now." Mane said. "H'bout we set up a few other trades while we get ready?"

"Like what? I won't deal firearms or hiked goods."

"H'bout Green?"

"There's a decent market for it?"

"Small one but it pays."

∗ ∗ T H R E E ∗ ∗

Jasmine smiled at the waiter who took away her plate. He avoided making eye contact and said a bit hopefully, "Will that be all?"

Mane had suggested they tone down their look but keep a bit of a dangerous edge. They made the young man nervous with their feathered earrings and leather bracelets.

"I'll have more coffee," Jasmine said.

"Same for me," Mane said. The waiter gave them a resigned grimace of a smile and they both watched him march off to the kitchen.

The after-work crowd that had shuffled into the restaurant half an hour ago, speaking of office politics with strained faces, had begun to relax—alcohol having its usual effects. They'd soon be ordering something to rev them up. Mane kept closer watch on a table of eight.

Jasmine scanned the room for anyone paying more attention to Mane and her than they should.

"Can spot them before they get in the door," Mane said. "Aren't any police in here."

It wasn't the police that worried Jasmine. Green Splinter though; they'd do a lot more that get her arrested if they suspected her of removing Yit.

Mane returned to his perusal of the room.

"You better get the bill," he suggested.

"Me? I paid last time." Jasmine nevertheless ran her card through the credit slot in the table.

"All we had last time was one drink. Doesn't count," Mane said as he spotted the small bowl of blues the table of eight had ordered to stimulate their party. They both sprang to their feet and Mane had his hand over the bowl before anyone could take one. The whole party held their breath while he sadly shook his head. Then he smiled and the whole party relaxed. Jasmine counted out eight yellow capsules and placed them on the table. Mane's card fluttered down beside the small ovals. Eyes widened. One man chuckled with amazement at the audacity of these two young entrepreneurs.

Jasmine and Mane left without a word.

They walked quickly down the sidewalk, hands in pockets, for a block before looking at each other. Then Jasmine caught the smile in Mane's eye and tension took flight with their laughter. They slowed their pace and looked around. They were in an area just outside the Core. Mane found a corner that gave them a good vantage point and they leaned against a wall like patient predators, letting the evening foot-traffic move around them.

The forty square blocks that made up the Core were still dirty, crowded and sometimes dangerous. Out here streets had been widened, not for vehicles but to put in green strips and to give cyclists more room. This area had an equal mix of residences and commercial development. Closer to the city rim, residences won out.

"I like the look of that one." Jasmine pointed to "The Purple Fig".

Mane looked doubtful. "Customers too close to dead. Need someplace with more action." With that they continued down to the corner and milled with the rest of the swarm waiting for the light to change.

A woman's voice called out, "Hey, Rochelle!"

Jasmine turned while Mane stepped away from her to lounge against a light post in case it would be best for him to disappear. Special officer Watanabe scanned her with deep brown eyes the same color as her skin.

"You still at it, girl?"

Jasmine shrugged and tried to shake off the stunned expression she was sure she'd displayed. The woman frowned with frank disapproval and she hadn't even spotted Mane yet.

"I've been looking for you." Watanabe was out of uniform but her posture was unmistakably police.

Jasmine hid behind the expression of distant indifference that most Core Rats used when faced with authority. They'd been too obvious collecting clients. The police were on to them already. Panic made her want to run.

Watanabe continued. "Martin Yit was murdered in an alley a week ago."

"I heard." Jasmine let the mask drop a bit, relieved now that she knew what the spot interrogation was all about. A self-conscious smile crossed her face. "It won't surprise you if I'm not fractured over it." The preliminary investigation had exposed Martin Yit and several others as members of Green Splinter. One of his pals was even accused, but the so-called investigation trial fell apart when a key witness disappeared and it suddenly seemed the accused had an unshakable alibi.

"Got any leads?" Jasmine asked.

"None I can talk about." Watanabe studied her. "I hear you've been back on the streets. Adrien didn't even know where you were."

Adrien would have denied she was even family if he could have. "Just trying to get my life spliced again," Jasmine replied.

"Here? Doing what?"

"Coping."

Watanabe's gaze fell on Mane. She took a step closer to Jasmine and whispered. "If he's part of you coping, you better watch yourself. He doesn't do anything unless there's big money in it." Jasmine tried to move away but Watanabe put a hand on her shoulder. "That includes making friends." She released Jasmine.

Mane came over and when Jasmine's arm went around his waist he draped his arm over her shoulders right on cue. Mane assumed an air of pleasant protectiveness while Watanabe scrutinized him. He remained silent, no doubt reluctant to spoil any story Jasmine planned.

"It doesn't seem right to just forget about the time you spent as Owen Lamberin's daughter." Watanabe said. "From what I heard, he had real hopes for you."

"I lost my parents thirteen years ago. I lost another father this year and Adrien is so buried in his work he doesn't know where I am. Anything here 'seem right' to you?" She hugged Mane a little closer. "I need to have some fun and I need some overhaul time while I decide what to do with myself."

Watanabe sighed and looked at Jasmine in a way that made her wonder if the woman had children waiting for her at home. "You got a number where I can reach you?" she finally asked.

Jasmine nodded and gave Watanabe her personal number rather than the business one. It could be traced and tapped but it was less suspicious than giving Watanabe the number to an untraceable line.

"Where were you when Yit was killed?"

"That was a . . . Wednesday night?"

"Tuesday."

"We were at that little place at 17th and Pillar."

"That's ten blocks from where Yit was found."

"Uh huh." There was no easily accessible evidence linking her to Martin Yit so being honest was just smart. Yit was a witness at the trial, not a suspect. Unless Watanabe knew more than she let on, in her eyes Jasmine would have no reason to go after him. Mane's tracking and the gathering of evidence could be traced but it would take a lot of time and money to do it. Jasmine doubted that Watanabe would bother unless she discovered a solid lead.

"Do you know anything about his murder, Jasmine?"

"Just what's been on the vids. Haven't heard any street talk about it. You don't think he was just fighting off a mugger?"

"He was tripped, then spiked. That plays more like a planned murder to me."

"You think it might be related to my father's murder? Is there any hope now of reopening the investigation?"

Watanabe looked away. "I think you better let that one go."

Good, she was still embarrassed about the collapse of the trial. Maybe Watanabe would spend a bit more time wondering why a witness had so conveniently disappeared than she would about whether Jasmine Rochelle had motive or opportunity to kill Martin Yit.

"You hear anything, you call me." Watanabe spoke the request as if it were a warning.

"Sure."

She frowned at Mane. "Rochelle, don't spend the rest of your life in mourning." With that Watanabe gave her a wave and left Jasmine and Mane among the rest of the side-walk flotsam.

"Y'know," Jasmine said softly. "Eventually we're going to have to think about protection. The way we've been collecting clients hasn't exactly been low profile."

"Mmm," Mane agreed. "That's the trade-off."

"When the cops catch on they'll try to set us up. We're not easy to miss."

Mane didn't answer. He seemed to have his own doubts despite his insistence that he knew just who to approach and that he had radar for police. She'd believed him, though, when he claimed Greens dealing wasn't an enforcement priority. The business-card game was the best fun she'd had in months but she was starting to worry about how exposed it made them.

"Just two more days," he said. "Then we can afford to use word of mouth. But you're right. Need a way to clear our clients."

"Too bad we couldn't run credit checks on them," Jasmine chuckled.

"Jasmine and Mane," he pronounced, "Providers of pleasure. Only the solvent need apply. Could have them fill out an application. Contact their employers and ask if the applicant really can afford to spend .5% of their wage on Green. We'd have them lining up at our door."

"I'm serious. We have to think ahead."

"Then we'll do credit checks," he answered, the matter decided.

"Come on. I was kidding. How?"

"The way it figures, we've still got a month before we attract any big attention. That gives me time to build a lending institution. Construct a console route to credit check anybody we can get a number for."

"Will any of this be legal?"

Mane looked offended. "Got a reputation to protect. Of course it won't be legal."

Jasmine's phone buzzed in her pocket and she pulled it out.

"Hi."

"Hey, Jas." It was Adrien

She braced for angry words.

"I still haven't had a chance to go through Dad's things. I was going to take some time off if you . . . I could use some help."

Adrien taking time off; and he was asking her back to the house, to what was left of their life.

"Yeah . . . um . . . sure," she stuttered.

★ ★ F O U R ★ ★

Jasmine hiked her bag up to her shoulder and started the short walk from the rail station to the house. Her father had told her that before the fifty year plague there were twice as many houses here. They had since been thinned out. She had tried to imagine houses so close together they had no lawns between them.

Fifty years of one disease after another. No one she'd ever met understood it—no one her own age, anyway—how it could have taken anyone by surprise. Hadn't people destroyed the ozone that protected their immune systems? Hadn't the ocean's plankton died from the same exposure to ultra-violet rays? Hadn't the world warmed until coastal cities and all the most fertile river valley farmlands were lost? Hadn't the weather systems of this wounded world created natural disasters that fed disease with the starving victims of typhoons and drought? Two out of every three people died. They'd almost destroyed themselves from sheer stupidity.

Jasmine stopped in front of the house, almost surprised to see it still standing despite the destruction of everything she'd known there.

The front porch was for communing with the neighbors, while the back overlooked a small garden for communing with nature. Flower beds took up most of the small back yard and contained all the government-approved domestic flowers (twenty-five kinds) as well as a few others snuck in for good measure. As anyone who knew Owen Lamberin would suspect, he had chosen to live in an entropic neighborhood and this house was unlike any others in this sector. The color, design and rough plaster finish on the outside were as individual as all the other houses here.

The door still reacted to her palm print and snicked the latch open. She stepped into the hallway and set her bag on the floor.

"Hey, Jas." Adrien's voice came from the living room. She met him in the doorway, his arms piled with papers and books, looking sheepish. "I've just been picking up a few things."

"Hi," she answered, wary of his good humor.

As soon as she saw the living room, it was obvious that Adrien spent very little time in the house. He'd gathered up scattered books but dust had settled everywhere—even on the covers hugging the keyboards in the corner. When Owen was alive, a day had never gone by that he or Jasmine hadn't played. Until now, dust didn't have a chance.

"I'll give you a hand," she said and went to get the duster from the closet, leaving Adrien to continue picking up.

"How's the clinic?" she asked while setting the particle size and weight.

He shrugged. "The busy part's over—I've got the apprentices all set with their new projects but Linda will have her hands full."

Jasmine listened half-heartedly while Adrien filled her in on the clinic's progress on various fronts. She had every intention of a quick run with the duster but every memento, holoset and book in the cluttered room pulled at her, reached into her memory until she had to stop and acknowledge it as part of Owen Lamberin's life. There were ancient musical instruments, paper books, and his favorite seashells. He had a collection cabinet full of brightly colored and intricately patterned shells. The sturdier ones he kept out on his shelves where people could pick each up and wonder at what creature could have made such a thing. The largest looked like a bumpy rock with spines. When Jasmine had first come into this house, she'd been a sullen little brat who only used words to lash out at anyone who dared to try to talk to her. The man who became her father had invited her to pick the shell up. It took two hands to hold it but it was lighter than she had expected and when she turned it over, she revealed a polished purple mouth whose opening led back into a shiny spiral deep inside. The first conversations she'd had here started with a thirteen-year-old Core Rat asking a soft voiced, bearded man questions about these unlikely treasures. She'd been saddened almost to tears when he'd told her the creatures that created shells like these no longer existed. Jasmine gazed at her distorted reflection in the purple polish while the spines dented her palms.

A tide of anger rose in her. There were only memories left. Her father could never explain to her again how these creatures moved over the ocean floor.

"At this rate it will take you all day just to dust," Adrien teased.

"How can you not be angry." She turned to face him. "How can you live here and not be angry?"

"Jas." He took a step towards her.

"They took everything from us!"

"I know. Give yourself some time. You'll eventually work through the pain and—"

"Is that what you've been doing? You've been hiding. When the trial failed, you shrugged and went back to work. You did nothing."

"Are you telling me I didn't hurt enough?"

Something nudged at her to stop but she couldn't halt the fury. "If you did, you didn't do anything about it."

"That's enough." Adrien turned to go.

"You were willing to let Green Splinter get away with murdering Dad."

He stopped and turned to face her. "And do you feel better now that you're a murderer too? Has killing Martin Yit made you feel better?"

"Yes," she lied. "At least I wasn't afraid to do something."

Adrien took a step towards her and just stared for a moment. She stood wide-eyed—waiting.

"You really are a vicious little bitch," he said, his voice low, "and when you first moved in I took it. I'm not taking it now because you're old enough to know better."

She recognized that look. This was as far as the conversation was going to go. The pain in her hands finally registered where she'd been clutching the murex shell. She tossed it in Adrien's general direction and turned away.

"Frass! Ouch!"

Apparently he'd saved it from the floor.

Jasmine picked her bag up from the hallway and stood looking at the door. This was her home too. The thought of Adrien made her want to run for the Core, but the comfort of familiar surroundings put its arms around her and she wanted to stay. It was her home too.

Jasmine walked down the hall to her room. It was just the way she'd left it except her flute lay on the bed like an offering. She plopped down beside it. She hadn't played since . . . Jasmine stood and ran a hand over the dresser like a hotel guest exploring an expensive suite. The flute tugged at her. She turned to the wall and smiled and reintroduced herself to the musicians in each of her posters. Then she held the flute, caressed its familiar buttons and keys. She flicked to the alto setting, and sat on her bed leaning against the headboard. After the first few notes, time disappeared and the music became all there was. She played her three favorite pieces, then laughed with delight, wondering how she could have gone so many months and not played a note. A Caribbean set she'd prepared for a class project came to her and she was transported to warm sands where the call of seagulls and the perfume of coconuts hung in the air. She stumbled through other sets she'd learned for school and traveled the world. Jasmine flicked to the soprano setting and continued to play. Several pieces later she looked up to think of another selection and found

Adrien sitting cross-legged across the hall. Despite the merry jigs she'd just finished, his whole body slumped under the weight of his sadness. But he kept coming back to her.

"Lunch is ready," he said, standing.

She followed him into the kitchen and sniffed at the aroma of vegetable chowder and fresh bread. Adrien took two bowls out of the cupboard. He was still angry but had an annoying ability to bury it.

She took her place at the table while Adrien brought over the steaming pot. She could always tell when he had been cooking. Half the cupboard doors were open and the counter was a clutter of utensils and bowls. It was probably his way of rebelling against the order he always kept in his lab. Jasmine cut bread while Adrien ladled chowder into her bowl.

"Did you check your console?" he asked.

"I didn't get the chance," she said through a mouthful of bread.

"There have to be at least twenty calls for you. Half of them are from Chanel. She even called me a couple of times."

"What did you tell her?"

"That you're taking Dad's death pretty hard, especially since the trial, and I'd lost track of you."

"I'm going to have to call her."

"A lot of people have been worried about you. What are you going to tell them?"

She stared up at him.

"I'm just curious," he muttered.

"Look, you're the one who invited me home. I've come. I don't know what else you want."

"I want you home. I want to go to bed at night hearing you at the keyboard. I—"

"You want Dad to still be here and for everything to be the way it was. That just won't sync. I don't know why you think that was such a great time. I was miserable."

Jasmine dug into her chowder. When she looked up again Adrien was watching her.

"No you weren't." He cut another slice of bread for himself.

"Don't tell me what—"

"Okay Jas, let's drop it before somebody says something stupid again."

"I just—"

Adrien stood. As if walking away ever solved anything. It just meant they'd fight about it again later.

"Sit down."

They continued to eat in silence. The house began to play 'Jail House Rock' and Jasmine couldn't help but smile.

"You haven't changed Dad's house music," she commented.

"Haven't had time to do the sort." He shook his head.

Here it comes, she thought.

"I'll never understand why you and Dad listen to the primitives when there's so much more sophisticated stuff out now. And if you need to listen to ancient music, why not J Jackson or Collins? At least they did interesting instrumentals. It's like staring at cave paintings when you'd really rather enjoy a Rustini."

"Adrien, you've told me this a thousand times."

He grinned at her. "I know, and I always feel cleansed afterwards."

Jasmine chuckled. "So how is Chanel?"

"Not bad. Her percussion group is playing the Neon Club some time next week. By the way, what did you tell her about me? She seems really . . . interested."

"Are *you?*"

"She's a little young," he replied, meaning maturity, not age.

✷　✷　✷　✷　✷

By late afternoon, both Jasmine and Adrien sat on the living room couch, the study door pulling at them. Behind that door, more than in any other room, the essence of Owen Lamberin presided. His personal mementos were scattered throughout the house but the issues that stirred his passions resided in his study. Going through that room would be like sorting through his mind.

Adrien looked at her and shrugged. "Let's go have a look." He rose from the couch and Jasmine followed him to the study door.

Adrien froze in surprise as the door slid open. "Somebody's been in here."

"Adrien—"

"Everything's different from how I left it."

"Adrien—"

He took a step back. "I'm calling Watanabe."

"It was me," Jasmine said as she stepped past him. "All she'd find are *my* fingerprints."

"You mean you came in here after the trial without seeing me?"

"We weren't exactly speaking to each other at the time." Jasmine surveyed the cluttered little room. Shelves were packed with books, vids, data scrolls. "Besides, I needed to know if Dad kept any physical files that Green Splinter was after him for and I had to link the console for Mane to have a look at it."

"You let that thug go through Dad's console?"

"Yeah, that thug you spent an hour talking medicine with a couple of weeks ago." Adrien didn't answer. "It was part of the job I hired him for. We needed to find out what Dad was working on."

Adrien shook his head as he sat down at the console and flipped up the wafer-thin screen. "You are unbelievable," he said then called up all unanswered messages. "More memorials have come in."

"How long has it been since you've been in here?"

"Not since I let Watanabe and her crew in before the trial. Let's go through these first."

Jasmine sat down beside him while he began to separate the memorials from the other messages.

"What did you get on Yit?" Adrien finally asked.

"I've got him on tape bragging to his Splinter pals about getting away with killing Dad."

"How . . . "

"Mane set up the surveillance. That's what took the longest. We spent weeks following Yit around before we got it."

"Was Yit working on his own?"

"No, probably an ordered kill, but the Green Splinter is tight. It took a lot of high-end surveillance gadgets and a lot of work just to find Yit getting together with his pals."

Adrien considered that for a moment, then spoke. "I talked to Watanabe after the trial. I asked her how we went from a suspect she was certain would be convicted to no key witness and an alibi mess that embarrassed the whole department. She said she was investigating but hinted she was being blocked by the force. If Green Splinter is being protected, there aren't many groups powerful enough to do that and the only one of those with a motive is the Emerald Warriors."

It would make sense, Jasmine thought. *Wherever there's Green Splinter pulling the trigger, there's an Emerald Warrior protecting them.* Proof of that would frenzy the news-people.

"Did you find out why it was Dad they were after and not somebody else?" Adrien asked.

"Not really."

He waited.

"He was the Raker." The opposition had plans to document corruption in the E.C. Watanabe's crew had found his correspondence files and they knew Owen Lamberin was helping with the investigation but no one had suspected what a pivotal role he played.

"The Raker," Adrien repeated.

"But killing him didn't stop the investigation Dad started. They replaced him a couple of months ago. That wasn't the reason."

"Did you find anything Watanabe missed?"

"Yeah, a batch of files with lists of Coalition land acquisitions. And one file even Mane couldn't get into."

Adrien stared at the screen for several moments.

"By killing Yit," he said, "you're taking on the same people who left our father speared in an alley."

"I would have invited you but you were too busy working."

"Come on, Jas—"

"You want to do this or not?" She challenged him to pursue the argument.

Adrien turned back to the screen. "Out of thirty-two messages, twenty-three are memorials."

Your fury blinds you. Best not to act when you can't see. Sometimes she remembered.

* * * * *

The next morning, Jasmine woke with eyes still swollen from the night before. Owen Lamberin had died over twelve months ago. Watching all those people talk about him had made it seem like only days ago.

Once she dressed, Jasmine took her tools to the backyard. The plants around the back sprinkler hung limp and brown. She'd noticed yesterday that the head wasn't working. She checked the sprinkler system circuit box for faulty electronics. When she didn't find anything there she checked the sprinkler head for mechanical damage. After taking most of the unit apart she found the smoked part and scanned the remake code. The shop could probably have a replacement for her by noon.

Jasmine was putting her tools away when Adrien appeared with two mugs of fresh coffee and handed one to her. Their moistened breath formed fog in the crisp air. They sat in the sun and gazed out at the jumble of green and yellow that was the garden.

After a moment, Adrien spoke. "Yesterday you said you'd been miserable here."

Jasmine sighed. Why couldn't he just leave her alone? Let her just be here?

He continued. "I don't think that's true, but where would a thought like that come from?"

"I've spent the last few years trying to decide what to do with myself."

"You mean career-wise?"

"No, I've been thinking about changing my hair."

Sharing your hopes helps you see them more clearly. She didn't want to share her hopes—she didn't have any now.

Adrien resumed his study of the garden.

"I was trying to decide between mech eng and music . . . I don't know. Desilva didn't like my compositions much. You're right though; I wasn't miserable so much as confused."

"Why not go with your music?"

"I enjoy it—I'm not bad at it but it's not important to anybody. If I never compose anything in my life, other people will still be there to do it. And anybody can engineer mechanical systems."

"You're still learning. I think your playing is incredible."

"I can't see doing it forever." Her eyes slid from him. "This VJX idea though, that really syncs me. Between me and Mane we can splice between the researchers who need it and the Core Rats who can supply it. Veejix is something that can make a difference to a lot of people."

"That's not why you're doing this," Adrien remarked. "You don't care about Lightning Madness. You're angry at Green Splinter and the E.C. You want to attack them for killing Dad."

"We are setting up a veejix artery."

"Dealing in Green puts you in the sights of the Emerald Warriors. You've seen what the Splinter can do and get away with. You're not going to accomplish much if they put you away or kill you."

"Give us some credit. How do you think I survived five years in the Core? How do you think Mane does it? We're ready. All we need now is to know acceptable purity percentages, acceptable cutting agents, and whether you can use stuff that's gone through a solvent process."

Adrien studied her for a moment. "You've really done your research."

"Don't look so surprised. We know what we're doing. Mane's been doing security work for years. He'll be able to protect the operation. Manda has made some long-term deals with her supplier so we're guaranteed a steady supply for the next 18 months, depending on how much the trials will actually use. We're waiting to talk to a researcher to find out how much they need."

Adrien warmed his hands around his cup and surveyed the garden, his eyes resting on the small tree that stood as the centerpiece. He sighed and closed his eyes for a moment. "You were right." Adrien stood. "They took everything. You may as well be gone too." He took his cup inside.

* * * * *

That afternoon, Jasmine and Mane went to The Frog. Adrien had remained distant and self-absorbed for the rest of the day. Nothing Jasmine said was answered in more than a few mumbled words. She had left him to it, knowing he wouldn't be able to stand himself that way for long.

Manda was busy talking business to a large man who worked too hard at seeming bored. Mane gave the man a big wink and the thumbs up as if to say keep it up, you'll do fine. Which rattled him even further since he'd never seen Mane before.

Jasmine couldn't figure why anyone would choose to be a patch-head. When recreational drugs were legalized, it was pretty much agreed that drugs didn't cause social problems, they were just symptoms.

Naltrexone and its clones had been used in dry-up clinics for years by that time to block the addictiveness of drugs and alcohol. Addiction then was seen as a matter of choice and addictive behavior treated with therapy. Unless you were like Manda. Like a lot of Core Rats, she obviously did too much of the stuff but didn't want therapy. Patching and popping had become a habit. Maybe she preferred seeing the world through the chemical filter of her choice.

"Time to pour the reserved stock," Mane said to the Frog's owner who stood behind the bar.

Jasmine found a table and sat where she could listen in on Mane.

The owner glanced at Jasmine, then back at Mane. "You two are starting your drinking a little early."

"Live to enjoy. Lots of time to rest after we're dead. You complaining about the extra business?"

The waiter joined in the conversation as soon as he spotted Mane. Jasmine smiled to herself. The Frog had become their office over the past few weeks.

The man talking to Manda now had desperation in his eyes and Manda looked back at him with the same dull expression she always wore. Jasmine had first thought that all the patching had made Manda a snail, but under that face that never seemed to smile her mind was plenty sharp enough to get the best deal she could. You could just never tell if she was high or sober and she was impossible to read. The man she'd been talking to grunted and stood, their deal done. Manda came over to join Jasmine, catching Mane's eye on the way there.

Jasmine nodded hello while Mane sat down and passed her a drink. "So, how much veejix is out there?" he asked Manda.

She shrugged. "Can get you point forty-three k over the next three months, maybe more."

"The supply has to be constant," Jasmine said. "What about after that?"

Manda looked at her and blinked. "No problem. If . . . " The rest of her answer died as a messenger dropped an envelope on the table and scurried out. Her motor-board putt-putted down the street.

Jasmine picked up the envelope since her name was scrawled on the front. She tore the top open and shook out a twig with five still-green leaves, the base shaped into a point. A miniature of the branch that had been used on her father. As soon as she stood, Mane's hand on her shoulder pushed her down again.

"She's just a messenger," he said.

Manda looked at them both, then discovered she had business with the bartender and left.

Jasmine sat and glared at her glass.

"Hey, Doll. This doesn't mean Splinter knows anything. They're just trying to scare you."

"I can't sit here any more." Jasmine stood.

When they had marched down the sidewalk a few blocks, she asked, "What do they want?"

"They're trying to fracture you into exposing information about Yit's death. They don't know anything."

Mane had assured her that his sources couldn't be turned—that the information he'd used to find the Splinter members in the city couldn't be traced. She'd trusted him but how would a Core Rat have access to such a tight source?

"What if they—" The rest of the words slammed against something in her throat and stayed there. The alley. She walked, then ran between the buildings, dodging garbage as she went. Of course there was no sign of what had happened to Martin Yit here. The blood had long since washed away. Then she looked at the wall. A dark smudge remained where they had burned him. She touched it. Was it soot?

"Jasmine!" Mane looked ready to carry her out to get her away. "This is extinction. What if somebody sees us in here?"

He took her hand and led her unseeing and stumbling back out to the street. Her legs went weak and her stomach lurched. Mane sat with her until her breathing slowed again and she pushed the horror deep where it could no longer hurt her.

*   *   *   *   *

Jasmine got off at the last stop before the city limits, so she could walk back the few extra blocks home. Farms and plantations grew right up to the last city street. A field of plants with starburst leaves swayed with the breeze.

The neighborhood probably wouldn't last more than another ten years. Hemp plantations were pushing in on all sides and every five years the plantation owners made applications to expand. One of these times they'd get the "go for" and the city would grow smaller. Sometimes it seemed the E.C. wanted most of the population squeezed into mass habitat buildings again—out of the way of their plans to restore the globe to a mosaic of preserves and plantations.

"Jasmine? Is that you?"

Marsha Wong waved from her back porch and, because this dynamo of a woman had been the first neighbour to welcome Jasmine when she joined the Lamberin household, Jasmine smiled and jogged over to the porch railing.

"Come join me. I can use a break." Marsha waved Jasmine into one of her porch chairs.

The stocky, brightly dressed woman ducked into the doorway for a moment and then emerged with a tray of glasses and fruit juice. "It's good to see you," she said as she poured a glass for Jasmine. "Yeah, me too," Jasmine replied and they both sat and savoured the tart red juice.

Gazing at the fields behind her home, Marsha sighed. "It's like an ocean straining to break off more of the shore." She turned to Jasmine and smiled. "We sure miss your father. With all the committee work he did, I don't know where he found the time for his teaching. Still no idea what he was working on to attract Green Splinter's attention?"

"No, and I've been asking."

Marsha pondered that for a moment. "The Suburb Preservation group held some sucessful rallys over the past months. I hate to say it, but since your father died, we've had more interest than ever from participants and the media."

Marsha settled back in her chair. "Something your father was always anxious to get started is a call to open the preserves so we can all enjoy what we've given up so much to build. That will be the focus for next month's rally. An appearance from you would really help—just to say a few words."

The field of swaying green mesmerised Jasmine for a moment. "I can't," she said. "This isn't my fight."

"What is?"

"Nothing."

Marsha looked at her as if expecting her to finish, to explain herself.

Jasmine shrugged. "I've done enough fighting in my life."

Thankfully, Marsha left it at that and they continued to enjoy the juice and the feel of the sun on their faces. Half an hour later, Jasmine made her way home.

When she got back to the house, Adrien sulked in their father's study, no more inclined to talk to her than before.

Jasmine unrolled the keyboard, set it on its stand and played, desperately needing to do something familiar. The sound filled her, filled the room until everything was the present and everything was sound. Sound pounded from the keys and thundered into the walls. Her flute was a plaything but this—this was something that came from inside and possessed all the richness and complexity she could control.

She switched from organ to grand piano to honky-tonk and the accompaniment was sometimes percussion, sometimes winds, sometimes vocals. When she ran out of selections she knew from memory, Jasmine scrambled to find the prompter and set it at eye level above the keyboard. After a while she found it harder to keep centered on the music as exhaustion made her clumsy. Finally she stopped. All emotion had emptied from her.

Adrien had come in and lay on the couch, eyes closed, moisture welling at his eyelids. Jasmine knew what was wrong. No matter how much time they both spent here, no matter how much of her music she played, it wasn't the same. It would never be the same. A chapter of their lives was gone forever.

He sat up to make room for her beside him.

"You were right," she realized. "Nothing I've done changes the fact that he's gone."

"How did you . . . What was it like going back?"

"It was incredible out there. Being in the Core was so different this time. Had a job to do and, because I knew all the information routes, I did it. In some ways, it's the most satisfying time I've had in years."

She laughed without humor. "If I had thought about what I was doing once we actually found Yit, I couldn't have killed him. I programmed myself to do it from the very beginning and I did."

Jasmine thought about Martin Yit's frightened eyes. She sat up and swallowed. She had put those feelings away, yet a rush of emotions was coming. Jasmine tasted the grief, the anger, the loss, the outrage as if it were climbing up her throat. And because she was sitting beside a friend who had seen her in every state of emotion imaginable, she finally let it come. Jasmine squeezed her eyes shut against the tears and her body shuddered with long sobs. She barely felt Adrien lift her from where she sat. She barely felt arms holding her but she knew there was someone taking care of her while she gave herself up.

The urge to cry eventually drained from her and though Jasmine felt exhausted, her head had cleared. She found herself curled up on Adrien's chest. He was half lying on the couch with his legs up on the table. She looked at him. His face was wet.

"What are *you* crying for?" she asked.

"You, I guess."

"He really is gone, isn't he?"

"Yeah, Jas."

Jasmine realized now what she had done, leaving him alone.

"Little by little we'll learn to live without him." Adrien wiped his eyes with the back of a hand. "But I don't think we'll ever stop missing him."

She hugged him and lay beside him until her breath no longer came in shudders.

Jasmine sniffed deeply and looked at the large wet spot she'd made on his shirt. "Look at you," she laughed weakly. "You're a mess." She got up to find some tissues.

"I guess we should send off all the mementos Dad left to people," she said.

Adrien sighed. "I'll get the list."

They spent the rest of the day packaging and mailing the items Owen Lamberin had left to his friends.

* * * * *

That morning Jasmine woke suddenly to the 1812 Overture blasting out at full volume—a trick she'd played on Adrien in the past and sure enough, he stood in the doorway taking in her reaction. He grinned and shrugged as she glared at him.

"I so seldom get the chance, I couldn't resist," he shouted above the music. "I've got coffee on." He turned the volume down on his way to the kitchen.

Jasmine was usually the first up in the morning. Familiar surroundings made her lazy today. Then it came back—that uneasy feeling that's left from dreams unremembered but unpleasant. Something about metal spikes and her arms feeling numb. It took an effort to shake off the anxiety.

She looked over at her wall-hung holosets while the now-muted music continued its cannon fire. The one wall was a tribute. Her dead mentors were all there: Vangelis, Collins, Morricone, Lemantar and Wendelela. Men and women who possessed the drive to make music their lives. She let her eyes close and wished she could understand their determination.

Jasmine woke again with a start, not sure how long she'd dozed off. She spilled herself out of bed and pulled on pants and a shirt, then followed the aroma of freshly brewed coffee to Adrien who took a tray to the back porch. He retracted the windows so the two of them could sit in the fresh morning air overlooking the garden.

"The VJX artery is ready to go," Jasmine said. "Mane is pushing to contact a researcher."

"Don't do this," Adrien answered.

"It's important. We're giving you a chance to partner with us."

"You enjoy breaking laws, don't you?" he said, realization clear in his eyes. "You just won't accept the consensus that makes laws. You have to challenge everything."

"I'll challenge what's wrong."

"You're challenging this just to attack the E.C."

"You are such a lump. Didn't you ever listen when Dad talked about civic responsibility?"

"I listened about as much as you did, which wasn't much. Don't use him as an excuse. You're doing this for revenge."

Jasmine glared at him. She'd come to help him. She'd tried to get him into partnership because Mane had convinced her what a good idea that was. Well, she'd tried.

"Sometimes I think *you're* the one who's adopted," she said as she went back into the house to pack her bag.

* * F I V E * *

The Neon Club facade doubtless looked more spectacular after nightfall with the neon tubes forming a show of glowing patterns—some colorful abstractions, others animals and sea creatures. Once inside, however, daylight held no influence and Jasmine and Mane stood within the doorway for a moment to get their night eyes in the relative darkness.

Jasmine had finally called Chanel during her visit with Adrien.

"Jasmine, I'm not going to harass you about getting behind at school but it doesn't make sense that you walk away from all your friends. I honestly can't imagine what it must be like losing a parent the way you did but you can't let that destroy you. At least keep in touch with us."

"Okay, okay." Jasmine had relented and accepted the invitation.

She blinked and the sparsely populated club came into view. She had insisted they come to the club early. She disliked starting an evening by squirming between tables trying to find room and beg enough table space for the number of people she knew were coming. Besides, despite Chanel's assurances, she knew she was in for some hard questions. She hadn't seen any of her old friends for the four months since she'd returned to the core. And she couldn't bear facing everyone at once. Mane waited for her to lead the way.

Mane's face had brightened when she told him where she was going and she didn't have the heart to exclude him, although she wasn't at all sure how to explain him. Now that she was here, she was glad to have him beside her.

He'd attempted to control his hair with two small braids on either side of his face. The soft green shirt threaded with gold looked as if it had been made just to suit his coloring.

Jasmine had spent at least an hour getting dressed. Nothing seemed quite right. Core clothes were out. Wanting to look good, she didn't need anyone feeling sorry for her, she'd finally decided on a bright turquoise body suit under a dark teal lace jacket and pants—dressy but still her. Her hair she left in the soft, shiny black spikes she usually wore.

A few early arrivals were scattered throughout the club. Dim overhead lights made the patterns of neon on the walls and ceiling all the more prominent. Motionless and unlit on the stage, Chanel's equipment waited.

"Hey, Jasmine," someone called; a high-pitched whistle seemed to say, over here! She turned to see Arri Deckert rising from his chair at a large table in front of the stage. He removed the trademark whistle from his mouth. She had never seen Arri look at her with anything other than amusement. Now he stood frowning at her. "We didn't think you'd actually come," he said as if to explain his initial speechlessness. "We missed you," he said accusingly.

Jasmine took a step back from him and swallowed the urge to run. "I didn't come here to end up fractured."

"Sorry," his tone softened. "What you've gone through . . . I don't know what to say. Except it's great to see you."

"And I didn't come for your pity." She took a step towards him. "The last thing I need is—"

"Hey, Doll." Mane's hand on her shoulder stopped her and she spun to face him, the venom dying on her tongue in the face of his calm.

As she turned back to Arri he enveloped her in a hug before she could stop him. "Don't ever leave us like that again," he said and against his warmth and with his short black curls on her cheek, some of the tension drained from her, leaving her merely confused.

Arri released her to take a closer look at Mane. "So this is the guy you left us for," Arri bowed. "Arri Deckert."

"Mane Silverstar," Mane answered, then lowered his voice. "Actually I'm her manager. She started a career as a dancer in the erotica pavilion at the dome. Quite a job. Wouldn't believe how many men go for short women," he said with such earnestness that Arri seemed close to believing him until Jasmine punched Mane lightly in the arm.

"I'll warn you. The man is a compulsive liar," she said. "Where's our table?"

Arri studied Mane for a few moments, no doubt wanting to enquire further. Instead he moved towards the table he'd chosen and Jasmine and Mane followed, seating themselves with Arri at one end.

"Chanel's in the back with Sven and Kari getting synced." Arri invited them to punch in their drink selections.

Arri glanced at her, still not knowing what to say next. Then he decided to avoid her altogether. Jasmine watched him welcome Mane. He could make anyone immediately comfortable. Arri Deckert had come into the circle through the side door. He was a chemistry major with an interest in music. While taking several classes with Jasmine, he became part of the group. Perhaps he found his fellow chemists boring.

Jasmine sat back and watched the club slowly fill while Mane easily deflected Arri's questions and turned the conversation to Arri's latest chemistry project. She felt a pang of protectiveness. Arri entered every conversation making you feel like you were the only person who mattered to him. Even made you feel like you'd made that rare connection that results in instant friendship. At least until you saw him treat everyone with that same intense interest. Jasmine had downloaded for him—and how. It had taken her three months to realize he flirted with every woman he met. She'd spent more months afterwards alternating between anger at Arri and anger at herself, over her infatuation. Jasmine still contended he should come with a warning label. She watched Mane for a moment and decided he could handle Arri.

Sally and Gowan arrived together and their animated chatter stopped dead when they saw Jasmine. She sat up straight, ready for more recriminations.

"Jasmine." Sally glanced at Gowan. "We're so glad to see you."

Jasmine smiled and said, "Yeah, me too."

Arri made introductions to Mane while Jasmine tried to think of something to say. She'd played with Sally and Gowan for class concerts.

Conversation stalled. It seemed everyone wanted to ask questions but couldn't figure out how.

"Power of zero about the trial," Sally said. "I guess they'll never find out who really did it."

Jasmine's discomfort became dread. What had made her think she could come here and splice with everybody again as if she had never left? This had been a mistake.

"I wish you had kept in touch," Sally said.

Jasmine flushed. "My father was dead, his killer went free, the news sharks were at the door every day and Adrien disappeared into his lab. I was just a little busy!"

"Hey," Arri said. "Don't go sheared over this."

"Don't tell me how to—"

"My fault," Mane said and everyone stared at him. He shrugged. "Been keeping her busy helping me with my investigation business."

Arri, Sally and Gowan considered this for several seconds and inhaled as one to ask another question when the lights dimmed, silencing everyone.

The instruments on the stage glowed. One set that looked like drums glowed white with internal lights, while banks of panels glimmered like luminescent patches behind. The lights in the instruments began to throb and the words "Luminous Flux" appeared in the air above the stage. The faint sound of tinkling became steadily louder. There were three black-clad figures on the stage and the banks of shapes vibrated as they were struck, producing a melodious hum as prelude to haunting single notes. Slowly a melody developed—the stage lighting made it look like the instruments communed with each other to make music without benefit of human hands. The audience was silent.

The music faded as the house lights slowly came up to reveal the three people on stage. The applause started with Jasmine and friends and spread quickly. The black figures bowed as the applause continued, most enthusiastically from Jasmine's table, to the amusement of the other audience members who no doubt guessed the band had invited their friends.

A familiar laugh made Jasmine turn and look up as Indra reacted to Arri's expression. He clutched his heart with both hands and gave her a beseeching look.

"You really need to see a cardiologist and get that fixed—looks painful." Indra smirked at him.

Adrien walked up beside her and she pointed to him. "Look who I found lurking outside. He obviously *has* no friends so I thought he'd enjoy flocking with you glitches." She took a look around. "Hey, Jasmine. Good to see you," she said as she squirmed into a chair. She surveyed the faces around her. "So, what's the glum?"

No one answered.

"Hey, Jas," Adrien said softly, sitting down beside her.

Chanel must have invited him, as if this evening wasn't already hard enough. She hadn't spoken with Adrien since she left the house a week ago. She was still angry with him. If he had agreed to a partnership, things would have gone so much smoother. Now she and Mane had to pick from a handful of researchers they didn't know and hope they could sync with whoever they chose.

"Hey," Indra called to her. "They been baiting you? Well, my girl, we *are* all angry with you. Can't be helped. That's what happens when you don't let people help you. What's the use of having a bunch of wonderful friends like us if you don't use us when things go sheared?" She shook her head, disgusted.

Was that really why people were annoyed with her? That made no sense at all.

"Good evening everyone." Chanel removed her hood and shook out her hair. "Welcome to Luminous Flux." Applause started up again then faded when the lights began to dim.

"There's The Fan." Sally nodded toward the bar at the back of the room.

It took Jasmine a moment to realize she meant the blond who stood with one elbow on the bar behind him, a drink in his other hand. Yellow hair in loose shoulder-length curls hid most of his face. Gowan leaned towards Jasmine. "He's been at every club Luminous Flux has played in the last six months. He stays for the whole show but never talks to anybody in the group."

"He's too shy." Sally sighed. "A lot of them are like that."

He didn't look shy. He looked like he was waiting for the world to come to its senses and surrender itself to him, like he could wait forever for what he wanted. He turned and saw Jasmine watching him, then was lost in the darkness as the lights faded completely.

Again an eerie performance began as the panels in the wall lit up a section at a time, struck by invisible hands. Single notes became a melody that faded and strengthened in an easy rhythm. This was the best Chanel had ever been. She'd entered that place where Jasmine had only ever been twice. That place where there is no need for the brain to send messages to the hands. The body just knows what to do and does it better than it ever has before and it seemed Kari and Sven were in that same place. No one here tonight would forget Luminous Flux.

At some point the melody had grown heavier, noisier, and booming drums became more pronounced until it sounded like the heart of the whole world beating. Jasmine sat enthralled; the rhythms of her body were being played out on stage. When it stopped, the room took a second to recover, then burst into applause.

Chanel, Sven and Kari stepped in front of the instruments, removed their hoods, and bowed. Out of breath and sweating, Chanel beamed at the audience. When the applause died a bit she shouted, "This is Luminous Flux. We'll be back after a break."

Jasmine headed for the dressing room before the applause had completely stopped. It was a tiny chilled room. Jasmine gave Chanel a big hug before she could react.

"That was power of ten. No lie," Jasmine said.

"Thanks." Chanel was breathless. "I don't know what happened out there. I just hope it happens again."

Jasmine hugged Kari and Sven while she was at it. "Where did you learn to play like that?" she asked.

The three of them rolled their eyes and chorused, "Practice, practice, practice."

Sven let out an indulgent sigh. "Shall we go and mingle with our fans?"

"Did I see Adrien out there?" Chanel whispered to Jasmine.

"Yeah."

Chanel stopped when they got halfway down the hall to turn and have a close look at Jasmine. "It's so good to see you."

As they approached the table, everyone stood and gave Chanel an ovation. Jasmine introduced Mane and Chanel smiled at Adrien.

"Chanel," he said, "if our ancient ancestors had heard the three of you tonight they never would have given up drums as a means of communication."

"I don't know," Mane mused. "Get a drum kit small enough to fit inside a phone . . . you'd need a tiny little drummer." But Chanel was radiant at the compliment. Jasmine reclaimed her seat beside Adrien and wondered why he was there. And why had he chosen to sit beside her when he obviously thought she was a failure for going back to the core?

Chanel quickly took the seat on his other side and began questioning him about the clinic, feigning interest in processes she barely understood. Jasmine sat back and tried to enjoy the company of friends she'd done without for too long. Even after her harsh words, these people were willing to take her back without any more explanation than she was willing to give. She didn't know what to make of it.

Sally and Gowan pretended to fight about something Mane said. Kari looked, as always, as if she wanted to be invisible—uncomfortable unless she was standing behind an instrument. Sven put on pompous airs that no one took seriously. Indra continued her rebuffs of Arri's overly dramatic flirtations—a game they'd been playing since they met a few years ago. Indra was an architecture student with a passion for techno-clatter. Every so often she condescended to go listen to the "dull popular stuff", especially when it came to percussion groups.

Arri motioned for attention. He lifted a jar of caps and grinned. "Last week I finished my class project and I couldn't think of a better occasion to sample it." The bottle made its way around the table and Jasmine took one as it came to her. The caps were red, code for euphorics. Hands under the table she slipped it into her sleeve, then pretended to take it just like everyone else. She looked up to see Mane smirking at her from across the table. Jasmine wrinkled her nose at him, then ignored him.

She'd tried recs before and hadn't cared for the fuzziness they caused. And now she was making a living selling recs. She'd never quite understood why there was such a market for Green recs when you could get the legal stuff at any store. Mane figured it was the mystique of the forbidden fruit—the excitement of having it come from the forests themselves. Although no tests she'd heard of had ever proven that drugs processed directly from preserve plants were any more effective than the synthetic ones, people still risked buying Green. Proving once again that there would always be illegals to deal.

She didn't understand why harvesting medicinal plants would be illegal anyway. The E.C. maintained that any taking of plants in the preserves had to remain forbidden because of the damage caused. Jasmine couldn't imagine the harvesting of a few plants having much of an effect.

She turned to the stage. Lonely instruments waited for Chanel, Kari and Sven, who had gone to prepare for their next set. If she worked hard and practiced hours every day, someone might pay her to be on stage herself one day. The prospect filled her with disinterest. She wanted to do something that would make a real difference and if she had to defy the E.C. to do it, so much the better.

Arri tried to include Jasmine in a conversation about university admitting policy that threatened to deteriorate into a series of quips with the help of Mane's chemically amplified wit and Arri's talking whistle. No one singled her out for questions—they just wanted her to be part of the group and Jasmine finally relaxed.

She checked her watch and decided there was just enough time to stretch her legs by feigning a need for the washroom. Other patrons apparently had that very need. She squeezed through the crowd mobbing the bar and washroom.

"You haven't performed for a long time," a voice accused in her right ear and she turned to see The Fan. He looked like a negative—blond hair and eyebrows against bronze skin, then his words sank in.

"I . . . I've had some family problems to sort out," she said, wondering why she was making excuses to a stranger.

"I know," he said as if that was all that needed to be said between them for him to feel her pain. For an instant she glimpsed an expression of sadness before his eyes shifted to a frank study of her. "Last two concerts you gave were brilliant."

The last two concerts she'd done were her own compositions—they were 'unrefined and raw but a good start' to quote her instructor. She laughed, incredulous. His confused expression made her add, "They were pretty rough."

"Yes, brilliant." He grinned. "You . . . " he searched for the right word. "You've got a chaotic hand."

She smiled. "Don't tell that to Celeste Desilva. She wouldn't see it as a compliment to her teaching skills."

He smiled and seemed to be waiting for the moment to pass so he could return to more serious matters.

"Who are you studying with?" she asked.

"I'm not a student."

The concert series was only open to students, instructors and their guests. "Who invited you?"

"My muse." His brown eyes twinkled and she realized he'd sneaked in. "Got . . . an interest in music," he continued, "and I like what you've done." He reached into a pocket and pulled out a data disc the size of a large coin. "Have a listen to this." He placed it in her hand as the lights began to fade. "Be real interested to hear what you think." He raised an eyebrow and turned away as the room darkened. Before Jasmine realized she didn't know his name, she lost sight of him in the crowd.

The talking and laughter faded. Luminous Flux was back a bit more quietly now. The first had been their "performance set". Now they played their standard mix, designed to be interesting but could double as background music. After several minutes of polite silence, small conversations sprouted all through the club.

As her eyes adjusted to the darkness, Jasmine made her way back towards the table, only to be intercepted by Adrien.

"I have to talk to you," he said.

"Can't it wait?" She didn't want him to spoil what was becoming the most fun she'd had for a long time.

Adrien shook his head and led her outside. Neon sea creatures turned them rainbow colors with their glow.

"I got a call from Nancy Salkov yesterday," Adrien said, looking expectantly at her.

Jasmine shrugged. "I said we were going ahead."

"She asked me why I wasn't already doing VJX trials since there was a supply available. She also told me she was impressed with the research you've done." He shook his head. "Anarchism must be a family heritage. How pure a product were you able to find, anyway?"

"About 7.3."

"What's it thinned with?"

"Carbohydrates or something. Mane's trying to find a quick test to tell what is used so we can check for ourselves." She watched Adrien intently. What was he up to?

"Try a node 12 iodide."

"I'll suggest it. We have to monitor the stuff for the first six months anyway. Suppliers sometimes try cutting purity after a few months hoping their customers aren't checking anymore."

"How do you know all this?"

"My other education."

Adrien smiled a little and nodded, then gazed down the street. "I promised her I'd find a cure. Not while she was alive, of course. Afterwards when it seemed possible. I never spoke the promise out loud—no one ever knew but me."

Adrien studied her for a moment. "You're ready to do this without me."

"Only if you won't partner with us."

He sighed. "Well, then. I talked to one of the research managers at the clinic. Her lab could be moved off site. We have an equipment warehouse across town she could use. She's really excited about the project. I just need to get her some VJX to start work on."

Jasmine stared at him, waiting for the meaning of his words to sink in. Adrien smiled at her confusion. "So, are we partners?"

She flooded with relief. "Of course." Then she was smiling, too.

* * * * *

Jasmine sat in the rail car in silence. Mane wasn't thinking clearly and was too drowsy to make an effort at conversation. Every meter they traveled towards the Core took her away from the warmth of her friends and closer to a cold world of Core Rats and Core Kings. All of them playing survival of the fittest with Darwinian hoof and fang.

Then there was Mane. He sat there and seemed to let himself give in to a night's recs and alcohol, trusting Jasmine to take care of them both for now. Somehow she couldn't believe he wouldn't sober in a flash if he needed to. She smiled at him though his eyes were closed, and felt in her pocket for the data coin.

Jasmine led Mane to their building, then to his room. She made sure he collapsed on his bed and not the floor, then locked his door behind her and went to her own apartment down two floors.

She was too tired to stay up. Jasmine sat at her console, put the data coin on the table-top and stared at it. The brown-eyed blond had apparently waited for her for months, hoping she'd show up to hear Luminous Flux. She wasn't sure whether she should feel uneasy or flattered. Jasmine inserted the data coin.

The Fan appeared in a head and shoulders shot. His head was cocked to one side and Jasmine couldn't decide if he was pouting or frowning.

"Jasmine Rochelle, I found you," he said, then leaned towards the screen. "Listen."

He faded into a still shot of a bird of prey frozen in the act of leaping from a perch in pursuit of some small creature.

"The longest time," his voice announced, then, in the sing-song voice of a song writer still searching for the music, told of a lifelong struggle failed against the loss of innocence, the loss of ideals, the loss of self in words so real and so powerful Jasmine had to pause the disc when he finished.

"I am an old and broken man, though it took the longest time." His words clung to her in the silence.

She skipped through the disc past four more spoken songs, then stopped at one with music. The vid showed The Fan at the keyboard. He sang of the despair of lost first love while the keyboard wept under his hands. At the end the vid cut back to him looking through the screen at her. "Tell me. Should I quit my day job?" Jasmine laughed out loud to hear him spout the ancient musicians' dilemma, then she noticed the question in his eyes. The screen blanked to nothing but a name and phone number. Jasmine leaned back in her chair, staring past the screen.

Curiosity made her consider listening to the four songs she'd skipped but she suspected his songs were better taken in small doses.

Jasmine fell into bed with the words "It took the longest time" and "Edan Loffler" running circles in her mind.

⋆ ⋆ S I X ⋆ ⋆

Jasmine walked up to the restaurant, surprised to discover she was nervous. She hadn't spoken to Edan Loffler directly, but in a series of messages, they had decided to meet here. It was mid-afternoon and the informal little café was empty except for Edan, who sat in a corner surveying the room. His only reaction when he saw her was to study Jasmine with a half smile as she squeezed between tables. She sat opposite him and placed the data coin on the table.

"Edan," she spread her hands. "This broke my heart. What are you going to do with it next?"

"Need music for the words."

"But your lament piece was beautiful."

"Light, easy to compose for." He leaned towards her and she noticed tiny scars at his eyebrows. His knuckles showed faint lines—the scars of a Core Rat. As short as he was, just slightly taller than her, he would have been thought of as an easy target in the Core.

"Need something primitive and raw to go with the melancholy, otherwise it's too sentimental. Only ever heard that rawness from one person." He sat back, his eyes narrowed into slits. "Like you to help me."

Jasmine stared at him. He had described the very qualities her instructors wanted removed from her work. "Have you tried the University? They—"

"Unfortunately I wasn't an orphan and up for adoption," he muttered, staring at a spot beside the table, then looked at her and found himself again. "Sorry. Didn't mean that the way it sounded."

He could have meant a number of things by it. Which didn't he mean?

Refusing to appear uncomfortable, he shrugged and looked away. "Maybe I did."

After a moment he leaned towards her again. "Had to make do with remote courses and any equipment I could get put together. Was a time when I would have given anything to have your education. Don't feel that way anymore. Heard what Desilva told your brother about your last concert piece. Follow her advice, you'll squash everything that's fresh about your music. No matter what you create, they'll put it on their mold and if it doesn't fit they'll take turns jumping up and down on it till it fits or it's destroyed. What would Desilva say about this?" He tapped the disc. "Call it maudlin and depressing because it doesn't fit into the commercial mold. Think she's right?"

"Of course not."

He sat back and ran a hand through the front of his hair. That's what was odd about his coloring. His hair grew in almost the same color as his skin and bleached blond in the light. She had to keep reminding herself not to stare.

"How long have you been following me around?" she asked.

He gave her a quizzical look.

"To know I'm an orphan," she added.

He smirked. "Who needed to follow you? Your whole life and your brother's were in the press."

"Oh . . . yeah." Owen Lamberin's murder.

"Ever listen to Vince Chapman?"

"Of course—he's a favorite from way back."

"I knew it."

Jasmine let herself be drawn into a conversation about comparative musical tastes. As the afternoon progressed she not only discovered Edan

Loffler's musical favorites but that he had parents he wouldn't talk about, had spent some very rough years as a Core Rat and now worked enough hours at a club in the Core to buy the courses and equipment he needed. He learned more about her life than he'd seen in the press and that Jasmine and Mane were partners in a security business.

Once, as he turned his head, a flash of iridescence at his neck drew her eyes to a long, thin feather that looked incredibly real as it caught the light. He wore a combination of mouse brown and moss green that hadn't been around for years. She wondered if he couldn't afford anything newer or if he wanted to be different.

It wasn't until the after work crowd started leaving that she thought to look at her watch. There was someplace she should—

"Jasmine," Edan whispered and she leaned closer. "My lyrics move you at all?"

"Are you kidding? Your lines have been floating around in my head all day."

His earnest eyes blinked and she knew she'd given the wrong answer.

"It's more than that," she groped. "The emotions have stayed with me all day too. There's real power in your words."

He waited as if wondering why she wouldn't tell him the truth.

"I felt like . . . you'd looked inside me and knew my deepest fear would be to become that 'old and broken man.'"

His eyes started a smile that slowly spread to the rest of his face till he grinned at her. "Help me find the music, Jasmine. Already worked up melodies but I need help to—"

Jasmine's wrist band prickled against her skin—Mane. She looked at the time again and groaned. "I was supposed to meet my partner an hour ago," she interrupted while searching for her pocket phone. "Mane? I got stalled."

"We still going?" Mane asked.

"Yeah," she said standing. "I'll be there in 15 minutes."

Edan raised an eyebrow at Jasmine.

"I'm sorry. I have to go."

He shook his head, somehow finding her amusing. "So am I, but remember, you still owe me an answer. Call me when you finish?"

"Yeah, I will," she mumbled awkwardly and suddenly couldn't wait to be away from him.

*　*　*　*　*

Jasmine and Mane walked between the large box-like buildings in the city's warehouse district to a relatively small one. This was where the clinic kept equipment it wasn't using—it was where Adrien had set up a first stage research lab.

Mane waved and pulled a face at a tiny indentation above the door frame—no doubt having spotted the entry camera. Jasmine rolled her eyes and pushed the buzzer. The door unlatched and Adrien motioned them inside with all the excitement of a new father.

"Welcome." He bowed first to Mane then Jasmine. They were surrounded by stacked crates. While pointing out all the moving they had done to make room for the lab, Adrien led them through a maze of container-lined corridors to an open door that spilled light into the dim warehouse.

As the three of them stepped into the room, a young woman with long black hair turned from her console to greet them.

"Jasmine and Mane," she said in a voice that made Jasmine think of her flute.

"A bright jewel worth looking for in these dreary surroundings." Mane bowed deeply while the woman laughed.

"This is Mei Komika," Adrien mumbled, his attention caught by the display behind her. "You're getting closer?" he asked, stepping forward to take a look at the jumble of lines and colored balls that hung above the console like a child's tangled toy.

"Not quite close enough," she answered. "Watch this."

Adrien reached to cup a section of the projection in his hand and the shapes began to change except for the section he held. "This is a molecular group from the capsule wall." Then, at the very end, the section he held shifted and the simulation ended. "We thought that might be the one part that VJX prevents from mutating." He grinned at Mei. "Guess it's still just a theory."

Adrien turned his attention to the rest of the room. "That's just something we're playing with. The real work is to conclude the toxicology tests so we can finish up the dosage development and start tolerance studies."

Jasmine had seen him excited about his work before, but this time she was involved in it and he invited her in to be part of that excitement. She and Mane had spent a lot of time setting up delivery schedules and payment timetables and that had been exciting, but this . . . they were doing something big here.

Mane surveyed the room. "Are you doing tissue trials for toxicology, or using simulations?" he asked.

Jasmine rolled her eyes. She wouldn't be surprised if Mane knew as much about VJX as Adrien at this point. She had given up trying to keep up with him though he kept sending her more material to read.

"It's easier and more reliable to use actual tissue."

Adrien motioned towards a set of screens showing human bodies with patterns of color patches that moved very slowly. "These are the beginning of tolerance simulations. They'll also tell us if the drug reaches the affected area and how long it stays there. The simulations take a matter of days to run through but we'll also have to use people. That test run could take two years. Only then can we actually start treating patients, assuming everything indicates VJX will work."

Mane seemed pensive. "Too bad you can't speed people's reactions up like a computer simulation." He shook his head. "Won't work. I've seen people sped up on vids. They sound like mice when they talk and you can't understand a word they say."

Adrien laughed then turned to Jasmine. "We had trouble with residues on the second batch of VJX you supplied us with. It was put through a Jacobson solvent extraction process that introduces impurities. They can cause side-effects. We need a standard supply that's residue-free or our results won't be useful." He spoke to her as if she were a colleague.

"I'll talk to Manda." she answered. "We'll get you a clean batch next time."

"Good." Adrien stared at her intently. "That's what we need."

Jasmine smiled at his serious expression. "It would help if we had a street test to use that would show up the impurities on a small sample before we buy."

"I'll get Mei to come up with something for you," Adrien replied. "You can access security through here," he pointed the console out to Mane.

Mane sat for less than a minute when he said, "I could break through this in fifteen minutes. Anybody else—might take thirty. Let me see what I can do."

While Mane continued his appraisal of the security system, Jasmine stood off to the side. Adrien's lips pursed as he listened to Mane's suggestions. The hollows under his eyes had all but disappeared. It seemed he was getting what passed for regular sleep for Adrien. Happiness for him swept over her like a warm glow. This project was giving him a way to heal. He'd been intense and excited before but not this content. She suspected his happiness had little to do with defying the Emerald Coalition and everything to do with pioneering research on a drug no one had thought to work on. He was risking his career to help the victims of Lightning Madness—and his career was everything.

Adrien turned and caught her watching him. He just grinned at her as if to say, isn't this the best fun you've ever had? She returned his smile.

* * * * *

Jasmine and Mane walked to their rail station. She pulled out her phone once they sat in their car and called Edan's number. It was well past midnight but he answered in a moment.

"Great timing. I'm off work in an hour. Why don't you come down?"

"I . . . ," she'd expected they'd chat for a few minutes then make plans to meet again in a few days. She'd been learning a new person. Her mind was already full to bursting with him.

He misunderstood her hesitation, "I can send somebody to the rail station to pick you up but it's not really that rough out there tonight."

"No, I can handle it." His enthusiasm for her made it hard to say no. "I'm on the train now. I'll be there in fifteen minutes."

"Great. 'kay."

"'kay," she replied and pocketed the phone.

"Loffler?" Mane asked.

"Mmm."

"So what does The Fan want? Not another autograph I hope."

"He has a name."

Mane put his hands up in defense. "He's been all but stalking you. From what you've said, he's knows way too much about you. Street talk says he's been stashed in his place for the past few years, only comes out to go to work."

"You've been checking on him?"

Mane shrugged. "Just keeping in practice."

"He's been buried in his music the past few years. He's worked really hard at it. He's amazing. His music and words—they're . . . sad, powerful, sweet . . . "

"Are you talking about his music or him?"

She frowned playfully at him.

Mane shook his head. "Already doomed." He stood. "My stop's coming up. Be careful with this guy. Don't let him throw your judgement."

"Was I a Core Rat? Stop worrying. Good night."

*   *   *   *   *

When Jasmine walked up to the club, Edan was already on his way out.

"Slow night," he said while putting on his jacket. "Got off early. Let's go."

"Where are we going?" she asked.

"My place. I've got—"

Jasmine had stopped dead. He cocked his head at her and she honestly believed he had no idea why she hesitated.

"Was hoping you'd play your requiem for me. My 'board's not great but . . . " He trailed off as he finally understood. Then his cheeks pulled in. Edan turned to look at the rail stop ahead. "Listen, if you'd rather send a recording—"

"Edan."

He looked at her over his shoulder.

Jasmine stepped in front of him. "Both of us survived the Core by not giving trust too quickly. Am I right?"

"Yeah," he admitted and his face softened. "At least let me walk you home."

They fell into step together and headed for the rail stop. Edan didn't speak as they walked. Even in the darkness his eyes were slits—as if opening them wider would let the truth spill out.

"From what I could tell," Jasmine commented, "you've got a couple of bad keys in your 'board."

"Can't get the tuner to sync them."

"Must be circuits if the tuner won't work. Have you got a kit?"

"Yeah, still in the box." His eyes brightened. "You know how to use a kit?"

"I guess you never followed me to engineering class."

"Wasn't stalking you," he said getting that insulted look on again.

"I'm kidding." She shook her head. It wouldn't take long to do a tuning with a brand new kit. "If I can get those keys tuned I'll play for you."

That really confused him. "You mean now? Tonight?"

"Yes tonight. But learn to take a joke, would you?"

"Sure, when you learn to take a compliment," he muttered.

*   *   *   *   *

It took almost an hour of tinkering before Jasmine was satisfied that she'd done the best she could to get Edan's primary 'board functioning. His music filled his living room including several smaller 'boards that could integrate with the main one.

Jasmine sat at the 'board while Edan took the stuffed chair opposite her. She was nervous and not just that extra little buzz that puts life into the music. She took a few minutes to limber her fingers over the keys, then started in. It had been a long time and every so often she stumbled, but most of the notes appeared in her mind just before they needed to flow through her fingers.

At the end she looked up just in time to see Edan wiping at his eyes.

"I can die now," he sighed. "Jasmine Rochelle has played my living room."

"I made six mistakes."

"Still think you're brilliant."

Jasmine sat on the couch, gave him a sidelong glance and said, "Thank you." She shouldn't be here but despite his intensity, she didn't feel threatened. It wasn't her his attention was on, it was on her music.

"You must have been pretty angry when you wrote that."

"I was." Jasmine leaned back and closed her eyes hoping it would stop him talking, freeing her to leave just as soon as she rested a moment.

"When was that?"

"No more questions," she murmured. "You've worn me out."

*   *   *   *   *

Jasmine woke to the dim light of morning and lay frozen until she could figure out where she was. Edan was asleep in his chair, the yellow mop of his hair hiding his face. She wondered why he hadn't gone to his bedroom for the night. He'd probably gotten some perverse pleasure from watching her sleep. Someone had put a blanket over her. She threw it on the floor.

"Good morning," Edan said while stiffly unrolling himself. "I'll put some coffee on." He sat there a moment with elbows on knees looking at the floor.

Jasmine ignored him and dug in the cushions for her other shoe. "I, of all people, should know better than to fall asleep with a stranger."

He chuckled. "We've never been strangers."

Jasmine checked to be sure she had both shoes on, then searched for her jacket.

"Hey," he said. "Will you at least give me an answer before you go?"

"Yes." There had never been any doubt. "Yes, I'll help you."

He grinned, watching her put on her jacket.

Her anger was dying. "Do you really have to be so smug about this?"

He pushed himself out of the chair. "Hey," he said. "Wouldn't take more than an hour to fix the opening phrase of that ballad."

She turned away from him for a moment still rooted at his door. If he hadn't just woken up, he would have looked earnest and hurt. As it was he stood just a breath away from her, eyes puffy and clothes rumpled, barely coherent, asking her for help.

"Didn't you say you were making coffee?" she asked.

Jasmine shed her jacket and sat at the 'board while he clattered in the cooking nook. Once he had coffee for both of them, he pulled out an old 'board and they played with each other and to each other for the next half hour.

"Wow," he muttered. "This is power of ten. Gotten more done with you in thirty minutes than I could have done alone in hours."

Why was she still here? Why hadn't she run? Then he looked up and smiled at her. A smile that took the ever-present pout from his lips and opened those guarded hazel eyes. A smile that made her hold her breath for a moment, hoping her face wasn't as flushed as it felt.

Panic crept up on her and, as if a curtain lifted, she realized she had only really met him yesterday and here she was sitting in his living room charmed out of all sense by him. She had to get away, to think. She couldn't trust herself here.

"I have to go," she blurted.

He looked surprised. "When can you come over again?"

"I don't know." Jasmine stood. "I'll call you."

Disappointment was clear on his face.

"Really," she insisted. "Tomorrow. Mane and I are working a case today."

She quickly grabbed her jacket and flew to the door before he could move close to her again. "This was great," she assured him before she fled, feeling like she had escaped a trap.

Jasmine and Mane walked from the restaurant for half a block, then laughed and ran all the way to the rail station. They'd picked up five clients in the past month already with their restaurant scheme—all of them well off. What seemed to come as no surprise to Mane was that some of these people found dealing with Core Rats exciting.

"Always on the hunt for excitement," Mane had said. "They've done most everything money can buy. Nothing gets them excited like danger, or dangerous people."

Jasmine squeezed in beside him on the rail car. He was silent for a moment then turned to her. "Can you handle Manda on your own?"

She squinted at him. "That woman from the Razzmatazz called you, didn't she?"

He shrugged, then smiled without meeting her eyes.

"You know," she continued. "We *are* only supposed to be selling recs." She shook her head. "Go. I'll handle the meeting with Manda."

"Thanks, Doll," he said and bolted from the car at the next stop.

Jasmine checked her watch. She was ahead of schedule for Manda. She got off a stop early to go for a walk and enjoy the first snow of the season. Snow at night always seemed to come out of nowhere. Tonight big scattered flakes slowly drifted from clouds invisible in the darkness above. As usual these days, her thoughts turned to Edan. After her abrupt exit the first time, he'd toned down the charm. That made their visits more comfortable. In the month she'd known him, she'd spent a number of afternoons at his place going through his lyrics and making suggestions, even fitting their sessions between meetings with Mane and Adrien.

He was convinced that the world was ready for more challenging music.

"When people don't have a lot of frass in their lives," he'd said, "they look for grief outside themselves. People need to feel despair and anguish or they're not really living. The world is full of people who are not really living."

Maybe he was right. The plague years were behind them, ecosystems all over the planet were in recovery, manufacturers had found ways to build factories that didn't pollute. The world had been on the brink of annihilation—those who were left to rebuild were grateful for the chance.

More and more often she'd been able to watch his scowl turn to a smile. He took such joy from each piece they worked on. She envied him.

Find your joy—the rest will fall into place around that.

Had she found her joy? Working the Core was a challenge—working the Core with Mane made it more fun than it had ever been. Adrien was more excited about his work than he'd ever been. For now it would do.

She strolled past shops for a while, then, checking her watch again, realized that now she had to hurry or be late.

She was still across the street from the Frog when she spotted a tall brunette woman waiting outside. She seemed to recognize Jasmine. Jasmine stopped—did she know her? The woman's grim expression made Jasmine reach in her jacket pocket for her stinger. By the time the woman made it across the street she apparently remembered she should be smiling.

"Hello, Jasmine."

Before she could answer, a stocky Asian man walked up beside her. Seeing them together, now she knew who they were. They were on Mane's vid. These two had chatted with Martin Yit when he bragged about killing her father.

"I think you got our message," the man said. "We've been waiting to talk to you."

It had been over a month since she got their leafy "message". Had they been softening her up? For what? She had to be very careful what she said.

The brunette stepped closer. "What do you know about Martin Yit's death?"

"How do you know Yit?" she asked. These people had celebrated with Martin Yit when he told them about his kill.

The woman smirked. "A friend of ours—"

"A friend of *yours* was killed? You people killed my father."

Both of them stepped closer. "Just tell us what you know about Martin," the woman said.

"Or what? You didn't bring a branch with you. Are you gunning people down now?" She had a mental image of her father, chest bloody from the protruding branch.

"No, we brought a spiker," the man growled though his hands were empty.

These people had smiled when Yit described the murder scene. Anger swept aside any caution Jasmine had felt.

She stepped towards him. "You're cowards. He was an old man. How many of you did it take to kill him? A spike in the heart is better treatment than any of you deserve."

The man lunged at her. Jasmine thrust her stinger into his hip. He yelped and fell, stunned. The woman grabbed Jasmine's arm and Jasmine took an unexpected step towards her. Using the woman's momentum, she turned it into a throw. Everyone she'd ever fought as a Core Rat had been bigger than her. Jasmine had learned to take advantage of her low center of gravity.

The brunette was on her feet again too quickly and Jasmine bolted back the way she'd come, searching her pockets for her phone as she ran. She ducked into an open alley. Jasmine had the phone in her hand, then the Asian slammed her into the wall. He'd anticipated her and cut her off. He grinned and took his attention off Jasmine long enough to stomp on the phone where it had fallen. Jasmine thrust her stinger at him but he grabbed her arm. The woman caught up and held Jasmine while he twisted until bone gave way and her arm was aflame with pain.

Jasmine fell against the alley wall. Every thought she had was replaced by fury.

The brunette held the man back. "What do you know about Martin Yit's murder?"

"Was assassinating my father Splinter's idea or were you somebody else's dogs?" Jasmine took a step from the wall.

The woman shoved her back. "Answer me!"

Jasmine stood to face her. "Did you run out of ideas for targets? Have to fight somebody else's battles?"

A punch that doubled her over brought Jasmine to the ground. She struggled to get up and fell, then realized it didn't matter because trying to fight now wouldn't change anything. There was nothing left to do but wait it out. The brunette held her up so the stocky man could get a few more punches in, then got tired and dropped her. They did the rest of the damage while Jasmine lay on the ground.

"Can't tell us anything if she's dead," she heard someone say. By the time she heard retreating footsteps, Jasmine lay face down in a puddle of blood and vomit. Every part of her body hurt. The sharp pain in her arm made her weep in hoarse gasps. Jasmine turned her head and let the snowflakes cool her face.

*   *   *   *   *

When Jasmine woke, her entire body was numb. She heard voices—Adrien and Mane, and peeked through slitted eyes.

"Found her, didn't I?" Mane's voice was a quiet drum-roll.

"Only because one of your patch-head friends noticed she was late for a meeting," Adrien answered, voice pitched high with anger. "Why weren't you there?"

Jasmine had never seen Mane angry. She'd seen him pumped, serious, relaxed, but she'd never seen his eyes so hard. She had the uneasy feeling that a very thin layer of control held back his anger now.

Jasmine flexed the fingers of her right hand and found she had enough strength to push the call button.

"She's a big girl. She can handle herself." Mane turned from him.

Adrien persisted and moved to face Mane. "Where were you?"

Mane had had enough and forced Adrien back a few steps with a shove to his shoulders. "Back off, doc."

Adrien stared at him. Jasmine was sure no one had ever laid hands on him in anger before. "This is a hospital, not the Core," he said as the nurse came in. The young man ignored the two combatants and came directly to Jasmine's side. There was a moment of silence while Adrien and Mane realized why he'd come in.

"Jas?"

"Hey, Doll!"

Jasmine ignored them and whispered to the nurse. "Tell them to get the hell out of here until they can talk to each other without yelling."

The nurse straightened and faced the two men. "I have to ask—"

"We heard." Adrien said. "I'm her doctor," he tried.

The nurse's expression didn't change.

"Okay." Adrien gave Mane a warning look. "We'll shut up."

Jasmine closed her eyes and drifted off.

*   *   *   *   *

Jasmine floated in and out of awareness and every time she woke, it was quiet. She was finally ready to open her eyes again.

"Jas?" Adrien bent over her. "How do you feel?"

"Numb mostly, for which I'm sure I should be thankful. How much damage?"

Mane was at her other side and took her hand. He just frowned at her.

Adrien sighed. "Broken arm, cracked ribs—your whole body is a bruise. Your face is in pretty good shape—a black eye is all."

"What happened?" Mane asked.

"Green Splinter," she said.

"Frass! They say anything?"

"Wanted to know about Yit. Didn't tell them anything we haven't already seen on the news."

"Then they . . . did this?"

"After they made me angry."

Adrien rolled his eyes and shook his head.

"Oh," said Mane.

"What do you mean, oh? They laughed when Yit told them what he did."

Mane gave her the strangest look, then. For a moment there was pain, pity and sorrow on a face that had only ever shown her bravado and laughter. He seemed to shrug it off.

"He's right," Mane said. "Should have been there. Knew Splinter would move eventually."

"No lie," Adrien muttered.

"Adrien! Leave him alone," she said. Why did she feel so tired? She struggled to stay awake. "They waited till I was by myself. If it hadn't been tonight, they would have found me some other night." She turned to Mane. "Hey, you know I like you but I don't want you with me everywhere."

Mane didn't smile. He came to her bedside and looked at her for a moment. "I'm sorry, Doll."

"Don't be," she tried to say but the drugs dragged her into sleep again. This time as she drifted in and out, soft voices kept her company. Stilted and awkward, but not angry.

She surfaced a while later to the sound of Adrien's laugh followed by Mane's voice. "Then I asked her what she wanted for the pair. She didn't come sheared. She just stuck her chin out and said she'd only sell if I could prove I had rhythm. Yeah, well . . . I haven't proved it yet." Mane's laughter rumbled through the room.

Jasmine's face crept into a smile. "What time is it?" she asked.

"It's eight a.m.," Adrien replied.

"Don't you people ever sleep?"

"You've been sleeping enough for the three of us," Mane replied.

"We have to decide what to do," Jasmine said. "If we don't make a display, they'll just keep harassing us. I'd like to see how many punches those two can take before *they* pass out."

Mane glanced at Adrien. "Let's wait till I can get more information on what they're up to."

"A spike in the heart would be better than they deserve," she muttered. "We fight back."

"You can't be serious." Panic was clear on Adrien's face. "Mane, tell her she's being reckless."

Mane smiled at her and placed a patronizing hand on hers. "You're being reckless, Doll."

"This is serious."

"Relax," Mane answered. "We'll think of a way to make a point and to finish this without getting ourselves killed."

Adrien shook his head, apparently unconvinced, then glanced up, surprised. Jasmine followed his eyes. Watanabe.

She stood in the doorway as if she'd been there for hours, arms crossed, leaning against the door frame. She nodded to them.

"I hear you got hurt," she said to Jasmine.

Jasmine tried to imagine what Watanabe read into seeing the three of them together. She frantically replayed the conversation. How much had Watanabe heard? Surely Adrien had spotted her as soon as she walked into the doorway.

"What happened?" Watanabe asked as she walked in past Adrien and Mane.

Jasmine shrugged. "Core Rats looking for a few laughs. Man and a woman. Too dark to see faces."

"All the street lights suddenly burn out?"

"I was too busy getting in the way of their punches to notice."

"You found her?" Watanabe asked Mane. "You have any idea what this is about?"

Mane shook his head.

Watenabe leaned in close so only Jasmine could hear. "You're in trouble, girl. I can tell from over here. What's going on?"

Jasmine turned away.

"Go home. Go back to school. Get away from Mane, he's dangerous."

When Jasmine didn't answer, Watenabe straightened.

"Who is it you're going to make a point with?" she asked. "What needs to be finished?"

Mane sighed. "Think this might be pay-back for some surveillance we did a while ago. We'll take it up with our client."

Watenabe waited for more information.

"Sorry," Mane shrugged. "We offer a confidential service."

Her gaze fell on each of them in turn. A warning? An appeal? She left.

"What are you doing?" Adrien said in a hoarse whisper. "Tell Watanabe what's going on so she can take care of this."

"Why?" Mane whispered. "So she can find out what really happened to Yit?" He shook his head and looked at Jasmine. "We can handle this."

"She was almost beaten to death tonight!"

"I've survived worse," Jasmine said. "We can handle this."

Adrien looked at them both for a moment. Mane shrugged. Adrien sighed and looked at his watch. "I've got a meeting in an hour." He shook his head at them and left. He just didn't understand that Green Splinter had just thrown them a challenge. If she didn't do something, they'd keep harassing her . . . or start on Adrien.

"So, what's our plan?" she asked Mane.

✶ ✶ E I G H T ✶ ✶

Rain had begun to fall at dawn and still splattered the already saturated green of the forest. Although he was protected from the rain by the porch roof, mist drifted in, moistening everything and running in droplets down the mock-wood pillars. Miguel Escalente took another sip of hot tea and closed his eyes to listen to the din around him. The birds were silent for now but a marvel of insects kept up a chorus despite the downpour. Their buzz and drone became white noise to the occasional series of chirps, trills and whoops that Miguel had been told by the area guardian were those of frogs. As soon as the rain stopped, the birds would start up again.

He had made the trip to the cabana many times but was able to see very few of the birds, insects and other animals which advertised their presence so insistently now.

Miguel drained the last sip from his cup, after checking to be sure nothing had flown into it, and stood. Part of his morning ritual was to search the porch for moths that had been attracted by the lights from the night before. When Carlos, who took care of the cabana, had first told him the porch walls were sprinkled with moths every morning, Miguel had thought it a story told to make fun of newcomers. Then he'd learned to spot the small bits of out-of-place wood and bark that were actually moths. Carlos had poked some of them and to Miguel's surprise, they stayed put. Some that looked like leaves fell to the mock-wood floor.

Miguel thought they were too fragile to touch and was content to find them and leave them alone. There were a few startler moths on the porch railings and he couldn't resist gently stirring one drab outer wing to see the moth quickly flash the bright colors underneath. It returned to its unassuming resting position and Miguel poked it once more, feeling like a child who, after repeated forbiddings, can't help but touch grandmother's most precious collectibles.

Several shrill whistles reverberated through the jungle announcing that the rain had stopped, and a few more birds began to sing although water still sprinkled the foliage, running off from leaves high above.

Still sheltered by the porch roof he stood at the top of the steps and gazed into the mass of green that rose in clouds of leaves fifty meters above him. No matter how many times he came, he stood awed by the miracle EcoTech had created here. Forty years ago all these plants and the animals that inhabited them were just genetic codes in the heritage vaults.

Footsteps broke into his solitude and reminded him he'd come with a five member press party. Shelly Vandaal stood in bare feet beside him, her housecoat wrapped around her, squinting into the mist.

"So many times I tried to imagine what a jungle was like—I never could have imagined this." She looked more closely into the still dripping green. Her shoulder-length blond hair framed a beautifully crafted face— blue eyes, full lips and perfect cheek-bones. She crossed her arms across her chest against the cool, damp air.

Miguel leaned on the rail beside her and smiled. As much as he preferred coming to the president's jungle cabana alone, it was heartening to watch people new to the forest.

Shelly slapped at her neck. The mosquitoes had found her. She retired into the cabana where netting kept most of the insects out.

Voices murmured and pans clattered in the kitchen. Bringing the press out here had been Simon's idea. "Let them see, smell and hear what we are trying to preserve," he'd said.

"I know I should be packing," Shelly called from inside, "but can we go up the elevator one last time?"

He chuckled. "You took it up so often yesterday, there's no push left in the cells."

"Then let's just take it as high as it goes. We've got time if we have breakfast on the plane."

Of course he gave in. It was refreshing to be around someone who treated him like a fellow human being rather than either a celebrity or a criminal needing questioning.

*　*　*　*　*

Lack of power made ascent in the elevator excruciatingly slow but Shelly didn't seem to mind. She peered through binoculars in one direction then another as the observation elevator crawled up the tower. Ten meters, twenty meters, thirty meters and . . . it groaned to a stop. They'd only gotten as far as the second canopy—no panoramic views today. The tower had been built so that visitors could have a close look at the jungle without damaging it. Miguel had spent hours in the elevator trying to penetrate the foliage with binoculars. He'd seen splashes of colour and glimpses of birds and flowers while the voices of hundreds of tiny jungle inhabitants sang, hidden by the green. Miguel leaned over the rail to look up and spotted the branch that was so close to the tower it usually brushed the elevator when it passed. What if one day he could reach out and grab that branch, then, hand over hand, like the gibbons in the nature vids, travel through the canopy and finally find all those creatures, fruits and flowers that had stayed hidden for so long.

It was impossible and besides, the branch would never hold his weight.

Shelly came to stand beside him. "I can't believe the Opposition thinks the Emerald Coalition has out-lived its purpose. If they could see this . . . you have to protect this."

Protecting the preserves was the least of his worries. The preserves had been started by his predecessors. Miguel had taken on cleaning up politicians. He was convinced that was a much harder task.

"I will," he said. "By the end of the year we'll have another 125 square kilometers under preserve status. Another 200 the year after that. Part of the Guatemalan parcel is still in the courts hearing eviction appeals." The appeals seemed to take longer each time. The Opposition had started to get involved, taking advantage of people's growing dissatisfaction at being asked to leave their homes to live in cities.

"Plantation fields and cities are wastelands compared to this," Shelly said. "Every centimeter for fifty meters up is packed with plants and animals."

He glanced at his watch. "We have to go." Miguel brought the control lever down and the elevator descended.

They walked back to the cabana without speaking, their boots thudding on the boardwalk.

✱ ✱ N I N E ✱ ✱

Wind drove rain against the picture windows of Miguel's Geneva office. He stared unseeing at his clipboard screen. None of the things that needed doing were appealing. There were days when he could take blade to the Emerald Coalition and cut out the cancers with zeal and without remorse. This was not one of those days.

The block leaders of the Emerald Coalition were more than happy to support his rise to party leader when they saw how popular he was for cleaning out corrupt officials as the South American block representative. They were less happy now that they realized he had meant what he said. He often felt he was the only one who had taken his election promises seriously.

"Nine months in office and the boy's already taking exotic holidays."

Miguel looked up to see a familiar black face crowned with tight black and grey curls.

"Old man!" Miguel stood to embrace his friend.

"Did you have a relaxing time?" Simon Bonsorte asked, his eyes crinkled.

"Yup, same as always."

"Then why were you looking so glum?"

Miguel sighed and sat back down on the couch. "Tell me again that the party is behind me on this cleansing imperative."

Simon sat beside him. "Take your time."

"I cleaned up Bogota. Why is this so hard?"

"In Bogota you had the unconditional support of the captain of the South American Emerald Warriors."

"Oh yes, I forgot," Miguel muttered with sarcasm.

"If you take this too fast you'll make too many enemies. You won't be able to do much good if the block directors don't cooperate, at least on the record."

"Yes, yes, I know." Miguel hated the politics that made it necessary to allow the Block directors time to clean up before he started legal proceedings. That had been the condition the party elected him on.

"You want to hear my report or not?" Simon asked.

Miguel nodded.

Simon sat up straight and put on his official voice. "Louisa Bartchenko, Director Europa: still comes up clean. Martin Nakakura, Director Asia: investigation incomplete. Sheila Michaels, Director North America: looks dirty but I haven't got anything solid on her yet. Carmen Perez, Director South America: is clean as they come thanks to you. Theo Zambuto, Director Africa: definitely dirty. Mick Haberstad, Director Pacifica: my people are still collecting data." He sat back again.

"Michaels. I hoped she was clean."

"She may be one of the few dirty ones willing to clean up."

"What about Ortega?"

"I don't know, son. Could go either way. We're still investigating."

That was not good news. If Miguel didn't have the global support of the Emerald Warriors, his plans were in jeopardy even though he did have the support of the South American arm. They were as close as it got to being an army. During the plague years, armies became expert at organizing aid and burying bodies. For 50 years, no one had time to wage war. Afterwards the people who were left scrambled to find a way to survive and slowly rebuilt their political systems around the major continents.

The recovery years left them little time to worry about starting fights with each other, so a military was never reestablished. Keeping order was left to local police.

"At least on the record you've got his full support," Simon reminded him.

"Good."

Simon frowned. "The Owen Lamberin case is still a problem."

Still. The Restoration party leader was doing her best to use his death against the coalition. She had come very close to accusing the EC of having Owen Lamberin killed through an alliance with the Green Splinter. After all, she had said, the goals of the Green Splinter are the same as those of the EC. Too many people were willing to take notice of the Opposition's warnings.

"What now?"

"The officer in charge of the investigation has reported that one of her colleagues was uncooperative and that her superiors are trying to shut down the investigation prematurely."

"What's her stake in this?"

"Professional pride is all I've been able to come up with. She accused the department of forcing the case into court too early."

"Has she made an official complaint?"

"No, but she's starting a snarl over this. Since that Martin Yit was killed, she's been concerned this could start a cycle of retaliation."

"Find out what she knows or suspects. We need to keep an eye on this."

Miguel got up and sat at his desk. "I've got another list of names for you to work on."

*　*　*　*　*

Miguel smiled as Shelly clutched at her hair in a vain attempt to keep the wind from having its way. She stood beside him gazing out over lake

Geneva. The ice was clearing and the surrounding bare scrub and small trees were tinged with green as their buds began to open.

Shelly turned and smiled when she caught him looking at her.

He'd agreed to see her because her style impressed him. From the beginning she'd treated him like a comrade in arms. It would be an amusing diversion to find out what she was really after. He smiled back at her. He'd played this game many times.

"Simon tells me you need some interview time for a documentary on the preserves."

She sighed. "I did some research when I got back from the trip. Two days ago I got a permit to take cameras into the Mitengo preserve." She looked at him slyly. "And don't say it's been done before. I've got a new slant. Did you know there are at least five illegal harvesting operations going on in the South American preserves?"

"That sounds about right. They already had problems with that when I started in Bogota."

She frowned. "When are people going to learn? EcoTech no sooner gets an ecosystem re-established and somebody starts to exploit it again." She looked out at the lake. "Anyway, I think it's past time people knew about this. They're becoming too complacent. Only a 64% vote for Emerald two elections ago. That's insane. Sure, the last one you got in at 73% but that was only because of strategy. If you don't deliver on the cleansing imperative, that could easily plummet again— unless you've got another hand to play, but I suspect that was your last card." She looked at him as if she had just realized who she was talking to. Charming.

Miguel smiled at her sheepishness and played along. "Relax. I wish my advisors were as blunt as you are. It would save a lot of time."

That was the permission she needed to continue her rant. Considering she was here to interview him, she was doing a lot of the talking.

"As long as there are people willing to exploit the preserves," she said, "we need the Emerald Coalition and the Warriors to protect them. That's the story."

"I'm convinced. When are you leaving and can you pack me in your suitcase?"

She looked at him with surprise, then finally asked, "Bad day?"

"Mmm. Shining armor can get pretty heavy." She considered him for a moment as if she were thinking, now you're being charming.

"Come on," she said. "Let's walk it off."

She led them down the path that followed the shore line. The lake was sprinkled with small boats. The ones with the big bins were the feeders; the one with the small nets was a sampler, checking fish for growth rates and disease; the ones with the big nets were harvesting along the north shore. Shelly stopped where they could have a clear view of the harvester boats between the trees and bushes. She shook her head. "Can you imagine boats ten times that size harvesting on the open ocean?"

Miguel had seen vids of ships harvesting from natural populations before the lack of ozone let in so much UVB that the plankton species that nourished the fish died. Replenishing generators had brought ozone levels up again but the plankton mix was still all wrong. EcoTech claimed they'd even be able to fix that, given a few more years of study.

Shelly grabbed his hand to start them into a jog and all he had time to think about was where to put his feet so he wouldn't trip over tree roots—until his phone rang. It was Simon.

"Theo Zambuto is still giving us trouble." Simon said. "He's still insisting on an extension of the cleansing imperative deadline."

"When is he coming?"

"He isn't. Says he's too busy but would be happy to send his assistant director."

Miguel was silent for a moment. Enough. Simon's research had already proven Zambuto dirty. "Pack your bags, old man, we're going to the dark continent."

"Trouble in Africa?" Shelly asked.

Miguel ignored her question and started the walk back to his office. "You'll need to reschedule."

"How long will you be away?"

"Why don't you call my office when you're back from the preserves."

"Where in Africa are you going?"

He stopped to face her. "Ms. VanDaal—"

She put her hands up in apology and wisely remained silent for the rest of the walk back.

* * T E N * *

Miguel put his datapad back in his bag and stood in the small plane to stretch his legs. Simon had fallen asleep.

Miguel sat back down and pulled out a tiny holoset he kept with him— his family's plantation house. He'd been barely old enough for memories when his family had gotten word that they were on the eviction list. Five hundred hectares in Brazil were being cleared to extend the Espirito Santo coastal forest preserve. A relocation site was assigned and a year later Miguel's family and the two families that worked for them moved to the Cartagena region where they had a hundred hectare plantation to take care of. They even received vouchers to have additional top soil dumped on their new land where it had eroded, washed away during centuries of misuse.

One day, just after the move, Abuelita Naves, his mother's mother, had harsh words for everyone but the children. Mother and father were angry about something. Then Miguel, his brother and two sisters, all older than he, were packed up by Abuelita and they went back to their plantation. They all had to be very quiet as they sneaked up the hill where they could see the house. They sat in the morning rain, dried again when the sun came out, and waited. There were people around the house and huge vehicles. In the distance, hills that had been green with banana trees were black. As they watched, the house crumpled into a cloud of dust, then a loud boom shook them. Abuelita Naves wept.

When they returned home, Miguel's father proudly displayed the new holoset of the plantation house his family had lived in for five generations. On the same plaque, below the house, was a hand-written note. "Your sacrifice has made it possible to move a step closer to restoring our earth. I thank you on behalf of Earth's people." It was signed by Margarete Demille, president of the Emerald Coalition.

When he was a boy, people were proud to help rebuild the Earth to its natural state. Now people were starting to balk. They didn't want to move or they didn't want to be confined to cities. If they wanted factories to keep producing, if they wanted plantations to grow raw materials and food, then people would have to make way to expand plantations as well as the preserves. The EC goal, the goal that had put them in power, was to cover sixty-five percent of every continent with natural preserves and to alter the cities so only native plants and animals lived there. If that's what people still wanted, they had to realize that the days of sacrifice weren't over.

The president's thanks still hung on the wall of the new Escalente family home. Presidents had a much more straightforward mandate back then. She wasn't fighting her own party members.

"Buckle up, everybody," the pilot called over the intercom. "They're not too happy with us down there, Mr. President. All their sentences are starting with 'If we had known . . .'"

Miguel wasn't surprised. This unannounced trip was meant to put Nairobi into a snarl.

Simon woke up and immediately got busy with his phone and datapad. As the plane landed, he put both down and sighed, looking at Miguel. "Zambuto says you'll have to wait. He's holding a Block Assembly."

Miguel smiled. Zambuto had been playing the insulted saint, blustering with indignation every time he caught Miguel's people doing their research. Zambuto was not about to cut his assembly short to meet with the man who'd been responsible for the offence.

Simon rolled his eyes. "I suppose now we're about to disrupt a Block Assembly?"

∗   ∗   ∗   ∗   ∗

Simon acted as the prow of the ship that was Miguel's meager delegation, cutting through obstacles to get Miguel into the Nairobi Assembly Hall. A hush of quiet murmurs ran like a wave in front of him.

Simon demanded the doors to the Assembly hall be opened, and because Miguel stood behind him, they were. About thirty people and fifty faces on screens all turned to him as Miguel walked in. He checked for the press and noticed several people in the background speaking softly to an invisible audience—good.

"Members of the Assembly, please pardon the intrusion." He walked down the central aisle. Zambuto stood. He wore shock plainly on his face but never lost the air of defiance he always directed at Miguel.

A calm came over Miguel. The situation was at a head. That meant it would be resolved by the end of the day. Either Zambuto gave up his petition or Miguel would start proceedings to have him removed.

Zambuto was smiling now as he stepped off the dais towards Miguel. "President Escalente. Since your concerns are so urgent we can convene to—"

"No, no. This won't take long and will be of interest to everyone here." Miguel smiled back at him. "I understand you'd like an extension of the cleansing imperative deadline."

Zambuto scowled. "I will not discuss this here."

Miguel ignored his indignation. "Why do you need an extension?"

Zambuto stared at him for a moment and then seemed to remember who was watching. "It takes time to sort out what is going on and who we want to throw out. For example, a few branches of the Emerald Warriors are taking bribes. You know how it works. A new recruit comes in and part of their initiation is to take bribes. To fit in, they do it and so cannot turn in their comrades. These are good people. They are trying to fit in so they can do good work."

It was taking time for Zambuto to erase the appropriate documents was more likely.

Miguel shook his head. "It's no secret that I didn't want to give any clean-up time at all. This is a compromise that has already cost the party some credibility. This isn't easy for any of us. You are being short-sighted." Miguel looked around at the Assembly. "I'm not doing this because I made promises just to get elected. The future of the Emerald Coalition is at stake here. The election before mine was won by only 64% and for the first time ever last year one of our legislations was voted down. We should all be worried. People are starting to listen to the Restoration party. And why shouldn't they? We're a single party that's been in power for almost a hundred years. A lot of people think we've out-lived our mandate and that party members are getting fat on corruption. If we don't prove them wrong on both counts, the whole party is through."

"We have made a great deal of progress," Zambuto insisted. "We have replaced thirty-four people already but we've got a long distance to go. We need more time."

Miguel frowned. Thirty-four people who Zambuto was annoyed with for some petty slight had been replaced by thirty-four others more eager to please. Unless he was a complete fool, Zambuto had to know Miguel would have him removed. Zambuto's only hope was to buy time to destroy evidence and find a way to protect himself.

"There will be no extensions." Miguel's gaze took in the entire assembly. "Not for anyone." He softened his expression. "I know this has been hard for all of you. Your efforts make the Emerald Coalition stronger."

He turned and left the hall.

"As soon as we get home," Simon muttered beside him, "I'll have to order more bodyguards."

Jasmine knew she was being a pest visiting Mane while he was trying to work, but at her place, messages piled up from Edan. Explaining a broken arm was one thing—she just didn't want him to see the kind of bruises any Core Rat would recognize as being the result of street action. Thanks to the eye-patches Adrien gave her, the swelling had gone down and most of the color disappeared from around her eyes, at least.

"Will they believe it?" Jasmine asked from the couch while Mane worked his console.

"Good chance," he replied. "Ever since Yit died, they've been in a snarl about a response. Some actually want to forget the whole thing and concentrate on other targets. Won't be hard to convince them the rest of their little group doesn't like what their friend Yit got up to." He sat back and studied the screen for a moment.

"When I accused them of working for somebody else," Jasmine said, "those two just got angrier—they didn't deny it."

"Yeah, if it were Splinter's idea to kill your father, we would have started a war with them by killing Yit. They would have gone after one Restoration Party member after another, but they didn't. It's like they were doing somebody a favor and they don't want to have to deal with the mess it made. Somebody paid them to kill Lamberin and to take credit for it."

"Who?"

"Don't know."

That didn't surprise her. It was power of ten that they'd gotten as much information on Green Splinter as they had—as *Mane* had. She'd stopped asking how he knew these things—who he knew who carried access to such detailed information about Splinter. And why would those people make the information available to a Core Rat?

"I wish we could figure out those files of Dad's."

Mane frowned and shook his head. "Take a run at those every few weeks. Just can't get in."

She couldn't help but think that those files held the secret to why her father had been killed.

Jasmine rubbed her cast though it did nothing to relieve the itching.

Mane smiled at her. "Have to ask Adrien why nobody's ever started a research clinic to find out how to scratch an itch under a cast."

She stretched, then groaned. Everything still hurt and sitting wasn't helping. She needed a walk. Besides, she knew Mane could work faster without her looking over his shoulder.

As she strolled out the building doorway, she stepped in front of Edan. For a moment he seemed as surprised as she was.

"Hi. Didn't answer and . . . " He took in her cast and looked more closely at her face. "What happened?"

Jasmine was so shocked, she needed a moment to think of an answer. "Come on up," she said. "I'll show you my place."

When Edan peered around at the room she realized how little she'd done with it. This wasn't a part of her life she wanted to show him. His eyes kept coming back to her.

"What happened?" he asked again.

"One of our jobs got a little rough."

He reached up and brushed the hair out of her face to have a closer look.

"It's um . . . it's being taken care of." That seemed to satisfy him.

He looked around again. "Your music isn't here."

"No." It didn't belong here. It belonged to her past . . . and to Edan. "I keep it at the house." She offered him the couch and sat beside him. "I'm sorry I didn't get back to you. This job we're on . . . " She shrugged. "It's complicated."

"'kay," he said, then took her hand and smiled at her, testing to see how far he could go.

She wanted nothing more than to have him touch her but the bruises and the pain made her keep her distance. She pulled away from him and cringed at the flicker of disappointment he showed. "My time should free up in a week."

The entry request chimed. The door recognized Mane's palm and he poked his head in. "Needed to ask you—"

"Mane," she said to stop him and give him a chance to notice Edan.

"Loffler," he said entering, then bowed. "Mane Silverstar."

Edan stood and bowed as well. "Met before." He cocked his head at Mane. "Ellie."

"How do you know Ellie?"

"Used to run with Winkler Moss—"

"And Missy and Peeps." Mane nodded. "Didn't figure you for a patchhead." He glanced at Jasmine as if he'd just made a point.

Edan shrugged. "Gave up Core Trash." He put a hand over his forehead. "Too much in here that needed to be music. No time to sit around and patch recs to see how stupid you can get. Haven't flocked in the Core for years."

"Missy and Peeps are dead," Mane said, watching Edan's reaction with what seemed like detached curiosity. "A year after you flew off."

Jasmine hadn't been in the Core for over eight years. It seemed she had missed a lot.

Edan glanced at her then back at Mane. "You and Ellie were deep spliced back then. Must have given her some ride—crashed for two years after you threw her out."

Mane scowled and didn't answer.

"She even tried to warn her friends off you." He smiled and turned to Jasmine. "He still a dead shot for the women?"

Mane's usual reaction to this sort of teasing was a witty comeback. He cocked his head at Edan for a moment then replied. "Was clean-headed enough to know a bad connection when I made one."

Jasmine looked at both of them and didn't know what to do. Mane was the one who smoothed things over in these situations.

"Weren't you the weasel for Mendosa for a few years?" Edan asked Mane.

Mendosa had imagined himself a Core King for years. Even when Jasmine flocked in the Core, his dogs had tried to recruit her, less than gently, into their gang. She answered, less than gently, that she enjoyed her independence.

"Was one of my first clients," Mane answered, hands on hips, practically daring Edan out loud to continue the accusation.

Jasmine spoke up. "Edan and I were just going for a walk. You need me for anything?"

Mane stared at her for a moment then shrugged, his face flushed red. "No, it can wait." He walked past Edan and left.

"He's usually . . . more polite," she explained to Edan.

Edan smirked. "Just being protective. You more than business partners?"

"No." Jasmine looked at the door. "What was he like when he worked for Mendosa?"

"Unstoppable when he was after information. Smooth when he needed to be, brutal when he needed to be. Could play people against each other like no one else I've ever seen. Hard on his women." He must have read the disbelief in Jasmine's eyes. "None of us are the same people we were in the Core," he said. "I wasn't this charming back then."

She laughed.

"Let's go for that walk," he said and held out his hand. She took it and he led her out. She couldn't shake the image of Mane in the Core, brutal and dangerous. It just didn't fit.

Then Edan's fingers twined through hers and she couldn't think of anything other than this young man with the keen eyes who wanted to hold her hand.

* * T W E L V E * *

Eight days after the attack on Jasmine, she and Mane were ready.

Travers and McMichaels. Surveilance showed they went to the Rage every Friday night. That was where Mane had taken the vids of them and Yit. Jasmine and Mane waited for them down the block in a dark alcove. The hired car waited half a block away. Mane frowned into the darkness. He'd had a sulk on since he met Edan. Jasmine hadn't helped. She couldn't shake the image of Mane as Mendosa's information gatherer.

Jasmine turned back to her perusal of the sidewalk and smiled as she glimpsed them coming and got her stinger ready. Tonight it sat in her hand loaded with tranques.

Jasmine and Mane stepped out behind their targets and stung them before they even knew they were in danger. The car pulled up and Mane dragged the unconscious pair inside.

The driver was a man Mane sometimes hired when it required an extra body to do one of their jobs. He helped Mane get Travers and McMichaels into the warehouse. While Mane paid him, Jasmine got busy with the strapping tape. By the time the two groaned awake, they were immobilized and sitting against the wall. Mane had already searched them for their identification.

Jasmine stood in front of them. McMichaels, the brunette, turned her eyes away. Travers glared at her. They bore the sullen look of toughs hiding fear. It had been so easy for them to gang up on her. Jasmine took out her knife. "You two messed me up pretty good. You." She leaned closer to the man. His eyes registered fear as the knife touched his throat. "You broke my arm."

She'd rehearsed the paths her knife would take. From out of nowhere came a memory of the smell of a body burning. Jasmine's stomach heaved. She controlled it—just. She lowered the knife and tried to shake off the memory. These two didn't deserve any better than what Yit got, yet her arms grew numb and useless. Jasmine looked up to see Mane watching her. Why couldn't she at least hit them, she asked with her eyes. He shrugged.

Jasmine took a firm grasp of the knife again. "You're going on a little trip."

Jasmine paced in front of them while Mane flipped through what he'd found.

"Somehow," she said, "the rest of your little gang are starting to think you two killed Martin Yit to shut him up. Why would they think that? Who wanted Owen Lamberin dead?"

"The forests," the man blurted out.

"Shut up!" McMichaels snarled at him.

"And the oceans, and the plains. Every part of the earth that we should be rebuilding, wanted to stop him."

"Why?" Mane asked when Jasmine was too stunned to.

"He wanted to stop the Warriors who protect the preserves."

"How could Owen Lamberin have stopped the Warriors? What did he know?"

"He didn't know a damn thing. He was a liar."

Jasmine stared at Travers with forced paralysis. These people hated her father, she realized. She'd known that before on some level, but now she stood in front of that hatred and saw it naked and ugly.

"What did he lie about?" Mane asked.

"The forests are pure—"

"Shut up!" McMichaels snarled.

Mane hunkered down in front of Travers. "What did he say about the forests that wasn't true?"

"Shut up," McMichaels said again. "They're devolved fools, just like that old man."

At that, Jasmine lunged at her with her knife. It glanced off the wall beside McMichael's throat as Mane grabbed Jasmine by the waist then pinned her shoulders against his chest with his forearms. She lifted her arms and dropped free of him.

Mane yelped. "Frass!"

He held one bloody hand in the other. He took a deep breath while she stared at his hand, then her knife.

"Hey, Doll. Put that away, would you?"

She continued to stare at him then sheathed the knife and put it back in her pocket. "Is it bad?"

"No. Just need to run some water over it." He turned water on in a nearby sink.

Jasmine looked at the captives. They wouldn't meet her eyes. "Like I said. You're going on a trip. Your Splinter pals think you killed Yit. Think about that when you wake up tomorrow and want to call them for help."

Mane came back with more tape and ensured that McMichaels wouldn't do any more talking. Mane asked Travers more questions but was met with silence, so he was taped too.

Jasmine pulled the patches out of her pocket and smiled at their panic while she applied one to each of their necks. As soon as they slumped into sleep again, Mane lifted them into the crates. Jasmine helped as much as her damaged arm allowed.

"Sorry about your hand," she said while he set the lids on the crates, his one hand taped to stop the blood flowing.

Mane shrugged. "I'll get over it." He turned to her and smiled to make sure she understood he wasn't angry. This was not the man Edan had described—not the man Watanabe had warned her about. Edan was right, none of them were the people they had been in the Core.

"When is the truck coming?" she asked.

"Pick-up is in half an hour. They'll be on their way before midnight."

The truck headed for the freight rail station, each crate destined for a different city. The occupants would wake in 24 hours, make noise, be released and left to restart without money, without identification and with their access numbers revoked. Something Mane could achieve in the next few hours since he had their identification cards. It would take them weeks to reestablish electronic identity. They had no reason to believe it was safe to come back since there really was a suspicion amongst the Green Splinter that Martin Yit was considered a liability by his friends.

"Ready to celebrate getting rid of the garbage?" Mane asked, hooking her arm in his.

"Don't you still have some work to do?"

"Can wait an hour."

"'kay, but only if we don't have to walk." She still ached where the bruises went deep and had enough walking for one day.

* * T H I R T E E N * *

A speck of light moved slowly across the night sky. Jasmine trained the binoculars on it. She and Adrien sat on the back porch in lounge chairs, each with a blanket to keep out the chill.

"I need an angle," Adrien said, the sat-guide ready on his lap.

Jasmine noted the tiny read-out at the bottom right of the field. "It's 42.7."

He punched it in. "That would make it Möbius 003. I'll add it to your checklist. What does that one do?"

"Weather mapping," she answered offering him the binoculars. "Aren't you going to have a look?"

He was busy entering the details.

"You can't put it on your own list if you don't actually see it. Being with somebody who's seen it doesn't count."

Adrien snatched the binoculars. "Okay, okay." He found the angle and started panning. "There it is." He entered his find. "I got a call from Arri this afternoon," he said.

"About the Neon Club next month?"

"No, he asked me about VJX."

She stopped breathing.

Adrien looked at her, satellite forgotten. "Why would he be asking anyone about VJX?"

"Mane asked him some questions about purifying veejix and before we knew it, he was offering to do it for us."

"Did you tell him it was Green?"

"He knows—he doesn't care." Jasmine didn't need to see his face. She could tell he was frowning. "Don't start, Adrien. Arri can make these decisions on his own and we didn't push him into anything."

Adrien didn't comment. He held the binoculars limply in his hand.

"Are you done with those?" she asked.

He passed them to her. "Why are you concerned about some contaminated VJX? I thought you had a steady supply of usable purity."

"We may need a bit of it to fall back on for a while."

"Why? How much VJX are you absolutely certain about?"

"You've got what we bought two weeks ago. Arri should be able to distil another .3 K from what we gave him. That puts us dead on for the supply schedule till May."

"And then what? That's only three months away."

"Our supplier is working on getting another lot in 6 months but we can push to get it before then. It may put us a bit behind but we should be able to catch up."

"Nothing about this sounds very certain. We agreed on a supply schedule. If you don't meet it, the research is in jeopardy. I can't just stop using VJX on the tissue trials till the supply gets back on track. That would negate everything we've done so far. I'll shut the whole project down first."

"You're over-reacting. It's just a supply glitch. One of the delivery copters was shot down. The supply will be back on schedule by May."

"How can you promise that? You don't control the supply."

"We'll do it." Jasmine started scanning for more satellites. Adrien was quiet for so long she finally put the binoculars down to look at him.

"I'm pulling out," he said, his eyes on the stars.

Her disbelief made her pause a moment.

"Give us some time," she finally said.

"For what? Every time I see you you've got fresh bruises. You were admitted to the Core clinic twice in the past two months with cuts needing sealing. Either Loffler's pounding on more than just his keyboards or you're getting into a lot of street fights."

"You're exaggerating. Territoriality is part of dealing in the Core."

He sighed at the sky. "And now I've either got a contaminated supply or no supply at all. None of this is working the way I expected."

"Give us time to push our supplier—to find somebody else if we have to. We've all put months of work into this project. How can you even think about pulling out?"

"I can't run a research program with nothing to research."

"This isn't about the project," Jasmine realised. "It's about me. You took this on so I wouldn't go to anybody else. Now there's a minor problem and you're using that as an excuse to pull out. So you can say you told me this wouldn't work—so you can go back to your safe little lab at the clinic—so I have to take up a safer occupation—so everything reverts back to the way it was and you can still say you gave it a try."

Adrien stood, ready to walk out on the conversation.

"Walking away isn't going to change the fact that you have no confidence in what I can do."

"You're ranting," he replied and headed for the back door.

"And you're a coward," she said as the door closed.

She threw the blanket off her lap and paced a few steps before leaving for the street.

The sidewalks were clear but wet from snow melt. Some waterlogged patches of snow still lay on the lawns from the winter's accumulation.

Jasmine went over the conversation until there was nothing new to take from it. She was losing the project.

Jasmine's walk took her by an overgrown yard and she stopped, wondering if it still lay there. Her father had shown it to her. Plaques and stump were invisible in the darkness, but she knew they were there beneath a lump of sodden snow. A mossy tree stump with two metal picture plates embedded in the surface. The stump was over fifty years old but preservatives kept it from rotting away.

The Emerald Coalition had outlawed the use of any unapproved plants for fear of them spreading into future preserves. Only trees with a habitat history for the region were left standing.

When they put the Campbell Street oak on the unapproved list some people didn't agree. Since the Declaration of Irretrievable Loss, such natural wonders were precious.

She remembered running her fingers over the plate that showed the tree lying on the ground surrounded by people, some with their hands covering their faces. Their father had brought her and Adrien here five years ago and told them about the fight to keep the tree. The appeals took three years to go through the courts, but in the end the Emerald Coalition won and the tree was lost. When it came time to remove the stump, the neighbourhood put its foot down. A battle of wills resulted with the Coalition insisting that the stump be destroyed so people could forget the past and move forward while the people insisted that the stump be saved. Money was raised to save the Campbell Street oak stump by installing a security system that would alert anybody for blocks that someone was tampering with the stump. Eventually the Coalition gave up and the stump remained as a symbol.

"Of what?" Adrien had asked.

"For some as a reminder of the price we pay to restore the world," Owen answered.

Adrien nodded understanding and Jasmine shrugged.

Owen's eyes crinkled and a sly smile came to his lips. The real answer was coming. "For others it asks the question: How far is too far?"

Adrien had cocked his head but Jasmine understood.

The grasses around the stump had caught snow all winter. Jasmine stood and stared at the spot until the cold air penetrated her jacket.

She had to make it work. Those dying people deserved to be treated.

Jasmine took stock of where she was and figured the shortest route back to the house She ran most of the way.

Adrien was still up when she came in. He sat on the living room couch, frowning. She dropped herself into the upholstered armchair.

Adrien barely glanced at her. "I wish you wouldn't take this so personally," he said. "It's a business decision based on what's best for the research."

"Here's your chance to prove it. Give me six months to get a supply established. If I don't, we shut down the project. If I do, you'll have to admit that I'm better at this than you gave me credit for."

"If you can't do it in three months, we'll have nothing to keep going with."

"You'll have what you need by the end of May," she replied, suspecting it was impossible. "Do we have a deal?"

Adrien considered for a moment. "Okay, but no extensions."

"I won't need any," she answered, hoping it wasn't a lie. "And don't even think of winding down before May 31. If you try, my spies will tell me."

A strained smile flickered across his face. He put his hand on her shoulder. "Jas—"

She stood. "I'm going to bed." She had to get away from him. She couldn't bear to have him touch her. The last few months had been the best she'd ever had. Mane was the perfect partner, the work was exciting, she and Adrien were as close as ever, and she was doing something no one had tried before. Now Adrien had the power to end all that. Even if she went to another researcher, word would be out that Jasmine and Mane couldn't deliver on their promises.

"Jas." Adrien stood in front of her. "I'm sorry it's working out this way."

She sighed. "No. You're not," she said hoarsely avoiding his eyes. "You're not sorry. This control is something you've always wanted." She walked to her room.

"That's nonsense."

"Yeah, sure." Jasmine shrugged. She closed the door on his broken china expression and wished she had just walked into Edan's room.

She picked up her flute, looked at it for a moment, then put it back on the side table. Jasmine called up some Luminous Flux from the house music selections. As she lay on the bed letting the thrumming wash through her, she told herself it was the music that moved her to tears.

* * F O U R T E E N * *

Carla Watenabe watched as the man she'd been following slipped into a restaurant. Once inside, she saw he'd joined a younger man at a table for two. It was just after the mid-day rush so Carla had her choice of where to sit. She found a spot that put her target in easy distance for the microphone in her datapad. She pointed it at them and pretended to get caught up on city news.

They spoke for several minutes about the menu. Carla ordered lunch.

"So why do *you* think they disappeared?" the young man asked the older in a whisper.

"I don't know but I don't like it. They were good friends with Martin. Now all three of them are gone."

"Do you really think they did him to keep him quiet?"

"No. Something else is going on."

The two fell silent as the waitress brought their drinks.

"You were right," the young man said. "He never should have taken that job—nothing but trouble."

"Yeah . . . well, can't be helped now. We have to move on."

They didn't say a word for several moments. When Carla looked up, they were both staring at her. She blinked, not having to pretend surprise at their notice, then went back to her reading. The trial—they must have seen her testify and recognized her. It only took them a moment to cancel their food order and leave.

Carla decided to stay and enjoy the rest of her sandwich. If she'd been able to keep this case active, she could have sent one of her crew to do surveillance rather than trying to fit it in during breaks between other cases.

This one had really gotten under her skin. The department had forced the trial early. She still wasn't sure why. She knew before it went to trial that there wasn't enough evidence, yet a bit more time and she could have dug up what they needed. She didn't like to think the force could be played with. Maybe that bothered her more than the expressions of disappointment and betrayal on the faces of Owen Lamberin's children when the verdict was read. The son had buried himself in his work and the daughter became a Core Rat . . . but not before hooking up with Mane Silverstar, the town mercenary. Their security work seemed legitimate, but living in the Core was no place for a young woman to mature. Talk from her street sources suggested Jasmine and Mane were dealing Green. That girl was in trouble. Watenabe couldn't help but think those kids' lives would be very different if Lamberin's killer had been found.

She shook her head, ran her card through the table slot and stood. There was no money to find Lamberin's killer, yet officers were still sent out to track down Greens runners who were doing little harm compared to the other Core trash.

Watenabe strolled out into the sunshine and watched people walk by for a moment. The killing of Martin Yit should have started a war between Green Splinter and the Opposition—it hadn't. It seemed now that Yit was likely Lamberin's killer, not just a witness. She'd always assumed Yit was killed by Owen Lamberin's Restoration friends but what if he wasn't? Maybe she wasn't the only one who figured Yit for the killer. Adrien and Jasmine, now there was motive. She'd always seen Lamberin's children as victims, too busy trying to put their lives back together to think about revenge. Maybe that had been a mistake.

When Watenabe returned to the office, a message from the divisional supervisor requested her immediate presence in his office. He started blustering before he'd even closed the door.

" . . . a case you have no authorization to pursue."

"Sir, it now seems likely that Martin Yit killed Owen Lamberin and Yit's murder was payback for that. I've got—"

"The case is dead."

Watenabe stared at him. How could they work this fast? She'd only been spotted an hour ago. Did the Splinter have a direct line into the police force? She'd always respected the man who stood ranting in front of her. She pitied him now. A man of his principles forced to swallow being told to hold off—to sabotage any efforts to solve the case.

She tried again. "I'm on the verge of figuring the connection."

"Do you *have* other cases?"

She frowned at him.

"Then I suggest you work on those. We don't have the money to spend on cases that are going nowhere."

"The evidence suggests—"

"It doesn't matter." His glare dared her to continue.

Because she had known him for so long, she caught a glimmer of regret under his gruff manner.

"Yes, sir," she finally answered, angry at whoever had been able to violate the department this way.

Carla spent the rest of the afternoon at her desk pretending to do research through her console. She'd been pulled off cases before but the reasons had always been good ones, usually lack of evidence. The reasons now seemed political, and though that made her angry, it also made her curious.

* * * * *

Watenabe walked up the sidewalk to the house and stopped to admire the yellow and white flowers that formed a sunny border in the front beds. She let the day's frustration fall from her and smiled. She never understood colleagues who spent home-time working at their consoles. Home was her refuge, a place where work didn't fit.

She palmed the door open and by the time she'd tucked her bag into the front closet, she was greeted by her saw-dust-covered husband.

"Hi sweetheart." He kissed her.

"Daniel, my clothes!" She pushed him away and tried to brush herself off. Daniel snickered and she couldn't help but smile back at him.

"Sorry," he said without much conviction. "I haven't started supper yet."

Of course he hadn't. Her work day officially ended at 4:00 but she rarely started home before 6:00. Today she'd left on time. While Daniel headed for the kitchen, Carla peered into the living room, expecting to see a new piece of home-made furniture displayed there. The household bills for mock-wood were getting higher all the time. But she only saw the familiar comfortable couches and the two guest chairs. The chairs were beautifully designed but no one who ever spent an evening squirming in one of them ever sat in them again.

"Hi Mom."

"Hi Mom."

Voices called from her son and daughter's rooms. Her children no longer ran into her arms when she came home. They were at the aloof stage. She poked her head into Becka's room. She sat on her bed reading from her data pad.

"What are you reading?"

Her daughter's answer was lost as Carla saw something with leaves on it laying beside the bed. She picked it up—a small branch with the end sharpened to a point.

Jasmine uncrossed her legs and stood. Sometime during the past two hours, the engines of the supply chopper had become background noise. The rumble was still loud enough that the two living members of the cargo had long since abandoned conversation. She squeezed between crates to stretch but there wasn't nearly enough room.

Mane had given up on being comfortable in anything but a horizontal position. He lay stretched out on a bed of whatever softer supplies he could find and slept, or at least pretended to. All his sharp edges were gone. Not just because he was sleeping; he'd changed after she was attacked. Despite her better judgement, she'd trusted him from the first time she met him but she always sensed he was humoring her and keeping part of himself hidden behind his bravado. Now he seemed absolutely committed to her as a partner. She was grateful but she didn't understand why.

By May first it had become clear that Manda's supplier couldn't come up with the VJX Adrien needed by the end of the month. Mane did the fastest hunt of his career and in one week he figured the source. But it took two weeks and all the cash they had to convince Gunter Vint to let them come into his operation to look around, as well as to pick up the VJX and the recs they needed. The hope was that this trip would establish a business relationship directly with the harvester. That way they could set up a supply schedule that was actually stable.

Jasmine kicked lightly at a crate with one of her new boots and smiled. As a bonus, she and Mane got to see a real jungle. Black market trips into the preserves were more expensive than what they'd paid. Jasmine sniffed at the air thick with fuel fumes and various odd odors coming from the packages around them. Those who paid black market prices probably received better accommodation. This "blind transportation" was only one of many conditions imposed by Gunther Vint, and for good reason—he didn't want Jasmine and Mane seeing where his base was.

Jasmine stumbled against a stack of solvent barrels as the chopper banked. Mane opened one eye and peered at his watch.

"Guess we're there," he said sitting up, careful not to hit his head on the ceiling.

Jasmine sat on the floor wedged between crates to avoid being knocked over by the next turn.

The flight had seemed to take forever. Fewer than 500 people were given regular access to the rainforest preserves, and she and Mane were about to see one of the first ever regrown.

She pulled the fabric sun hat down over her head. A hat was recommended and she had read somewhere it was less to keep out the sun and more to keep debris and insects out of her hair. She and Mane had watched everything they could find to prepare for the trip and both wore the requisite light cotton shirt and pants with over-the-ankle boots. A real jungle— the most complex ecosystem on earth. She glanced at Mane and he grinned at her with happy anticipation. He'd tied his hair back to keep it under some control. She noticed he'd tucked his pants into his boots and she did the same. The chopper banked again then jolted backwards to a stop. The engines grew quieter and Jasmine and Mane heard voices outside. Jasmine stared at the cargo door—a door they had sworn not to open without invitation. Her excitement was dimmed by the recognition once again that she and Mane were here by the sufferance of their host and once they had stepped into this chopper, were totally under Gunther Vint's control.

The door clanked and Jasmine squinted in the bright light. She stood frozen for a moment. She couldn't see much at first, blinking into the sun. Warm air flooded the stale cargo hold. It held the scent of coconuts and vanilla so there was no doubt about where they had landed.

"Out of the way," someone said and she was pulled through the doorway to stand in a clearing that, by all appearances had been made to give the chopper a place to land. More pungent odors wafted up from the ground, reminding her of wet grass. Jasmine looked down at bruised and trampled plants. She could almost see the aroma rising off them in the heat.

Jasmine gazed up at a wall of green foliage. The chopper had landed in what appeared to be an enormous well walled by the jungle trees. The clearing must have been a quarter of a city block wide. Jasmine searched for Mane and spotted him standing within listening distance of the pilot who was arguing with a young man.

"If you wanted me to wait till 11:10 you shouldn't have told me 11:05," the pilot said as she climbed back into the now-silent chopper for her bag. The young man she spoke to shook his head at her and turned away. Mane shifted to stand beside Jasmine and let his gaze fall on the green surrounding the clearing.

"They timed the landing to come between sat passes," he said in a whisper.

Shouted orders made them both turn back to the chopper. Four people held 3-meter poles erect. A sheet of flimsy metallic fabric attached to the tops was being dragged over the landing area.

"Sat shielding," Mane muttered. "Let's get our stuff." He grabbed her arm.

Jasmine ducked as the fabric rustled over them. She was close enough to notice that the poles the sweating workers carried were made of a fibrous material. Wood? Could it be real wood?

Mane pulled at her and she climbed back into the cargo hold to get her bags. Not only did they have to pay Gunther Vint for the trip, he'd insisted they bring their own food. Jasmine and Mane jumped back outside with packs strapped on. The shielding hung above them now and took some of the heat away. Mane pointed in the direction several people laden with supplies were headed. Jasmine followed him, watching the people ahead of them as they, one by one, were swallowed by the green wall. The trees easily stood as high as the ten storey buildings still scattered through the Core.

As Jasmine and Mane strode into the jungle, everything changed. The air was now cool and heavy with moisture. It took time for eyes to adjust to the darkness and the towering green was overwhelming. Nothing Jasmine had seen before ever made her feel so small. She knew the forest they were in was composed of a collection of different trees and plants, but she found herself unable to tell where one plant ended and another began—it was all just shades of green.

The small vehicle, with its trailer, sat chugging on a path. Two people could crowd into the cab. The platform behind it was already stacked with barrels and the long narrow trailer was half full of crates of supplies. Jasmine and Mane added their packs to the pile.

Jasmine looked up and tried to see evidence of the sun shining. At occasional bright spots, the sun lit up leaves, passing through them as if through green glass, but no ray of pure sunshine made it to the ground.

Nothing moved. She could hear what could have been invisible birds, insects, and frogs forming a background noise of quiet chirps behind the sound of the small transport's engine.

"The tourists have arrived!" A voice as big as the trees accosted them. Gunther Vint stood beside the transport, hands on hips, grinning as if he'd just played a joke on them. He was almost as tall as Mane and easily as large a man. He spoke with a hint of an accent. Jasmine couldn't place it more than deciding it was European.

Jasmine stepped forward and gave him a slight bow. "Thanks for letting us look around. We'll do our best to stay out of the way."

Vint laughed so loudly in the quiet that Jasmine wondered why everyone wasn't cringing at the intrusion his voice made into the forest.

"Everyone!" At his command the group of six put down their loads to stare at Jasmine and Mane. "These are our guests. And they've promised to do their best to stay out of the way." He said it as if Jasmine had said something absurd.

Eyebrows lifted but no one said a word. Vint leaned towards her.

"These people," Vint's gesture took in the six standing behind him, "these people stand between you and the darkness in there." He pointed into the green. "You will do more than just stay out of their way. You will do everything they tell you. Understood?"

Jasmine and Mane nodded.

"Wonderful!" Vint's smile was back. He slapped at his leg. "Welcome to the home of the perpetual itch."

Vint leaned towards them. "How long do you think you would last out here alone?"

Jasmine just stared at him but Mane considered the question as if he could actually come up with an answer.

"Pah! You'd be lost in an hour," Vint decided. "The dark tangle," he whispered and behind him the pilot rolled her eyes and, taking her lead, the rest continued loading supplies on the narrow vehicle.

"It's not as beautiful as it seems," he continued, oblivious to the resumed activity. "And how would you survive? There are many fruit trees, yes, but how to get at the fruit? Could you climb that?" He pointed to a huge tree trunk devoid of branches for at least twenty meters. "And the plants themselves—eat them? They contain the most poisonous toxins known. If you didn't poison yourselves first, you'd starve to death." He straightened. "Be very careful."

It wasn't just the jungle they needed to be careful of. Jasmine was certain no one on a black market trip was treated this way by their host.

"Tourists ride in back," Vint announced. Everything he said was less like giving orders and more like merely a confirmation of the way things were.

Jasmine and Mane cleared a corner of the back of the trailer and sat on the tailgate, legs hanging over the end. Mane's feet caressed the ground. The vehicle had cleared two tracks down to the soil with the steady passing of its tires. Behind them the motor hummed and a sudden lurch started the whole transport moving. Passing over tree roots spread like huge, unruly cables on the path very nearly bounced them off several times.

Jasmine stared into the green, trying to make sense of all the shapes. She said to Mane, "After watching all those vids I was ready for a paradise of plants and animals. This place seems . . . "

"Dangerous," Mane finished for her. "The dark tangle . . . Vint could be right."

"Yeah," she replied gazing at the jumble of huge trees and plants, wondering how anyone had managed to clear a road here, even such a narrow one as they rode on. Many of the trees she glimpsed were so huge they seemed out of proportion with the world around them, as if some optical illusion made them appear much larger than they really were. The trunks of some formed enormous folds that extended to the ground. Buttresses—the word sprang to her head.

"The layers," Mane mumbled.

"Huh?"

"That's what makes it so confusing. Not just the horizontal layers of small plants, larger ones and the stories of the canopy but the larger trees forming a base for other plants to grow on them." He continued to squint into the green darkness. "Must be a way to make sense of it. People used to live in forests like this. I don't think they got lost. I think they got to know their way around as easily as we can find our way in the Core."

Jasmine examined the plants around them and still only saw a confusion of green with an occasional oversized tree trunk. Her mouth dropped open as they drove right beside such a giant. She looked up, but the crown was lost in the distance. As they passed by she examined the trunk. Several buttresses had been cut off to allow the road to pass. The cut surface looked like an open wound, though it must have been cut a long time ago.

"You think that hurt the tree?" she asked.

"Probably anaesthetized it first," Mane replied.

"Mane!" She shoved him and he pretended to almost fall off. "I mean, made it weaker somehow."

"Don't know." He returned to his study of the tangle.

Jasmine watched the wounded tree recede and thought of a colossus with his toes cut off.

The transport passed through two more such maimed trees before stopping in what seemed like a clearing, at first only because some sunlight was able to reach the ground. When the hum of the transport engines stopped, Jasmine could hear a clamor of music coming from one of the huts.

Jasmine and Mane dropped off their perch. Several structures the size of small cabins sat scattered through the trees. Their frames were covered by a fine-meshed grey fabric topped with translucent plastic roofs.

Mane looked up. "Enough trees to form a satellite shield," he said softly.

"Welcome to Vint-town," Vint boomed. "Population seven . . . no make that nine for now. Don't forget to visit our chamber of commerce. It's a rustic little town with no crime to speak of. Oh . . . except that it's based on an illegal economy. Small matter." His laugh reverberated ahead of him as he walked, empty-handed, to a cabin at the far side of camp.

He called back from his door, "Tourists! Time to earn your keep. Help with the unloading."

Vint's crew took the barrels to a cabin almost out of sight at the back of the camp. Mane put one over his shoulder and followed a harvester who carried one of his own.

"These go to the kitchen," said a young man as he stepped in front of Jasmine to pick up a small crate. She did the same and followed him onto a pathway of planks that led to a cabin more solidly built than the others. Inside stood rows of sealed lockers and a single large freezer. Jasmine set the crate on the table then touched the table top. She scrutinized the floor then reached out to feel the wall.

"This is wood—it's all real wood." Jasmine was appalled. No one had built anything out of real wood for a hundred years. Trees had died here to provide building materials for buildings that could easily have been built with plastic-based mock-wood.

"Yeah," the youth replied. "It kinda grows like trees around here." He shook his head and walked out to retrieve another load.

Jasmine looked at the planks of the path and realized they too were wood. She stepped onto the surrounding earth. Jasmine knew there would be surprises on this trip—this wasn't the kind of surprise she expected. She stepped back onto the boards and proceeded to get another crate. This was "Vint-town" after all. She'd play by his example for now.

* * S I X T E E N * *

When Jasmine woke the next morning, it was still dark. She had woken many times during the night, startled by sounds that were no longer there when she listened for them. This time she woke to the splattering of rain on the roof. A constant chorus of chirps creaked from all around. Jasmine imagined it was the sound of frogs perched on tree branches happily commenting to their neighbors about what wonderful weather they were having.

Darkness hung like a black velvet curtain in front of Jasmine's eyes. No place in the Core ever got this dark. Jasmine turned to lie on her back and waited for the sun to come. The night before, the sun dropped from the sky with such speed it was as if a switch had been turned off. No lingering twilight. She waited for the switch to turn on again and wondered if Mane still slept. Vint had assigned them separate huts, no doubt as a reminder that he controlled everything and everybody in the camp. He wasn't the first to assume she and Mane were more than just business partners.

It had taken till dark to put away all the supplies. The rest of the evening was spent preparing supper and watching vids.

The drops became a drizzle punctuated by occasional splats as water ran off leaves onto the hut's roof. The frogs grew quiet. A buzz and whine was audible now that she couldn't place as being caused by any of the machinery she'd seen the day before. Whoops and trills occasionally sounded, echoing through the trees. Some calls sounded like birds, the rest remained a mystery.

There it was—the translucent ceiling turned grey and showed black silhouettes of leaves and other forest droppings that lay on the roof.

In the growing light, Jasmine glanced over at the two women who shared the hut. Both snored softly. She quietly slipped out of her bag and grabbed her hat on the way out. She'd kept her boots on after hearing stories of spiders crawling into footwear overnight.

By the time she stood outside the hut, enough light came through that she could make out the other buildings in the camp. Everything was wet and now she understood the plank walkways that kept her out of the mud. Jasmine wandered around quietly, hoping to catch a glimpse of the animals that called from out of the green. The high-pitched buzz she had noticed earlier came from all around the camp.

Jasmine walked to the edge of the camp clearing and peered into the forest. The richest ecosystem on land and all she saw in the brightening gloom was green and brown. Her boot scuffed the ground and came against something soft. She looked down for a few seconds before noticing a tiny thread of blue. She crouched to get a better look. A small black frog with bright blue stripes took several lazy hops, then pushed its way under a leaf to disappear again. The plants hid everything. To find the animals, one had to be able to see past the plants. Once the sun was higher, she'd search again.

Jasmine saw a path she hadn't been on yet. It must be the one to the lab outside the main camp. As she approached and smelled the acrid and unnatural odors that came from it, she could guess why. Jasmine peered in through the mesh. The full barrels from the chopper stood just inside the door. It looked more like Arri Deckert's lab than Adrien's. She let herself in. Sealed cupboards breathed in as she opened the doors. They held jars of chemicals. Bales of leaves were stacked along one side and pieces of apparatus filled the far wall. Two large sinks boasted running water, one still held the odor of solvents. Jasmine searched for the fermenter under the sink. Arri had shown her the one in his lab and Jasmine still found it hard to imagine that microbes could live in that solvent mix, much less digest it. She only found an exit pipe. It had to drain into an external fermenter. She went outside to look—just a thick black pipe that ran into the tangle. She followed the pipe, brushing shrubs out of her way. Just a bare pipe. Jasmine looked back and barely saw the lab through the trees. She couldn't get lost with the pipe to lead her back. She was determined now to find out how the lab effluent was being treated.

After what must have been twenty meters, the ground became marshy and Jasmine looked for a way around the big puddle that the pipe crossed. She chose a colossal tree trunk for a landmark and was making her way to its side when the sound of thrashing branches made her freeze.

"Whoop, whoop, whoop," came the calls above her. Jasmine gazed up and could only see patches of dark brown moving between branches that bounced under the animals' weight. She took a few steps to follow the racket in hopes of glimpsing the animals that caused it. There, a monkey, brown and black, swung from one branch to another, then he and his friends were out of sight. Jasmine heard the crashing of branches in the distance. She stood quietly for a moment, mouth open, gazing into the trees. She'd finally seen one of the mammals of the forest.

Jasmine searched for the landmark tree and spotted several giants. She made her way to the one that seemed most familiar. Was it the same tree? If so, the puddle it was standing beside had vanished along with the pipe. Wrong tree. She looked for another. Jasmine bounced from tree to tree three times before she took notice of her racing pulse and realized she was in a state of panic. Her mind was locked into an almost uncontrollable need to run from one place to another until she found her way. Jasmine forced herself to stand very still, then sat on the huge root that extended from the last tree she'd tried. She closed her eyes and tried to push the dread away by taking a few deep breaths.

Her first morning in the jungle and it had taken, she checked her watch, twenty minutes to get lost. At least she had the rest of the day to find the camp. Lots of time to think. She listened—the high pitched buzz she'd heard before had stopped. So had the earlier trills, whistles and barks. The forest stood silent . . . except for the sound of running water! The river? Jasmine could easily imagine the treated camp effluent being piped to the nearest river. She slowly got up and made her way towards the sound by winding between the trees. She was stopped by a wall of vegetation. Judging by the bright light shining from beyond the green wall, she had reached the river bank.

Jasmine struggled to find a way through the small trees that grew in loops with both ends rooted. She squeezed and broke her way through, ripping her shirt in the process.

The cool of the forest gave way to bright sunshine and a view of a small river. Luckily the water level ran low enough to expose a bed of gravel and rocks that she could stumble along. The river moved slowly if at all—the sound she had heard came from a small stream that flowed into the four-meter-wide river. The water evaporated from her clothes and boots and she was soon sweating in the broiling sun. Jasmine kept a slow, steady pace until she noticed a discoloration on the bank up ahead. The pipe end was visible. A wide rim of yellow and brown plants grew around a bare circle at the base of the pipe's opening. Jasmine got close enough to smell the trickle of fluid that ran out—solvents. The same odor she smelled at the lab sink. Chemicals that could corrode the skin off your hand were being released, untreated, into the river.

How could these people live in this beauty and be so careless? The lab could have been fitted with a fermenter for less than a hundred dollars. She plopped onto the gravel and sat beside the circular ruin of plants.

It had seemed natural to assume that anyone who went to the trouble to live here would see the beauty of it all and make an effort to fit in with that beauty, not to constantly challenge it. Gunther Vint and his camp were at war with the forest. This debasing of the river was another way for Vint to show his domination of the "dark tangle."

Jasmine gazed down the river. It was lined by a wall of leaves on either side. Occasionally a flash of butterflies or the iridescence of dragonfly wings flitted over the water.

Now that she'd found a way back, she didn't want to leave. She'd never seen anything like this before. Imagine living here—being able to come to the river any time you wanted.

Movement caught her eyes as a blue and white bird plummeted into the water and emerged with something silver and wriggling in its beak. How could anyone dump solvents into this river?

The last thing she wanted to do now was to return to Vint's clamoring camp, but Mane would be worried.

Jasmine sighed and looked at the pipe again. No matter what she had to go through, this time she would follow the pipe.

* * * * *

By the time she stumbled back to the lab, Jasmine was soaked and filthy and her shirt had too many holes torn in it to count, but at least she was back. The noise box boomed again and sounds of activity came from the lab. She stepped onto the path. Footsteps made her turn just as Gunther Vint slapped her hard across the face, knocking her to the ground. When she looked up, her view of Vint was blocked by Mane who stood hands on hips facing Vint without a word. Jasmine swore. All they needed now was to have Vint angry with them.

"I'm fine," she said, jumping to her feet though her face stung and the inside of her cheek felt raw.

Vint stepped aside to get a clear view of her. "Don't ever go anywhere but where you're told!" he shouted, though he kept his distance. Thankfully, Mane kept his mouth shut. "You missed breakfast and there is no time to clean up. Both of you are going with Helmsly to clear the chopper pad. Now!"

Jasmine and Mane turned away and walked towards the vehicle where Helmsly waited.

"Got time to get your water bottle," Mane said softly.

"No she doesn't," Vint's voice thundered.

Mane stopped dead and turned towards him. "You want us to get some work done or do you just want to watch us pass out?" Mane didn't wait for an answer. He and Jasmine walked to the hut she'd stayed in to get her water bottle.

Once at the vehicle, Mane gave her a questioning look. Jasmine shrugged, unwilling to go into detail in front of Helmsly.

"I got curious and wandered too far following some monkeys. It took me a while to find my way back."

Mane waited for a few seconds, then gave up on getting more from her. He got in beside the driver and began questioning Helmsly about how the base camp had been set up.

*   *   *   *   *

Under the sat shielding, Jasmine and Mane slashed and hacked at the parts of the jungle that tried to reclaim the chopper pad while Helmsly lay on the back of the vehicle and slept.

They were up to their knees in the tangle and maybe that's what it took for Jasmine to finally see what the vids had shown—the tangle swarmed with insects. She kept pausing to look at ants of all sizes and colors of black, brown and red. She saw beetles that looked like a naughty child had haphazardly glued extensions on them and then spray-painted them with the most unlikely colors.

Every time she saw a creature more bizarre than the last, she wondered if EcoTech hadn't slipped up just a few times and inserted mutated insects into the mix, but the engineers had insisted that all the organisms came directly from the genetic codes in the heritage vaults and that no aberrations had occurred. EcoTech had actually made quite a fuss about that guarantee in hopes of being hired to do the coral reef retrieval next. It seemed to have worked. Despite protests from other genetic engineering interests that the technology was being used before being properly tested, the prospect of reestablishing ecosystems was so politically attractive that the Global Government had all but given EcoTech the whole planet to re-sow—for a reasonable price, of course. Standing in the middle of one of their first projects, it was hard to argue with that decision.

Jasmine heard Mane chopping and went at her patch with enthusiasm to keep up with him. She tried not to think about what small creatures were being trampled while they hacked at the small plants. The camouflage netting they worked under cut out some of the sunlight but the suffocating heat forced them to move slowly and, despite their water bottles, their legs were shaking by the time the pad was cleared to Helmsly's satisfaction. Jasmine had to catch Mane twice as his legs buckled on their way to the vehicle. Helmsly muttered something about heat exhaustion as he started the little transport back towards camp. Mane was white and nauseous while Jasmine felt a headache starting at the back of her head.

On the way back to camp, the forest pushed past on either side, unseen and unremarked upon.

Once back, Jasmine put Mane to bed after giving him salt tablets and more water. She felt dizzy and realized she hadn't eaten all day and it was past noon. By the time she retrieved some of her food from the cookhouse, her headache was worse. She noticed Vint watching her with amusement as she made her way to her hut. He chuckled when she caught his eye, but didn't give them any more assignments.

When Jasmine woke to a grey ceiling the next morning, she groaned. Her arms and shoulders ached and a long thunderstorm had kept her awake for most of the night. The sun had blistered her skin through the torn holes of her shirt and the cuts from her wandering seemed to be scraped raw by her bed bag every time she moved. But, as tired as she was, she was unwilling to miss any part of the day. She lay listening to the buzz and a constant tweet-twee-oo for a moment and then stiffly got out of bed.

Mane was up and wandering through camp. Jasmine could see his red-gold hair between the trees. She went over and found him studying a crumbling tree stump.

"Hey," she said. "You feeling any better?"

"Yeah," he replied, though he still looked pale. In the humid heat, his size put him at a disadvantage. He gazed into the forest at the fallen tree. A path of red-brown wood-chips led from the stump to the cut trunk. Mane followed the trail to examine the cut surface. "This is where the wood for camp came from," he muttered as he reached up to measure the trunk's height. Over 2.5 meters, his hand reached the top of the severed trunk. The roundish cut was laced with growths of grey and green. Together with the green fur of moss and the tunneling of insects, the jungle managed to obscure the marks of the saw.

"Incredible, isn't it?" Gunther Vint's voice startled them both. "It was only a month ago we cut wood for more planks." He scraped some grey away with a finger-nail. "The dark tangle attacks anything that can't defend itself." He turned to look at them both. "Everything crawls with life here. If you stand still too long, the dark tangle finds you. Crawlers and flyers will think you're just another bit of the tangle to burrow into—to eat the crust from—to cut into smaller pieces to take away into dark, damp holes."

Vint studied their faces a moment, perhaps to see what impact his words had. Apparently their stunned silence was just what he was hoping for. He grinned and turned to leave, saying over his shoulder, "Breakfast in ten minutes."

Jasmine and Mane continued to stare at the cut surface of the tree that couldn't move to save itself from the saw any more than it could escape the lichen, moss and insects taking advantage of the exposed wood. And Jasmine felt a shiver up her back because Vint could be right. If he was, those minions of the dark tangle moved like a hidden force behind the protection of all that green, the tree leaves, the ground plants, the moss, the leaves that littered the ground.

Mane turned his attention to the length of the tree and walked beside it. Jasmine followed for a few steps and wondered what would happen to all the plants and animals that made their homes in what had been the upper reaches of this tree. It didn't seem fair to disrupt them just for wood.

"At least they only needed to cut *one* down to get all the wood they needed." Mane said as he returned.

*   *   *   *   *

During a quick, gulp-down breakfast, Vint reminded everyone of all the refining and packaging that still needed to be done for the next day's air lift. Then he looked at Jasmine and Mane with that grin that was starting to make Jasmine nervous whenever it was directed at her.

"Tourists!"

Behind him, everyone got up to head for the lab except the tall, large woman who'd been introduced as Silvie.

"We are going hunting," Vint continued. "You need to take water and lunch."

Once outside the cook house, Vint hung a bag of equipment over Mane's shoulder and handed Jasmine a bag containing several more large cloth bags. Following Silvie, they slowly marched into the forest. She seemed to navigate using a combination of landmarks and a pad with satellite readouts. Mane tried to get close to her to see how she was doing it, while Jasmine was content to hang back and take in as much of the sounds and glimpses of jungle life as she could.

Every time Silvie paused, Jasmine scrutinized tree trunks, lifted leaves and scuffed at the ground finding many insects and other small creatures, now that she knew what to look for. They were busy carrying, burrowing, eating or attacking. She constantly thought of Vint's swarms from the dark tangle. Even now his voice was a constant intrusion into the peace of the forest as he played tour guide. He pointed out several plants to Mane. Vint then pulled them up, roots and all, and brought them to Jasmine to put in a bag. She followed again until the group paused in a light gap. Several trees, no taller than Mane, had managed to take advantage of the patch of sun. All the plants seemed to be engaged in a slow-motion battle for sunlight. Vint handed Jasmine and Mane clippers.

"Now," he stated, "we take all the leaves that are not blemished." He watched for a moment, then continued his lecture. "The old leaves lose toxins over time and insects start eating them. We want the young leaves with high concentrations. Hah! The tangle's toxins are our recreation."

Then, seeming unable to stand idly by watching others destroy a part of the forest, he picked up a pair of clippers and joined them with glee. The leaves filled one of Jasmine's bags.

Jasmine let the rest of the group move on. Vint's voice was a beacon she could follow to catch up. She stared at the trees that were now sticks with a few sorry-looking leaves attached, and wondered if they stood a chance of surviving the pillage of their foliage. A motor started up and Jasmine figured the group wasn't moving for a while.

Was it worth it? These trees would die to produce a handful of caps. The motor revved up and Jasmine considered going to see what Vint was up to. She scuffed at the ground to see if the vids were right. Jasmine uncovered a mass of white thread-like roots within a bit of soil—not the centimeters-deep topsoil of home. It was a wonder anything could grow in this little soil, let alone the giant trees that surrounded her.

She lifted the bag of leaves to feel the weight, then gave an unspoken apology to the two stripped trees. Jasmine followed the sound of the motor and stopped when she heard a loud crack. She ran towards the sound of smaller cracks and got there as the huge tree crashed into the ground. The smell of freshly exposed wood washed from the cut stump. Vint stood there like a triumphant warrior, the saw in his hands.

"Are you insane?" she demanded.

Vint laughed. "How did you *think* we got veejix?"

He took a step and Jasmine blocked him. "This can't be necessary."

Vint's expression grew serious. "It is necessary to the operation. I'm running a business here."

Nothing had changed. The same mentality that wiped out the buffalo, the rhino, the forest, was right here, standing in front of her, a hundred years later.

"You want the veejix and the recs, but you don't like how we harvest—"

A shutter fell over her mind. A learned response to the anger that constricted her throat and caused her to tremble. Mane stepped beside her. His aura of good humor included her—allowed her to retreat, to let Vint's words wash around her without touching her.

"What are you going to do?" Mane spread his hands. "Tie her to a tree until she admits her mouth is bigger than her brain? I've tried that—it didn't take. Believe me, she's hopeless." This stopped Vint's rant cold.

"Give her a chance to recalibrate." Mane continued softly. "It's our first time ex-city. We've never seen a harvesting operation and some of your methods are . . . a bit of a surprise."

A surprise! More like illegal and immoral, but Jasmine kept her mouth shut, remembering the bruise on her face and that Mane would also pay for whatever she said to Vint.

This was as much as Mane could dare since Vint could as easily let the tourists die in the forest as send them home.

"She doesn't understand this," Vint said darkly.

"She's a city kid." Mane shrugged as if he weren't.

Vint eyed Jasmine and when she was silent, turned and made his way along the fallen tree.

They walked along the trunk for 25 meters before they got to the first branches. The crown of the tree formed a roughly spherical mass of branches, foliage and epiphytic plants that grew among the branches. Some of these hangers-on were in bloom. Silvie called out, "Orchid, bromeliad, fern, mistletoe . . . " to Mane's questions.

Faced with the chance to see the hidden part of the tangle, Jasmine slowly forgot her outrage and joined the exploration of the tree crown. Careful to heed Vint's warning to look before placing a hand or foot anywhere, they climbed through the branches and came across beetles, frogs, ants and snakes.

The four of them spent the rest of the day exploring the crown and pulled off every plant Vint or Silvie thought was useful.

Even Vint carried several bags of plants on the way back to camp. Tired groans greeted them at the lab when the lab crew saw the bags. Vint assured them these plants didn't need to be refined for tomorrow. Jasmine noticed the bales of leaves she'd seen the day before were gone.

Supper, like all the meals seemed to be, was quick and utilitarian. Each evening's meal was apparently rice, beans vegetables and yogurt.

Jasmine and Mane spent the rest of the evening laying leaves on racks to dry and sorting the plants onto shelves so they wouldn't rot before the lab crew got to them.

After finishing, Jasmine sat at the table where the lamp glowed brightest, and held a small drab bromeliad with its rosette of spiked leaves, and examined the roots. They were crusted with a grey material—the mold that contained VJX. The mold that needed the magical mist of the forest in order to grow. Adrien had told her about the failed attempts to grow the plant and the mold in the lab. The balance of trace elements that could only be found in rainforest mist couldn't be reproduced, and until its bioactivity was better understood, VJX couldn't be synthesized. This unassuming mold was the only thing that worked.

She placed her chin on her hand and stared at that fragile crust in wonder, then sadness. The drive to harvest this and other plants was leading to the destruction of the forest all over again. By being Vint's customers, Jasmine and Mane were part of that destruction.

*   *   *   *   *

The next day Jasmine and Mane had helped load the chopper and squirmed into their places with the cargo. Mane finally couldn't take her sullen mood any more.

"All right, what is it?"

She knew exactly what he meant but she didn't know where to start.

"Vint, his camp—it's all so ugly." She stared at the packages beside him. Then looked up at Mane. "The day I got lost I was following the effluent pipe from the lab. All their waste is being dumped, untreated, into the river, including the solvents."

Mane sighed and stared at his hands.

"Mane, we can't do this. They're not harvesting in there, they're pillaging. Vint took everything. Didn't leave enough behind to regrow. He didn't need to strip those two trees. How many plants did we see him destroy to get at the few he brought back? Vint's causing damage that will take fifty years to repair. He's ready to move through that forest, pillaging as he goes, for as long as he can make money doing it." She looked away from Mane's cocked-head gaze. People like Vint could destroy that beautiful river without even noticing. "I can't support him or anyone like him. It's bad enough we've helped him destroy part of the forest already. We're pulling out."

"Last time I checked this was still a partnership. I don't like Vint or his operation either but for now, he's all we've got to supply Adrien with."

"It doesn't matter."

"What about those people dying of Lightning Madness?"

She studied him for a moment. "That seems like a good reason, doesn't it? But how do you think people justified destroying these forests to begin with? It was build more farmland or starve. There's always a good reason to destroy forest. I won't be part of it. There must be another way to find a cure."

Mane was silent and when she looked at him again his face said this wasn't over.

They spent the flight in a silence that made the three hours seem like six.

* * E I G H T E E N * *

Jasmine stood outside Edan Loffler's door. The time in the chopper had made Jasmine more resolute and turned Mane's annoyance into smoldering anger. The subsequent plane trip had been no better. She wanted to be somewhere that wouldn't remind her of VJX, so she'd called Edan.

He gave her a bemused smile as he invited her in. "How was the business trip?" he asked, taking in her boots and sweat-soaked shirt with a puzzled look.

"The deal's extinct. But," she added as explanation, "we did get to see some preserves." Jasmine ran a hand through her hair. It was matted and tangled. "Um . . . I guess I'm a mess. Mind if I use your shower?"

He looked ready to laugh at her again. "Help yourself."

Jasmine stared at herself in the bathroom mirror and couldn't believe she hadn't just gone home. Her cheek had a greenish tinge from the bruise Vint had given her two days ago. She pulled off her shirt and was surprised to find her blisters and scratches were still red and puffy. She'd have to see a doctor in the morning. She started the water running and wondered why she constantly felt drawn here.

When they worked on the music, time flew by. She felt like she wasn't keeping up with him somehow. Once she passed all her musical skills on to him, which was happening much too quickly, he would leave her behind. For now she enjoyed basking in his seemingly unconditional admiration for her ability.

Jasmine toweled off and looked at her hair. All the set had washed out. She didn't have any but Edan might . . . no. She'd made him wait long enough. She dried it and let it fall into a shaggy mass of short black strands. Edan's intensity scared her sometimes. He must have noticed because he'd stopped his advances. That made her more comfortable but . . . it disappointed her, too.

Edan raised an eyebrow at her when she came back into the living room, grinned and said, "Got to listen to this."

The melody that flowed from his set was pretty, but slow and repetitive. The violins played each strain with more sadness than the one before until Jasmine had to swallow a lump just to say, "This is too sad."

"Yeah," he replied happily. "Ancient, an adagio by Barber—"

"I mean it, Edan. Turn it off." Her partnership with Mane was about to go sheared. She'd come here to escape the feelings that came with the realization. "I don't need sad tonight—can you play something angry?"

He smiled and sat at his board. "How's this?"

He started on familiar notes. Having learned her requiem, he pounded it out with all the fervor she'd felt while composing it—more. More? How was he doing it? She leaned forward and watched his hands. When he finished she still studied his hands.

"Again," she said, her eyes on the 'board. He began again and halfway through she sat back and watched his face. He winced as he hit the notes. It was his punctuation that imbued her piece with more rage than she'd ever been able to play.

"That was power of ten," she said when he finished.

He laughed. "It's *your* piece."

"Not any more," she replied, certain that she'd never play it that well herself. She shivered, more from fatigue than from cold.

"Want your jacket?" Edan asked, reaching into her bag from where he sat.

"Thanks."

He was about to toss it to her when he felt something in the pocket and pulled out two blue caps.

"You doin' recs?" The question was an accusation.

"No," she replied. "A friend was passing them out and I didn't want to be rude."

He brought her jacket and sat beside her, the blues in his hand.

"Used to like these. Got on a real cycle: reds, blues, reds, blues. Then tried a bunch of both all at once. Pretty disappointed when the medics were able to revive me." He sat back. "I was an unhappy kid to begin with, but this stuff—it killed me for a while. Never should have been legalized. It ate up eight years of my life then spit me out in a dry-up full of hating myself, full of anger, full of pain. Spent another two years pulling myself together."

Jasmine wondered at how many ways people could find to hate themselves. At least she'd had Owen and Adrien. Edan had to recover alone. She wanted to touch him—to let him know he wasn't alone.

"Don't get started on this shit—it's poison." He closed his hand over the caps and went to the washroom. Jasmine heard the toilet flush. Any thoughts she'd entertained about telling Edan the truth about her trip disappeared.

Edan still looked shaken when he returned.

"Let me hear what you've been working on," Jasmine suggested and they spent the next few hours fine-tuning his songs.

Jasmine was always the first to tire at these sessions. She stared blankly at Edan when he finished the piece they were checking and he laughed at her.

"Sorry."

"Spend the night here if you want," he offered as he sat beside her.

"Thanks." She looked at her watch. "I already have." But she didn't really want to leave. Edan studied her for a moment.

"Your trip that bad?" he asked, then took her hand.

Her ability to think of a reply was almost swallowed by the touch of his hand on hers. "Yeah, I think I'm losing Mane as a partner."

"Power of zero," he muttered and seemed truly sorry about the news. He didn't ask any more questions, except with his eyes. For that, she was grateful.

"I have to go," she stood.

"Really?" he asked as if he knew she didn't have any reason at all to leave those beautiful hazel eyes behind.

When she reached for her bag, he leaned in and kissed her—a gentle brush of her lips with his. Jasmine froze as he pulled back, then she cocked her head a bit and smiled. He smiled too as he kissed her again, longer and with more urgency. His yellow curls hung around their faces like a curtain. His arms came around her and hers around him. Jasmine let herself sink into the warmth of his body.

Jasmine hugged him, clung to him just so she could hold on to someone solid and warm. Someone who wanted to kiss her. Edan nuzzled her neck then whispered, "let's at least get comfortable," then led her to the couch. There she entangled him again and they lay entwined. The softness of him in her arms kept away the despair that hung on the periphery of her thoughts and finally, the exhaustion of the past days let her sleep.

* * * * *

When Jasmine woke, Edan was still asleep, his face smooth—released from the grimness he so often wore. She brushed long, blonde curls away to see his eyes. She was certain if he opened them now, in that instant before awareness, his eyes would be soft and open and unsure.

Jasmine gently extricated herself from him. She found his 'board and set it to piano, quiet piano, and played tinkling, melodious music until he woke.

"Frass," he said. "There's a happy person in here somewhere."

She smiled and kept playing. Then she felt him behind her as he knelt and put his arms around her so she stopped, turned and kissed him. He watched her as she pulled away again, his eyes soft, mouth set in a smirk that broadened into a smile that crinkled his eyes and she felt like she'd been given a gift.

He sighed and looked at his watch. "Work."

She'd have to go back to her place, to Mane.

"Hey." Edan studied her expression and must have read the dread there. "Need to go retreat? Stay here."

"No . . . I'll be fine."

"Stay," he said as if stating the obvious. "Off by nine. Can go to that club I told you about. I'll call later."

*   *   *   *   *

Jasmine spent the day smiling to herself. She studied Edan's things as if she could know him better by holding them.

They went to a club that evening, held hands and spent more time looking at each other than the band. She should have gone home that night but instead spent it curled up beside Edan, dreaming of tangles of trees and swarms of small creatures that made the forest floor heave.

She spent the next day walking, trying to think about Edan. How good it felt to have someone beside her all night long, but her thoughts kept drifting back to Vint's camp. The ugly buildings, ugly smells, ugly racket, ugly people.

What would she do now? Go back to those narrow-minded music professors? Try to have her compositions accepted without the compromises they insisted on? Or become one of a flock of mechanical engineers designing nuts and bolts? She and Mane could continue their security work, if she could convince him to give up selling Green, and make barely enough money to survive.

There was nothing.

If only those harvesters could just do a few thing differently—it would be so simple. Just use a fermenter to break down any dangerous materials in the lab effluent. Find a way to get at the plants they needed without cutting down entire trees. Surely they'd still make a profit.

Jasmine pulled her jacket on and walked out into the rain.

She supposed Mane had taken Adrien the VJX they'd brought back. What would he do? Those poor people—who would tell them there was probably a cure but their lives weren't worth cutting down trees?

Why was this so hard? Every step she and Mane had taken had gone sheared. Manda dried up, they found her supplier. He tried to over-charge them, they found the harvester. At this rate. . . At this rate they'd soon be doing *everything* themselves. She nudged the edge of that idea, not daring to take hold of it.

Edan was already home when she got back. She didn't meet his eyes and shrugged off his kiss.

"Luminous Flux is playing the Neon Club tonight," he tried.

"I can't. I can't sit there with all those people who know me and pretend there's nothing wrong. My whole life is going sheared."

"But I thought . . . " He was trying to understand what she meant.

Jasmine looked at the boards, Edan's music collection, saw his passion laid out there and it only made her angrier. "I've got nothing left."

"Don't need professors to make music."

"I don't want to spend the rest of my life hiding in a dark room play-ing to myself." And when she looked into his baffled eyes, she knew he deserved better treatment than this, but she didn't know how.

"You always push people away right when you need them?"

"You can't help with this."

He looked at her with that smirk that seemed to say he knew every-thing and was just waiting for her to come to her senses.

"Oh, stop it," she said. "If you know so much why are you spending half your days washing dishes and the other half pretending you're a musician?"

His eyes narrowed then but he didn't say a word.

"I'm leaving," she said and stomped into the bedroom to pack her things. With each item she found and shoved into her bag, her anger diffused until none of her problems were so important she couldn't take a moment to explain to Edan. She carried her bags into the living room only to find him gone.

Jasmine plopped onto the couch and let the day's events run through her head. She didn't know how long she sat there, her mind racing, not accomplishing anything—as if the same data coin played in her head over and over at fast forward. Stuck there.

The entry request chimed. She gave a cry of relief but in the time it took her to get to the door, she realized if it were Edan, he would have let himself in. She pushed the door release to reveal Mane.

"Figured two days was enough time to think about this," Mane said, scanning the room for Edan.

"He's not here. I was just leaving." She didn't meet his eyes.

Mane grabbed her pack. "Let's go, then."

It was a sparkling night—rain had wet every surface and every surface reflected neon and street lights.

Just having Mane beside her seemed to clear her head.

He led her to a bench and finally spoke. "Can't just call this whole thing off."

"I know," she realized as she sat beside him.

"We can look for another harvester."

"That's not good enough." Jasmine remembered wooden planks and cabins then saw a mock-wood bunk house, fermenters on all the plumbing. . . "We need to control the whole operation or we'll never get anywhere."

"How?"

The vids she and Mane had watched to prepare for their trip showed the jungles as full of life—a place where the ancestors of humans had been born. They had made trees their homes, not their enemies. That jungle was nothing like Vint's dark tangle.

"Let's put Vint out of business," she said and saying it out loud made it seem possible.

Mane squinted at her for a moment, then caught her meaning. "Set up our own harvesting operation? That's impossible. We spent three days in the rain forest. You got cuts and blisters that wouldn't heal. I spent half a day throwing up from the heat."

"People lived in the jungle for millions of years. It's time we did again—but not like Vint."

They could live there in that green wonderland without spoiling it. Live in an actual jungle. She could walk to a river's edge any time she wanted without asking permission.

Even her father would have approved. *Do they want to keep us out forever? Then who are we reseeding the globe for if not for us?*

Mane was silent for a moment. "We have no expertise."

"I know." It didn't matter. She knew it could be done.

"Operation like that would cost at least three hundred thousand just in start-up."

"Yeah." Jasmine was grinning with excitement. "Come on." She stood, grabbed his hand and pulled him to his feet. "Let's find someplace dry. We've got a lot of planning to do."

Then he grinned, too.

✶ ✶ N I N E T E E N ✶ ✶

Jasmine scrolled through another page of references for solar charged power cells and groaned. Fermenters, power cells, building materials, plumbing—it was overwhelming.

The console chimed and Adrien's face appeared on the screen. "Weren't you ever going to call me?" he asked.

Jasmine shrugged. "Did you get your Veejix?"

"Yes. Mane dropped it off. So here goes," he said and began reciting from memory. "I, Adrien Lamberin, admit without coercion that Jasmine Melanie Rochelle is the best and most reliable VJX supplier in the city and I will continue to do business with her until such time as Frontal Sclerosis is eradicated."

She laughed in response and he smiled. Adrien didn't often need to apologize but he made it seem so easy.

"Give us some time and your supply troubles will be over. We're going to set up our own harvesting operation."

"What? You can't be serious."

She laughed at his shocked expression. "We figure it will take us a year to get the money together. That's more than enough time to do the research we need."

An hour later, Adrien signed off. She hoped she'd convinced him she was serious.

The screen stood blank, waiting for her to call Edan. One of the first things Owen Lamberin had taught her was to apologize for the pain her anger caused, but despite the fact that she'd had more practice at it than anyone she knew, she hated it. Many times it was easier to just walk away— she didn't want to walk away from Edan. She sighed. He was off work today.

* * * * *

Jasmine put her ear to Edan's door. He was playing—sad and slow. She laid her hand on the palm release and the door slid open. Edan shook the hair out of his eyes to look at her and played out the last verse.

"That was beautiful," she said. "Everything you play is beautiful." The next words stuck in her throat. She should have rehearsed something. "I'm sorry. I wasn't really angry with you. It's just that . . . "

He nodded as if he agreed. "You and Mane spliced?"

"Yeah."

"Everything's fine then." He waited a moment to be sure then stood and reached for her. She fell into his arms with relief.

"Missed you," he murmured in her ear. He released her and kissed her lightly on the cheek. His lips fluttered over her lips, cheeks, eyelids, ears, throat until her whole body tingled at his touch. She gasped with excitement. Edan led her to the bedroom and kissed her again. She slid her hands under his shirt and caressed his smooth brown skin while he undid her pants. He pulled her onto the bed and they made love slow, long and sweet.

* * * * *

Jasmine watched Edan heads down with Sally and Gowan about the trends in percussion rhythms over the past fifty years. She'd brought him to meet the "Neon Club Gang" because neither of them could have sat still at his place tonight.

"What he lacks in size," Adrien said in her ear, "he makes up for in intensity."

Jasmine smiled in agreement and hoped the low lighting hid her flush. She'd been blushing all evening.

"Does he know about the business?" Adrien asked.

"Same as everyone else. Mane and I are doing investigations for hire and the cases are too confidential to talk about."

Adrien just nodded as if he understood something she didn't. Then "Luminous Flux" came back on stage and riveted everyone's attention except Jasmine's. She watched Edan.

He sat at the other end of the table, rapt by the music. She watched him observe the players as if he could see through them into their own thoughts. Maybe that's how he did it—spoke feelings so easily through his music, because he absorbed other people.

He was beautiful: golden hair, brown skin and hazel eyes that displayed boldness, sadness and strength—all those qualities were propelling him towards something big, something important. Her body ached just looking at him.

He turned to find her and smiled that precious smile.

★ ★ T W E N T Y ★ ★

Shelly paused to let the images behind her sink in. The faces in the hall before her reminded her that talking in front of people was a lot more exciting than talking into a camera. She could see their reactions, could give more information when they strained forward—pick up the pace when she lost eye contact.

She'd spent the last hour telling anecdotes about her visits to the preserves and using the holoprojections her crew had gathered to impress these people who had all paid outrageous prices for the privilege. It was a benefit of sorts for the preserves.

Frame after frame of saw-molested trees and filthy water-ways had been flipping through behind her.

"It's incredible, isn't it? Just over a hundred years ago we were devastated by the declaration of irretrievable loss. It wasn't until the irretrievable loss of aquatic ecosystems in 2069 that we finally paid attention. It was hard to convince people in 2053 that the irretrievable loss of grasslands was a disaster when they saw fields of grain where grasslands once stood. It was hard to convince people that a jungle containing seventy percent banana and plantain trees was a plantation and not a rainforest when the irretrievable loss of rainforests was declared in 2075. Then, when the oceans went dead and there was no longer a perpetual source of fish and shellfish, people noticed. But, it wasn't until total irretrievable loss was declared in 2095, that people were ready to have political action taken."

She watched the reactions of the guests in front of her. It wasn't enough. They were disgusted but how long would that last—a few hours? It wasn't enough.

"Irretrievable—EcoTech proved that part wrong when they created these forests. Working with the Coalition, they brought the Earth back. All the same plants and animals in the same ecosystems will be brought back. All the relocations, political battles and reclassification of farmland were worth it. People are returning to the cities and leaving the land to heal. The Coalition has done its job. So what now? Is the Coalition obsolete? Redundant? You can't possibly believe that when this kind of pillage still happens." She let them take in the broken tree behind her.

"Who can stop this? You can. Two elections ago the Emerald Coalition was voted in by sixty-four percent . . . sixty-four. When that falls to forty-nine percent, who will fight for these forests? We used to think it was just modern society that destroys ecosystems, but what about the destruction of the North American plains after European colonization? World fisheries in 2053? We've been doing it through the ages. It's human nature to destroy the Earth. People aren't going to stop now. The partnership between EcoTech and the Coalition must continue and Emerald Warriors must continue to keep these preserves safe."

Brows were wrinkled now. That's what she wanted.

"Thank you all for your kind attention." As applause welled up, Shelly bowed slightly and smiled at the audience, then marched off stage.

Shelly checked herself in the backstage mirror and straightened her jewelry. The opal earrings from Mick Haberstad, Emerald leader from Pacifica—the beaded broach from Theo Zambuto, Emerald leader from Africa. She'd soon have a piece collected from Emerald Leaders from every block.

A stray strand of hair waved in front of her and she tucked it back where it belonged. She was expected in the reception hall. Her eyes blanked—she'd just made a political speech. She was supposed to be a journalist—the impartial eye. Her presentation was to have been nothing more than a documentation, even though the evening was hosted by EcoTech. When her producer found out what she said . . . his chief reporter getting political . . .

"Come on Shelly," the event coordinator said as he stuck his head in the doorway. "They can't wait to meet you."

As soon as she made her entrance, Shelly was surrounded by curious audience members. She was inundated with questions about her travels more quickly than she could answer them. This was another reason she preferred living audiences to cameras. She could tell immediately how she'd gone over—no ratings to wait for.

After an hour of being "on," a pleasant smile had frozen onto Shelly's face and her mind was going numb. Someone took her arm and a woman's voice quietly said, "I have some questions of my own." Shelly allowed her rescuer to lead her to the door before she turned and could see it was Marina Fasal, a cheif director from EcoTech. Marina smiled at Shelly's recognition. "But *my* questions I'd like to ask in private."

Shelly followed her down the hall to a small office. She'd only met Marina once before, while doing the line-work to get filming permits for several preserves.

"I'm sorry," Marina said ushering Shelly into the tiny office. "This was the best I could do on short notice."

They sat on the couch and Marina peered at Shelly. "You look exhausted."

Shelly smiled. "I'm just not used to being on for more than a show at a time."

"I've been watching you closely ever since you took your crew to the Mitengo preserve. And I've been thinking about making this offer for some time. But what I heard tonight . . . well. The voice of News Port shaking it up. Nothing I could have said would ever have made that kind of impact." She placed a hand on Shelly's shoulder. "EcoTech needs you—needs your voice. I'd like you to consider a position as director of public information with us."

Shelly was stunned. "You've got trained staff being spokespeople already. What makes you think I'd be any better at it?"

"Because of who you are—Shelly VanDaal—trusted journalist. People believe you. You'll bring a level of credibility to EcoTech that we need. Shelly." She leaned closer. "I've been worried myself about support for the Emerald Coalition falling off. You're right. People are becoming too complacent and they don't think the Coalition is necessary. But it's the Coalition that's made our work possible. If the legislations that allow evictions and insist on high standards for industrial emissions are weakened, EcoTech's dream to reseed the globe is in danger of dying. Will you help me?"

Shelly didn't know what to say. "I need time to think about this."

"Of course. It's a big step and I can only afford to offer you five hundred thousand." She sat back and studied Shelly for a moment. "You brought up some interesting history about mixing humans and natural areas. How do you feel about providing free access to preserves?"

Shelly shrugged. "I don't think it's time yet. I don't know if it will ever be safe to let humans and preserves mix."

Marina smiled. "You look ready to crash. I'll call a car for you."

"Yes . . . ," Shelly replied. A car? Now that was luxury. "I'll think about your offer." Five hundred thousand was almost twice what she made now. Shelly let herself be led to the building's entrance.

*   *   *   *   *

As soon as she arrived at work, Shelly spotted Raul Martinez waving her into his office. He frowned at her.

"You were on the news yesterday," he said.

"I'm always on the news. It's my job." She was buying time.

"It's not your job to *be* the news. There were a couple of reporters at your little speech last night."

She shrugged. "I told you I was doing a docu on my preserve trips."

"You didn't tell me you were giving a political speech."

"I got carried away." She sighed.

"You've always been passionate about the issues you report on. That's part of your audience appeal. But you have to keep a balance. We've talked about this before."

"I'm sorry. I knew it was wrong . . . " she looked back at him. Raul stared at the top of the desk.

He looked up at her. "I'm putting Tony on EcoTech coverage."

She laughed. "All he knows is what I've told him. I know more about EcoTech than anybody else on staff."

"Really. I've heard EcoTech has failed its own purity imperative, that genetic aberrations are being introduced to the preserves on a huge scale. I've heard EcoTech, a private concern, has been dictating policy to the EC. I've heard EcoTech has a secret mandate to keep the preserves closed indefinitely. Why haven't I been hearing these allegations from you?"

"Because there's no evidence."

"How much time did you spend looking?"

"As much as I needed to to see there was nothing to those rumors. The Restoration party is stirring up anything it can to discredit what the EC does."

Raul stared at the door for a moment.

"Are you sleeping with Miguel Escalente?"

Shelly glared at him. "Don't be stupid. I've only spoken to Escalente twice in person."

"Shelly." He leaned towards her. "Your credibility as an impartial journalist is going sheared." He sat back and frowned at his desk top. "I'm taking you off international political coverage and giving you a two week vacation effective today."

She stood. "You better make that two weeks severance pay."

"Take some overhaul time. That's all I'm asking."

"No. That's not all. You're asking me to stop talking about the most important issue in front of us today. That's not going to happen. You just keep listening, mister. You'll be hearing more from me than ever."

The door made a satisfying bang behind her.

* * T W E N T Y - O N E * *

Shelly set her bag onto the seat beside her on the rail car. The flight to
Geneva had done little to calm her anger. She'd threatened to quit before
and always went back when Raul relented. This time he wasn't relenting
and Shelly couldn't imagine doing her job while watching Tony cover
EcoTech. This time Raul had gone too far.

Shelly had arranged another interview with Miguel and he'd actually
shuffled his schedule for her. What she needed the interview for, she was-
n't sure. She just wanted to be around people who would understand her
concerns and interviews with Miguel weren't like work at all. He was so
easy to talk to and didn't put on airs. There was a man who understood
how powerful public perception was and she admired him for it.

There were even more large men and surly women lurking in the corridors than last time—security. Twice now, gun-fire had gone off too
close to Miguel. He was soon to go on record as the most fortified political leader in history.

Simon was there when Shelly got to the office. His dark eyes crinkled
with a smile when he saw her. Miguel stood and bowed a fraction in
greeting. Blue-black hair framed a brown, smooth face that would remain
unetched by time for at least another ten years. She'd often wondered if
people underestimated him, believing him to be younger than he was.

"Oh," Simon said from the door. "How was your Amazon adventure?"

"Simon." She answered. "Those forests are a wonder. I've never been surrounded by so much green. But the amount of illegal harvesting going on is destroying so much of what we've built."

Miguel sighed. "You had to get her started."

"Hey." She turned to Miguel. "You know, you're not helping the situation. They need more Warriors to fortify the preserve borders. And they need a way to legally spot-search perimeter homes for Green. EcoTech investigators believe the bordering plantation owners are helping with Greens smuggling."

Simon shook his head. "The Warriors already have too much power. Honest people are more afraid of them than the smugglers are. Just a few weeks ago they killed a farmer who was breaking into the preserve beside his plantation. He was just curious—wanted to spend some time in the forest."

"He was armed," Shelly countered. "I got there just after it happened. They shot him in self-defense."

"That's what the Warriors told you? I thought you were a journalist."

"That's right. I investigate what's going on and *then* report on it."

Miguel leaned back on his desk. "EcoTech's gotten used to getting their way. Sometimes they forget that they're just contracting to the government to do a job. A lot of changes were made to the law to allow them to do their work effectively. I can't see making more changes now. Besides, the Warriors work for us, not EcoTech. They're under scrutiny like everyone else right now. While the investigations run, that has to be my focus, not finding more ways to make life easier for EcoTech."

Shelly couldn't hide her disappointment. "But the only way to stop the smugglers is to fortify the borders and put up more surveillance satellites. And the preserves are expanding. That will require more, too."

"Yes, I know."

"No," said Simon. "We don't need more borders. We need to start letting people in. People aren't going to stand for increasingly less land being available to live on. We can't expect everyone to go back to living in boxes piled on top of each other."

"We are nowhere near ready to let people into the preserves." Shelly was shocked by the notion.

"Shelly," Miguel gave her a small smile. "What's this interview about?"

Simon took his cue and moved to the door again. "Good to see you, Shelly." He waved at her and left.

"That man is going to hurt your career."

Miguel sniffed. "That man has *made* my career. Every thing I've done, I've done with him behind me." He motioned her to the couch.

She was still thinking about rebuttals to Simon. She couldn't imagine herself not being able to express her concern for the preserves.

"Are you here?" he asked. "You look a bit fractured."

"Miguel. I'm really sorry I've wasted your time." She stood. "I don't need an interview. I'm quitting News Port," she said as she realized it. "EcoTech has made me an offer."

Mane used his Core swagger to cover his unease as he walked into the Police Station. It had been three years since Martin Yit, but being around police officers still made him nervous—always had and probably always would. It didn't help that his size and bearing made the officers bristle. Taking a deep breath, he walked up to the desk.

"Here for Dustin Sedwick," he said to the uniformed man who raised an eyebrow in surprise.

No doubt he was wondering why a Core Rat was coming to pick up the son of one of the richest families in the city. Mane wondered the same himself but smiled. "I'm his nanny." He handed the man his card. Perhaps the Sedwick name carried enough influence to give Dustin his choice of custodian. "What's his bail?"

The officer looked at the card and, without using it, handed it back.

"No charge, just sign him out." He pushed the data pad towards Mane. "The kid's at the end of his warnings. Next time he'll be fined and that will go on record. We've told him that but it may need to come from you."

Mane grunted. "His parents would love me as a role model."

Dustin was brought out, as sullen and angry as Mane expected. It wasn't being caught building climbing again that angered him—he always wore that look. Dustin scowled at him as he started on a long series of documents. Mane winced, having seen the same expression often enough in the mirror. Dustin was a muscular kid with short blond hair and features that were usually harsh but sometimes melted into a smile. If he'd been taller, he could have been Mane ten years ago. Mane also recognized the hurt in his eyes—Dustin carried that with him wherever he went. It didn't come from bruises—it came from betrayal. Mane was confident that the Sedwicks had never laid a hand on their son just as he was certain they'd battered him with words as soon as he showed signs of thinking for himself.

Dustin nearly got by him before Mane realized he was on his way. He mumbled something that could have been thanks, then headed for the door. Mane grabbed the back of his jacket and yanked him up short. Dustin pulled away and faced him. "What?"

Mane smiled at him. "You owe me."

"Frass!" Dustin dug for his wallet.

"No," Mane said. "Money's too easy."

They walked out the front door together.

"Want to go home?" Mane asked.

Dustin gave him a look that said he questioned Mane's sanity.

Mane smiled. "Didn't think so. Come on."

They walked past the rail station—the kid could stand to burn off some energy. After a long silence, Mane asked, "Why climbing?"

"I don't have to talk to you."

Mane shrugged and kept them walking in silence for at least ten minutes.

"When you're climbing," Dustin said, "the rest of the world goes away."

"How?"

Life was coming into the young man's eyes. "Because a wrong move can kill you," he said as if Mane had asked something stupid.

Mane wasn't any closer to understanding why anyone would climb a thirty story building once, let alone several times. That must have been obvious because Dustin continued.

"It's the focus. Every time you take a hand-hold or a foot-hold you have to ease into it. If your balance is off even a little . . . " He smacked his hands together. "When you have to concentrate that hard, there's no room for all the other frass in your life."

"Officer who called me said this is your fourth warning. Why do you keep doing it?"

Dustin gave him a crooked grin. "It's the way my DNA stacks up."

"What's different about this time? Why call me?"

His eyes went dead. "I've got a climbing trip planned next month. A thousand meters up an actual mountain. My parents threatened to cancel it if I got caught city climbing again."

His sullen mood was back. "They care more about what their flock thinks of them than they do about what I'm doing."

Mane let him go on. He knew the words and the anger from memory. For Mane it had been his father who was the worst but it was his mother's habit of watching their fights and not helping her son that made Mane finally go. When Dustin was played out and silent again, Mane remarked, "I know."

"Get synced." Dustin sniffed. "Are we done yet?"

Something made him think of Jasmine—how quickly and fearlessly she had trusted him. How that trust had given him the first bit of real acceptance to hang on to for a very long time.

Dustin stared at him, angry, ashamed, waiting for an answer.

"Ever hear of the Stanton Family? Toronto?"

"Their son was kidnaped and never returned. My parents have been trying to keep me out of the Core with that story for years." He squinted at Mane who grinned at him. "You kidnaped him?"

Mane chuckled. "Guess I did, in a way. Kid, that was over ten years ago. I was a few years younger than you are now."

"You're Alden Stanton? You're a Core Rat!"

"Yeah. I am." Mane laughed and, as understanding spread over Dustin's face, he laughed too.

Jasmine and Mane looked at the huge house from across the street. The bright lights illuminating the grounds, kept night at bay.

"I can't believe I let you talk me into this," Jasmine muttered, beginning the ritual.

"Good money for a little acting," he replied. They'd been doing party appearances for the past year. "Every party's a step closer to setting up our operation. Just four more months to go." They made three times their normal profit on everything they sold at Sedwick parties, and if they were entertaining enough, they picked up more clients.

Sounds of the latest pop trash wafted from the door. They looked at each other, smiled and said in unison, "Edan would hate this party."

Before crossing to the house, Jasmine put on her Core Rat attitude to go with the feather collar and leather vest, then marched towards the front door.

Mane shook his head and smiled as he came into step beside her. He cleared his throat and took on the attitude too. The irony was that the act came easier to Jasmine than it did to him. He was constantly fighting the urge to laugh at himself.

The doorman stepped aside for them without a word. A tall golden man and short grim woman, both in Core clothes, could only be Jasmine and Mane, Greens dealers. Mane carved a familiar route through the party guests while Jasmine followed.

Those who'd never been to a Sedwick party that featured Jasmine and Mane stared at them, enthralled. Mane found it difficult to keep a straight face. He envied Jasmine's ability to believe the role so strongly that once in the front door, nothing would fracture her.

The two of them took their positions in the darkened hallway. Their first customer was a regular—a man in his forties who enjoyed flirting with Jasmine. Mane took a step back and let her handle him.

Jasmine eyed the man and looked him up and down. "Something I can do for you?"

The man's face flushed. "Yeah, need more reds," he answered in an unconvincing Core accent.

Jasmine appraised him again. "Show me what you've got."

He caught his breath at her double meaning. "Forty five dollars for eight reds."

"Buy you four," she replied.

"It'll buy me eight." He lost the accent entirely in his excitement. Mane straightened.

Jasmine instantly had the man's shoulders pinned to the wall. What she lacked in size, she made up for in ferocity. "Going extinction on me?" she snarled into his face. The man just stayed there without a word, savoring the moment.

Mane shook his head and leaned back against the wall. What was it about this crowd that they couldn't take all that money of theirs and do something real with it? Instead they wasted it on show-off parties and to hire Core Rats to scare the guests. Well, if they couldn't find a good use for it, "Jasmine and Mane, Jungle Entrepreneurs" would happily do something worthwhile with it.

"Four will be fine," the man finally whispered, his eyes wide.

Jasmine released him, pulled out four red caps and exchanged them for the man's money. He was practically giggling with excitement when he left. Jasmine glanced at Mane, relief in her eyes. Mane winked at her—she blinked once and then ignored him.

Nancy Sedwick, lady of the house, was the next to find them. She walked past Jasmine, directly to Mane. She smiled slyly as he straightened to stand taller, knowing the shaggy fur vest he wore made him look larger than he was. He glowered down at her, waiting.

"I'd like twelve blacks," she said, pulling out fifty dollars.

She wanted to haggle. Mane glanced at Jasmine. She was already busy with two more customers. Mane took a step towards Nancy. She flattened against the wall. Mane stood with his arms folded. "You think because you own this place you can insult me?"

"This is all I've got. I need those blacks."

She'd backed right up to the end of the hall as Mane followed her. Mane slowly unfolded his arms and placed a hand on the wall either side of her head.

"The price is one-thirty."

She reached into a fold of her dress and pulled out several more bills. "I've got eighty."

Mane turned away for a moment then slammed his hands into the wall beside her again with such force that she yelped with surprise.

"Price is one-thirty," he repeated, hoping she'd give in. Last party a customer took the game so far Mane actually had to hit him.

Nancy leaned her cheek against his hand. "Why don't we find a bedroom and I'll make the rest up to you."

Before he could answer, Jasmine ducked under him and was face to face with Nancy. "Don't have the money—don't play the game." Mane backed off. Jasmine turned to face him. "Been selling your own self on the side?"

Mane put two hands up in appeasement. They pretended to be jealous lovers sometimes when customers expected sex with their recs.

Nancy glared at Jasmine and fled.

"Sorry," Jasmine said. "Did you *want* to sleep with her?"

"Frass, no!"

She smiled at him. It didn't take acting for him to feel protective of her. She was the most precious thing in his life. He'd suspected as much when he met her but knew it for certain the night he found her beaten and broken in the alley and knew he'd almost lost her.

He couldn't help but think if it weren't for Edan Loffler... She'd been with Edan for two years now, yet she often came to Mane first when she had tears to shed or triumphs to report. Edan didn't seem to mind having Jasmine constantly pulled away on business. But Mane had had several women friends who couldn't handle the "sullen little glitch" who had the power to end their night out with a phone call.

A sound at the hall doorway made him look up. Dustin was watching them, his mouth curled in disgust, then turned away. Was it Mane or his mother he was disgusted with? It mattered—it mattered enough that Mane left Jasmine to deal with more customers while he looked for Dustin.

Mane found him at the bar. Dustin frowned at him. "Got a job for you."

Mane raised an eyebrow.

"I need you to arrange a kidnaping."

"What happened?

"This happened." Dustin gestured around the room. "Don't you see how disgusting this all is?"

"Yeah, these people all have a piece missing. They're looking for it." Mane turned back to Dustin. "How was the climbing trip?"

Dustin glared at him, probably wishing Mane would be as angry about this lifestyle as he was. He had been. Sometimes anger ferments into pity over time. "Best time I ever had," Dustin finally said. "Makes having to come back here even harder."

"Don't need to be kidnaped, you just need a plan. What I did wrong was I ducked out too soon." He'd had little choice. Mane had gotten out before being stripped of his self respect. He'd given up a lot to keep it.

"Don't want to end up the entertainment at some party, do you? When I kidnaped myself, hadn't even finished school. Became a Core Rat. Set up my own investigation business but to my clients I'm still a Core Rat. Took remote courses, I was still a Core Rat. All the people I got to know were Core Rats—do all their thinking with their pockets and what's between their legs." He looked around the room. "Think that's an improvement over this?"

Another woman left Jasmine's hallway grinning. When he was assigned to help her, it started as another job. Opposition agents paid him twice what Jasmine could to help her find Owen Lamberin's killer. He got two paychecks for one job. It didn't get any better than that, even in a Core Rat's dreams.

Jasmine had trusted him when she shouldn't have. She took him into her life as if she'd been waiting for him. Why? He didn't know. She introduced him to a group of people whose values he understood and shared and because he was at her side it didn't matter that he was a Core Rat—her friends became his.

Surely he could have done that without her. Yeah, he could have, but before Jasmine, it never occurred to him that anything had been missing—at least nothing a Core Rat should aspire to. Maybe his parents had taken more from him than he'd been willing to admit.

Dustin followed his gaze towards Jasmine. "Why do you flock with a glitch like her? She's got no sense of humor and—"

"Hey," Mane wasn't sure if Dustin asked out of curiosity or to provoke him. He grunted. "She helped me get back what I threw away when I left my parents." He watched for a moment while Jasmine stood at the entrance to the hallway, waiting, never letting the persona lapse. She hated this game but she played it with the same determination she had when Mane helped her track Martin Yit and when they tracked Yit's friends. This time the goal was to gather enough money to start their own harvesting operation.

"Sometimes you meet people," he realized, "who can go places you can't. If they invite you along for the trip, you're a fool to say no. She's going to do something important."

"Like what?"

Mane smiled. "Going to walk beside her to find out." He glanced at the sullen young man next to him. "Stay with it. Let them pay for a live education for you—then run. By that time you'll have the support you need to stand without them."

Jasmine caught his eye with a look of appeal as two men approached her.

"Have to get back. Find you later."

Mane helped Jasmine with the two men but as soon as they left, she turned to him, panic clear on her face. "Edan's here," she whispered.

"What?"

"He's the entertainment."

"Thought *we* were."

"He's playing here."

"Hates pop trash." Mane glanced behind her only to see Edan making his way through the guests towards them. "But I see money can buy anybody."

"Jasmine?" Edan's usually brooding expression was full of frank surprise.

Edan and Jasmine studied each other for a moment, both hesitant to speak. As if they both understood something irreversible was about to happen and neither wanted to be the first to start it.

"It true?" Edan's voice was almost a whisper. "You're selling recs?"

"Yeah. It's true." Her voice was a challenge.

Edan's mouth set into the grim clench of lips he used for his most angry performances. "How long?" he asked.

"Two years, maybe more," she replied getting on the same anger.

"After I told you what that shit did to me?"

"Grow up, Edan. We're selling something that's in demand and if it weren't Green, it would be legal. What people choose to do with the stuff is up to them."

"Lied to me the whole time we've been together."

Mane thought of stepping in but, this time, he wasn't sure he wanted to help.

"Oh," she answered, "and what is Edan-too-good-for-pop-trash-Loffler doing playing a pop trash set?"

"It gives me a chance to play off an audience."

"And you couldn't tell me about it? Like everything else you won't talk to me about. I have to listen to your lyrics or ask the strangers you sing to, to find anything out about you."

"Because you always want to take the pain away—as if it's something evil. Pain is natural, I need it—it feeds me."

"That's sick."

"Like selling recs is something to be proud of."

The altercation was starting to draw a crowd. Mane stood between them. "We're here on Sedwick time," he said. "Let's get back at it."

For the first time since they saw each other, Edan and Jasmine seemed to realize there were other people in the room. Edan turned and walked away.

Jasmine snapped into her Core Rat persona, ready for the next customer. Mane took a step back and watched her as she surveyed the room.

*   *   *   *   *

It wasn't until they were on the train home that Jasmine let her face soften again. She laid her head on Mane's shoulder. He put an arm around her.

"I'll talk to him when he's more rational," she said.

"Yeah, doll."

As always she assumed she could fix any situation just through force of will. The same way she handled every problem. If she could convey enough of the facts, she was convinced she could get anyone to see the situation with the same clarity she did. She was usually right. Mane didn't have the heart to tell her that being in love doesn't work that way.

★ ★ T W E N T Y - F O U R ★ ★

Jasmine gazed up into twelve stories of branches, leaves, epiphytes and vines, her head light and heart pounding. Today. Today would make it all worth it. Two years of territorial squabbles in the Core, of being party entertainment, of dodging Watenabe. After four weeks of learning to work in this heat, learning never to leave insect repellant behind, shooting climbing cable leads into the trees twenty times to get one good shot over a load-capable branch. She shook her head and smiled. Today the dream comes true.

Jasmine removed her weathered canvas hat and replaced it with a climbing helmet. Although Dustin insisted it could save her life, Jasmine suspected a helmet wouldn't do much for her if she fell from forty meters up, but it stopped debris and small fauna from settling on her head and prevented damage from bumping against tree branches. Sweat already dampened her shirt. The temperatures were comfortable enough—a steady room temperature or a bit warmer, but the high humidity kept everything sticky—nothing evaporated. Mane had joked that if you waved your hand through the air it would come back wet.

Dustin checked her harness—again. "Don't forget to keep this safety line on when—"

"Dustin." Jasmine put a hand on his arm. "Don't go fractured. You passed me on all the practice climbs. Let me just do this."

"Okay." He backed off, sheepish despite his worry. It was hard to imagine he was the same reckless, silver-roach she'd met two years ago. While the rest of the group had been practicing their climbs on smaller trees, only about seven stories tall, Dustin had been running the cables to set up a harvesting area. This week he had finally felt confident enough about his cable network to let the others use it. Along with Levi Maclaren, the crew's botanist, he chose the best sites and best support trees. There were a lot of trees tall enough for the web, but surprisingly, many of the species were too weak and brittle to support a climber.

Levi was ignoring them, bent over some pink flowers he'd found scattered on the ground. In the month they'd been here, she'd seen more of his backside than she had of his face. Arri had found him at University of Glasgow while making enquiries into VJX three years ago.

"Hey, Levi!" she called.

He looked up and blinked at her from under the large brimmed hat pulled over his fine brown hair, torn between his study of the wilting flowers and watching her ascent.

"It's calling us." He gazed up. "Promising nectar if we come and spread pollen." He seemed to realize then that she was waiting for him. He tucked a few blooms into his ever-present sample vials and came over.

Jasmine checked for her own sample bags. It was inevitably the case that whenever any of them went anywhere without sample bags, they found something worth collecting. Dustin handed her a coiled climber's cable. It was thinner than climbing rope and would stand up to continued wear from clamps. Although it was as light-weight as they could find, she had to carry 150 meters of it—it would make the climb hard work. She pulled the coil over one shoulder and across her chest. Once clipped onto the ascending cable she gathered slack by leaning her weight into the line and pushing her top ascender clamp higher each time. When she figured her next "step" would take her off the ground, she looked at her two companions. Levi peered into the green above them with eyebrows raised. Dustin was frowning.

"You're doing nothing to instill confidence here," she reminded them. Dustin smiled. "You'll love it."

Jasmine shook her head at them, stepped into the stirrups and started the climb. Climbing was a tedious repetition of stand in the stirrups, reach up right hand to set the top ascender, shift weight to the harness, reach with left hand to bring up the lower ascender which held the stirrups, then repeat until exhaustion set in. Each step took her up by one third of a body length.

Jasmine was wet with sweat by the time she'd gone five meters up. The familiar vertigo hit when she got about three stories high. Nothing but empty air on every side and Levi and Dustin were much too small. Jasmine climbed faster knowing the feeling would ease once she put some foliage between her and the ground. She looked up and saw the cable disappear between leaves—no visible attachment to take comfort from. The cable wound through the crown of one of the lower canopy trees. Brushing against the branches, she dislodged soil and stirred up the resident ants. Any branch thicker than her wrist was covered with its own garden of epiphytes growing in the humus collected there.

Soon leaves were below her and she felt sheltered though she knew full well the branches would never break a fall. She stopped to enjoy the cooling effect as her sweat actually evaporated in the drier air. As she continued up, Jasmine reminded herself to stop often. She didn't need to add heat prostration to the challenge of the climb.

"Shree-oo?" Dustin's whistle asked.

Jasmine whistled back, "shreet!" so he'd stop worrying. Arri had come up with the code. The shrill whistles cut through the green much more clearly than voices could. It also meant they could rely less on electronic equipment that could be overheard by one of the constant satellite swarm.

As she passed through several more patches of branches, she noticed Dustin had clipped some to make passage possible, but she still had to squirm through openings, hoping she wasn't about to dislodge wasp nests or angry ants. Several times she caused ant swarms as the tiny insects burst from hidden nests to protect their homes. She sped her climbing past these so they didn't have a chance to get into her clothes.

Jasmine stopped to catch her breath and looked glumly at the ascender at her chin. She and Dustin had come up with a motorized harness that would have made this an easy trip up, but the crew were having problems keeping all the solar cells charged. Who would have thought that at the equator there would be such a shortage of accessible sunlight?

Practice climbs had only taken her up twenty-five meters—she was way beyond that, now. As Jasmine reached the forty meter mark, she broke through the last layer of leaves to reach the sun.

Dustin had run the horizontal network of cable to three emergent trees whose crowns reached high above the upper canopy. It was as if she'd found the ocean's surface. Waves of green spread from her in all directions, broken only by a few other emergent trees.

It was huge. The green sea went on as far as she could see and she was so small. What was she doing here? Jasmine clung to the cable. The surface looked deceptively solid.

She closed her eyes and pictured Dustin and Levi, waiting for her on the ground, until the panic passed. Opening her eyes, she climbed higher. This time, when she looked across the green she felt weightless. As if flying, having invaded a place where only birds could go.

After a month surrounded by oppressive green, Jasmine was finally able to see past the living ceiling to clear open sky and sunshine.

She hung suspended above the forest, twelve stories above the ground, and laughed. She could barely see where the cables ran across the green ocean. They'd done it! It was going to work!

"Wahoo!" she shouted her arrival to the trees. "Yee-ee-ow!" she hollered and laughed again.

"Shree-oo?" came a whistle from far below. She blew "Shreet! Shreet! Shreet!" in answer.

Jasmine enjoyed the view for a few minutes, then continued her climb up to where the cable ends were tied. Dustin had strung a triangle of perimeter line joining the three trees. An internal cable ran from the tree Jasmine was in to the line that ran between the other two trees. The web could be configured to drop a harvester anywhere within the triangle.

Jasmine had talked Dustin into letting her drop the first harvesting line, though he insisted on preparing the knots for the clamp himself. Levi had suggested where to drop the line. Dustin then made the adjustments on the three cable attachments to the tree not trusting anyone else with his web. All Jasmine had to do was travel the internal line to the point where it attached to the perimeter cable. She clipped her clamp onto it, keeping the safety line attached until she'd transferred both ascender clamps, just as she'd been instructed. Now she hung from the horizontal line.

She'd worked out the engineering with Dustin. To prevent the pull of the cable from snapping branches, she'd designed a sag of three meters into the line. She should have known better than to simply release her clamps. First she plummeted, then shot along the sharply angled line. The clamp buzzed against the cable as she sped feet first past tree tops and whooped with sheer exhilaration. Until she saw that her weight, plus that of the bundle of cable she carried, was causing the line to dip into the crown of a tree. Jasmine tried to tighten the clamp and it slowed her down a little just before she crashed into the branches. It took several minutes to untangle herself and her collecting bags from the tree boughs.

"Shree-oo?" Dustin asked from below.

"Shreet!" she replied, bruised but unbroken, then proceeded with more caution along the cable until it joined the perimeter line.

Carefully unwinding the top end of the cable from her bundle, she clipped the end to the connection point. Then she released the coil and watched as it plummeted down, disappearing beneath leaves long before it hit ground.

Jasmine descended and when she got below the upper canopy, she used her binoculars to slowly scan the trees around her. Levi had suggested this was a good site for several bromeliad and orchid species that were on the target list. She spotted a promising branch laden with moss and clumps of epiphytes. She pulled out the hook, strapped it to her harness, pointed the rod at a horizontal section of the branch and cranked the extender with her other hand. The hook had a reach of three meters and was just barely able to grab the branch. Jasmine reversed the crank and pulled herself close enough to reach the plants she was after.

Carefully, she searched through the mat of vegetation and found a target plant. A clump of narrow, pointed leaves radiated from roots embedded in the thick moss. A thin crust of soil had formed on several of the older leaves where several seedlings had taken root but it was a hopeless substrate. Jasmine scraped all seven of them into a vial, then slowly pulled up the parent. Holding it over the branch, she turned the cluster of spiked leaves upside down and shook out the inhabitants. A frog, various insects and spiders all scurried for cover as they landed amongst the branch's garden. Taking them to the forest floor with her would mean their death—their DNA was stacked to allow them survival here, not down below. After stuffing the plant into a bag, Jasmine took one of the seedlings, a tiny tuft of pale green spikes, and tucked it into the humus that still clung to the spot where she'd taken out the parent plant.

Jasmine continued her harvesting for the next half hour till her arms and shoulders ached from the constant pulling she had to do.

"Shree-ee-eet!" came from below. Trouble.

"Shree-oo?" she asked.

"Shree-ee-eet!" came the answer. Something was very wrong. She had to get down.

She answered "Oo-oot!" and hoped her calculations had been right and the line would reach as far as the ground. Jasmine loosened the ascenders and, remembering her bruises from before, kept her speed controlled as she rode the cable down. Jasmine maneuvered through several patches of branches that the line had tangled over when she dropped it. She reminded herself to slow down several times with Dustin's warning that "Panic makes people stupid."

She was soon clear again but worry kept her from enjoying the ride. More whistles sounded asking Mane for the medical kit. If he was at camp, it would take him at least ten minutes to get to them. Jasmine hit the five meter knot with a jolt that bounced her up and down several times before letting her just swing there. Dustin's fetish for safety—the knot prevented a released ascender from plummeting a climber to the ground. Jasmine carefully moved the ascenders past the knot and traveled the remaining several meters to the ground. She released the stirrups first, then the upper ascender. As the line was freed from her weight, it flew up past her, bouncing back and forth while she tried to orient herself among the tree trunks. She actually didn't need to use her data pad—the shapes were familiar and she knew which way to go to find Levi and Dustin. Mane was right—the crew had soon become as familiar with the landmarks in their patch of jungle as they were with those in the neighborhoods they grew up in.

"Dustin?" she called.

"Here," Levi answered.

Dustin lay on the ground, head and shoulders propped against a fold in a huge tree trunk. Levi was busy talking into his datapad. Dustin was pale, his eyes clenched shut and his breath was ragged from pain or fear.

"What's going on?" she asked.

Dustin opened his eyes and mumbled something as Jasmine went and crouched beside him. Levi continued his frantic questions into his pad. Dustin's left arm hung at his side, the sleeve torn open top to bottom. "What happened?"

"Got bit," he answered.

A welt covered half his forearm and the rest of his arm was puffed into an angry red. A piece of rope tied around his upper arm was obviously meant to slow blood circulation. His hand was so swollen it looked like he'd never be able to bend his fingers again.

"Anti venom?" she asked. Surely Levi had already tried it.

"None of the spider stuff is working much."

"How do you feel?"

He gave her a sidelong glance. "It hurts like hell."

Levi held a collecting jar in front of the data-pad camera. Inside crouched a large black and red spider. Levi sighed, put down the jar and turned to face Jasmine. He scowled at her. "I'm a botanist," he said. "Plants don't usually bite people."

"What happened?"

Levi showed her the jar. "Dustin made this little fellow angry and got bit. We were looking for mold under that bark. It jumped on his arm, then I grabbed the wee monster."

It would only occur to Levi that his first reaction should be to collect the culprit.

"Trina's been trying to identify it for ten minutes now." Trina was a colleague who thought Levi was on a research trip. "Adrien is standing by, as well."

Jasmine took the jar and peered at the spider. The eyes were a scattering of round jewels set into a black head. The hairs on its body shone a hard black and brilliant red—nature's universal warning for poison.

Levi put his hand out for the jar. "I have to decode it."

Jasmine tightened her grip. "You can't homogenize this." Surely she'd mis-heard him.

Levi stood, cocked his head at her then glanced at Dustin. He whispered, "I have no idea how serious this is." He snatched the jar from her hand.

Jasmine stood between him and his kit. "You will not kill anything here without talking about it first."

Levi reached around her and grabbed his decoder kit. "If I don't know what this is, I can't help him then, can I?."

"You don't need the whole spider for this."

He deftly popped the lid from the jar and snapped it into the homogenizer in one quick motion.

"Levi!" she cried with disbelief.

Fluid ran into the jar causing the spider to jump and scurry in panic. Blades descended.

Jasmine stared at the jar as the black and red was beaten into a grey slurry.

"Hey, Dustin," Mane's voice called as he and Arri arrived out of breath. Mane knelt beside him with the med kit.

"Don't move him," Levi warned. "We should try to get the swelling down and give him something for the pain. He needs to stay still to stop the venom spreading. So far it's stopped just below the shoulder."

Jasmine still glared at Levi busy with his decoding. A few hairs or a single leg would have been enough for the assay. "This isn't over," she spat in a hoarse whisper. If the crew didn't follow its own rules about how they treated the forest, they'd soon end up another version of Gunther Vint's camp. Levi ignored her.

Arri rooted through the medications.

Mane checked his watch then looked at Levi's open data-pad. "A sat pass in two minutes," he said. A few seconds later, the pad chimed a warning. The crew risked detection every time they used sat bounce communications. Mane kept a careful schedule of satellites that could pick up their transmissions. He was working on getting them their own untraceable line.

Levi glanced at Arri who was applying patches to Dustin's arm. "And better not make him laugh," Levi warned. "He needs to stay still."

"Why is he in so much pain?" Jasmine asked.

"According to Adrien," Levi said, "spider venom doesn't just kill the prey, it starts digesting it. He's been injected with enzymes that are trying to digest his arm. The anti venom we've got counteracts that but it's not nearly powerful enough or it's not acting against the majority of the toxins."

Levi stared at the screen, obviously hoping for a reply from Trina before they went into blackout. "She can't find the code in the banks yet but came close. Adrien has a suggestion I can't even pronounce. Arri, look at this, could you?"

Arri sprinted over, took a look, and said, "Okay, you can turn off. I think we have something close." He went back to his rummaging in the med kit.

Dustin seemed more relaxed, perhaps even asleep—the pain killers doing their work. Arri applied more patches and everyone stood around Dustin waiting for a sign—any indication that he'd survive. They all seemed to realize at the same moment that staring at him wouldn't help. Now he needed time.

Jasmine checked her watch—4:00. She looked up, unable to see the sky. There was no hint above them that it would be dark in two hours. She missed the sky. In the forest there was no sky to read for weather. The only hint of a coming storm was the tossing of treetops high above the ground and the patter of rain as it hit the upper layers of leaves.

"It'll be dark soon," she said. "How are we getting him back to camp?"

"We're not," Levi answered. "Moving him will only spread the venom through more of his body."

Mane grunted. "Guess we'll be sleeping here tonight."

"It doesn't have to be all of us," Levi said. "I can watch him."

Mane stood and stretched. "Somebody has to bring back food and sleeping gear . . . " He looked at Dustin. "It'll be all of us."

Jasmine moved to join him.

"You've been climbing all afternoon," he said. "Stay here. I'll go back with Arri. We'll get supplies for the night."

"You can take our first harvest with you. I left the bag just over there." She led Arri and Mane to where she'd landed. This should have been a celebration.

Jasmine went back to Dustin and flicked off a fly that landed on his cheek. She hadn't known him very well before they set up camp, but he and Mane had been friends for several years now. She had no idea why a rich kid would take up with a Core Rat but here he was, stringing up their harvesting lines. He was two years into an engineering degree when he pulled out to join the crew. Mane had tried to insist he continue with remote courses but, so far, there hadn't been time. His studies weren't all he had walked away from. His parents had forbidden him to go when he explained he'd been hired for a research expedition. Dustin had spent their last three weeks in the city living with Mane.

He'd given up so much to follow her into the forest and now he could be dying. Scarcely breathing, his heart barely beating.

Levi's data-pad chimed and he went back to his communications with Trina. After a few minutes, he switched it off and sighed. "There's no match in any DNA records on that spider. Can't do a thing more for him."

Jasmine thought about that for a moment. There were probably a number of species in the world that were still not decoded, but this was an engineered forest. All its inhabitants were recreated from embryos frozen in the heritage vaults that were set up when it was clear all ecosystems would be lost. Nothing in this forest should exist that didn't come from the heritage vaults.

Levi seemed to be thinking in the same direction. "This forest is less than thirty years old," he said. "Even with all the growth accelerators, that's not long enough for evolution to produce a spider whose code is that different from its closest relative."

The obvious answer was that EcoTech's methods had created genetic aberrations.

"Do we have the codes for Veejix?"

"Yeah."

"Check it against the DNA records."

Levi's fingers danced over his data-pad. He must have already used up the day's com ration and was well into tomorrow's.

Jasmine waved a mosquito away from Dustin's arm. Insects were beginning to stir and their whirs bumped against the afternoon stillness. Whistling calls and whoops occasionally rang out above them, signaling night-fall.

"Trina says no," Levi said. "She can't find a match in any of the records and there's none she doesn't have access to." He stared at the screen for a moment and Jasmine came to the realization with him. "Bloody hell," he whispered. "Could that be why EcoTech wouldn't give Adrien the research permits?"

"Maybe," she answered. EcoTech had made VJX by accident.

* * * * *

Two hours after night-fall, the crew sat in a circle in the dark. The lamp was posted a distance away and cast stark shadows that made them all look like eerie forest spirits. Arri started a beat—ta ta tum thum thum. Mane joined in, thumping on his jungle kit. Jasmine listened for a few minutes, then took out her pencil and note pad and rapped along with the beat. They did this every night for at least half an hour and Jasmine was grateful. Unlike Arri and Mane, she needed to go retreat at the end of the day. And for the half hour they drummed, it kept Arri and Mane quiet.

Levi didn't join in. Several times he got up to check Dustin. Mane had lifted him into a hammock so he at least could rest off the ground. Levi had laid a blanket dowsed with insect repellant over him.

The drumming subsided and the crew sat and listened to the sounds of the animals around them.

"How is he?" Jasmine asked Levi as he joined them with good news clear on his face.

"His pulse is finally stronger. He's stabilized. Seems the worst damage has been done."

They sat in silence with their relief, grateful Dustin would be safe but worried about the damage.

Levi gazed into the dark. "I know some people who could probably engineer a virus now that we've decoded it."

Jasmine stared at him—he was suggesting they eliminate every spider of the species! "Don't even think it."

"Why not? It's an aberration. Doesn't belong now, does it? Where's the harm in destroying it, then?"

"We all agreed to the Code."

"The Code—that's brilliant, that is." For the first time, Levi's anger showed. "If Dustin had been bit any closer to his heart, he'd be dead now. This thing is too dangerous and it's not natural."

Mane said softly, "you can't be sure. The records may have holes. That spider might belong as much as they do." He indicated the noisy insects around them. Mane probably knew himself how unlikely that was.

"We either go by the Code or we don't. And if we don't, we'll end up just like the people who destroyed these forests the first time."

"Can we make a species-specific anti-venom?" Mane asked Arri.

"Depends," he replied. "Did you cryo-stat any of it?" he asked Levi.

"Yeah. About 0.3 ml."

Arri shrugged. "If we send it out with our next supply drop I can find somebody to do a venom analysis. From there we should have something within the year."

"And what do we do in the meantime?" Levi was persistent.

"We're more careful looking under bark," Jasmine replied.

Levi glared at her.

Mane put a hand up to stop Levi's reply. "Let's continue this discussion tomorrow."

Arri took out his tin whistle and started a light, repetitive tune while Mane kept beat.

Jasmine's anger slowly submerged. She gazed into the dark around them and watched, mesmerized by the tiny pulses and streaks of pale green light that marked the aerial dances of fire-flies and click beetles. The way forest species were so scattered, it was unlikely they'd run into one of those spiders again soon. Jasmine hoped there weren't too many more surprises like that one.

Voices brought her attention back to the group.

"I did the last dirty job," Arri insisted. "It's your turn."

Jasmine assumed they were arguing about which one of them would walk through the swarm of insects at the lamp to turn it off for the night.

Mane shook his head. "Remember, I'm the one who found out the kitchen fermenter was down and cleaned it."

"Some job you did. I had nightmares for two nights running from the remaining stench."

Dustin had been too busy running cables to keep a close watch on the fermenters. Jasmine could figure the mechanics of the system but no matter how much reading she did, keeping the right microbe mix to digest waste was beyond her ability.

Mane folded his arms. "Cleaning that mess is worth at least three insect swarms."

Arri shook his head but stood. "Okay folks. One minute to lights out."

*   *   *   *   *

They all lay curled up in their blankets, but Jasmine doubted anyone slept. At least a dozen times during the night she saw a pocket light dance over Dustin as one of the crew decided to check on him. Together they kept an unspoken schedule of looking in on him every half hour, heartened by his strengthening pulse.

Jasmine stood under the front eaves of the cabin. She leaned against the wall and watched the forest slowly shed its overnight shower. Rain had stopped falling half an hour ago, but was still taking its path through layer upon layer of leaves to eventually hit the ground where it quickly soaked into the porous soil.

Jasmine brushed away debris with her toe and exposed a tiny patch of thin bare soil. Creating soil had been EcoTech's first step. A combination of plant and animal waste and bacterial inoculants had been laid down over the preserve area. Then, for ten years the area was seeded with plants and animals grown from the heritage vaults. Daily, nutrients and growth hormones rained down on the infant forest. In twenty years, a forest that would have taken one hundred years to grow had established itself. That was as much as most people knew. Details about the technology were property of EcoTech.

She could hear activity behind her in the cabin; the crew waking up. Jasmine was first up, most mornings. It gave her half an hour to relax with the forest before having to deal with the demands of the day.

"How is he?" Arri asked someone inside.

"Seems fine . . ." The rest of Levi's reply was lost in the clatter of cups.

The cabin she leaned against served as bunk-house and cook-house and had a toilet in the back. Eavestroughs caught about five liters of water a day from the roof. The only other building was Arri's lab. Mane had worked out a supply route to get in what they needed. They'd tried to be as self-sufficient as possible. Every time the supply plane made a drop, they risked detection.

Mane came out and brought her a cup of whatever Levi had brewed up this morning. He was experimenting with the local flora. She took it and it barely warmed her hand.

Mane winced. "We're short on fuel."

"The fermenters again?"

He nodded.

"Is absolutely nothing going to work here?" she asked. The waste fermenters were to supply at least enough methane for cooking. "The fermenters haven't worked to specs since we got here. We lost a crate of food to a swarm of . . . something that got past the seals. Monkeys stole half our solar cells. We're already on a four-hour-a-day power ration. And to top it all off, EcoTech's monsters are biting my crew. Just one morning I'd like to start the day with a hot cup of coffee."

Mane leaned against the wall beside her, gazing into the trees. "Has anybody done this before?"

"No."

"Then why should we get everything right the first time?"

Jasmine listened to the frogs chirp for a moment. "Dustin's been overworked. I'm going to see about getting somebody in to work with the fermenters and the solar cells. Indra keeps pestering us to get her involved."

"Let's ask the group what they think." Mane put his hand on the door. "Come on. Levi's cooking up the plantain he found yesterday."

Now that was worth cold tea. Levi was convinced they could supplement food supplies using local plants and as long as he kept to the harvesting Code of taking less than 30 percent of available edible matter, she was happy to be eating something other than rehydrated rations.

"Is it still wet out there?" Arri asked as they came in.

"Hmph. Same as always," Jasmine replied and joined him at the table.

The cabin had a translucent ceiling and fine mesh walls. Hammocks hung along two walls and everyone had their own section on the floor to pile their belongings. She still had to build some open shelves. Anything that sat in a pile grew mold before long.

The other two walls were taken up with lockers for food and a wash-up area. The large table was the center-piece, where the group gathered for meals and for planning. Jasmine and Mane had built the place while Arri set up his lab, Levi got used to being in a real jungle and Dustin strung cable.

Levi was busy in the midst of a clatter of plates and Dustin was struggling with his shirt. Jasmine got up to help him. It had been two days since his painful encounter, but his left arm was still swollen and one huge bruise from fingers to shoulder. Jasmine did his buttons up and when he looked up at her, his eyes were filled with tears. She didn't know what to say. If he thought this was unfair, he was right. No one had expected a spider could do so much damage.

"Hey," Mane said. "I could use your help with some building. It'll be dull," he warned. "No swinging through trees involved."

Dustin smiled a bit but still looked fractured.

Levi grinned as he presented everyone with a plate of hot plantain. The starchy fried bananas were a welcome change.

"Mmm. Let's make Levi our permanent cook," Arri said.

"No thanks." Levi joined them with his own plate. "I've got better things to do than keep you glitches well fed." He looked around the group and seemed satisfied that everyone was silenced by their enjoyment of breakfast. "Whoever's on water duty—I'm almost out."

"That's me," Jasmine said. "I'll go out this morning."

"I did the last harvesting on the line yesterday." Mane said.

The cable would have to be adjusted for the next site.

"I can't . . . " Dustin's voice was a hoarse whisper.

"That's fine," Jasmine said. "Don't push the arm, but we've got a schedule to keep. I know the web almost as well as you do. I can make the adjustments."

"I need to check the connections."

"Don't worry. I'll make sure—"

Dustin stood and walked out the door. Mane shook his head at her and followed him. Arri and Levi stared into their cups.

"What?" Jasmine finally asked.

"It's *his* web," Arri remarked.

"No, it's *our* web," she replied. "And we've got a schedule to keep."

Jasmine took her cup and plate to the sink. She got outside just in time to see Dustin walk into the forest as Mane watched him go.

"What's going on?" she asked.

"He needs some time to himself."

"I don't like him going off by himself in this mood."

"Well, we can't all live our lives to please you."

Jasmine's face flushed.

"You really don't know why he's upset, do you?" Mane asked.

"He's angry with me because he doesn't want anybody else messing with the web."

"He's angry with himself for letting you down."

"That's . . . " Of course it was silly. But Mane had a way of being right about these things.

"We're all here because you were willing to walk through anything and anybody who stood in your way. I walked beside you on that path. These people want to walk beside you, too. Let them. Don't push them out of your way just because they see things a little differently."

Like she would have walked through Adrien if he hadn't agreed to work with them. Like she and Mane walked through the Green Splinter. Like she'd walked through Edan.

"You can't build something like this without sacrifices," she said. "We both knew that—we both made them." She was well aware of what their partnership had cost his social life.

"But we can't do this by ourselves."

She was beginning to think that would be easier than trying to deal with four points of view every time a decision had to be made.

"Let Dustin have the web," Mane said. "So we can't harvest for a while. I've still got building to do and Arri could probably use some help getting the harvest processed before it rots. Adrien says Dustin should start using his arm to get the strength back. He'll be able to start climbing in a week. Don't break his spirit for the sake of a schedule."

Jasmine sighed. "Tell him we'll wait harvesting for him. I need to go get some water."

She went to the lab and pumped the water caddy dry, running the water into a smaller container. Empty, the meter-tall plastic canister was easy to set on its wheels. Jasmine pulled the three-wheeled contraption out the door. She tugged it behind her down the path towards the river.

The mornings were usually the worst, Arri always concerned about time lines. Too much harvest meant he couldn't keep up—too little and the production schedule fell behind. And Dustin constantly slowing everyone down with his attention to safety. Four other opinions to consider at every turn. Some days she wanted to scream and tell them all to go home and let her do this herself.

And some days, when they sat around the cookhouse at night drumming, she'd felt like she *was* home. All of them working together for one goal. That's how her father must have felt all the time.

It hadn't hit her until the funeral. He had work and political friends who all quite sincerely told her and Adrien what a great man Owen Lamberin was. And the stories they told—they loved him and included Jasmine and Adrien in that love. What did her father do to gain that kind of support? That's what she wanted to do—what she needed to do, but she didn't know how.

She moved faster. Jasmine loved the feel of her legs pumping her along. She'd been more active and felt in better shape in the past two months than she ever had. A chittering began in the trees above her and she looked up. Some animal scolded her from behind the leaves. Finally Jasmine caught a flash of movement and of blue. She continued to look up. It was all so huge, so out of reach. She was tiny and without camp or her crew there, she suddenly felt very vulnerable. Wonder turned to awe and fear. She looked down at the ground—at the path. *Her* path—something familiar, and her heart rate slowed again.

When she got to the back-lit green wall that marked the river, Jasmine checked her watch—8:30. She had an hour and a half till the next sat pass. She steered towards the bright patch that indicated the opening they had cut to get to the river bank. Jasmine walked out from under the trees and looked up at blue sky.

"Hey!" she shouted. "Wake up!" An indignant quack answered her, then a whole chorus erupted from a tree down the river. A group of herons were roosting too far away to be seen as anything but grey shapes in the tree. Yesterday they'd scared her out of her wits when they started quacking right above her. Waking them again today seemed quite fair. She'd looked them up, only to find their name unpronounceable, so she called them "Big-eyed Herons".

Jasmine tossed the hose into the water and started pumping. The ruckus she'd caused died down as the herons went back to sleep, oblivious to the rhythmic chug-swoosh of her pump. The sun hadn't had a chance to move to this side of the river, but she was still sweating by the time she was half done. If only they'd been able to use the solar cells the way they had intended. She'd be able to use the motorized pump.

Experience had taught her to pace herself in the warmth, so by the time she finished, she only had ten minutes to get the water caddy and herself under cover. The walk back to camp would take at least an hour with a full load of water. She needed a short rest. Jasmine sat just under cover of the trees and looked out over the river. Something black against the sky caught her eye. It was still there! The experimental solar cell had not been stolen or destroyed by monkeys or whatever had taken all the others. She'd forgotten about it. The river provided a ribbon of space clear of trees where the crew had hung the cells to charge. They'd lost twelve to animals. Levi thought animals were attracted to the shiny patches and made off with the cells as treasures. Jasmine had taped over all the shiny bits with flat black tape. It had worked.

It would take thirty minutes for the invisible satellite to pass over before she could retrieve the cells. Jasmine looked for the strangler bound tree she'd noticed last time. A large tree was surrounded by the roots and trunks of a strangler tree entwined in chaotic braids that flowed up from the ground along the old tree's trunk. The tree had continued its growth and the patches left bare by the strangler bulged out. Eventually the strangled tree had died. The branches and foliage that reached out high above were those of the strangler, not the original tree. She stared up at them for some time, wondering how long it had taken for the old tree to die.

She walked around the tree several times and eventually spotted a hole that might just be large enough for her to enter what seemed to be a hollowed trunk. The original tree had been dead long enough that parts of the rotted wood had broken away. She shone her flashlight into the hole, leaning on the wood. It gave way. She'd unintentionally made the hole wide enough for her to crawl through. High pitched squeaks sounded from high above her and the place stank. The space inside was the size of a large closet. She looked where her hand sank into the ground to find a spongy mix of bat guano and writhing insect larvae. Jasmine quickly scooted out again. If she really wanted to explore the tree, next time she'd bring gloves and a nose filter.

She checked her watch. The thirty minutes were up. Jasmine went out to lower the solar cell and found it was not only in perfect condition but fully charged. Jasmine smiled, then pulled the tape off the contacts and clicked the hand-sized cell into the water caddy's motor. She switched it on and it whirred into gear. All she had to do now was steer and help it over tree roots. At least something was working.

She could barely see movement between the tree trunks and the cabin was only visible because she knew it was there. Its brown and grey blended in with the trees. She smiled and her heart ached with satisfaction. She'd done it. After two years of selling recs and being party entertainment, she and Mane were able to put together the start-up money. They spent countless hours in front of their consoles researching materials, rainforest ecology, surveillance technology, small scale energy systems—anything that would help them create this.

My girl, you will be and do whatever you want to. You've got the hunger for it. She chuckled out loud at the memory, breathed deep and continued down the path. It felt good to be out of the Core. Even her nightmares about Martin Yit had stopped now. The Core had been exciting at first but then the squabbles with other dealers and constantly having to watch for Green Splinter became tiring. And Watenabe had been constantly under-foot. Jasmine's dream of creating the forest operation had gotten her through the past two years.

* * * * *

"I'm almost finished," Jasmine assured Levi as he tried setting the table around her. She'd taped five solar cells already and hung them over the river and had spent the rest of the afternoon taping another five.

"Hey, this isn't a workbench," Arri admonished with a smile.

"Don't complain," Mane said as he sat. "Anything that increases our power supply is worth the inconvenience."

Jasmine finished quickly and Levi handed bowls around. Supper was the usual—rice with whatever struck the cook's fancy. With Levi that usually included some herbs he'd asked to collect along with vacuum-packed vegetables. If they could get the fermenters to produce enough fuel, they could power a freezer. That would make meals a lot easier to prepare, not to mention more tasty. No more dried food.

"I spotted some more targets." Levi said. "But I'm still not sure what taking out fifty percent will do to the whole community." He looked at Jasmine. "As a plant hunter, I'm your man, but it's going to take an ecologist to tell you what our harvesting percentages should be."

"Any suggestions?" she asked.

"Trina's taken a wee interest in our aberrations," he replied. "She has it figured that we're on a preserve. She's mentioned a few times now how she'd be interested to see how engineered species fit into the biome."

Mane smiled. "How would she feel about our . . . legal situation?"

"Academic curiosity." Arri shook his head. "It becomes the most important thing in your life to the point where the outside world, including its rules, just doesn't matter."

Jasmine had seen academic curiosity in action since Adrien started at the clinic. "We need help with keeping track of what we do and what effect we're having on the forest," she conceded. Adrien had already reminded her that he had to go public with his results if the therapeutic trials showed VJX was effective. When that happened he'd have to defend the whole harvesting operation and so would she. Arri and Levi kept records of what was harvested but they needed someone with credentials to determine what effect their harvesting was having. "Let's think about it. We can't afford a bigger crew right now."

Dustin pushed food around his plate with his fork. Levi watched him for a moment and said, "We should vote on what to do about that spider."

Jasmine frowned. What did they need to vote on? The Code was clear. "'We will kill no plant or animal unless for study, for harvest or for food,'" Jasmine quoted. "If we're not going to follow that simple rule, then we may as well send for chainsaws and go to it."

"I'm not saying we're to throw out the Code," Levi replied. "Just don't apply it to organisms that don't belong in the system. Trina's in the guild. She's got access to every DNA signature ever recorded. She didn't find a match."

"Not for Veejix either," Jasmine replied. "Do we destroy Veejix because it doesn't belong? Who decides? For all we know, that spider venom may be a cure for something. No! Somehow, these aberrations live here and have become part of this ecosystem. They belong here, now. *We* have to find a way to live around *them*. Just like we live around the bush masters and bola spiders."

Mane put a hand up. "I vote we leave them alone."

Jasmine raised her hand as well, then Dustin raised his.

Levi and Arri shared a glance in silence.

"At least let's allow collection for analysis," Levi suggested.

Jasmine nodded. "'Kay, but only one of each new species we find."

At that everyone sat scowling at the table-top.

"NewsPort," Mane said and with no small amount of relief, the crew pulled their stools over to the main console. No matter how low the power rations got, they watched NewsPort every night. Not because NewsPort was the only way to get news—it saved power when everyone watched at once and six o'clock was the most complete download of the day's events.

The biggest news story was the setting of a date for the next global elections. That meant for the next six months the news reports would be clogged with campaign rhetoric. Then, "And tonight's arts report features Edan Loffler, the music industry's fastest rising star."

Edan? Jasmine sat up. He'd just gotten his first disc out this year. The critics had called it nothing more than street opera, but every song of his she listened to held the same emotional power that his first had.

His music was all she had left of him. At first he'd remained too angry with her to reason with. Then it had become easier for both of them to concentrate on their work than to try to find a way to be together.

"Didn't take him long," Arri commented as Edan appeared.

Edan sat across from the interviewer. He'd trimmed his hair so he looked less like a walking mop. As soon as he opened his mouth she could see he hadn't lost the charming intensity that made her heart flutter. He sat there talking to Sandra Yee as if the cameras weren't even there. How could he be so calm? NewsPort was broadcast globally.

"What have you tapped into," Yee asked him, "that other musicians have missed?"

"The world is ready to weep," he told her as if she were the only person there. "Because there are no wars, no real poverty, people need something to weep over. I want to wake people up emotionally—make them feel what they may never have a chance to otherwise."

"Your music has been called Street Opera."

He smiled as if about to tell her a secret. "It's a great label. I'd been looking for something to call what I do."

Yee didn't hide her surprise. "I don't think the critics meant it as a compliment."

He shrugged. "I'm using the concept for my first concert tour. I'll have the show ready in eight months. 'The Suicide Tour.'" He grinned.

A tour. Was that the real reason he played Pop Trash at parties? To finance a tour? The whole world would hear his music. He would have let her walk beside him.

Yee turned to the camera. "Watch out for this one. I think we'll be seeing a lot more of Edan Loffler."

Jasmine had no doubt they would. For a moment Jasmine imagined them together, on stage, side-by-side. It was what he'd wanted from the first.

She looked up to see Mane studying her reaction.

"He's lost his Core accent," Arri commented.

Mane started a beat.

*   *   *   *   *

Jasmine woke to the insistent ringing of Levi's data pad and the mutterings of her roommates. Levi's face was lit in the glow of the screen. Mane turned his lamp on.

"Trina's in a panic," Levi said. "EcoTech paid her a visit last night and the police did a security check on her lab just now. She figures her inquiries into the heritage vault records were traced and questioned."

"Wouldn't be surprised," Mane said. Levi looked at him expectantly. Mane shrugged and caught Jasmine's eye. "Could just give her a secure line."

Levi handed him the pad.

"Hey Trina, Mane here. If you're willing to let me in, I'll reconfigure your system so it'll do everything including make us breakfast."

She laughed at his audacity and Mane got down to the business of giving her a secure line to the heritage vaults.

Rain pummeled the lab roof while Jasmine and Arri worked. She clipped the remaining roots from the Veejix epiphyte, careful not to lose a scrap of the Veejix-bearing mold that encrusted them. The rest of the plant, she tossed into a rubbish pile that would go to feed the lab fermenter. Arri sorted fresh plants and leaves from the collection sacks onto drying racks. Most of them would be processed into recs. That's where they made their money so they could continue to supply VJX. Six months into the project the crew was ready to refine the fourth shipment.

"Hey, you two," Mane called from the house. "Adrien's on the line."

From the lab she could make out silhouettes in the house and Mane leaning out the doorway.

"Coming," she replied while picking up her rain poncho. Arri closed the lab door behind them as they ran flapping along the mock-wood planking to the house.

Adrien's smug expression greeted them from the console screen.

"Preliminary results are in from the therapeutic studies." His excitement gave away the results before he even said, "VJX is going to work!"

Arri and Mane whooped and applauded while Jasmine, Dustin and Levi laughed and clapped along with the rest.

"This really *is* going to work," Adrien said.

"*Now* you decide it's going to work?" Arri laughed. "Give us some credit."

Now she could make some plans. The crew would be in the VJX supply business.

"There's more," Adrien said. "How do you feel about doing some prospecting? Two researchers have asked me about certain plants with possible bioactives they'd like to investigate. Another has asked about a beetle with bioactives in the carapace. She hasn't found a way to lab rear them. I told them they'd have to pay prospecting fees until you find a supply and they didn't bat an eye. What do you think?"

Jasmine looked at Levi. He shrugged. "Plants I can find, but insects I'd have to learn about. Trina's already an expert," he said hopefully.

"Ask her on board," Jasmine said. "Arri, how would you like to invite Indra to join the group?" His grin was all the answer she needed.

Jasmine turned back to the screen. "I guess prospecting just became a sideline."

"Great." Adrien grinned back at her. "You have time for some family gossip?"

"Sure," she replied and the crew returned to their tasks.

"Chanel said to say hello."

"How is she?"

"Trying to decide whether to go into teaching."

"She'd be good at it."

"That's what I keep telling her." Adrien studied her for a moment. "You're not angry anymore, are you?"

Her face flushed and she shrugged. She had to admit, living here had its challenges but the routine and the support of her crew had allowed her to relax.

"I haven't seen you this excited and content since you started university."

"All that rain must agree with me," she replied.

The warning chimed.

"Sat pass. Gotta go."

"Take care of yourself," Adrien said and signed off.

"Now that we've got some money coming in," Dustin began. "Could we get—"

"More cable," everyone chorused.

He grinned.

Jasmine pulled her hat down more firmly against the wind stirred up by the chopper blades. The river bank was being used as a drop-off point this time. Since the cargo being dropped included Trina and Indra, the pilot needed the room to manoeuver. He didn't want them swinging into trees.

A compact, dark-haired figure that could only be Indra, descended down the line. She no sooner stepped out of the harness, than Arri tackled her with a big hug that lifted her off her feet. Arri winked at them, still holding Indra.

"That's enough." Indra pretended indignation. "I see jungle life has only made you worse." She kissed him on the cheek.

"See? She missed me. I knew it."

Indra turned to Jasmine. "My God, girl. I can't wait to see it all."

Jasmine chuckled at her enthusiasm. "Welcome to paradise under a rain cloud."

"Come on." Arri took Indra's hand. "Let's get under cover." He led her into the trees.

Mane steadied the brown-haired woman now in the descending harness. Her features were frozen into a calm mask until her feet touched the ground. She smiled her appreciation at Mane then turned to greet Levi.

"We need to get under the trees." Mane guided her to where the rest of the crew waited. The chopper had already disappeared over the rise of foliage to return after the sat pass.

After waving the chopper off, Jasmine joined the others. Indra was chatting with Arri while Trina gazed around her.

"It'll take a while before you can see all the critters," Jasmine suggested.

Trina smiled. "Not surprising. Most of them spend their lives hiding from other critters that want to eat them, like mammals with sharp eyesight." She tapped a finger beside her right eye.

Jasmine was puzzled by Trina's easy acceptance of something she had found so frustrating herself her first trip to a jungle.

Trina stepped towards the dense foliage that basked in the light beside the river bank.

"*Euterpe edulis, Monstera, Philodendron,*" Levi recited following her gaze. "Even some monocots, *Musa*—"

"How can you see all that from here? How can you tell them apart?"

Levi shrugged. "Different shades, leaf shape, growth pattern . . . "

"They're all just green to me. I know," she said before he could interrupt, "It's like learning faces. I've just never had so many new faces to learn."

"It's not so bad now when it's quiet they are," he murmured. "Sometimes, when they all want attention at the same time, it's too much. Your mind freezes and you can't see anything but green. Then they settle down and you can make out the individuals again."

To Jasmine's surprise, Trina nodded, understanding.

Chopper blades thudded against the air and the group stepped into the clearing again. Indra looked up. "Here comes your luggage, Trina."

"Hey," Trina protested.

"Oh yeah, *one* bag is actually mine."

"Is it my fault I had to bring all my own equipment?" Trina replied, squinting into the cloud-hung sky.

The group headed for camp with Arri and Mane taking turns describing to the newcomers what it was like to live there.

Jasmine led Trina and Indra into camp. "Lab, toilet and dorm—that's all there is. We've got running water and a fermenter each," she blurted out, then realized that they knew all this. "Trina's equipment will have to go in the lab. There's no room in the house. We'll be pretty crowded in there." She turned to Indra. "We can't decide whether to put on an addition or build a separate bunk-house."

Indra laughed. "I've never seen you so talkative and excited. You're like a proud mother." She took another look around. "And you should be. You've built something wonderful here."

Jasmine looked at the house again. She and Mane had banged it together themselves. She smiled. Yeah, they'd built something wonderful here.

Indra inspected the roofing material, scraping it with a fingernail. Moss had just started to gain a foothold. "They make a denser version of this now. It would still let in as much light but the surface is less porous and won't let anything grow on it."

The rest of the crew entered camp pulling the equipment behind them.

Mane walked up to the two new women. "It's time for initiation."

Trina and Indra shared a worried glance. He took two button-sized trackers out of his pocket. "These are tracking beads." He gave them each one. "Wear them all the time. That way if you get lost or in trouble, we can always find you."

"Getting lost here is easier than it looks," Arri said knowingly.

Trina and Indra tacked the beads onto their collars.

Indra spotted Dustin inspecting a bundle of new cable.

"So, you and microbes—not a happy marriage, eh?"

"The lab fermenter is working close to specs but—"

"Never mind. You've got Indra's magic fingers working with you now. Soon we'll have so much methane we'll have to declare the place a fire hazard. Let's have a look."

Trina stood gazing up into the trees in wonder-induced paralysis.

"So," Arri stood hands on hips peering at Trina's pile of equipment. "That's how much room I have to find." He shook his head and headed for the lab. "I'm not saying it can't be done," he muttered.

"He's teasing," Mane assured Trina.

"Can I see the harvesting site?" she asked.

"Sure," Mane answered and Jasmine followed with Levi.

"It's so open," Trina remarked. "I pictured us having to cut our way through to get anywhere."

They walked in silence for a while.

"Has EcoTech been giving you any more trouble?" Mane asked.

Trina beamed at him. "Not since you got into my console." She shook her head. "Seven species so far. No record of them anywhere. I'm still trying to figure if the codes are close enough to what we have on record to be accelerated evolution from the vaults or if they are aberrations caused by their process. I can see why EcoTech is worried."

Jasmine couldn't. "It doesn't sync," she said.

"Sure it does. EcoTech doesn't want to admit it failed the purity imperative—that they've created these aberrations."

"Does it matter?"

"What do you mean?"

"EcoTech has already admitted that the number of species is a bit lower here than the original rainforests but the system works. Does it matter what exactly those species are?"

"It's not the same ecosystem. The whole point is to recreate what our ancestors destroyed."

"What if we can't?"

"Then we do more research until we can."

"The rope is just up here," Mane interrupted.

Jasmine still couldn't understand why one species wasn't as good as another. Aberrations were no better or worse than the natural species from the heritage vaults. It was a ridiculous reason to refuse the acceptance of VJX.

Trina looked up the rope and shook her head.

"I brought a harness and helmet," Levi suggested, "if it's a closer look you're after."

Her eyes widened and Jasmine could swear she went pale.

"I probably shouldn't take the time today," she answered. "Arri must be ready for me to move my equipment in and I should give him a hand if I'm going to stay on speaking terms with him."

Levi shrugged and they made their way back to camp.

* * * * *

That day the rain waited till the crew sat for supper, then drummed the roof as they ate.

"Have you had a chance to figure how you're going to study what we're doing?" Jasmine asked Trina.

"I've got it all worked out." Trina got up and pulled two electronic pads out of her bag. "There's one for the lab and one for the house. Everything we take needs to be recorded. Even if it's only one leaf."

No discussion, just "all worked out" as if this was already hers. Jasmine looked at Mane for a sign that he felt it too but he just sat beside Trina nodding at everything she said.

Trina continued. "I need proper nomenclature plus location to four decimals. So don't pick anything without an accurate location reading first. I'll also need to know if you've taken leaves, stems, bark or inflorescents. For insects—"

"For insects you'll be lucky if we can tell an ant from a beetle," Mane said.

"Not all of us are biologists," Jasmine reminded her. "You'll have to settle for our best guess on insects or plants."

Trina frowned into her glass, clearly disappointed. "Then if you pick something and don't know what it is, describe it. I can easily show you what identifying features are important. Then I can identify it myself."

"Speaking of plants," Arri said, "Levi, tell them your secrets-of-plants story."

Levi glared at him.

Arri just grinned at the group. "You'll love this."

At that, most of the group retreated to the more comfortable seating of their hammocks.

Arri and Levi had struck up a friendship based on their mutual interests in botanical chemistry and on Arri's constant attempts to draw Levi out and make him laugh. Arri had found the perfect audience in Levi—one who never challenged him for the spotlight. Only Arri could have convinced Levi to speak in front of the group. He never told after-supper stories.

"Plants lead secret, silent lives," Levi started self-consciously to a chorus of "oooh"s.

"No, really," he insisted. "They don't communicate by sound or sight. They live their lives governed by . . . chemistry and gravity."

Jasmine was unsure if his melodrama was intentional, but he had his audience's attention.

"Micky Temkin," Arri urged.

Levi's brow wrinkled with concentration and he gazed at the far wall. "Micky Temkin, now, he was new to the forest. He walked the path to the river each day to the wee dock. On his way there, he'd marvel at the plants he saw—it was a beautiful place, magic, but when he got to his wee dock, he'd sit and look down the river, the only open space there was, and dream of home. Where the air didn't weigh a man down with wetness and the heavy scent of flowers, fruit and decay.

"One day, after his morning journey to the river, Micky Temkin got up to return to his little shack. He was taking . . . um . . . UV level readings and had to check the instruments. Right. He got up and started to his shack when he caught the smell of sea spray. He froze in place and slowly turned round and round trying to catch it again to get a direction. There it was, through the trees. He took a few steps more and it hit him like a brick. Ocean waves smashing themselves to sea spray on the rocks of home. The smell of it tugged at his heart so much, it did, that he didn't think how odd it was. He followed the smell around trees, through stands of thorn bushes, into swampy moss until he could almost feel the fresh cool mist on his cheeks.

"Then he stumbled against it. He'd seen it before, but before it looked like a tall tree stump—all green and brown and crusty-like. Now it had split open at the top and inside it was dark, red velvet. He touched it—a finger sank into the red. Warm, it was, and soft, and his hand came back smelling of . . . of perfume—the kind his Angie wore. He leaned over this monstrosity of a flower and peered into the deep folds. Nothing but something clean and white in its throat.

"It looked like it should have smelled of raw meat or rotting flesh but . . . roses? Closer in he leaned, just to be sure he could smell Angie's roses from the bush she nurtured at home. Closed his eyes, he did then, and breathed deep. Warmth caressed his face. His eyes flew open but all he saw was red and he couldn't scream because red velvet filled his mouth."

Levi returned his gaze to the group, waiting for a reaction.

"That's it?" Indra asked. "That's disgusting." But there was awe in her voice.

Trina smiled and shook her head. "Power of ten," she murmured.

Arri started a slow, pensive beat. The rest of the group joined in, imagining the alien world Levi had described.

The crew sat staring at their cups while Trina continued her scolding.

"Document, document, document, or I've got nothing to work with." Her eyes were wide with wonder that they could take making their log entries so lightly. "There's a harvest log in the kitchen—another one in the lab. How hard can it be to just write down what you take?"

"How about an incentive?" Mane asked. "Last one who forgets to make an entry is on cook detail for a week." He grinned and looked at Levi who had picked leaves for tea two days ago.

"Well then." Levi smirked. "That would be those berries you brought in yesterday."

"Frass! That wasn't harvesting. I just wanted to know if they were edible." Mane looked at Trina in appeal. She shook her head. "It was just a suggestion. Do we really need incentives—"

"Oh, yes," said Levi.

"The integrity of our work depends on it," Arri chimed in.

"He's right," Trina said through their snickering. "I'm trying to work with EcoTech distribution charts and map out what we find so I can develop our own—"

"Trina," Jasmine interrupted. "We know. We'll try harder." Jasmine was certain everyone was happy to cut off another of Trina's academic diatribes.

"Let's get to work," Mane stood.

"Document everything," Trina called after the crew as they dispersed for the day's chores.

*   *   *   *   *

Jasmine and Dustin laughed at Mane who was attempting supper.

"You know, we're trying to concentrate here," she said.

"Oh, please continue," he insisted. "Never mind that this frying pan has the worst heat distribution. That's got to be why I keep burning this."

Jasmine and Dustin rolled their eyes at him and continued their study of the map Mane had prepared of possible new harvesting sites.

"Trina asked for a line through here." Dustin pointed. "But Levi figures this spot will give us a better yield."

"Then let's go with his suggestion. I'm not going to plan lines based on Trina's curiosity."

"We can make them both happy if we string it through this way. There's a strong enough tree here."

"Good. We can get them to approve it when they get back." She checked her watch. "Which should be in another hour."

Levi and Trina were out surveying for ideal harvesting spots. Arri worked in the lab conversing with his equipment, no doubt counting the days till Indra got back—one more week. She'd gone home for a few weeks to visit her grandmother for her eightieth birthday.

This was a lazy day. She and Dustin were able to pull themselves away from other duties long enough to make some plans. Now that Trina was here, she and Levi did the surveys together, freeing Dustin to work out the engineering with Jasmine. Mane combined their notes with the sat images so that, with the survey information, Dustin could choose the three perimeter points based on which tall and strong trees they had to work with.

Jasmine peered through the mesh wall. Light was dimming. The days always felt too short. There were only ever ten good hours of light to work in, which meant the sorting and drying was often done by lamplight into the night. And if they used all the methane for lights and dryers, there was none to cook with the next morning. A few times the harvesting had gone too well and it was morning by the time everything was sorted and drying.

Arri had insisted that no matter how busy they got, there was at least half an hour at the end of the day for them to drum. She was convinced it was Arri who kept them all sane.

"This tree's in the way," Dustin muttered and pointed to the map.

Jasmine looked at the species annotation, M.l., and had no idea what the tree looked like but the code told her it was tall but too weak to support a perimeter point.

"Can we pulley to one of the branches and divert the line?"

"I'll try the calculations." Dustin punched measurements into the console.

Jasmine wiped sweat from her forehead with the back of her hand. Just sitting gave a respite from the heat. It had been a warm month. Mane had suffered the most. He struggled with debilitating headaches if he didn't constantly watch his fluid intake. Arri figured Mane's size made it hard for him to keep cool.

There were times when she got so tired of the heat, she wanted to spend entire days immersed in the river. And the bugs—they were everywhere. Outside the house it was impossible to sit anywhere without either crushing them or becoming a new substrate or a meal for them.

It had only been recently that she'd been able to admit to herself how many times she'd wanted to walk away and go home. She watched Mane happily muttering to the stove then smiled at Dustin who was intent on the map and his numbers. This was not one of those times.

She heard Arri's voice, raised. Something in his tone made her get up. Through the screen wall she could see him standing in front of the lab, hands raised.

"Mane—"

A blast turned Arri's head brilliant red and he crumpled. A figure in Warrior uniform bent over him while others ran towards the house.

"Come on!" Mane cried in a hoarse whisper. "They're not taking prisoners."

Dustin dashed off and Jasmine and Mane ended up running side-by-side, heedless of the gunfire that kicked up dirt around them. After seeing what happened to Arri, they knew stopping wouldn't save them. Mane led her in a chaotic pattern that, judging by the decrease in gunfire around them, seemed to be putting distance between them and their pursuers. When they got to a light break filled with dense foliage Mane pulled her onto the ground and under the bushes.

Three Warriors ran past them—they would likely double back here once they realized they'd lost track of their quarry.

"I have an idea," Jasmine whispered, and they were running again.

Her heart pounded as quickly as her feet. As soon as she saw the green wall of leaves that marked the river, she veered off the path directly to the hollow tree.

"Get in there," she gasped to Mane who stared at the impossibly small opening. "Break it open," she urged while she pulled out her knife and cut down a nearby bush. She followed him in, dragging the bush behind her to cover the opening they had made.

The stench was as bad as she remembered and their panting made them inhale the dust and spores they stirred up. They convulsed in an attempt to keep their coughing quiet and, with shirts pressed over their faces, eventually breathed normally.

Mane moved to sit down. Jasmine put a hand on his shoulder and shook her head. A close examination of the writhing insect larvae and guano on the floor made him wrinkle his nose. The wall of the trunk muffled the sounds of the search but they could hear the voices of the warriors. As her eyes grew used to the dim light, Jasmine could make out the walls of their refuge. They were spotted with fungus and patches of colored slimy substances. A group of cockroaches crouched in formation on the wall, all of them facing upwards. Gunfire made her start. Who were they killing now? Mane's arms enveloped her and she held on to him. Volley after volley of shots rang out and she saw Arri's ruined face time after time.

"They didn't follow Dustin," Mane whispered. "They're just shooting up camp."

There were a few minutes of quiet. A deeper silence than she had ever heard.

An explosive charge went off and the ground trembled. Then another and another. They were destroying everything—everything she had built here. Fury shook her through, till not even the pressure of Mane's arms around her could stop her shaking.

Silence came again and slowly she calmed. There was a faint odor of smoke. She and Mane leaned against the cleanest part of the cavity wall. Mane stared at the moving floor, eyes unseeing. He was here because of her. The rest of the crew had come to be part of Jasmine and Mane's dream. Now Arri was dead because he'd followed her. What if Levi and Trina came back to camp?

"We've got to warn them," she whispered.

"We can't," he replied. "All we can do is try to find them when we get out of here."

She sighed and looked up. Faint light showed where the hollow opened to the outside, high above them. No doubt it was a doorway for the bats that squeaked occasionally up there. She leaned back and waited for night to come.

When it came, the wooden hollow filled with a darkness that draped them so completely, it blinded them. They were insulated from the sounds outside but the hollow filled with strange sounds of its own. With her blinded eyes Jasmine seemed to see tiny patches of green glow.

"See that?" Mane whispered.

Something dropped on her head and she shook it off. It could have been anything from bat guano to a large insect.

"Frass!" Mane whispered.

She could feel him jump.

"Something trying to nest in my shirt," he explained.

It went like that all night long. They passed the time whispering stories to each other so they wouldn't have to think about Arri or about the floor creeping up their legs.

*   *   *   *   *

With daylight came relief. Jasmine and Mane crept out of their pungent sanctuary. The odor of scorched vegetation clung to the air and Jasmine's apprehension turned to anger. She took several steps towards camp before Mane caught her.

"Have you gone sheared?"

"I want to see what they've done."

"Something they might just expect. Let's concentrate on finding the others."

This didn't feel right, they should be fighting back, not running.

"Empty your pockets," Mane advised.

Mane pulled out his knife. Jasmine always kept her jungle kit stashed in her pants pocket. Knife, whistle, first aid, water tablets, energy bar, tiny flashlight, insect repellant, three different anti-venom injectors, several small tools . . . tracker!

Mane grabbed it. "Great. Let's find Dustin first." He set the dial for Dustin's tracking bead and moved the small gadget in a slow arc around him. "Levi and Trina have kits with them but Dustin has no way to find us."

Worry lifted from his face a bit when the tracker blinked green.

They carefully followed the tracker readings, stopping often to listen for sounds that didn't belong. They soon found themselves at their harvesting site. Jasmine looked for the rope and didn't see it.

"Dustin?" Mane called softly.

"Shree-oo?" Jasmine whistled.

Branches rustled high above and they jumped out of the way of the rope as it fell. About two stories up, Dustin swung out from a tree branch he must have perched on through the night. He landed wide-eyed and Mane grabbed him in a relieved hug.

"Arri," he said when Mane released him. "What happened?"

Jasmine told him what she'd seen. "He can't be alive," she said in answer to the question in his eyes. Dustin attempted an answer but no words came. He took a step away and gazed into the trees.

Jasmine looked towards camp. Everything they had accomplished there was burned to ashes. Mane's hand fell on her shoulder. "We still have people to find."

It took two hours, but finally Levi and Trina answered from between trees and the group was reunited into a laughing tangle of relief.

"We were ten minutes from camp when we heard a shot," Levi gasped.

"Then all that shooting and explosions," Trina said. "We took off and spent the night out. Was it Warriors?"

Mane nodded.

"I'm glad we didn't decide to go back," she said. "All we have to do now is find Arri."

The joy drained from her face when she saw Mane's reaction. He recounted what Jasmine had seen.

"Oh, no," Trina cried softly. "Oh, no. Why would they do that? We don't deserve to be killed for living here." Her voice rose with hysteria. "Why would they do that?"

Mane put his arms around her and gently pulled her into him. Her chatter gave way to sobs.

Levi had gone retreat. He allowed Jasmine to hug him but he wasn't even there.

Dustin looked from one person to another with tears running down his face and seemed to be trying to make sense of what had happened.

Jasmine looked at her crew and the fury that was still there smoldered. Whoever was responsible for this would be made to regret it and if the Warriors thought they could keep her and her crew out of the preserves, then they needed an education.

After pulling themselves together again, the crew sat in a circle around their belongings and chewed on a corner of their ration of three energy bars split between them. They had three jungle kits, a data pad with a dead cell, some tools, notebooks, collection bags and vials, and Levi's tree hunting map.

"Six days till Indra gets back," Mane said.

"We could starve in six days," Trina muttered.

"People used to live in forests just like this," Jasmine said.

"Great," Trina replied. "We can try learning to make blowguns and bows and arrows while we starve."

Monkeys chattered above them the way they often did when a troop found a tree full of fruit. The crew looked longingly upwards. Without their ropes, whatever fruit was up in the trees was totally out of reach.

*　*　*　*　*

After four days, the water purification tabs ran out. Jasmine stared at the collection vial of untreated water. It looked harmless enough.

Jasmine stood too quickly and the forest spun around her for a moment. Everyone was hungry all the time though Levi did his best to find edible roots and stalks. A few times Dustin climbed smaller trees to retrieve fruit.

The nights were the worst. Sleeping on the ground made everyone food or substrate for the constant insect swarm that lived just below the thin cover of dead leaves.

Mane was quiet and grim. Jasmine suspected he was afraid to drink all the water he really needed. Jasmine and Trina had finally convinced him to conserve his strength for the walk to the chopper landing and let the others go food hunting.

Jasmine was beginning to think they should have decided to try to walk out rather than wait for Indra. At least the activity would have kept them busy. They could have made it to one of the plantation houses in five days—given a constant food supply, something they didn't have.

Trina walked over and stood looking at Mane where he lay. "This is insane," she said. "The whole idea of coming here was insane." She turned to Jasmine. "What were you thinking dragging us out here?"

Trina stomped off, probably wishing she had a door to slam behind her. Jasmine lacked the energy to care.

"She doesn't mean that," Mane said.

"Shut up," Jasmine gently replied. "I know."

Trina stomped back and announced, "We've got to find a way to boil water. Build me a fire," she said to Jasmine and stomped off again. Jasmine had no idea where she got the energy for all that stomping. Her own anger and panic had faded to acceptance—for now.

*　*　*　*　*

Relief washed through her as Jasmine heard the chopper blades. Mane still lay where he had collapsed after the long walk and showed no indication of awareness, though Dustin squeezed his hand and told him help had come. Trina crouched beside him and wept with relief. Levi had gone to meet Indra.

A few minutes later, Indra came running. Jasmine hugged her and choked back tears of her own.

She spotted Mane. "How is he?"

"Just weak, I hope. We all are. We've been living on roots and berries for six days."

"We'll take a crate of food with us. Levi is stashing the rest of the cargo under cover. I should go back and help. He looks as bad as the rest of you lot." She looked around the clearing. "Where's Arri?"

Levi hadn't told her. "Oh, Indra."

"He's lost?"

"The Warriors executed him."

Indra nodded slowly, eyes unfocused. Then she smiled briefly. "At least there's something that can be done for the rest of you. We'll have you in Bogota in an hour." She struggled to keep her voice from breaking.

Jasmine lay on the cot listening to the sounds of the city. Only the core of Bogota was left and it was filled to the brim with people while plantations and cattle ranches surrounded the buildings. Mountains surrounded those.

After a number of small meals and a night's sleep uninterrupted by insects, Mane had recovered along with the rest of them. He, Trina, and Dustin were still sleeping. Indra sat at the table with a cup in her hand, and Jasmine swore she hadn't moved a muscle in an hour. Indra had been uncharacteristically quiet since their arrival.

The datapad rang and put an end to sleep. Adrien was returning her call.

Indra flipped it open on the table and Jasmine joined her there.

"Jas, you look awful," was the first thing he said.

"The roots and shoots diet," she answered and then told him what had happened while the rest of the crew drifted in.

Adrien just stared at her for a moment when she finished. "Then um. . . I'll call Mei—"

"And tell her what? We're not quitting." Jasmine had had six long days to make plans. "I've already called Manda. She can get you enough through her suppliers by March. That's two months, we'll be up and running again by that time and supply—"

"What?" Trina said. "We're not going back out there!"

Mane put a hand on Jasmine's shoulder. "We'll take a vote."

A vote. It had never occurred to her that the crew wouldn't go back.

"I want people to know about this," she said to Adrien. "About Veejix, about Arri, about how we're harvesting. Arri was executed—the Warriors didn't give him a chance. People have to know about this."

Mane leaned over her shoulder. "Doll, we'll discuss it."

"Discuss what?" she turned to them. "Do you all want to go back to city life? Have you *looked* at Bogota? Give EC another ten years and all the cities back home will look like this, with people piled on top of each other so EcoTech can have more land. I don't want to live that way.

"And don't tell me we're going to let the Warriors get away with murdering Arri."

Mane smiled at Adrien. "She'll get back to you," and disconnected.

"You can't just—"

"Hey!" he said to shut her up. "Let's go for a walk." He took her arm, leaving her little choice.

"We're not giving up," she muttered.

"I know."

After walking down sidewalks for five blocks she felt better. She really didn't need Mane to tell her, her anger could cost her the crew. The anger that she had nurtured after the death of her parents, that had made it possible for her to do what she did in the Core, to survive before she had Owen and Adrien. She knew through experience that, outside the Core, it did more damage than she could repair once it escaped.

But she'd expected everyone to be eager to return once they got out of the jungle. Instead, they were all moping as if everything was over—as if there was nothing left to do. They couldn't let the Emerald Warriors stop them. Maybe it was the shock of Arri's death. But they'd had a week to get over that. How could they even consider not going back?

Mane kept her out all day. There seemed no reason for conversation and their mutual lack of energy kept them looking for scenic places to sit most of the afternoon.

"Hey doll." Mane finally addressed the cause of their silence, " So far this has just been our dream—yours and mine. If you want it to be theirs you have to give them a say and discuss decisions with them. We can't do it without them."

It made no sense to quit . . . but, yeah, she knew.

Before taking the rail again, Mane made a call. He came back smiling. "Let's get back."

By the time they stumbled through the hotel room door, Jasmine was practically asleep on her feet.

The whole crew was there and looked at her sheepishly. Indra got up and hugged her. "Arri was so excited about this project. Every time I talked to him he was bursting to tell me about it. And when he finally did, well . . . it just sounded like so much fun I had to wriggle my way in. I was never sorry I did. Not even now. He would want us safe, but he would also want us to keep going. If you're in—we're in."

Jasmine looked at each face just to be sure. "Thanks," was all she could croak out.

*   *   *   *   *

Jasmine stared at the numbers and hoped she'd missed something. They needed at least 150 thousand for building materials for what she really wanted to create.

She'd tried taking Mane's advice, and got the rest of the crew involved in deciding what equipment they needed and what it would cost. But funding, that was something she and Mane had to figure.

"Hey, Doll." Mane came in and straddled the chair beside her.

She raised an eyebrow at him.

"Trina took Indra to the market. She figured Indra could use the break. She's still pretty fractured." He nodded at the screen. "You don't look happy."

She sighed. "We've only got twenty thousand left. That would only build a shack on the ground. That's not good enough. If we don't want to be raided again, we have to do better than a ground-based lab and cook-house."

"Is that with using an outside contract to do the refining?"

She nodded. "Saves us a hundred thousand in equipment costs."

"What about picking up what we stashed?"

"Comes to about thirty thousand."

She shook her head. "I wish we knew what went wrong. How did they find us?"

"Already on it."

"What," she said with a smile. "You've got Warrior headquarters bugged?"

"No," he smirked. "I have sources."

Like the sources he'd used to find Yit—like the sources he used to find her attackers. Since they partnered, there wasn't anything she hadn't told him, yet Mane was still keeping things from her.

"Who are they?" she asked.

That surprised him. "People I found a long time ago."

"I'm basing our plans on what you find out. I want to know where your information is coming from. No secrets—that's our partnership deal."

"I had this source before we were partners." He didn't meet her eyes.

They had both proven their loyalty to each other countless times. His secrecy now baffled her.

"I made a promise," he said.

"Yeah, you made a promise to me."

He got that look on as if he were about to make a crack, then just shook his head.

"I'm not letting this go," she warned.

"I know." He leaned towards her. "Got a line into Opposition intelligence. Your father's Restoration friends."

"You got them to help you track Yit?"

"Doll, they hired me to track Yit."

But . . . he'd done the tracking for *her. She* had found *him,* hadn't she?

"Then why were you working for me?"

He sat back. "They wanted Owen Lamberin's killer found but didn't want their connection to a separate investigation known. They figured if you found out who did it, you would take care of it without involving them."

They had used her to get rid of Yit so they could stay clean. She had killed Martin Yit for them, with Mane's help.

"And you just watched." She leaned forward. How could he have done this? "I had nightmares for years. I have to live the rest of my life knowing I ended someone's life. I hope they paid you real well for that."

"Doll, they just wanted the assassin found and you where they could watch you. Didn't pay me to kill him."

Paid to watch her. How much of their partnership had been a lie?

"Did you partner with me because they paid you to?"

"What did you think I was when you first met me? I did things for people for money because doing things out of friendship only ever gets you hurt. I was a mercenary. Then you came along and treated me like a partner when I was still just in it for the money. That's when—"

"You know what I thought? I thought we were friends because . . . we were friends." Everything they had worked for was based on a false partnership. She'd let herself dream of doing something big with him and he was tearing it apart. Jasmine stood and rage filled her.

"We are finished."

" No," Mane said and smiled sadly, "we're not."

He stood and faced her, his expression impossible to read.

She continued. "You've destroyed—"

"That's enough." Mane gave her a shove that sent her plopping back in her chair. "You're not going to make me walk out of here before I'm finished."

He let so much pain show in his eyes that she stayed seated.

He went to the cupboard, pulled out two containers of fruit juice and put one on the table in front of her. "Papaya okay?" he asked when she didn't open hers. She just stared at him, his pain cloaked again.

Her rage was gone but she was still angry. She had every right to be angry.

"I don't work for them any more," Mane said sitting across from her. "Since Splinter sent you to the hospital that night, I stopped sending the Restoration agents any more information." He shook his head. "You got to me. The way you just pulled me into your life. The way you trusted me when you shouldn't have. They stopped paying me three months later. I walked away from them because of our partnership." He paused as if waiting for his words to work on her. "I've still got the money."

"What?"

He shrugged. "There was no way to spend it without you asking where it came from so I never did."

"How much?"

"Hundred thousand."

It was enough. They could start to rebuild. Mane waited for her reaction. Would he ever have told her if it weren't that he had to explain the money he was offering?

"Why are they still helping you?"

He smiled. "They enjoy watching you kick the EC in the balls."

"It helps, but you can't buy your way out of this."

"Yeah, but it means we're still partners." He grinned at her.

Jasmine picked up her bottle of juice and walked towards the door and stared at it for a moment. No, this wasn't over. She turned back to tell him so, but Mane sat there with his head in his hands. Jasmine fled into the dusty streets.

Adrien stood in the study doorway and gazed at the living room, his eyes finally resting on the covered keyboards in the corner. He sighed. Even when Jasmine had first run off into the Core with Mane, the house hadn't seemed this empty, but now that Jasmine had created a life for herself without him. . . He was spending even more time at the lab because it was less painful there. He'd had some strange notion that working with Jasmine would keep her close—she was only as close as a weekly com ration. He smiled as he recalled that thirteen years ago he'd begged his father to get rid of her.

He turned to the console. Mane had sent pictures. Adrien stared at one photograph after another on his screen. Green jungle with a black wound the area of a city block. Mane had found the sat records and pulled out the photos from routine passes over the camp. The warriors had burned a city block of jungle to destroy the camp. Adrien stopped focusing on the screen and let the images pass again and again. He'd been preparing for the battle to get VJX out in the open and accepted, but this . . . this made it more than just a battle with red tape.

The door chimed, then clicked open as it recognized a palm print.

"Adrien?" Chanel called. She'd insisted on dropping by after he'd called her about Arri.

"In the study," he answered.

After a moment he turned to see her in the doorway, standing hands on hips and glaring at him. "How could you not tell me? A confidential security job out of town—hah!"

"Jasmine didn't want anyone to know."

"I was her best friend . . . at least until Mane came along."

"She asks about you every time I talk to her," he offered.

Her frown still in place, Chanel sat beside him. "You've got a lot of explaining to do.

"Is that it?" she asked, seeing the screen. Adrien led her through the succession of shots, pointing out Arri's body. It had been left for the jungle to swallow. Arri's parents were still fighting to have it brought home. Perhaps the EC was stalling in the hopes that Arri would soon be unrecognizable. Chanel shook her head. "And after all this, she's going to rebuild."

"She tells me she's setting up an invisible camp this time." He often wished he was there, far from the battle with his peers he was about to have. Sometimes he felt he'd been abandoned here in the city.

"She's not coming back," Chanel said after a moment. "You really should stop waiting for her."

"What do you mean?"

Chanel didn't meet his eyes. "Since I've known you, both of you, she's been the center of your world. After your father died, I think you fell in love with her, trying to hang on to some of the life you had as a family."

"Get synced, Chanel. She's my sister. She needed a lot of help growing up and—"

"I've known you for six years and I've never seen you fall in love."

"I've been busy."

"You've been comfortable and that's the kind of love you can handle. No passion, no months of obsession, no giving yourself to the falling." She leaned toward him, full of concern. "You really should try it. It's frightening and wonderful all at once."

Adrien frowned at her. "Can we please get back to the part where you're yelling at me for not telling you about Jasmine?"

Chanel slumped in her chair. "Fine. So tell me what on earth got you into this."

"My therapeutic studies show VJX is going to be a cure for Lightning Madness."

"Power of ten! No wonder you've been so smug for the last month." She put a hand on his arm. "Now tell me the whole story from the beginning."

When he finished, Chanel was frowning. "Three years after the planning starts and I find out about it at the same time as everyone else."

"No, no. Everyone else won't be finding out for at least a few days yet."

Chanel wrinkled her nose at him.

Exposing VJX would be easy. He was just days away from finishing the documentation. Exposing how Arri had died would be harder.

Chanel glanced at the screen. "I should let Edan know what happened."

Adrien raised his eyebrows.

"I still keep in touch." She shrugged. "We have music friends in common."

*   *   *   *   *

"Lamberin! Have you gone sheared? You'll ruin us!"

"Morning, Max." Adrien tried to hide a giddy smile. Exactly twenty minutes earlier, he had sent the whole staff a preview copy of his VJX findings as a courtesy before publishing.

"Sit down. Linda's on her way with coffee." Adrien picked his data charts off his desk and prepared to join Max Hunter in his nook.

"I don't have time for this. You've created a public relations disaster."

"A public relations coup, actually," Adrien replied. "Sit down and I'll let you in on the plan."

"You've associated this clinic with the criminals pillaging the preserves."

"Do you remember meeting my sister Jasmine at the graduation reception? Played the entry march?"

"Yes. I saw her recital the following month," he answered, confusion clear on his face.

"She's my supplier."

At this, Max studied him for a moment, sighed and plopped into the nearest chair.

The door opened and Linda brought in a coffee tray. Max stared at it as she set it on the table.

"Cheer up." Adrien dropped the charts on the coffee table and sat across from him. "How often can the clinic take credit for a cure?"

"At what cost? You did all this work in secret. That is your first violation of procedure. Then you falsify your budget, then you work on an illegal drug. How can we expect our funders to trust us now?"

"All those violations of procedure protect you. You're not going to suffer from my transgressions because you didn't know about them. Believe me, evidence of a cure is going to more than balance out against my illegal actions."

Max sighed and took a sip of his coffee. "Tell me the details."

Adrien sorted through his charts and started to explain the research he and Mei had done over the past three years. When he finished, Max lounged back in his chair and stared at his hands.

Voices gathered around Linda at her desk. Max didn't seem to notice. "I had a cousin die of Frontal Sclerosis," he said quietly. "It worked like lightning all right." He looked up at Adrien. "Have you got proof you requested research permits for VJX?"

Adrien nodded.

"How soon before the clinical investigations are done?"

"We can put VJX on the market in a year if the side effects are minimal."

The commotion of voices outside the door became heightened in energy. Linda's voice pleaded, then the door burst open.

"You've had enough time with him, Max," accused Wanda Lipowski, a colleague. "Come on Adrien. We're taking you for lunch."

At that, the crowd in the hall erupted into applause.

Wanda took Adrien's arm. "Now you're going to tell *us* all about it."

"Linda!" Someone shouted. "We're taking the rest of the day off."

Adrien let himself be pulled along. When he glanced back, Max stood leaning in the doorway, shaking his head but smiling.

*   *   *   *   *

Adrien chuckled as Mei blinked at the controls in front of her then entered the readings.

"How long did you stay at the celebrations last night?" he asked.

"Oh, shut up." She yawned. "You don't know what a relief it is to finally be able to tell everyone what we've been working on." She cocked her head at him and smiled. "Hmm, I guess you do."

Adrien perused the cramped lab. In the past three years it had gone from an assay lab, to dosage testing to tolerance simulations. So they wouldn't have to go to other staff, Mei had become a chemist and a pharmacist as well as a molecular biologist. Keeping a secret with the doctors treating patients with VJX had been the hardest. Adrien hadn't told them exactly what the drug was, he just gave them enough of Mei's tests to convince them to try it.

"Hey!" Mei shouted across the lab. "NewsPort."

He joined her in front of the screen. Adrien had sent the sat photos to NewsPort that morning and was curious to see what the news crew would do with them.

" . . . continue with the mid-day report. There's trouble in the jungle and linked with NewsPort is EC president Miguel Escalente to shed light on what's been happening."

The interviewer swivelled to look at her own screen. Miguel Escalente smiled at her. One of the sat photos showing scorched jungle took up a small square on the bottom of the screen. "President Escalente, there are reports that Emerald Warriors burned several square kilometers of jungle in the Columbian preserves to get at some Greens harvesters."

Escalente seemed amused by the suggestion. "Let me clarify those reports. These harvesters cause a lot of damage. What happened in this case was an explosion in the processing lab that set the forest on fire. If it hadn't been for the efforts of the Emerald Warriors, the fire could have been much more widespread."

Adrien sat frozen, stunned by the boldness of the lie.

"This incident has prompted us to take a closer look at where the Warriors can be more effective at stopping the Greens harvesters to prevent more damage." Escalente now addressed the audience. "Not only are these illegal harvesting operations a fire hazard, but they can poison entire watersheds with the solvents used in processing. These preserves are the most precious thing we have on this earth so—"

Adrien didn't hear the rest. He grabbed his jacket on the way out. NewsPort needed an education about Greens harvesting.

*   *   *   *   *

Adrien had little luck being taken seriously in the NewsPort lobby until someone referred to him as the Veejix guy. The producer suddenly became available.

Raul Martinez stood and bowed as Adrien entered his office. "Dr. Lamberin." He peered into Adrien's face. "What can we do for you?"

Adrien's indignation stalled as he was confronted by those intense eyes. Martinez was not a large man but he had enough energy to fill the room.

"For one thing," Adrien said, "you could do more with those photographs I sent you than let Escalente use them to make the Emerald Warriors look like heroes."

Martinez spread his hands. "At least we made him sweat. That's all we could do with what we had." He motioned Adrien to the chair in front of his desk. "By the time they got the chemist's body out of there, it was too decomposed to give a clear cause of death."

"I don't care how decomposed his body is, it's still clear to an autopsy that a bullet went through his skull. And if they wanted to look, the investigators would find a hundred bullets embedded in the ground."

"If you've got evidence that the Emerald Warriors are lying, I'll run it. Otherwise, there's no news in it."

Of course he didn't have the evidence. Who would believe eyewitness reports from a crew of Greens harvesters?

"Yeah," Martinez said, nodding. "Talk to me about Lightning Madness."

"What?"

"You came up with a cure for a disease that can wipe a person's brain clean in less than two years. There's news in that."

NewsPort had already run a short clip on VJX. At this point more publicity could only help him. The more public this fight got, the cleaner it would have to be. Adrien told the recorder on Raul's desk abut VJX and Lightning Madness.

He left the NewsPort offices confident that Raul Martinez had enough interest in his work to keep it in the news for a while. But Arri— he felt a terrible guilt to think that Arri's family and friends back home were expected to believe that he'd died of his own incompetence. He'd have to track them down and tell them the truth.

* * * * *

"Special Officer Watenabe to see you," the entry request said.

"Show her in," Adrien replied. Here it comes. He'd published his VJX findings just a day ago and had lived in a state of nervousness ever since.

"Dr. Lamberin." Watenabe shook her head. "I volunteered to bring you in for questioning."

"About what I expected," he smiled at her and put on his jacket. "Did they actually read my paper or did they just watch the fifteen-second clip on News Port?" He chuckled, light-headed.

She stepped towards him. "This is a lot more serious than you think."

"Yeah, this is going to be power of ten."

"Adrien," she put a hand on his arm. "If what they tell me is true, you're facing possession of an illegal substance and if you don't cooperate with the investigation, that's obstruction of justice."

"I've been waiting for this fight to start for three years now. I'm ready. Don't try to depress me. Can't be done."

"You and Jasmine, why can't you get normal jobs?"

He shrugged. "It's the way our DNA stacks up. Let's go."

*　*　*　*　*

Watenabe stopped him just outside the police station. "There aren't just police officers in there," she warned. "Two reps from the Warriors showed up this morning."

Adrien smiled and shrugged. "Lead the way."

"There's the Lamberin kid."

Adrien looked for the source of the voice and smiled at the two men watching him. Detouring from Watenabe's lead, Adrien walked over to face them.

"Dr. Adrien Lamberin." He bowed. "Are you the gentlemen who asked to see me?"

The men's brows furrowed. "We'll be there in a minute," the darkhaired one said to Watenabe, then turned back to his companion.

Watenabe took him to an interview room and silently waited with him. When the two men entered she smiled weakly at Adrien and left.

They sat at the table with Adrien and frowned.

"You've been using an illegal substance in your research," the balding one stated without pausing for introductions.

Adrien was ready. "I went through all the proper channels to get harvesting permits." He placed a data coin on the table. "Here are the records if you're interested. After a year of EcoTech's denials that VJX existed, I gave up. I had an opportunity to obtain it three years ago.

"You've got harvesters in the Columbia preserves. Where are they?"

Adrien shrugged. "I don't keep track of them."

"Don't be stupid. The chemist was a friend of yours. He was working with your sister and some of your college buddies. Don't tell us you don't keep in touch. Tell us where they are."

"So there can be another unfortunate accident for you to heroically clean up? Maybe you can tell me how someone can die from a bullet to the head in an explosion. Maybe you can tell me why there are bullets scattered through the burn site."

The dark-haired one sighed. "Think of your research," he said. "You could be tied up with court proceedings for a year."

"Do you have any idea what Frontal Sclerosis, Lightning Madness, is? It's a disease that terrifies people. Do you really want to go on record as the people who stalled my research for a legal battle?"

"Where are the harvesters operating?"

"I don't know," Adrien replied truthfully.

"How do they get their supplies in?"

Adrien shrugged.

"How do they get the Veejix to you?"

He shook his head.

The questioning went on for at least another half hour. The same questions over and over, with Adrien giving the same responses. The dark-haired man finally sighed and paused his questioning for a moment.

"I can see you're concerned about your friends," he said. "We can guarantee they won't be hurt, but only if you cooperate. Otherwise . . . " He shook his head.

"You're saying that if you find them without my help, you'll kill them. I hope your recorders are getting all this." That gave him an idea. "How much damage do you think those harvesters are doing? Did you find evidence of trees cut down? Water table contamination? Of course not. They have a Botanist and Ecologist on the crew to ensure they don't do any damage to the preserves. You would hardly know they've been there."

"That's something EcoTech decides, not any bunch of thugs with a taste for the outdoors."

A buzzer chirped and the men looked at each other. They left without another word.

Adrien had to wait for twenty minutes before the door opened again. A tall blond woman came in who he had seen before, but couldn't remember where for a moment.

"Dr. Lamberin," she bowed. "I'm Shelly VanDaal."

The voice of NewsPort, he realized.

She studied him for a moment. "I'm a director with EcoTech." VanDaal sat at the table across from him and as if they were having coffee at a café, smiled and leaned toward him. "I'm curious. Why are you doing this? More people die of farming accidents every year than of Lightning Madness. Yet you are risking your career to find a cure."

"I've studied disease and so, in a way, I've studied death. I've lost both my parents—one to disease and one to violence. For my father, death came quickly. I mourned and eventually went on with my life. Imagine that pain, of grief and of mourning, being extended by eighteen months. Imagine knowing you are losing what makes you not only a human being, but that particular human being. And you get to watch the brain empty itself month by month. There are diseases that kill more people—that are more infectious. There are none that are as terrible.

That's why I found the cure and why I'm still working to understand how it works."

He didn't say that it made him angry that anyone could tell him not to use VJX. He didn't say that it had been a way to hold on to Jasmine. And he didn't say that he had more of his father's spirit in him than he had realized.

VanDaal was still smiling. Smug, Adrien realized. "There's no denying you've done something wonderful here. But you're risking it all by using an illegal substance and by supporting an illegal harvesting operation. You must know, if we press charges, your research will be shut down."

Shut down the lab? He figured the worst they could do was arrest him, that Mei would keep going without him. Shelly VanDaal was still smiling that confident stage smile. He had no doubt he was sitting in the same room with the woman with the power to shut him down. She may not be an EcoTech executive but she wasn't just the eyes, ears and mouth her title suggested either—they wouldn't have trusted her with this meeting if she were.

She looked at him sadly then. "If you tell me where the harvesting site is, I can personally guarantee the safety of your friends."

No, this wasn't going to happen. "You are seriously thinking of shutting down the facility responsible for giving hope to people who see their lives slowly slipping away? Let me clarify the position you're in. Four years ago, EcoTech denied that VJX existed. That's why I had to go underground. There's documentation that shows I went through all the proper channels to try to get research permits. When that becomes known, EcoTech isn't going to come out looking very good."

She smiled and shrugged. "The request must have gotten lost in the line-work. Anyone can sympathize with that."

"I gave an interview to NewsPort yesterday. I didn't mention why EcoTech denied VJX."

Her smile faltered just a little. "Now you're being clandestine, Doctor."

Adrien looked around the room. "Are you sure you want this recorded?"

"We're not being recorded."

Not being recorded. This couldn't be normal procedure. He wasn't sure what to make of it. "The purity imperative," he finally said.

She cocked her head.

"EcoTech rushed their methods. That's how they got their bid accepted when the EC first hired a nature restructuring company. EcoTech only got the contract because they agreed to the purity imperative when everyone else in the business said it couldn't be done." He leaned towards her. "We compared the DNA map of the VJX mold to the heritage vaults and found it shouldn't exist. It's an aberration. EcoTech knew that when I asked for a harvesting permit. You're failing your own purity imperative."

"That's an interesting allegation."

"One that I haven't mentioned so far and don't see any need to," he said, relieved to see her smile freeze on her face.

"You've made yourself clear," she replied, no longer smiling. She stood. "I don't see any reason to interrupt your work just now. But we will be watching your progress." She bowed. "Dr. Lamberin." And left.

Adrien laughed out loud once the door closed behind her. He'd gotten Shelly VanDaal to back off.

* * * * *

Light spilled into the hallway from the open door to the lab. That door was never left open. Adrien ran to the doorway and stopped dead. Destroyed—everything was destroyed. No glassware remained intact. No screen un-smashed. The imagers had been torn apart—Mei. She should have been in by now.

"Mei!" He searched behind counters and desks for her. "Mei!" He spotted her pocket phone in the rubble outside the incubator. She'd been here during the attack. Thump—he turned to the incubator and as he opened the door, Mei fell out. She groaned, but didn't seem hurt. Adrien helped her sit up, near to tears with relief. She was soaking with sweat.

"Did they leave the plumbing intact?" she asked. "I could use some water."

"Sure," he said and searched the rubble around the sink for a mug that wasn't broken.

"They came in last night," she said, then gulped the water down. "I couldn't stop them. I'm sorry."

"It's not your fault." He sat beside her on the floor.

"They locked me in there but I could still hear them. Smashing and shouting." Her breath caught in a sob. "They were like animals."

He put his arms around her and let her sob until no more tears came. He could only imagine what it had been like to be locked into that hotbox while listening to them destroy the work that had been done here.

As he ran more water into the mug, he noticed an unbroken screen. It was his own console—why hadn't it been destroyed? He punched keys but it remained blank no matter what he did. What had they used it for? He pulled out his pocket phone and called the clinic.

"Linda, check my office console, would you?"

After a moment she came back. "I can't—I can't get it to do anything."

He tried not to let the dread show in his voice. "Try to get through to my home system."

It took several minutes before Linda came back. "Nothing," she said. "What's going on?"

"Dunno. 'Kay."

He stared at the phone. He'd been wiped. The equipment could be replaced, but the data . . .

He sat beside Mei and handed her the mug. "All the data's been wiped," he murmured. "Including the backups at home and the office."

The two of them sat in silence.

Mei stood. "I'm going home to clean up." She glanced at Adrien. "Why don't you do the same?"

"Yeah." He walked Mei to the door. A color out of place caught his eye. Propped against the doorway was a small, pointed branch with several leaves.

*   *   *   *   *

Adrien stumbled through his front door, not knowing whether to expect the house to have been ransacked. Nothing looked out of place. He shouldn't have felt this tired. It was just late morning, yet the day weighed him down like a physical force. He wandered around like a lost man. The kitchen phone rang and he stared at it till it stopped. Finally he went into Jasmine's room and dropped on her bed.

He woke to the phone ringing again but continued to lie there. Only days ago he'd been riding the euphoria of proving a cure, of knowing he could help the victims of Lightning Madness. He'd thought of every angle—even out-maneuvered Shelly VanDaal. But in a matter of less than an hour, Green Splinter had destroyed everything and there was nothing to be gained by blaming an outlawed band of zealots whose only agenda was to eliminate those who posed a threat to their vision.

He should have been angry; he had been. But now he couldn't see a way to continue—now he just felt relief. The decision had been made for him. He could go back to concentrating on the research he was actually being paid for. No interrogations, no secrecy, no danger to the people around him.

The entry request chimed. Adrien groaned, but before he could decide wether to answer, he heard the door snick open. "Adrien?" Chanel called.

"In here."

"I can't believe I have to keep barging in here just to—" She saw his expression. "What's wrong?"

"The lab—it's been destroyed." He told her what had happened. "All the data's been wiped. They got into my work console and the one at home."

"That's why . . . " she mused. "I've been trying to reach you because something strange showed up on my home console. I think it's yours. Is Jasmine's still working?"

He nodded, afraid to let her suggestion sink in. After a moment at Jasmine's desk, Chanel turned to him. "Look at this."

Adrien stared at a list of file names, all of which were familiar. "Mane."

"What?" Chanel let him take her place.

"He put in the security system. I tried to watch him but I lost track of what he was doing about halfway through. This is what he did—used you as a hidden back-up. Guess he figured we'd stay in touch."

"This is wonderful. You can keep going."

He turned to her. "That was Green Splinter. They could just as easily have killed Mei as lock her into the incubator. In a matter of days they found a lab that I've kept a secret for three years. How can I keep going?"

* * T H I R T Y - O N E * *

Jasmine rocked in her hammock as the wind rattled her home perched four stories up a tree. Whistles made her look up from her reading. Indra was calling Levi and Dustin up for tea. The crew used Arri's whistle system all the time now, expanding the vocabulary when new words were needed. It had been easier not to think about Arri during the rebuilding. Construction material had to be chosen, hauled in, hauled up. Trina and Levi kept busy harvesting the whole time. The days were too full for contemplation and in the evenings, everyone was too exhausted to think. But now Indra sometimes had fits of melancholy that drove the rest of the crew into hiding. She seemed happiest when building and solving the associated problems.

Levi had retreated into the shy, preoccupied academic she'd first met. He spent more time than ever buried in his journals and drawings.

On the shelf beside her, Jasmine had arranged a row of the most bizarre seed pods she had found. Most were a shade of brown, some tinged with green or red. Some strangely shaped and smooth, others with spiraling extensions or frills or wings. The glint of metal caught her eye. Her flute lay in the far corner. Adrien had sent it, hoping it would be a pleasant distraction after Arri's death. Adrien didn't understand. It was part of what she had left behind to come here. Adrien didn't understand leaving things behind. He clung to the past as if it were a lifeboat.

She held the flute in her hands. It had taken Adrien a week to call her about his lab being destroyed. She'd never seen him so fractured.

"Two days," he'd said. "It only took two days and they found a lab I've been keeping a secret for three years."

"Will they give you research space at the clinic?'

"It doesn't matter. Anywhere I go with this puts people at risk."

"Well, you can't just stop."

Silence.

It had never occurred to her that he *could* just stop.

"I'm not about to die for my politics, Jas."

Not like their father had. "Are you still angry at Dad?"

"Yes, I'm angry. He knew that what he was doing was dangerous. But his ideas, his politics were always more important than us."

She couldn't, and didn't want to, imagine her father not constantly in an outrage over some injustice.

"You should be proud of what he did. The Restoration Party has never been this strong. They based their last attack on the EC on what we found in Dad's files."

"He's gone."

"His politics were his passion. You can't ask somebody not to have a passion. He'd be proud of what we're doing. He'd—"

"Is that what this is? You feel guilty because you never had a social conscience when he was alive and now you want to make him proud? He was proud of you when he thought you were going to be a musician. Don't pretend to do this for him. You're doing this because you like pissing on the rules and you've found some people willing to do it with you."

Jasmine's face burned with anger. She knew better than Adrien did how their father would feel, but anger wouldn't win this.

She blinked to clear her head. "Your passion is the puzzle. That's why your work became such an obsession—you spend all your time solving the puzzle of what makes a disease work. You figured out that Veejix works on Lightning Madness. You still have to figure out why."

"There are other diseases to work on."

"You can't walk away from this—you can't let them win. When Splinter came after me, I fought back. When—"

"You left the country." He shook his head. "Jas, I'm done."

Then she'd really gotten angry and he broke the link.

How could he have let himself be defeated by a group of fanatics?

After a day of growling at her crew, she'd decided to call Chanel.

"I'm worried about Adrien," she told her, not knowing where else to start.

"Me too," Chanel sighed. "When your father died, Adrien was sad, angry, buried himself in his work. That's normal. Now he's all that *and* constantly agitated—fractured, but in a secret, hurting kind of way. And he doesn't seem to be snapping out of it. I can't understand it. He was so happy when he made the announcement even after he was taken to the police station. I don't know what to do with him."

Chanel's insight surprised Jasmine. "How often do you two get together?"

Chanel looked at the bottom of the screen and shrugged. "Pretty regularly, actually."

Then she looked up, smiling at Jasmine, and Adrien suddenly became a clear picture. "You're the reason. He doesn't want to leave you behind like Dad left us behind. You've got to convince him to keep going with his research."

"You've tried, some of his coworkers have tried. He's not going to listen to me."

"Yes he is, because he needs your permission to keep going."

Chanel frowned. It took a while to convince her, but by the time they broke link, Jasmine had Chanel's promise to try.

Another gust shook the tree-house and Jasmine looked out the window. She swung the screen out so she could look up. No sign of sunlight. It had been overcast all day. The canopy of leaves and branches swayed in

the wind, making the swaying of her own tree seem even more pronounced. Looking along the cable that connected her to Trina, she
noticed a drifting of pink petals. Trina's tree was in blossom, the flowers
hidden from view in the very upper reaches. The wind picked off the
petals, freeing them to flutter to the ground. She watched to see where
they fell but lost sight of the pink specks through the branches. In some
spots, squared-off boulders peeked through the ground-cover, the rubble
from Miraflores. When EcoTech acquired the lands, the small city was
evacuated and levelled. So many people left their homes so EcoTech
could have more land to add to the preserves.

Mane had chosen the field of boulders grown over by forest for the
site. Unless you knew the paths, it would take a person more than an hour
to stumble through the old town site. The cable system that Dustin and
Jasmine had installed took the crew over the area in minutes. No sane
person would think of putting a harvesting operation at this site and the
crew was counting on no one looking for them here.

Mane's sources had found out that the three Emerald Warriors who
destroyed the camp had stumbled on their operation and panicked—
probably expecting the kind of shoot-now-talk-later reception they
would have gotten from Gunther Vint. A dull anger swept through her.
That didn't excuse what the Emerald Warriors had done to an obviously
unarmed man and an unarmed camp. Everyone who didn't know Arri
now thought he'd died from his own carelessness.

At least when Owen Lamberin died, everyone knew it was because he
was trying to uncover corruption. And by executing the man who killed
him, Jasmine could tell herself she'd repaid his death with justice. Her
arms ached at the memory of her rage.

She shook off the stiffness and looked out at the green. When they'd
first come to this site, Jasmine had wondered that anything could grow
on rubble. Then Trina had reminded her that the rest of the forest also
grew in a thin layer of soil on rock. These trees had taken hold in the soil

scattered over the site by EcoTech's soil generation process and had wrapped their roots around the old city foundations.

Emerald Warriors could walk, or stumble, through this site and never see signs of a camp. Even if they looked up, all they'd notice were some unusually large clumps of epiphytes growing in the trees. Indra had made sure to build the homes out of porous mock-wood. It had already grown a thin layer of moss and leaves in the past months.

The single ground building had been built of the same material. It too had taken on the color of the forest. That was where the harvest was dried, packed and stored. Levi still lived there. Indra had worked with Jasmine and Mane to build four treehouses so far for Jasmine, Trina, Indra and Mane. Dustin was happy to set up his hammock in Mane's place for now. Indra had invited Levi up with her but he seemed to prefer the solitude of the shed, even if he had to walk 500 meters of winding footpath just to get home.

The floor jerked slightly—someone was on the line. She opened the door and glanced at the door frame. A single bolt held cables that led to Trina, Indra and the ground. The line from Trina's was taut and she could just make out Mane between the leaves, swinging in the wind like a drunken pendulum as he inch-wormed towards her.

Jasmine closed the door and sat in the hammock to wait for him. He knocked and opened the door. The perfume of Trina's tree came in with him and Jasmine wondered how long he had spent there to have picked up so much of the fragrance.

"Getting pretty windy out there," he said as he sat on the only stool.

Jasmine rocked in the hammock as the entire tree swayed in the wind. She waited for him to tell her why he'd come.

"Have an idea about the food lockers," he said. "The newer section of town had basements. A perfect place for the lockers. Found . . . " and he went on about microblasters, the porosity of the rock, the storage problems they could solve. He told her this as if they were still partners, as if she wanted him to sit in her home and make himself comfortable, as if a breakfast meeting wasn't a better place to bring this up.

Shrill whistles sounded outside but Jasmine barely paid attention. Then the whistles were lost in the rain as it began.

"The flooding would be too big an issue," she countered after a while.

"Told you, the rock is porous enough that it's not a problem. The drainage is really good. Talked to Trina about it. She thinks it would make a good place for specimen storage."

"So the two of you are going to present a united front about this at breakfast instead of just bringing it to the whole group."

He looked at her with a blank expression.

"Why bother?" she said. "You always get your way anyhow."

"Oh, that's enough." He stood. "I have put up with your constant sniping for two months because maybe you needed to get your anger out and because maybe I had it coming, but this is enough."

Mane was finally angry. Jasmine almost smiled. Now she had something to fight against. "You want me to pretend you never lied to me?" she shouted above the rain.

"One lie—four years ago—before we even partnered," Mane shouted back. "If we're going to keep working together, we've got to splice this."

"Maybe we shouldn't be working together."

Mane shook his head at her in disgust.

Of course, that wasn't an option.

The entire tree house jolted violently, sending Mane to the floor and causing Jasmine to wonder why the sound of running water came from so close by. The water pipe above the sink had come apart at the filter and all the water that had been collecting in the cistern above was emptying into and past her sink. Mane jumped up and pushed the pipes together. "Tape!" he said. "Lots of it."

Jasmine climbed onto the small counter, tape in hand, to reach the pipe. Just as she finished, another jolt sent them to the floor again. The house swayed so much, they were both stumbling. Thunder rumbled around them.

"Uh, oh," Mane pointed at the water running down the the tree trunk that the house had been built against. Somehow the house was being pulled away from the tree.

"The cables," Mane said as he made for the door. With all the cabled trees swaying, the cables were being snapped taut, ready to pull the house right off the tree.

"Drop them," Jasmine shouted.

"We should get down."

"No time. The whole thing could go any second." Jasmine squirmed past him and started to undo the bolt that held the cables. She struggled with one hand in the wet then felt Mane grab her harness to steady her as the tree swayed. Experience told her not to look down. The violent tossing of the branches around her frightened her enough. She leaned out further to get a better hold and in seconds she had the nut loosened and the bolt was yanked out by the weight of the cables. Mane pulled her in and shut the door against the rain.

The wind was blowing rain through the windows. Jasmine released the rolled up shutters while Mane checked the damage. The ceiling had been pulled away from the tree trunk and so had part of the floor. The floor creaked a little under his weight but it seemed to be holding.

They sat on the floor, not trusting their footing in the wind. The floor had been built in three blunt wedges that circled one side of the massive tree trunk. There was a large screened window in each of the three outer walls. One end wall had shelves and Jasmine had hung the hammock there. The other end wall formed the bathroom nook. The roof was made of the dense translucent material Indra had found but let in no light now—it had grown dark.

"Well," Mane said. "We're too high up to tie bed sheets together." He got up again and took the locator out of his pocket. "Let's see where everyone is."

Mane leaned out the door. The whistling she'd heard earlier was probably a warning from the rest of the crew. She and Mane had been too busy arguing to pay attention. Now the rain, wind and thunder made whistles impossible to use.

"They're all on the ground," he said ducking back inside. "Probably spending the night in the shed."

His hair and shirt were soaked. Jasmine got up and tossed him a towel then found him a blanket. The crew wouldn't risk a rescue in the dark and storm. She and Mane were stuck till morning.

Jasmine pulled out her lamp and lit it against the dark, placing it on the floor so it couldn't fall off anything. She found a dry shirt for herself and changed. When she turned back to him, Mane sat there on the floor with the blanket wrapped around bare shoulders, his wet shirt hanging over the chair and for an instant, before he saw she was watching him, his expression was sad and miserable like a child just learning that the world wasn't fair. She missed him, but didn't know how to stop being angry with him.

Mane put on a grin. "I'll have to remember this trick next time I need an excuse to spend the night with a woman."

Jasmine stumbled as another gust shook the house. She sat against the wall a distance away from him. Thunder cracked and she looked up at the ceiling. Lightning cast hard silhouettes on the roof. In the dim lamp glow she watched Mane gazing upwards, waiting for the next flash. She couldn't do this without him—of that there was no doubt.

When they first collected the crew, Jasmine assumed they were willing to put up with the heat, the bugs, and the wet for the sheer novelty and adventure of it all. That may have been true at the beginning, before Arri was murdered. Why had they followed her back to the jungle where they could be killed by Emerald Warriors, or a fall, or from the exhaustion of building a camp over a boulder field? She couldn't help but think it was Mane they'd followed, not her. A small anger welled in her throat and she let it sit there for a moment until she recognized it as jealousy.

But she was getting better at it, she told herself. At first she'd grown impatient with Mane's insistence on discussing every decision until she realized the crew wanted a say—they didn't want to be "her crew"; they wanted to be partners in the operation. She sometimes felt her dream being realigned during those meetings—like other people were making changes almost too small to notice, but changes to her vision and Mane's, nevertheless. Now she was more willing to let them have their say—now that she trusted them to have the same vision for the project that she did.

Mane still stared at the ceiling, focusing on nothing in particular. He glanced down to see Jasmine watching him. He sighed, gazed at his hands for a moment, then looked up at her again. "You were never wrong about me," he said softly. "*I* was." He leaned toward her. "When we decided to partner, you thought it was because we synced, we were power of ten together. I thought it was because somebody paid me to. Who was right?"

He shook his head. "Frass, I can tell you the exact second I realized it. Green Splinter had just beaten you into the pavement and you were lying there battered and bruised and absolutely fearless about returning the favor." He paused, then looked at her. "Was seeing my contact that night for instructions. That's why I didn't go with you to meet Manda. Maybe I should have told you then."

If he had, she would have walked away from him. She would have lost her anchor. She would have let Yit's death destroy her.

Mane stood and paced a few steps. The tree was no longer swaying as much and the thunder had stopped. Rain still thrummed on the roof. He turned to her. "Doll, no lie. I'm here now because together we can build something important—something we couldn't build without each other."

"Yeah," she admitted, "I know."

"So we're partners?" He extended a hand. "I mean, really partners?"

Jasmine reached out and he pulled her up to stand in front of him. He put both hands out palms up and with a great sense of relief, she placed her hands in his. "Partners," she said. "I missed you," she added.

It seemed inadequate, but Mane pulled her into a hug. When he released her again he looked into her eyes, searching for something. What did he want? She didn't recognize the look but she stepped back, suddenly uneasy. Mane sighed and looked at the tree-trunk wall. Water still ran down it to disappear through the fist-wide crack where the floor had separated from the tree.

Mane shook his head. "So now you'll want to get off harvesting duty for a few days so you can fix this up." He sat back down again and Jasmine sat on the floor beside him.

The rain eventually stopped and the night chorus of chirps, buzzes and hoots slowly came to life. Jasmine and Mane waited for daylight that still had eight hours to come.

*   *   *   *   *

It took all of the next morning for the crew to get Jasmine and Mane to the ground and to string a new cable. Dustin had to shoot a new line up and find a way to connect it securely. Finally he rode the cable down, the counterweight slowing his descent. Dustin set the catch that prevented the counterweight from dropping and unlatched himself.

He handed the cable to Jasmine and grinned. "Your staircase," he said and bowed, cocky and sweet all at once. He'd only started wearing short-sleeved shirts a month ago, less self-conscious now about the red mottled skin on his fore-arm—sixteen months since that spider bite and Jasmine's first climb into the leaves. That little silver roach had stuck with the team, become intent on everyone's safety and been everyone's laughing kid brother. She was suddenly filled with gratitude that he was part of the crew. "Thanks," she said. He looked at her, surprised. "For hooking me up again," she explained. "Good work."

"It's my job." He shrugged, smiled then glanced at Mane as if to say, See? I told you I was power of ten at this.

Jasmine almost laughed with delight then. Instead, she latched herself in and pulled herself, hand over hand, up to her home, the counterweight making ascent effortless. As she reached her platform, whistles and cheers came up from the crew watching below and she waved, unsure if they could see her. She unlatched so Indra could follow her up.

Once there, Indra stood hands on hips assessing the damage, then glanced sidelong at Jasmine. "That's a pretty drastic measure just to spend the night together."

"Hmph, yeah," Jasmine said, then looked blankly at Indra who seemed to be waiting for an answer.

Indra laughed. "Oh, come on. You two are too synced not to be deep-spliced."

"Well . . . we're not." For the first time Jasmine wondered what the rest of the crew was thinking about her and Mane. "Who thinks we are?"

"Everybody. We figure you two are having a fight because Mane's been paying so much attention to Trina."

"He has?"

Indra threw up her hands. "That does it—you are definitely not deep-spliced." She seemed to study the wall for a moment. "Why aren't you?"

"I don't know," Jasmine replied honestly. "I guess I got comfortable being partners and never wanted to change."

"You mean, he was never interested either?"

Jasmine remembered his grim acceptance of Edan—his openness with her the previous night. "No," she replied less truthfully.

"Hmm." Indra seemed skeptical.

"I've needed a friend more than I needed sex, 'kay? They don't come in the same package."

Indra opened her mouth to reply.

"Look at this," Jasmine said. "Will four extra struts be enough?"

Indra shook her head and resigned herself to discussing extra supports and a new cable attachment system.

When Indra stood in the doorway ready to leave, Jasmine put a hand on her arm. "When we came back from Bogota, who did you follow, me or Mane?"

"Both of you. We all did."

"You can be honest."

"The truth, then. You and Mane may think you're nothing more than partners, but what's obvious to everyone around you is your unconditional support for each other. That's hard to come by and when people see it, they want to be part of it."

"Ha, you should have heard the argument we had last night."

"So you were angry about something he did. It never occurred to any of us that you wouldn't fix it. We all have different reasons for being out here from here," she tapped her temple. "But from here," she put a fist over her heart, "we want to be part of your partnership." Indra gave Jasmine's hand a squeeze, then latched to the descender.

Stunned into silence, Jasmine watched Indra disappear below her under the branches and leaves.

Once she was below the lowest branches, Jasmine released her clamps and rode the cable down as fast as her nerve and Dustin's warnings allowed. It was hard work to get up that far; at least she could enjoy the ride down. She whooped as she was brought up short by the safety knot. Jasmine rode the rest of the five meters down more carefully to protect the harvest hung in a large bag below her.

Indra waited to help her. "You're just lucky Dustin isn't here," she said with a grin and unlatched the harvesting bag, then shouted for Trina. "She's down!"

Indra was already rooting through the bags when Jasmine unhooked herself and removed her helmet. Jasmine went over to the small pile of equipment and found the printout Mane and Trina had prepared. Jasmine had taken the harvesting percentage of everything of value she could reach from where the line now hung. She'd have to climb up and across to adjust the perimeter cables so she could drop down to harvest where the map indicated.

"Whew." Trina plopped down her bag and pruning pole. She'd been clipping leaves from small trees—her favorite harvesting activity.

"Did you finish?" Indra asked.

"I took a little less than quota. Those trees were—"

"We're here to make a living," Indra said. "We're not here just to support your research."

Jasmine stepped in. "Is there a problem with the quotas?"

"No, I just—"

"Then we take the quota," Jasmine stated.

Trina's eyes narrowed but she didn't speak.

In the awkward moment that followed, Jasmine remembered part of her catch. "I grabbed something I haven't seen before." She sorted through the bag's contents. "Thought you might want to do a scan on it."

Trina had been keeping track of all the aberrations they found. She'd discovered sixteen so far.

"At this point we probably know more about EcoTech's mistakes than they do," Indra commented.

Trina shook her head. "Shatter company loyalty. Any ecologist with a conscience wouldn't let this go on."

"I still don't see the problem," Jasmine said as she found the plant she was looking for. "As long as everything's in balance, who cares if there are a few new species?" It wasn't a new argument. She and Trina discussed aberrations almost every week—she should have let it go but she couldn't help herself. "We've been trying for so many years to recreate what we destroyed. Maybe we can't. Maybe we have to be satisfied with reseeding the globe with ecosystems that are different from anything we've ever had."

"That's admitting defeat," Trina replied, taking the plant. "We destroyed it—we can rebuild it." She peered at the leafy mass in her hands. "I don't recognize it either. Levi might." She stashed it in her own bag. "I've got three more trees to do."

"And I'm going to do one more new line," Jasmine said.

"Whistle when you're through," Trina replied as she grabbed an empty bag and started off, her curls bobbing as she walked.

"Take the whole quota this time," Indra called after her.

Jasmine replaced her helmet, latched onto the line, and started the long climb up past layer upon layer of branches then finally emerged above the crowns of most of the trees. Once she reached the horizontal line, she pulled up the harvesting line and moved along the horizontal to its connection in a supporting tree. There she reeled cables in and out until the harvesting line could be dropped into its new position. It took two hours to reset and harvest the line. Indra was her safety and catalogued what they had harvested so far, making bundles as she recorded. "Dustin's rules" dictated every climbing party had to have at least two members with all beacons active and recommended a third person within earshot of a whistle. Jasmine landed with her harvest at 4:00, giving them a scant two hours to get back to camp.

Jasmine got the climber's load, half the weight the other two carried since she'd already nearly exhausted herself climbing. Indra and Trina stood ready with a bag slung over each hip and backpacks strapped on. Jasmine carried the collecting gear.

Trina walked in front of her. Tall and straight despite the load she carried. She'd done her share despite her fear of heights which everyone now knew about but nobody mentioned. She'd even pulled off a few climbs, landing white-faced and shaky. Even then she'd never apologized for herself. Jasmine had never seen her self-confidence waver. Maybe that's why she was so hard to like, though Mane didn't seem to think so. In the two months since Indra mentioned his interest in Trina, Jasmine had been watching them together. They'd developed quite a friendship. At least somebody wanted to spend time with her—things could have been uncomfortable for Trina otherwise.

The tired harvesters got to their ruins an hour before sundown. Jasmine's legs ached. She'd be happy once they got the harvest to the shed and she could sit down. The small hut was only 200 meters away but the path getting there was twice that long.

"I hate this part." Indra took a deep breath and started the winding path to the shed. It was a low little building built with screen walls to help the air flow and shutters to close against the rain and for camouflage. With the shutters closed the shed became just a large lump amongst the boulders. Half the shed could be closed to become one huge dryer with racks and fans. The other half had a corner for Levi's writing table and his hammock. The rest of the space was taken up by air-tight lockers where bales of dried plants were stored before being shipped.

Levi frowned at them as they came in. "Bloody brilliant this is," he said. "More plants to sit here and rot. The second time this week I've run out of methane for the dryers."

"I checked the fermenters two days ago," Indra said. "They're working to capacity."

"If I can't get the dryer running tonight, we'll lose at least twenty-five percent of this."

The only methane left in camp was what was in each home's individual waste fermenter. Jasmine whistled for Dustin and Mane, then turned to Indra. "Can you and Dustin get all the fermenters drained?"

"Sure," she replied. "Another morning without coffee. Maybe we should all eat more roughage so the fermenters have more to work on."

"How was the haul?" Dustin asked from the doorway.

"Good," Indra answered, then sighed and put his arm in hers. "Come along, my young apprentice. They've given us the nasty job again. Soon you'll be able to do this on your own."

"Not likely," Dustin grumbled.

Moments after they left, Mane poked his head in the doorway. "Need some help?"

"Yes," Levi replied. "We need to get this stuff spread out as much as possible so it can start drying on its own."

Trina had already begun to unbind the bundles.

The crew worked into the darkness, spreading leaves on every rack and surface they could find. Indra and Dustin came back with enough fuel to run the dryers on low all night. Dustin was then chased out of the overcrowded shed to help Trina who was cooking a communal supper in the only cooker they had that ran on fuel cells.

By eleven o'clock the crew made their way to Trina's. Jasmine was so exhausted she barely made the climb up. Mane tread gingerly and peered at the floor as he walked. "We're really testing Indra's design tonight."

This was the first time the entire crew had been together in Trina's tree-house. Rather than being built around a main trunk the way Jasmine's was, it was a box nestled between three splayed branches. Everyone scattered on the floor while Trina and Dustin handed out bowls of plantain soup. Rain splattered the roof while they ate in tired silence. Jasmine spotted one of the two geckoes that had made their home with Trina. It clung motionless to the wall, apparently believing it was camouflaged there. Trina was convinced they ate any insects that made it through the netting.

Jasmine almost nodded off several times while she ate. Then, with a stomach full of hot soup, she felt the work of the day in the ache in her arms and legs. Nothing could have made her move. Mane got up to help Trina with clean-up and their laughter got everyone else laughing with them and shrieking when wash-up turned into a rather cramped water fight. She closed her eyes and drifted in and out of a doze while tired, contented voices moved around her. This was power of ten.

*   *   *   *   *

Jasmine woke in her hammock to the bleating of her com unit. She was smug when she saw the link was from Adrien. That feeling fled when she saw his face.

"I can't believe you'd drag Chanel into this."

"She was worried about you."

"No. You saw another way to get to me. You can't—"

"Adrien. You said from the start you wouldn't do the research unless part of the plan was to eventually go public with what we're doing. That's started. You've got NewsPort interested. The more public this gets the less danger you'll be in."

He wanted to believe her, she could see it. He didn't want to walk away from the people he could help, or from the most dangerous puzzle of his career. She just had to give him enough reasons to keep going.

"Destroying one illegal lab isn't going to put too many people in a snarl, but if you move your research into the Clinic, Splinter can't go after the whole research facility."

Adrien stared at the bottom of the screen for a moment. Then he looked up at her. "Agree to an interview."

"What?"

"Martinez has been asking to talk to you. Let's show the world both sides of the operation." He had a half smile on his face.

Jasmine searched for a way to say no. She didn't want her world invaded. The secrecy made her comfortable.

Adrien gave her a sly look. "The more public this gets . . . "

"We're not ready to be exposed," she replied.

"You've got nothing to hide. Trina's been documenting environmental impact. Time to go public."

"We're still partners?"

"If you agree to an interview."

She didn't want NewsPort invading her home, but what Adrien was asking had the ring of fairness.

"We'd need time to set up the security."

"Shree-eeoo!" A whistle urged her to join the rest of the crew.

"They're waiting for me," she said. "Fine—set it up."

Adrien didn't look relieved, just resigned.

"You'll thank me," she said. "Not working on this would have killed you."

"And working on it might still. I'll talk to Martinez and get back to you."

Jasmine gazed at his image on the screen for a moment. It had been over a year since she'd seen him in person. He'd set up his research without her. He'd found Chanel without her. She missed him.

"What?" he asked. She seemed to be amusing him.

She smiled. "I'm glad you're still with us, that's all."

"Shree-eeoo!"

"'Kay," she said and broke the link. She grabbed a fruit bar and rode her cable down.

Normally morning meetings were held in the shed, but it was so full, the crew stood outside. Even the table and benches had been covered with drying leaves.

"We have to make do with what we can get here," Indra was saying. "If we have to start buying fuel our shares will be even less."

Levi shook his head. "We can't base all our decisions on economics."

"Hey!" Indra replied. "If I were doing this for the money, I'd have left long ago."

"What if we convert the dryers to fuel cells?" Mane asked.

"We'd need to buy at least ten of them," Levi said.

Indra frowned. "Then find a place in the sun to charge them once a week. We've already got sixteen for the com system and it takes us a day a week to charge them and change them."

Jasmine didn't like either option. If they could just find a way to increase the amount of organics that went into the shed fermenter. The waste that people put in their own home fermenters gave them enough for their own use.

"How much more biomass would it take to keep us up to rations and run the dryers?" she asked Indra.

"Maybe one k per day," she replied.

"Near the river, there's a thicket of brush on either side." Jasmine turned to Trina. "Could we harvest some to feed the shed fermenter?"

"As long as we don't take more than ten K a week and take it from along both banks there won't be any negative effects. Levi and I can check it out but . . . "

"It's against the harvesting code," Jasmine finished for her.

"As long as we take below our harvest quota and use every scrap for the fermenter," Mane suggested, "it's no more harmful that harvesting for food."

"Let's make sure the fermenter sludge makes it back to that spot," Trina added. "At least we replenish the nitrogen and phosphates." The others nodded agreement.

"It'll take a vote to change the harvesting code," Levi remarked.

A few other alternatives were discussed and dismissed as too expensive or impractical. A vote was hardly necessary. She didn't like it. Once they started changing the rules, it would be so easy to change more until they *were* doing damage.

"Dustin and I are going to check out the harvesting site Levi suggested," Mane said.

"I'll collect enough methane to run the dryers this morning," Indra said. "Hope none of you were counting on a hot lunch."

The group was about to break up when Jasmine remarked, "I got a call from Adrien this morning. His lab was destroyed a month ago." She told them what had happened and about her final agreement with him. To her surprise, the crew seemed angry.

"You could have told us when this happened," Trina said.

Jasmine shrugged. "Until Adrien made up his mind, nothing would have changed. I didn't want people to worry until I'd tried everything to keep him in. I'm responsible for—"

"No, you're not," Indra said. "Stop treating us like *your* crew. Ever since we came back you've been trying to protect us. Stop it!"

Indra's anger confused Jasmine even more. "I just—"

"You can't make up for Arri's death. You can't prevent it happening again. No one can. Just let us work *with* you."

"I'm sorry." Jasmine wasn't, but it was the only thing she could think of to say. "I'll let you in on any other glitches that come up."

That seemed to satisfy Indra. Everyone else sat in painful silence.

"I've agreed to do an interview with NewsPort," Jasmine said.

The silence didn't waver. Then Levi finally asked, "Why?"

"When Adrien agreed to partner with us it was on the condition that we go public eventually. I told all of you about this when you joined up. Adrien's done it on his end now that VJX is out in the open."

They remembered but obviously didn't like the idea.

"You'd be making us a target," Indra said. "Right now the Warriors don't look for us any harder than they look for anybody else. I don't want to be set up for another raid."

"The perimeter security net is almost finished," Mane said. "If anyone carrying a com device comes within ten kilometers of our base, we'll know."

Jasmine took stock of the crew as Mane spoke—they weren't convinced.

"As long as we're treated like criminals, we'll have to spend any money we make on security," Jasmine reminded them. "Wouldn't it be power of ten to be able to do our jobs—being able to talk to each other using sat com—without fear of being traced? To be able to walk home to a little cabin out in the open? We'll never do that as long as the only voice people hear about this is EcoTech's. We all know that what we're doing is not wrong. Let's convince the people who make the laws."

Indra shook her head. No one looked happy, but no one offered any more arguments. Without meeting her eyes, everyone but Mane left to do their day's chores.

"What just happened here?"

"Doll, if you don't let them in on the problems, they feel like they've got no control over what happens to them."

"But I only—"

"Want what's best for everybody," he finished. "We know. But let the rest of us be part of the solution. You keep this up, you'll wear yourself out. Let us worry about ourselves."

He glanced around and said softly, "I've got some news. I'm moving in with Trina end of the week."

She frowned. "Indra's got building supplies for your house coming first of the month. You won't have long to wait for your own place."

He smirked. "She can build it for Levi," he said, then laughed at Jasmine's confused expression.

"Oh," she replied and felt herself flush. "Then I guess I should be congratulating you both."

Mane grinned at her and she couldn't help but laugh herself. He folded her into a hug and whispered into her hair, "Doll, this won't change our partnership one bit, no lie."

Her confusion turned to dread—of course their partnership would change.

It seemed he'd been staring at the same image all night. A life-sized human body with massive organ failure. Every simulation Adrien tried ended the same way. Of course, Mei had been getting the same results for months. The simulations were based on the tissue trials. Exposure to VJX at doses sufficient to be effective against Lightning Madness caused dramatic damage to cellular structure. With the simulator, he and Mei could try various drug combinations and dosages. Nothing worked. When he announced the VJX results eight months ago, he knew there were still some dosage problems to work out, but that wasn't uncommon. He assumed they'd have an answer by now. A first human test case had even been lined up. He'd promised to call them tomorrow to decide what option to take.

Adrien blinked as the overhead lights flickered on. Was it morning already? Mei peered around the side of the sim screen at him.

"Don't you have a home to go to?"

"Morning, Mei."

"Cheer up. I may have a lead on a process we can use."

She hung up her raincoat then joined him at the sim screen. "I got word from a friend who had the same toxicity problems. She came up with a solution she hasn't had a chance to publish yet." She fed data into the simulator and they watched the time lapse proceed. It would take the rest of the day to run.

The vid screen chimed and Adrien turned to see Kevin Maravitch looking back at him from the screen.

"Dr. Lamberin," he said with rehearsed calmness, "I'm pulling out. Even if your drug works, I can't live like this."

Only eighteen years old and he was walking away from his life. "We may have a way to prevent the toxic effects."

"When?"

"Within six months at the longest."

"No," he said listlessly. "I've had enough. I almost killed a nurse two days ago."

The violent stage—Kevin was already there.

"I won't live like this. Your cure can't reverse the damage, can it?"

"No, it can't."

"Then that's all."

Kevin was replaced by his older sister. Her tired green eyes studied Adrien for a moment without accusation. "I support Kevin's decision." She glanced away for a moment, perhaps at Kevin. "Kevin wants his death to mean something. You mentioned one time that politics delayed the research on Veejix. NewsPort has asked to film Kevin until . . . A death watch, they call it. That way the world will know what a terrible disease this is and no one will stand in the way of a cure. Kevin wants to go ahead with it. I told the NewsPort people I needed your support. I . . . " she paused to gather the words. "Could you handle the logistics for us? Make sure they don't do anything . . . inappropriate?"

How could she be so composed? Adrien felt like he was ready to fracture completely, yet this woman calmly told him she was ready to watch her brother die. In the face of that strength, all he could do was to choke out, "Yes. I'll handle NewsPort." Just six more months. He thought for a moment of trying to convince Kevin not to give up—to wait for VJX, but Kevin knew all the choices and their consequence. There was nothing left to tell him.

"I'm so sorry," Adrien said.

"I know," she replied, and smiled in an attempt to comfort him. He stared at the screen while she thanked him for his efforts and signed off. Mei finally reached past him to break the link.

Kevin Maravitch was going to die. Adrien was a researcher. He didn't have the relentlessly constant experience of doling out life shattering news. He couldn't do anything else for Kevin . . . except deal with NewsPort. Adrien punched in the link.

Raul Martinez grinned back at him. "Hey, Doc. Kevin said I needed your agreement to go ahead."

"How can you do this?"

"A death watch could do a lot to help you and your sister."

It also wouldn't hurt ratings. "I don't like it. You're asking permission to exploit someone's suffering for good vid watching."

"We'll be putting a human face on Lightning Madness. The more people know about it, the more support your treatment will get."

"Send me a proposal—keep it tasteful." Adrien said. "And Martinez—you owe me for this." He waited for a nod of acknowledgment before signing off.

There being nothing else he could do, Adrien sat and let his mind wander over all his efforts to use VJX to cure Lightning Madness. He remembered how it had taken nine months for the light to fade from his mother's eyes. She was 38 years old and her family was relieved when she died. That was the pain and the guilt Kevin's sister had ahead of her.

"Adrien."

He blinked and looked at Mei.

"We *are* going to figure this out," she said.

"Maybe."

Adrien stood and walked out of the lab, out of the clinic, into the daylight. He kept walking because it kept him moving, kept him doing something.

He walked all day past shops and cafés, through parks and playgrounds, through parts of town he'd never seen before. Two thunderstorms played out around him, the sun drying him after each noisy shower.

Finally he walked into familiar surroundings. Just half a block away from his house he saw Chanel sitting on his front steps. Before he could bolt, she saw him and hurried down the sidewalk to meet him. She hugged him while he stood there lifeless as a scarecrow and wished she would just go away. She took his hand and led him home without a word.

In the front hall, she took a close look at him. "Now," she said, "we are going to a concert."

"No." He finally found his voice.

"I'm sorry. Did you think I had given you a choice?" She took his hand again. "Come on. I'm not taking you looking like this."

She pulled him into the bedroom then turned to him. "Mei told me about Kevin. People have been dying of Lightning Madness for years. Kevin is only *one* more. The last one before you find the answer to making it a useable cure. You're so close. Mei said you could have the toxicity problems solved within six months."

It would be too late for Kevin. Kevin's personality would continue to disassemble itself over the next thirteen months while a cure was only six months away.

All Adrien could do was stare at the wall over her head while Chanel unbuttoned his shirt and pulled it off. He numbly inserted his arms into the clean one she held for him and stared at her while she undid his hair and ran her fingers through it to let it hang to his shoulders. She smiled back at him. "Believe me, you need to get out."

*　　*　　*　　*　　*

As they sat in the concert hall listening to the first composition, several facts elbowed their way through Adrien's tangled thoughts. Chanel had seen this same show two nights ago. He also remembered that this was her regular rehearsal night and she never missed rehearsal.

Frass! He could be so self-absorbed at times. Adrien sighed and took her hand in his, interlocking their fingers. Surprise passed through her eyes, then happiness settled there. She leaned closer towards him and he rested his head on her shoulder. Adrien found she was right. This helped.

"I should get home," Mane said. It was already midnight. He and Jasmine had spent since eight that night planning security measures for the interview. They'd been able to put NewsPort off for two months with getting the security system just right, then working out the technical protocols.

She tried not to show it, but Mane could tell Jasmine was still nervous, not about the technical connection, but about the interview itself.

"What's the toughest question he'll ask?" Jasmine said from her hammock, barely visible in the lamplight. Mane took his tea and sat on the floor, leaning against several cushions devised from rolled up blankets.

"Who does you hair now that you're not in commuting distance of a Foxy Locks?"

Jasmine didn't answer and he could picture her frown.

"Okay," he said. "Martinez said he wants to know why we're here, what it's like to live here. He might also ask why we're willing to come out in public about what we're doing. They'd be stupid not to ask about Veejix."

"I just hope he asks about Arri."

The two of them continued to chat about interview questions until they dozed off.

Mane didn't wake till rain splattered the roof just before dawn. He stretched out on his stomach hugging a blanket and lay there for a little while longer, then groaned and got up.

Jasmine still slept, so he quietly stepped out the door and clipped his ever-present harness onto the cable that took him home.

He switched the lamp on low when he got there. Trina was sleeping. Her chestnut hair made dark waves around her face in soft, round swirls of rich color and that was what she was. Round—her face, her body, who she was. There were no sharp corners to her. She was unlike any woman he'd been with. There was no harshness to her, no cynicism, she'd been unmarked by time. It still surprised him that a wonder like her could love him. He wanted to kiss her but was dripping with rain. He stripped and grabbed a towel, then climbed into the hammock and snuggled into her.

"You just get in?"

"Been here all night," he said, indignant.

She chuckled. "You're a liar."

"Yeah, I am." Mane nuzzled her hair and kissed her.

After a few moments Trina got up. "I waited for you," she said.

"Said I'd be late."

"You whistled late, you didn't say you'd be out all night."

"We had a lot to go over. Setting up the interview site is going to take some tricky line work. She's a little fractured about this whole thing."

"Oh, she's pitiful. Can't you see what she's doing? She kept you there to show me she could."

Trina must have seen the dismay in his face.

"Why is everyone always protecting her? No one really likes her but no one is willing to say so."

The crew didn't dislike Jasmine, did they? Even if they found her a bit harsh, they owed her a lot. "Why should they say anything? Without her, no one would have thought to build an operation like this. Without her we would have quit when Arri was killed."

Without her, Mane would still be a Core Rat. "Not even thirty and she's been orphaned twice. She climbed out of the Core then reached down and pulled me up with her. She deserves some respect for that if nothing else."

Trina started water boiling for coffee while Mane looked for the insect repellant. Uncharacteristically silent, Trina banged kettle and cups, then finally turned to him.

"I heard what she said last week when you suggested the north-west line. Why do you let her get away with that?"

He shrugged.

"It's insulting."

"She's got a lot on her mind. She's focused on her vision—"

"She wouldn't have accomplished any of this without you. She'd be doing this by herself, without you to keep all these people together. She's a hot-headed—"

"Trina," he warned.

"Is she above criticism now? I didn't realize I'd joined a cult."

"What hurts her, hurts all of us."

Trina was right. He wouldn't have tolerated the fits of temper and coldness from anyone else. But Jasmine had been so wounded when he first met her and she put up such a brave front, he couldn't help but help her.

Mane pulled on a dry shirt. Every woman he'd met since he partnered with Jasmine had put him through the same routine. Trina shared his work. He'd expected her to understand.

"She's always going to be there, isn't she?" Trina asked. "It'll never be just the two of us."

Mane went to her and put his arms around her. "Hey, it's you I'm in love with. If Jasmine were any more than a friend, I wouldn't have gone looking for you." He couldn't help remembering that it was only months since he'd looked into Jasmine's eyes hoping to find something more than friendship, finding only that she stepped away from his scrutiny, having offered him everything she could.

"Shree-eeoo!" Levi blew the ten minute warning.

"Breakfast!" Mane said. "I'll get it. You get dressed."

It took ten minutes of rushing and they were the last there but Trina and Mane made it in time to join the rest of the crew.

"Don't forget," Jasmine was saying, "we'll need to cut com rations in half till after tomorrow." There was a communal groan. "We need almost all the cells to run the cameras and microphone."

The rest of the meeting was the usual planning for the day's tasks.

* * * * *

Mane adjusted the camera he had pointed toward the foliage according to the instructions in his ear. NewsPort had requested two cameras, one on Jasmine and the other showing the jungle. Initially they wanted live feed from camp. Mane refused—it would be too easy to trace them and would give away their camouflage.

Jasmine fidgeted. "Is it too late to cancel this?" she asked.

Mane smiled. "I could tell them you were carried off by a passing troop of monkeys."

"Tell her she looks fine from here," Raul Martinez said through the link in Mane's ear.

"Martinez says you look great," Mane passed on. He looked at the monitor, then glanced at his watch. Almost there.

"Hello, I'm Matt Scarpulla and this is a NewsPort special report. Harvesting the preserves—is it pillage or progress? With me is Shelly VanDaal."

VanDaal's image took up half the screen. "You may remember her as a reporter for this station—now she represents EcoTech. Jasmine Rochelle joins us from her jungle harvesting operation."

Jasmine's image replaced his over half the screen—small and brave.

"Ms. Rochelle, you've set up a harvesting operation in the south end of the Columbian preserves?"

"We've set up in a preserve somewhere in South America, yes."

Mane smiled. She sounded calm, though he knew the effort it cost her to appear that way.

"You've chosen to live in a place that most people have only seen on vids. Tell us about living there."

Jasmine told him what their days were like while Shelly VanDaal sat poised and patient. Mane's shots of the surrounding foliage replaced her image while Jasmine spoke about the jungle.

It had taken four hours to haul the two security cameras, monitor and transmitter this far from camp. Dustin had helped with the setup. The rest of the crew was busy with the harvest schedule. The broadcast wasn't until 4:00—it would be dark by the time all the equipment was fit to travel again. Dustin had been sent back and Jasmine and Mane would spend the night out and haul everything back the next morning. Mane had insisted on going to all this trouble. In case their signal was tracked somehow, at least the location of camp would still be safe.

The chatter in his ear brought Mane's attention back.

"Give her one more question then let Shelly in," Raul coached Scarpulla.

"You're not the only harvesters in the preserves, are you?"

Jasmine waved at a small swarm of flies that hung in front of her and looked earnestly into the camera. "No. There are others, but they have a different attitude. They see the jungle as the dark tangle—an enemy to battle with and dominate. For us, the jungle challenges us to find a way to live there and harvest. We are the only harvesters I know of who don't cut down trees or strip plants."

"Despite your claims, there are reasons why harvesting from preserves is illegal. Ms. VanDaal?"

VanDaal put on a slightly hurt expression. "These preserves are our only hope for reseeding the globe. They are extremely precious and must not be tampered with. History shows that humans destroy whatever natural areas they live in. Oh, we always start with good intentions. We need buffalo for food, we need Pacific Yews for medicine, cutting a bit of mahogany for furniture can't hurt. But once we start, we never know when to stop."

VanDaal leaned towards the camera. "EcoTech grants research permits, but we're not about to let people live there and harvest for profit. Next the preserves will be overrun with entrepreneurs and we'll be back where we started when irretrievable loss was declared. This illegal harvesting is very dangerous."

"Ms. Rochelle, you've described a tough lifestyle in the jungle and if you're caught, you face years in prison. People have found less dangerous ways to make a living. Why do you do it?"

"Because there's no other way for some researchers to get the drugs they need. We can get those drugs."

"You also harvest recreational drugs, don't you?" Scarpulla asked.

"Recs help pay the bills. Researchers can't afford to pay much." She winced a smile.

VanDaal interrupted. "What percentage of your harvest is bought by researchers?"

Jasmine shrugged. "About forty percent."

"Sixty percent of what you harvest goes to support the criminals who sell Green recs."

"Recs aren't illegal." Jasmine flushed and grew grim.

Stay calm, Mane thought at her and tried to catch her eye.

"The ones you harvest are," VanDaal continued. "There's simply no need to do what you're doing. EcoTech has made provisions to provide harvesting permits to researchers. We don't stand in the way of legitimate research."

"Then why are three of our clients being forced to use illegal harvesters to do their research?"

"Perhaps because it's cheaper to buy from you. Researchers aren't immune to greed."

Mane heard Scarpulla say, "I'm losing it here."

"Let VanDaal take it," Raul answered. "This is great."

"Why are you coming public with your operation?"

Jasmine relaxed a bit—this was the kind of question she and Mane had prepared for. "We want people to see what can be accomplished by working with the forest. We want people to realize that it's time to open the preserves."

VanDaal was incredulous. "Based on what you've told us? You can't expect us to take your word—you're a gang of criminals trying to justify what you're doing."

"We're doing nothing wrong. The laws have to change."

"Before you were adopted, you led quite an . . . adventurous life. Police records show you were arrested for petty theft and assault."

"That was a long time ago. My father gave me a chance to change and I did."

Mane winced. This was *not* the kind of question she and Mane had prepared for.

The announcer whined in Mane's ear. "I wasn't told this about her. Where did Shelly get that? Who did my research?"

Jasmine looked ready to bolt from her seat. VanDaal smiled with insincere understanding which made Jasmine tense even more. "I think you did," VanDaal said. "Until your adopted father, Owen Lamberin, was killed. Now you're going back to a comfortable habit of criminal behavior."

"I'm not a criminal," Jasmine stood and leaned towards the camera. "*You're* the ones who killed Arri Deckert. *You* destroyed my camp and the surrounding jungle with it. Who's the criminal here?" She plopped back into her seat. "Not me."

There was excitement in the studio. "She'll walk out if we're not careful," Scarpulla said.

"Let her," Martinez replied. "It'll make great news."

Mane smiled. He'd never known Jasmine to walk out of a room in anger—the targets of her anger usually did that.

VanDaal continued. "There are very good reasons for the government to continue to protect EcoTech's—"

"Hey!" Jasmine leaned forward. "Is this an interview or a lecture? Is Scarpulla dead?"

Mane could hear Martinez tell Scarpulla to wait. Come on, he thought. Enough is enough.

VanDaal smiled and said, "The kind of exploitation—"

"Did they hire you back?" Jasmine said on top of her.

Martinez relented. Matt Scarpulla's smiling face filled the screen. "Well, this has been an interesting debate, ladies, and I hate to cut it short."

Mane glanced at his watch. They were cutting the whole interview by two minutes. Jasmine had done it again.

Jasmine sat staring at the ground in front of her.

"Martinez says thanks," Mane said. "He's happy with how it went."

"Nothing about VJX," she muttered standing. "Nothing about Lightning Madness, nothing about Trina's studies."

"You made a good start."

"Didn't ask about Arri. If nobody investigates his murder, if nobody is punished, he will have died for nothing. People will still think he blew himself up." She looked down at her hands as if surprised by them, then shook them out and stomped through the forest in the direction they'd come. That was one of the problems with jungle life, there were no doors to slam and you couldn't just run with feet pounding pavement and the wind in your hair till frustration bled away. He missed that about the Core and he was certain Jasmine did too.

Mane began to put the electronics away and hoped she'd be back before dark.

Jasmine returned in time to help him raise the tarp and hang the hammocks and mosquito nets in silence.

They had the cart packed by the time it was full daylight. Jasmine shouldered the pack with their provisions while Mane strapped the cart to his harness. It bounced along behind him as they made their way home. Rain started before they'd gone half-way. Mane's tracking bead chirped. Three times it chirped; danger.

"Frass!" he said. "They got the transmission coordinates. I'm going to kill Martinez."

"Come on," Jasmine was ready to run for camp.

"No," he said, remembering the damage the guns had done last time. "They're looking for us now."

Mane pulled the cart under a leafy bush. After a moment Jasmine found a hollow to stash the pack and sprinkled it with dead leaves. Then they each found tree roots to hide behind.

Mane had designed the alarms to be triggered by any electronic equipment that didn't belong to the crew. All it would take to set it off was a stranger using a communicator.

Jasmine and Mane stayed hidden, rain drenching them, for two long hours and didn't hear or see anything unusual.

For another two hours the two walked through the dripping trees, afraid to use communications in case they were traced. Jasmine and Mane didn't call out when they got home. Mane set his tracker for Trina and Jasmine set hers for Indra. They stumbled over the rubble following Jasmine's tracker to the underground shelter. It was a squeeze between damp boulders for Mane to get in. Indra and Dustin were illuminated by a small lantern and a screen. Indra lit up when she saw them and hugged them both. Dustin sat staring at the read-out—worried.

"Trina and Levi were out scouting," he said. "There's been nothing triggered for over two hours now. It was just these two corner ones that were set off." He pointed to the alarm map.

"I think they just glanced off on their way by," Indra suggested.

"That's the way I read it, too," Mane replied, but he couldn't relax. Trina and Levi weren't here.

"Let's go find them," Jasmine said, heading for the doorway, tracker in hand.

They found Levi just fifty kilometers into the forest, on his way home, shaken but relieved.

"Where's Trina?" Mane asked, his tracker on her still blank.

Levi shrugged. "Her bead's dead—for hours, now. We were out scouting. I wanted to stay and study some flowers so she got ahead of me. She was to come back for me but then the alarm went off." Levi looked at the faces around him. "I hid and I'm glad of it. I heard voices once, so they were close, but didn't find me. I waited a long time before coming out. By then, I couldn't track her."

Levi went on to describe his stealthy walk home but Mane stopped listening. Life had drained out through his feet. He tried not to think of what had happened to Arri. Mane sat cross-legged on the ground. Dustin sat beside him.

"Show us where," said Jasmine. "Where were you supposed to meet her?"

Levi just stared at her for a moment.

"We've only got six hours of daylight left, people," she said. "Dustin and Indra, we need food and water. The rest of us will map out a search pattern." That got everyone moving.

By the time Indra and Dustin returned, Jasmine had a search plan ready. For four hours they fanned the area, their whistles asking for Trina every few steps. The search gave them all a focus and for a while Mane could hope that Trina was still hiding and her bead had just malfunctioned.

The crew trudged back into camp in the dark—without Trina. Levi and Indra rummaged through the food lockers to put a meal together. Jasmine paced and muttered, taking Trina's disappearance as a personal affront.

During the search, there had been a sense of excitement. It had faded into dread.

"NewsPort," Dustin announced.

Mane tagged along to watch. There were the usual political reports then . . .

"—a report on illegal harvesting in the rainforest preserves of South America. A feisty young woman who runs one such operation is Jasmine Rochelle. She had this response to questions."

"I'm not a criminal. You're the ones who killed Arri Deckert. You destroyed my camp and the surrounding jungle with it. Who's the criminal here?"

The image of Jasmine's enraged expression froze on the screen for several seconds.

"Shelly VanDaal of EcoTech had this to say."

"EcoTech grants research permits but we're not about to let people live there and harvest for profit. Next the preserves will be overrun by entrepreneurs and we'll be back where we started when irretrievable loss was declared. This illegal harvesting is very dangerous."

"NewsPort will continue to report on this important debate."

No one looked at Jasmine. No one knew what to say. They'd all watched the entire interview the night before.

"Out of the whole interview," Indra said, "that's what they show."

Jasmine left without a word and in a few moments, Mane heard her climb home.

Indra started a beat but Mane didn't join in. He hadn't seen the shot that killed Arri, but he'd been the first to see the sat photos of his body. Is that what was happening to Trina? Dead, with the jungle feeding on her? He let out a ragged breath. Dustin put a hand on his shoulder the way Mane had often done with him. "We'll start looking again at first light."

That night Mane lay awake, too alone in the hammock to sleep. In exhaustion-induced dementia he became more and more angry at the insects and frogs that persisted in their calls. How could they go on with their lives, as raucous as before, while Trina was missing? The whole jungle should be hushed, waiting for her return. At last a rain started, forcing the night chorus into quiet and he almost slept.

The next morning they searched again, and again found nothing.

Every day for five days he went out to search, Dustin his constant shadow, replaced occasionally by Jasmine when Dustin was needed to set the cables. And if Jasmine felt he was wasting his time and hers, she never said so.

"Was that Jasmine?" Chanel asked as Adrien came into the kitchen. "Any news?"

"Still nothing. All they've found are patches of broken brush where the warriors came through."

"Didn't Jasmine say one time they've had raids come through before? What happened this time? What went wrong?"

"I don't know. Usually the perimeter alarms go off, everybody hides, and some Emerald Warriors show up. Remember the time the warriors just circled the rubble field? The second time a group of four of them walked through the site but didn't find anything. Jasmine figures this time EC sent at least twelve warriors who swept through the broadcast site after she and Mane were gone. Trina must have been spotted as the warriors moved through, before they got close enough to the camp to set off the alarms.

The phone chimed and he picked it off the wall.

"Dr. Lamberin? Martinez here."

The blood drained from Adrien's face.

Martinez calmly continued. "I want to reach Jasmine—"

"After what you did, you expect her to talk to you?" He could barely keep his voice from shaking.

"The interview? She's the one who—"

"The raid."

"What raid?" Martinez said with believable surprise.

Was it possible he didn't know? "Twelve hours after the interview, Emerald Warriors raided the broadcast site. One of her crew is missing."

"Sorry, but nobody found out from this end. Can you tell her that?"

"I'll tell her you said so but she won't believe you."

"I want to get some footage of her—"

"Hey! Did you hear what I said? Jasmine's broadcast site was raided and one of her crew is missing. There were only two ends to the line—hers and yours. You let them find her."

"No, I didn't. Only my tech crew could have traced her signal. Why would I sabotage my chances to get another interview?"

"The least you can do is find out what happened to Trina Josell. Surely there's news in that."

"Fine. In return I want you to consider—"

"I'm not even going to talk to you until you find Trina."

Adrien set the phone back on the wall. He turned but Chanel was gone. He looked out the back porch windows. With sunhat and gloves she'd hunkered in the garden. He'd let his father's garden go into a thicket of weeds. Every weekend Chanel spent a few hours digging out the invaders from around the few flowers that struggled there.

Chanel had been right. After his father died, he wasted so much time waiting for his life to fall together again the way it used to be. He'd tried to hold on to Jasmine but she was all but lost to him—no longer a part of his daily life. Yet over the kilometers, from her jungle home, she had made it seem like the most inevitable chain of events that he research an illegal drug despite the threat of arrest or violence. Would he have done the research without her to throw him the challenge—without her expectations to live up to? He wanted to think he would have done it to solve the puzzle of the most feared disease there was, and because of his promise.

Jasmine may have been the catalyst but she wasn't there to share the little triumphs along the way or the frustrations and stalls.

And though he'd never asked her to, Chanel was there for all those times. Her friendship never wavered and now he couldn't imagine being without her. Perhaps he hadn't given himself to her with the passion and abandon she would have liked, but he loved her in his quiet way and that seemed to be enough. She'd slowly become an essential part of his life.

Chanel spotted him and, hands on hips said, "Are you going to watch me work all morning or make us some tea?" Then she smiled and Adrien let worries about Trina and Martinez slip away.

He made a show of wincing but stepped outside. "I'd rather kiss you," he replied and pulled her close.

They kissed in the sunshine for a moment. When his hands ran over her hips, she pulled away.

"I'm all dirty," she protested.

"Mmm. I love it when you're dirty," he said and found her mouth again.

★ ★ T H I R T Y - S I X ★ ★

"Is everybody there?" Adrien asked, still putting on a solemn voice.

"Yes!" Jasmine had grown impatient. "What did you find out?"

"She's alive and she's unhurt."

He could see everyone let out the breath they were holding.

"Where is she?" Mane demanded.

"In custody in Bogota. She's on her way to the North American Block. Martinez found her, so now the Warriors have handed her to the police to deal with."

"They've had her for six days," Mane said. "They can't detain somebody in secret for that long."

"Apparently they forgot about that law till NewsPort reminded them. She'll be making a statement on NewsPort tonight. She's anxious to talk to you but doesn't trust the com lines."

Jasmine pushed past Mane, who seemed in shock. "Does she need a lawyer?"

"Probably. They're just laying charges today. Of course EcoTech is pushing for maximum fines. Trina will probably talk about what the charges are during her statement."

"Let us know if you find out any more," Jasmine said watching Mane, worry clear on her face.

Adrien was surprised. He'd expected shouting and ranting from Jasmine.

She turned back to the screen. "We'll wait for her statement, then figure what to do. 'Kay?"

"'Kay," he replied and broke the link.

*   *   *   *   *

"Has it started?" Chanel asked as she came in. Adrien shook his head.

"Five more minutes."

Chanel joined him on the couch and kissed him. "I can only stay till seven," she said. "More recitals tonight. Argh! Why does every student choose the same piece of music?"

Adrien smiled and put an arm around her. "They're all just trying to impress you."

"And now," the announcer said, "for a NewsPort closeup. A week ago we spoke with Jasmine Rochelle about her harvesting operation somewhere in Amazonia. A member of her crew was captured shortly after the broadcast. Our correspondent joins us from Bogota."

A young man stood beside Trina with a microphone. Trina's hair hung in dark strands and her eyes were hollow, but she seemed alert and in good spirits.

"This is Matt Scarpulla with a special report. Trina Josell was apprehended six days ago and kept here in the Bogota jail. Can you tell us what the last few days have been like?"

Trina smiled into the camera, perhaps a smile for Mane, then turned solemn. "It's been frightening. I wasn't told why I was being held, just questioned repeatedly about our harvesting site."

"Have charges been laid?"

"Yes, finally. Trespassing and poaching."

"You're an ecologist. Why would you want to be a greens harvester?"

"Because more than anyone else, I can see we're not doing harm. I'd like to challenge my colleagues. You know where our first site was. Take a look and see if there's any sign we were there, other than the patch of jungle burned by the Warriors. We harvested in that area for sixteen months. I've kept detailed records of everything we took at the new site. I'd be happy to make those available."

"EcoTech indicates that it isn't time yet to open the preserves."

"EcoTech is trying to convince us that humans and natural areas can't mix—that humans should continue to live in cities or plantations. They believe humans have no place on the preserves. They want more and more land and they're getting it, evicting people and forcing them into cities."

"Humans don't have a good record in natural areas."

"Recent history says otherwise. In the past fifty years our parents and grandparents made huge sacrifices once irretrievable loss was declared. We were on the brink of making this planet unlivable, nearly destroyed ourselves, but learned a very important lesson. We are ready to reclaim the Earth, all of it, for ourselves. Not just for Emerald Warriors and EcoTech but for everyone. Jasmine's harvesting operation is showing us how and that's what has EcoTech frightened. We need—"

"Miss Josell, what's your response to the charges laid against you?"

"What I've done may be illegal, but it's not wrong. This legal battle is the beginning of a lobby to start licensed harvesting in preserves."

"Thank you." The announcer turned to the camera. "Now we speak to EcoTech for their views on recent—"

Chanel frowned. "Why are they laying charges? Trina didn't say anything about aberrations. That's your deal, isn't it?"

"The deal only applies to me. Besides, laying charges is the only way they can hang on to her. If they let her go, she'll just disappear into the jungle." Adrien sighed. "I guess she'll need a lawyer."

The phone rang—Martinez. "There you have it; Trina Josell. What have you got for me?"

"You owed me for Kevin Maravitch. The way I see it, we're even now."

"Why not let Jasmine decide for herself?"

"Until you can prove you didn't trace her transmission to her camp, she's not going to want to talk to you."

Martinez was actually quiet for a moment. "I'll be in touch."

"Hey, thanks for Trina."

"'Kay."

Adrien found Chanel still on the couch.

"This is getting too big," he said.

"What do you mean?"

"Before long, we'll have no control over where this goes."

*   *   *   *   *

"It's time to ask for what we want," Adrien insisted. "Trina requests a harvesting permit for a year with no restrictions on harvested species. If they go for it, EcoTech will probably insist we only take VJX. We can compromise on a list of species including what you need to harvest for recs."

Jasmine didn't look happy, but nodded. "They'll want to see the operation to check what we're harvesting."

"Let's offer to send everything through your pilot in La Paz. They can check the harvest there."

Jasmine sighed. "I don't think they'll go for it."

"We have to try. We'll have a better chance in the long run if we're seen now as trying to compromise."

"I doubt EcoTech will agree without outside pressure. We've got a better chance of convincing the EC to let us harvest legally."

"You might be right."

"I was being sarcastic."

"Think about it. A lot of opinion shows have tackled this now. Whenever they need to hear opposition to opening preserves, they don't go to the EC. They go to EcoTech. But, if we ever get our harvesting legalized, it's the EC that needs to change the laws. They've been very quiet about the whole thing."

"This is impossible."

"Yeah, just like building an invisible camp in the jungle."

Miguel leaned forward to get a better view from the back seat. Bogota kept changing. Even since his last visit, he could see the population growth. The city was thriving. After the plague years, city council had decided to centralize the city and bulldozed everything but the middle of the core. As people moved in from the outlying areas where the plague had done less damage, new homes were built for them and the people displaced by the preserves.

Miguel eyed the driver and two body guards—they hardly seemed necessary here. He was home. Simon was right, though. Miguel could never take anything for granted. Not his own safety and not the safety of the party.

Even after completing the cleansing imperative, the election two years ago had only brought him sixty-four percent of the vote. Now the Restoration party was making the most of Trina Josell's interview with NewsPort. They were also constantly challenging eviction proceedings, Owen Lamberin's legacy. It was the "Raker's" investigation six years ago that actually gave Miguel a way to save the party. The Raker began to expose small scale corruptions that had worried Miguel and got him thinking party reform would save the EC. Now he was convinced if Owen Lamberin were still alive, he wouldn't find much to complain about. He wished the old historian *was* still alive. Perhaps his children would have found more ordinary careers.

Before Owen Lamberin started digging around, the Restoration never ran expecting to win. Voters saw the Opposition as watchdogs making sure the EC kept its promises. In the past ten years, they had become a serious threat.

The car stopped and the driver opened Miguel's door. He stepped out into the sun and took a deep breath of the warm spicy air.

"Escalante?" said a surprised voice, then, "Escalante!"

The lump of rags piled beside the building's entrance came to life and moved towards him.

"Why is my son dead?"

One of his guards stepped beside Miguel, but the old man was clearly unarmed.

"They killed my son!" The old man pointed to the doorway. "Can *you* tell me why? They won't tell me why. They will tell *you* if you ask."

Miguel's security stepped between him and the old man, and Miguel took a step back.

"Why is my son dead?" the man persisted as Miguel turned to the doorway and walked into the Emerald Warrior offices. Ten years ago he would have stopped to talk to the man, but Miguel had learned since then that he was a target for any lunatic who recognized him.

He was unexpected so it took a few minutes of surprised expressions and panic-induced whispers before Ortega could be found.

Ortega worried him. He seemed more concerned about keeping EcoTech happy than he did the EC. Simon's research showed a clean record for Ortega though he had a reputation for toughness and bending the rules. The opposition was making noises about Arri Deckert's autopsy report being incomplete and suggesting that the farmer who was killed in the preserves three years ago had been unarmed.

Miguel had been a team with this man's predecessor. Together, Miguel and Alberto Misoto had cleaned up the South American block. That had exhausted him, and Alberto retired after Miguel became party leader. Ortega was his pick to replace him. He had assured Miguel that Ortega was passionate about protecting the preserves, but his passion for shooting poachers made him a danger to the EC. If he continued to work in isolation and with a heavy hand, he could cost the EC badly needed support.

After a few minutes, Miguel was led to Ortega's office. As tall, brown, and craggy as ever, Ortega smiled and bowed. He indicated the couch but as Miguel sat, Ortega remained behind his desk. Alberto would have sat beside him. Miguel always felt there was an unnatural orderliness forced on this man's body and was always a bit unnerved when Ortega could bend enough to sit. If he was at all surprised about Miguel's visit, he didn't show it.

"What can I do for you?" Ortega asked.

"Tell me about Trina Josell."

Ortega spread his hands. "We figured her for extremely dangerous when we brought her in."

"Did she have weapons?"

"No, but she was wearing a tracking device and her pals could have come after us any time."

"Did you question her?"

"Sure—for a couple of days."

"Do you have the tapes?"

"No, she didn't say anything worth keeping. We have some notes."

Miguel frowned. Nothing Ortega had done was illegal in the strictest interpretation of the law, but . . .

"We have to be very careful," Miguel said. "It's fortunate that no one was killed in the raid. Since Lamberin and Josell have been talking, public attention is turning your way."

Miguel scrutinized the carefully composed expression. They were supposed to be fighting the same fight here, but Miguel felt no connection between them.

"That farmer your warriors killed three years ago—there's talk now that he was never known to carry a gun, that he was probably unarmed when he was killed. We can't afford to be heavy-handed here."

Ortega just looked at him, no acknowledgment. Miguel sat back in the couch. "What would you do if you were me?"

Ortega smiled. "Pull warriors off all the preserves for three months and sweep through Amazonia. That way we could cover every square kilometer and burn out the camps as we advance. That would show them that poaching the preserves won't be tolerated."

"What about the people?"

He shrugged. "Deal with the ones who fight and arrest the rest."

From his tone, Miguel thought few would survive to be arrested.

"Then double the man-power at the borders. And double the satellite coverage."

"Lamberin and Josell have painted their harvesters as a group of unarmed young people harvesting a drug that would otherwise be unavailable. If we slaughter all the harvesters we find, it would be a political nightmare. I'm being pressured by the scientific community to make the preserves more accessible, not cut them off." He leaned towards Ortega. "Make no mistake. What you do reflects on the EC and if our support continues to slip, you may be out of a job. Think about it. The opposition wins and starts reversing the legislations we've worked so hard for. Then, if we don't reclaim office in eight years, there is no EC any more. The borders will be opened and your precious preserves will be overrun with tourists and entrepreneurs. If you don't want that to happen, go softly. We have to continue to act reasonably."

Miguel stood. "Your only option is to fall into the rules and to keep my office properly informed. Finding out about Trina Josell's capture only hours before it becomes news is not acceptable. I don't want to hear any more rumors about bending the rules. Clear?"

Ortega stood as well. "Clear, sir."

"Now." Miguel smiled. "Does Rosita's Grill still make the best saltenas in town?"

Ortega's features softened. "Yes sir."

Miguel headed for Rosita's with his entourage and wished he'd come in better circumstances so he could actually savor what he felt were the best saltenas in the *world*.

Simon leaned in through the office door. "You just got a call I thought you'd want to take yourself. It's Jasmine Rochelle."

"The jungle woman? Trace it while I talk to her."

Miguel's screen flickered on to reveal Jasmine Rochelle set in a backdrop of tree-trunks hung with moss. She blinked with surprised. "Oh, I didn't think they'd put me through." Recovering, she continued. "I have a proposition for you." She took a deep breath. "I think if you had a chance to see our operation for yourself you might feel different about what we're doing here."

"What do you propose?" he asked as much out of interest as to keep her talking.

"We're offering you a chance to visit us for two days. You fly in blind, you won't know our location and you can bring one person with you. Either an unarmed body guard or a camera-hand. We'll show you the whole operation. After you see what we're really doing, I don't think you'll be as opposed to letting us continue legally." Her expression softened having recited her carefully memorized request.

"Why?"

That stumped her for a moment. "I don't want to live my life hiding like a criminal. What we're doing here may be illegal but it's not wrong. I want my crew to be able to visit friends and family without fear they'll be followed back home."

Home. She was calling the jungle home. "Tell me a bit—"

"That's all I have time for. I'll call for an answer in a week." She flickered off the screen.

Simon shook his head. "The signal has been bounced too much. We need twice that long for a trace."

"What do you make of her?"

"You should go."

That possibility had never occurred to him. Miguel leaned back in his chair. It just didn't seem a safe proposition. "What if it's a trick? What if they just want to kill me or take me hostage?"

Simon shook his head, "They're playing a public relations game. You'd be safer with a camera-hand than with three armed guards. It would be suicide for them to let anything happen to you."

Simon leaned towards him. "Miguel, you can't keep the preserves locked up forever. I know that's what EcoTech wants but it's just not feasible. Part of the reason the opposition has gained so much ground *is* the corruption issue, but after all the work we did to clean up, we still only won by sixty-eight percent. A big part of that is the public seeing us as redundant, no longer necessary. The environmental crisis is over but we still don't let them into the preserves and if they knew EcoTech plans never to let people in, they'd have us out this year. If we're not willing to change with the times, we may as well pack our bags now."

"Are you saying we should condone what Rochelle and her gang are doing?" He couldn't believe Simon was being so empathetic to this young criminal.

"No, but be open to some possibilities. She's offering you a chance to play the humanitarian leader. Go—see what they're all about and if you think they have a legitimate operation, take steps to allow harvesting on a regulated basis, or after this election the opposition will do it for you."

"It was private enterprise like harvesting and tourism that destroyed so much a hundred years ago. We can't go down that road again."

"When the coalition started, people wanted their natural world back, but for what? So it could sit in huge patches that no one can ever see? The dream was that every person could walk out their front door and be in a natural area within half an hour, the way they could over a hundred years ago."

"We're not ready for that."

"That's EcoTech talking and I've come to suspect they have a reason for not wanting people in."

"What is it?"

Simon shook his head. "I'm not sure. After Trina Josell challenged the scientific community to check out the old harvesting site, a group of three biologists applied for permits to do just that. EcoTech buried the request. All three have disappeared from their jobs. Something is not right."

Simon looked down at his steepled fingers for a moment, then looked up at Miguel. "A special officer Carla Watenabe was in charge of the Owen Lamberin murder case. She's been poking into connections between Green Splinter and some other political groups. She's also developed a lot of contacts that might be useful for us if we want to go ahead with investigating Green Splinter. She's not afraid to dig and she's not afraid of EcoTech. I'm making her an offer to head up the investigation team."

"Good. We need to get these suspicions cleared up."

Simon continued to update him on the investigation but Miguel's thoughts kept returning to the nervous young woman who called the jungle her home.

✶ ✶ T H I R T Y - N I N E ✶ ✶

Miguel hoped there was ground somewhere beneath him as he was lowered through the trees. When he dropped under the bulk of the foliage he saw the pile of bags and supplies. Nadia had landed before him and stood by the bags as if guarding them from the two people facing her. Jasmine Rochelle was there to steady him as he landed.

"Welcome," she smiled with a warmth he hadn't expected. She looked much more relaxed than she had on NewsPort or during their short discussions to plan his trip here.

"Thank you," he replied while stepping out of his harness.

"You have several choices," a voice rumbled behind him. Nadia stood hands on hips, face to face with a tall blond man. "We can send everything back," he continued. "We can leave it here for the monkeys to pick through. Or you let me scan everything."

Miguel was surprised she was making a fuss. With her training she should know better.

"If you're afraid I'll damage something, I'll let you watch." The tall man smiled. "You can bill me for anything I break."

"Just make sure the scanner frequency won't damage the circuits. That's all I ask." She stepped back, inviting him to continue. He did and then proceeded with a full body scan.

The blond frowned at Jasmine for a second. Did he suspect Nadia already? These young people were not what Miguel expected. They weren't patch-heads or militants.

The blond sauntered over and introduced himself as Mane. Miguel allowed a body scan as well. Mane stepped back and asked, "What's going to happen to Trina?" in a tone Miguel would expect from a colleague.

Without thinking, Miguel answered honestly. "EcoTech is pressing charges. She's looking at some heavy fines."

"Only money." Mane sniffed. "Remember, NewsPort is watching how you treat her."

"Let's get the supplies loaded," Jasmine said.

The supply packages were stacked onto a cart. Nadia and Miguel carried their own bags.

Without the aid of boardwalks or paths, the group made its way through the forest, free to walk wherever they chose. Jasmine assured him that her crew had done a full harvesting sweep through the area. He found it hard to believe her until she pointed out several small trees only three meters tall that had been clipped of some leaves and branches. Nadia followed their conversation as best she could with her camera. She handled it like a pro after only two weeks of training. Her real job was security. She'd worked for Miguel for two years after four years of combat training and he had no doubt that she could take on this whole camp and win if she needed to.

When they came to a huge patch of overgrown boulders, Mane asked Nadia to stop filming. Miguel expected they'd be making their way around it. Instead, Jasmine led him to a spot where the rocks opened up a bit and he stumbled after her. They seemed to be headed for a large green and brown lump.

As they neared it, Miguel made out a shed covered with moss and small plants. When they got there, he parked himself on a bench while the crew bustled with their supplies and Nadia took their bags inside. He watched transfixed as these young people treated the forest like it was theirs—as if they weren't under the canopy of the most wondrous thing EcoTech had created.

After she unloaded her share, Jasmine came to sit beside him while Mane ducked into the shed.

"Welcome to Jungle Haven," she said.

Before Miguel could answer, Mane backed out of the shed. "Hey, doll," he said. "Trouble."

Nadia followed with her gun drawn. Without thought, Jasmine rushed at her but Mane stopped her when she reached him. Nadia didn't flinch.

"If you're going to shoot, you better do it now." Jasmine had effectively made it impossible for Nadia to aim at anyone other than her or Mane.

Jasmine and Mane moved apart. They were getting ready to try to disarm Nadia. That could only lead to someone being shot.

Miguel stepped forward. "That's enough," he said. "Hand it over, Nadia."

She frowned but gave it to him. Jasmine again put herself between the gun and her crew.

"Is this the only reason you came here?" she asked. "To kill us?" She took a step towards him. No one had guns here. Someone would have pulled one out by now if they did. No chainsaws—no guns. This was no ordinary poaching gang. He popped the charge out of the weapon and gave it to Nadia. He handed the gun to Jasmine. Mane took it from her. "She was working on her equipment when I came in. Think she'd just put this together. She's not just a camera-hand."

"This was a stupid idea," Jasmine said, flushed with anger. "You're the same people who stalled the investigation into my father's murder, who killed Arri—" Mane winced and put a hand on her shoulder. "You came here to destroy us," she continued.

"I'm here to find out why anyone would risk arrest to live out here." Miguel had to save this. Even without weapons, Nadia was more than capable of protecting him, but he couldn't let it come to that. "If you had been invited to Geneva to see me, wouldn't you have planned some back-up in case things went wrong? That's all this is. We are not here to inter-fere." That could come later.

Jasmine glared at him, then turned away. Miguel hoped she was thinking she had everything to gain by getting their meeting back on track. Mane went to talk to her.

Miguel glanced at the crew. They had frozen in wide-eyed silence, look-ing not at all like the seasoned scrappers most poachers were. Jasmine and Mane though, they seemed confident enough at defending themselves.

Mane returned and approached Nadia with a smile. "You and I are going to go through your equipment one more time. If I don't find any-thing, I'll just confiscate it." He put up a hand to stop her response. "If I do, we'll be storing it in the river till you leave tomorrow."

Miguel shrugged when Nadia looked at him for instructions. She cer-tainly didn't need weapons to be effective and they needed to make a show of compliance for now. He approached Jasmine, who still scowled. "I'd be interested to see how you're keeping records."

She looked at him for a moment as if she hadn't understood. "Levi," she said. "He's been keeping track of everything while Trina's gone."

Levi rolled his eyes and muttered. "I don't know how Trina ever got any other work done. This takes bloody forever. No plant or animal is too tiny, she says." He led them into the shed and sat at the small screen there.

Jasmine started an explanation of their harvesting catalogues while Levi called up various pages. Her expression softened with pride after a few minutes. Who would have expected a gang of poachers to be spend-ing time keeping records? They seemed serious about having their work accepted as legitimate.

Miguel's first climb was a short hoist to Jasmine's home in the trees. Mane pulled the thin rope over a pulley to lift Miguel the several stories to Jasmine's landing. He ducked into the cramped, mock-wood box wrapped around one side of an enormous tree trunk. The huge windows made the place seem larger. After acknowledging the cistern plumbing system, home fermenter and single methane burner, his gaze was pulled again to the view from the windows. Jasmine swung the screen out so he could lean out to see the maze of trees and branches. Miguel peered through the branches and listened to the hidden birds and insects until the light was lost to sundown.

Back on the ground, Jasmine gave him a small light to use as he followed her through the alleys of the boulder field to the shed. Levi and Dustin bustled to get a meal prepared.

After the meal of heavily spiced chicken stew with rice and plantain, Indra started drumming. The others joined in and kept it up for half an hour. Once he got the beat, Miguel joined in, too. He had to keep telling himself that these people were poachers. They didn't act like poachers—he was reminded more of summer work camps when he was a university student.

"Arri Deckert taught us that," Indra told him.

"NewsPort," Dustin announced. Everyone turned their attention to a small vid-screen to catch up on the day's news.

Levi finished the evening off with a story about a girl who became a forest spirit to escape abusive parents.

Miguel and Nadia slept in hammocks in the shed while Levi sat at the table lit by his screen. He worked all night on the records, perhaps because Miguel had taken his hammock, perhaps because he wanted to keep an eye on the visitors.

*   *   *   *   *

Miguel looked at the climbing harness in Jasmine's hand then again at the foliage above them. If Nadia were here, she'd try to stop him dangling from a rope depending on instructions from a bunch of outlaws. But she was confined to the shed with Indra, and Miguel had a chance to touch a world he had only ever seen from a distance. Mane had Nadia's camera pointed at him. He accepted the harness and Jasmine helped him into it. She insisted he wear a helmet. Despite Jasmine's warnings to go slow, he was panting by the time he reached the first ceiling of leaves

A tree limb full of epiphytes caught his eye. Several bromelaids held stalks of red and blue flowers and a Christmas cactus cascaded a magnificent clump of magenta flowers. He took out the hook and pulled himself closer. With his free hand he touched the moss then looked inside the bromelaid. Tadpoles swam in the water and tiny squiggles, insect larvae, squirmed. A bromelaid pond. He'd only ever read about them. Now he could touch one. He dipped a finger-tip into the water and laughed with delight when he saw a small larva squirming there. Swishing his finger in the pond, he released the tiny creature.

When he descended to the ground forty minutes later, he was giddy and exhausted and didn't mind sharing with the camera that he'd been to see something truly remarkable. Jasmine smiled at his enthusiasm and reminded him they only had an hour before the chopper came for him and Nadia.

* * * * *

Miguel stood outside the harvesting shed and munched on the cereal bar and fruit he'd been given. He wondered what small city the rubble had been. Impossible to say. Countless towns had been swallowed by the preserves.

Miguel gazed at the trees around the site and once again could see no sign of human activity except the worn path to the shed and some large shapes in several of the surrounding trees. Maybe Simon was right. Maybe letting a few people in wouldn't hurt if it was done carefully. And stopping the harvest of VJX would be a political nightmare. Lately, he couldn't walk through the Geneva offices without hearing staff discussing the Kevin Maravitch death watch, what his sister had been wearing to visit that day, how the conversation went, how he'd thrown his tray at the nurse, how his memory was starting to go, how terrible it was they hadn't discovered VJX in time to help him. It was as if people had no lives of their own to live.

But it meant everyone knew what Lightning Madness and VJX were. That it killed fewer than a hundred people a year wouldn't matter to all those people who now counted Kevin Maravitch in their personal circle of friends because they looked in on him every day.

Allowing VJX harvesting might even get people excited again about EC's accomplishments.

Miguel spotted Jasmine and Mane at the table outside and went to sit across from her.

"I have to say, I'm impressed with what you're doing here. If you stop now, I'll see about getting EcoTech to take a closer look at permits. Veejix is becoming important enough that EcoTech has to grant permits for it."

Jasmine looked at Mane and a smile came and went before she let her attention come back to Miguel. She shook her head. "We can't stop."

"I'm offering you a way out. The warriors are going to find this camp. It's just a matter of time."

"My brother has lots of experience waiting for EcoTech to process permits. If we leave, all we do is go back to waiting for EcoTech to let us go to places everyone should have access to by now. Besides, what would we do? Leave our homes and get arrested as soon as we set foot in an airport? And what about all the other medicines we harvest? Where will they come from? No. We won't stop—we can't."

Her impertinence surprised him. He was offering her a way out. "EcoTech will—"

"Who's running these preserves? I thought EcoTech worked for the EC, not the other way round."

"EcoTech is in the best position to know what's good for the preserves."

"How can you give them that much power when they can't even pass their own purity imperative?"

"Hey, Doll," Mane warned.

"That's the real reason the permits for Veejix were never approved," she continued. "EcoTech has known for at least ten years now that they produced aberrations when they made this forest."

That was impossible. EcoTech had gotten the contracts because they'd been able to convince the EC that they were the only natural restructuring company that had the technology to do the job.

"They've based their reputation on being able to recreate ecosystems without aberrations," he began.

"And that's why they want to keep the preserves closed," Jasmine answered. "So no one finds out. Veejix didn't exist before EcoTech built this forest. Neither did the spider that bit Dustin."

"EcoTech may be using DNA banks you don't know about."

She shook her head. "They were right in 2095. The loss is irretrievable. We can't ever get back the ecosystems we destroyed, not the same way they were."

She was saying the EC was doomed to fail. EC had been built on the promise it made to restore the world to the way it was—to reverse the Declaration of Irretrievable loss. "All we need is time," he said.

"It's too big. No matter how much technology we develop, we can't put it back together the way it was. We should stop trying."

"That's absurd. We can't stop trying."

"Look at this forest. It's power of ten—it works. Even though Trina found seventeen aberrations. A few new species in the mix isn't going to make the whole place go sheared.

"Trina and Levi are always talking about how the forest works as an organism. You can't assume that people are the only force at work here— that we decide if the world lives or dies. What about this forest? Forests are living systems that survived asteroid collisions and massive volcanoes spewing toxic gases. This one is trying to heal itself."

No. Ecosystems the way they were—no aberrations. That was the deal with EcoTech. Otherwise there was no telling what could be unleashed on the world. Jasmine's suggestions were reckless. No doubt her father had filled her head at an early age with the Restoration propaganda that the EC and what they stood for were no longer necessary.

"A few more species in the mix," he commented, "could be a disaster. EcoTech would never allow it."

"But they already—"

"I need to finish packing." He stood.

"We won't leave," Jasmine said. "But we'll agree to try for permits again."

"You're breaking the law by living here." What made her think they could just keep living here and make demands? "I won't negotiate with criminals."

"Who's the criminal here?" Jasmine stood to face him. "I saw Emerald Warriors kill Arri Deckert—an unarmed chemist. They shot him point blank. Are *they* deciding who's a criminal?" She took a step towards Miguel but Mane put a hand on her shoulder.

Miguel didn't budge. "If you come out, we can talk. Otherwise, you're wasting your time."

Mane's hand dropped and Jasmine took a half step back. "We're not leaving," she said. "Too many people depend on what we do here."

Miguel shook his head and walked away. This woman was dangerous. Her whole operation was dangerous. Not to the forest directly, but to everything the EC and EcoTech were trying to accomplish. With her as an example, people might become convinced that the EC was doomed to failure—that EcoTech couldn't be trusted.

Jasmine and her crew would be less dangerous if they were typical poachers using chainsaws to harvest.

Miguel wandered through the boulders as if in thought. He pulled the homing device out of his pocket and, without looking at it, dropped it. He absently kicked at leaf litter to cover the tiny device. Turning it on would no doubt activate Mane's security net. Turning it on would wait.

Miguel looked up at the lumps of epiphytes that indicated the homes of the crew. They didn't belong here—no humans did. They would only undo what EcoTech had struggled for so many years to accomplish

✴ ✴ F O R T Y ✴ ✴

Miguel drank in the smooth line of her bare arms as Shelly poured whisky over ice. Shelly, who had never been awed by him, who had treated him as an equal from the first time they met, whose passion for her work infected him with new hope that people still held the preserves as precious. Shelly who had also become the best diversion from his work he'd ever had.

The casual dress she wore fell over her hips and fluttered around her thighs as she came towards him. She handed him a drink.

"What did Nadia do next?" she asked.

Shelly had been interrogating him about his jungle trip. "Not much. She stayed confined to the shed and kept her eyes open from there."

"You know, that was a foolish risk," she scolded as she sat beside him.

"Mmm," he commented, then kissed her. Their drinks sat forgotten on the coffee table as his hands moved over, then under the dress she wore. They moved to the bedroom and he lost himself in her for a time.

Shelly lay with an arm draped over his chest. "Did you find out where they are?" she asked.

"Who?" It took him a moment. "Oh . . . no. They were pretty adamant about keeping their location a secret." Did she have to keep talking about this? He wanted to escape for a while longer.

"And you didn't take any trackers with you?"

He smiled. "I didn't say that."

"When are the Warriors going in?"

"Not for a while."

"Why wait?"

"Activating the beacon will likely set off their security sensors. That means they'll have time to prepare for a fight and if they fight Ortega, we'll have more deaths to explain. It makes more sense to keep talking for now and make them realize we won't allow them to stay so they better give up and get out."

Shelly nodded slightly as if she agreed.

"They've made up some interesting allegations," he added.

"Such as?"

"Their chemist was actually shot by Emerald Warriors, they've found genetic aberrations, and EcoTech purposely ignored requests for research permits."

"Do they have evidence?"

"How can they? It's absurd. They're just trying to justify their own paranoia."

She didn't speak for a moment.

"I don't think you should wait," she said.

"Why?"

"God, Miguel. They're laughing at us right now. They know they're breaking the law and they refuse to abide by it. Why are you negotiating with them? Set off whatever gadget you left there and get them out of the preserves."

"It's not that simple."

"It should be. Is every law EC brought in over the years open to challenge now? You can't let that gang of pillagers get away with this."

"I won't. But they've got some political leverage with this Veejix business. I have to be careful."

The living room console chimed a reminder.

"Come on," he said. "NewsPort."

By the time they dressed and made their way back to the couch, Matt Scarpulla was already smiling out at the audience. "Miguel Escalante went to visit the VJX harvesting operation we've been featuring in some of our special reports. It's a move some are calling brilliant, others foolhardy. He made it back without incident. During his stopover in Bogota this afternoon, we spoke with him."

"President Escalente. Is it true you were invited to have a look at the jungle camp?"

"The invitation came from Jasmine Rochelle, yes."

"Why did you go? Wasn't your safety a concern?"

"Not really. Rochelle and her crew are businesspeople, not thugs. They would have nothing to gain from harming me. But make no mistake here. They *are* dangerous to the preserves through their own actions and the example they set. I went to see for myself what the jungle crew are doing."

"Why the invitation?"

"Jasmine Rochelle wanted an opportunity to justify what she's set up. She'd a businesswoman. If she can get permits and not have to spend money on an elaborate security system, she'd make more money from what she harvests."

"Did you see evidence of harvesting?"

"That's difficult to answer. In an environment so lush with species, how would the average person know if one or two species were missing? True, they weren't cutting down trees but harvesting anything in an uncontrolled manner is dangerous, no matter how it's done."

"Are they keeping records as Trina Josell suggests?"

"Yes, but still, they aren't the experts—EcoTech is."

"Can you offer any insight into why Jasmine Rochelle has set up her jungle operation?"

"I'm not a psychologist, but I believe she is an angry young woman who is striking out at the world with this scheme of hers. Unfortunately, she's been able to convince a group of bright young people to throw away promising careers in order to help her pillage the preserves. She's been orphaned twice and had a very difficult adolescence. Now she's angry, intense and charismatic and holds a sway over her crew that's difficult to understand."

"You sound almost sympathetic."

"It's hard not to sympathize when a young person has chosen the wrong path in response to such difficult circumstances. It's inexcusable, however, that she's breaking the law and has coerced these friends of hers to help her. She's extremely dangerous and must be stopped."

"Were you able to locate the camp?"

"No, I have no idea where they are."

"Surely you must have some plans to arrest the jungle crew."

"Well, yes. Make no mistake. Rochelle and her people will be found and soon, and will be held accountable for what they've done. We have to be careful to enforce the law without anyone getting hurt."

"Thank you, Mr. Escalente, for taking the time today—"

"Well done," Shelly commented.

"Let people think about that for a while. Then we pull the jungle crew out of there."

★ ★ F O R T Y - O N E ★ ★

Edan blinked in the brightness as he woke. Selina had drawn the curtains back. Slumped on the window seat, she looked out to the street below. It must be Saturday—visiting day.

He stared at the white ceiling. Selina had insisted they take this room. I don't care if you want to record in a black box, she'd told him and his crew, but we're sleeping in a white room. He couldn't blame her for wanting a break from the darkness his music flourished in. She had her own dark corners to fear.

With a sigh, Edan swung his legs over the side of the bed. Selina wiped her eyes, hearing him.

Edan put a hand on her shoulder. "Hey, love."

"I can't do this anymore," she said, not looking at him. "If I don't go, he won't even notice."

"And you'll be even more miserable than you are now," he said softly.

"He remembers things we did when we were kids, but doesn't even recognize me."

They'd had the same conversation every Saturday morning for the past three weeks.

"I'll go with you," he offered.

"The cameras," she said. "Those damn cameras. I don't want to drag you into this."

"Some news shark is going to catch us together eventually. Let's do this on our own terms."

She looked up at him through strands of red hair, her green eyes shining with captured tears. This week she might just give in.

"Could you . . . ?" she choked on the rest and tears were freed to roll down her face.

He knelt in front of her and held her hands in his. "Sure, love. Sure."

He was relieved. He'd never liked the thought of her going alone, but didn't want his celebrity to detract from Selina or her brother.

*   *   *   *   *

Edan's presence beside Selina in the hospital corridors attracted only mild interest from the staff who had only ever seen her visit alone. He'd pulled his hair back tight and wore regular casual shirt and pants. He hoped the look was different enough from his most recent stage persona that he wouldn't attract attention.

When they got to the room, he was relieved to find the NewsPort camera-hand was on a break. Kevin was asleep. Edan glanced around the room as Selina sat beside her brother. The camera-hand wasn't there, but Edan counted at least three cameras keeping watch from corners of the room.

At the sound of the door opening, Selina was up again. "What's that machine for?" she demanded of the doctor.

"It's just a different kind of blood pressure monitor."

"You know he doesn't want any life support."

Didn't want. Kevin signed all the appropriate papers when he was still legally coherent. At eighteen, he'd been barely old enough to sign them himself.

"Yes, Miss Maravitch." The doctor smiled. "I wanted to talk to you about trying some medication that might slow the deterioration."

"Can it bring him back?"

"That damage is impossible to reverse. But what we can discover—"

"Hasn't he done enough? Now you want to use him to test some drug that's going to keep him like this even longer? Are you insane?"

"Give us a minute." Edan's tone left the doctor little choice, and he left shaking his head.

"There will be no drugs—no machines." Selina swept the monitor onto the floor before Edan could react.

"Just let him die." She turned, but Edan caught her in his arms before she could do more damage. She sobbed against his chest. "Just let him die. Why is it taking him so long to die?"

"Who's there?" Kevin called out. "Who's dying?"

Edan grabbed Selina and fled the room and the cameras. He found a private alcove, sat her beside him and waited for more tears. She'd put on such a brave show the past few weeks, it was just a matter of time before she fractured entirely. He held her as she cried.

Almost a year ago he'd been here to see Kevin Maravitch for himself. He'd never heard of Lightning Madness before he saw Adrien featured on NewsPort. The more he learned about it, the more it fascinated him—a disease that leaves the body alone and step by plodding step destroys the mind. When the death watch on Kevin started, Edan's curiosity drew him here. He'd met Selina here. She recognized him immediately, called him a ghoul and eventually admitted she was a fan.

Even tucked away in their alcove, their privacy lasted for only ten minutes before a young man, obviously looking for someone, found them.

"Edan Loffler," he announced as if Edan had to be told who he was.

"Yeah," Edan replied.

"Walt James, NewsPort," he bowed. Edan nodded but kept an arm around Selina.

"You know Miss Maravitch?"

"We've been friends for some time."

"Is this the first time you've come to visit Kevin?"

Edan grinned slyly at him. "Is this an interview?"

"It could be." Walt smiled back.

Edan shook his head. "This story isn't about me. It's about Selina and Kevin. I'm not giving interviews today."

"If you could tell me—"

"Really, I'm not." Edan had a reputation for being a good interview. Putting off one reporter wouldn't hurt. The young man seemed ready to speak, then thought better of it, aided by the grim look Edan gave him. He shrugged and left.

Edan and Selina exchanged a glance, then went back to Kevin's room. Kevin was gluing plastic sticks together to build a house. He peered up at them as they came in.

"Hi, Kevin," Selina said. "I'm your sister Selina and this is my friend Edan."

Kevin had a hollow look that Edan hadn't seen since he left his patch-head friends behind in the Core. Edan had watched with the rest of the world as Kevin grew sad, angry, vicious, then duller by the day.

"Good to finally meet you," Edan said bowing.

"I seen you on screen," Kevin said while he continued his gluing. "You had a 'board."

Selina sat beside him. "Tell me what you're making."

Edan had watched her here, being so patient, so strong when he knew what she wanted most was to run from the room and never come back. His heart nearly broke for her. He felt helpless watching her. The phrase, "won't you let me fight your demons and do battle with your fears," came to him and he searched his pockets for something to type it into.

✲ ✲ F O R T Y - T W O ✲ ✲

" . . . he'll be thrilled to see you," Edan heard on the periphery of his attention. He continued recording notes.

"Hey you! Back to the real world," Selina said.

He looked up.

"Guess who's here?"

He gazed at her blankly. This had to be important. She never interrupted him needlessly.

"Jasmine," she said.

Before he could think what this meant, the entry request rang. Selina opened the door to a small, dark haired woman in three-year-old street clothes and a stained canvas bag over her shoulder.

Jasmine dismissed Selina with a cursory smile and stepped towards Edan, her face a mixture of curiosity and hesitation. "Hi, Edan," she said. "I . . . " and ran out of words.

Jasmine Rochelle stood stammering in his hotel room. It was Selina who welcomed her.

"It's wonderful to finally meet you," she said, and surprised him by giving Jasmine a big hug. "I'm Selina."

Edan overcame his paralysis and hugged her quickly, just long enough to feel some of the tension drain from her.

"I figured," she said, "if I came in person you'd find it harder to refuse to see me."

"It's great to see you," he said.

Selina started asking about Jasmine's trip here and what did she want to drink. Edan tried not to stare at Jasmine. He'd finally realized what her and Mane's secret really was when he saw her interviewed. The realization that she wasn't a Core Rat dealer but slogging through jungle to provide Adrien the drugs to cure Lightning Madness had him fractured fro a week. First he'd felt guilty, then angry that she'd kept such an important secret from him.

"Why didn't you tell me?" he blurted.

It only took a second for her to realize what he meant. "Green Splinter was after us. You would have been in danger, too, if you knew anything."

I would have forgiven you. I would have kept loving you, he wanted to say, but for Selina's eyes on him.

"I guess you saw the interview?"

He nodded.

"And Escalente's travelogue?"

He nodded again.

"Then you know I need help dealing with reporters. Trina has no trouble saying the right thing on camera so I know it's not impossible."

So she started in. No how have you been—no, hope I haven't come at a bad time. She just assumed that if she presented the facts, the simple logic of it would get her what she wanted.

"The only thing keeping Adrien out of jail or buried in fines is that he has a secret EcoTech doesn't want revealed. We can only keep it a secret for another year at the most. By then, even if we say nothing, the scientific community will find it." She folded her arms and paced a few steps. "Escalente is ready to declare war on us. If he does, it's all over. If he pulls all the Warriors together and sweeps through Amazonia, he'll find us. But if we can keep this fight in the public eye we stand a chance he won't risk the bad publicity of destroying the operation responsible for getting VJX to hospitals all over the world. No matter what Trina and Adrien say, I'm seen as the spokesperson for the Jungle Haven. So far, NewsPort and Escalente have made me look like a Core Rat with delusions of grandeur playing with people's lives and a fragile new ecosystem. I need a plan that will make us politically untouchable. NewsPort keeps asking me for interviews and I've got to turn my image around—be more sympathetic." She smiled at him. "And you're the best I've ever seen on camera."

"Yeah?" Edan smiled back. "Guess I've got everybody fooled."

"No, really." She paused, then said without apology, "It's the sympathy part I'm having trouble with. I could use some coaching."

"Be glad to help."

Even asking for help, she was intense. Always so strong, so in control. He admired her for it and hated her for the distance it had put between them.

"How long can you stay?" Selina asked.

Jasmine glanced at Edan as if asking permission.

"We've got at least one room free," he said. "You're welcome to it."

"It sounds decadent, doesn't it?" Selina said. "But we only rent out the wing when we're in production. It saves time to have everyone in one place."

Jasmine cast him a look of helplessness as Selina ushered her out. Edan sighed. Selina and Jasmine flocking together—this couldn't be good.

The phone buzzed. "If we spend any more time warming up, we'll be too tired to rehearse."

"'Kay, I'm coming," Edan replied.

*   *   *   *   *

Kath sat at her board in the recording room, her eyes glazed over as Edan continued to shake his head.

"What now, mister?" asked Duff.

"That doesn't sound enough like a cello," Edan grumbled.

"Have you ever heard a real cello?" Rico replied from the mixer.

"Only recorded ones," he admitted. There had to be a way to get a richer tone. What if they could get a real one? All gleaming wood and dancing bow . . . what a sight that would be. "What if we don't do an opera with voice? What if Cartiffe pulls out his cello, a real one, and plays out what he's feeling instead of singing it?"

Selina and Jasmine were a vague flicker in his peripheral vision as they came in.

"Selina, think you can find me a real cello?"

"Dr. Nakama used to have one," Jasmine said.

"And Carmina could answer him with . . . What's pitched higher than a cello?"

"A viola," Jasmine answered.

"Yeah." The novelty alone would make it a hit. No one had recorded or performed with real strings for decades. For so many years, real wood instruments had been considered obscene but other materials just couldn't capture the fullness of the sound.

"Could you find one of those?" he asked.

"Take about three calls," Jasmine replied.

"Come listen to this." He led her to the playback rack. He played the first song, a whimsical romp to introduce the young heroine.

"What instrument?" he asked.

"Violin," Jasmine replied. "I assume she dies before the curtain falls?"

"Of course," Kath answered with a snicker.

"You could pull out some melancholy strains from later . . . I assume there are some?" she asked Kath who smiled and nodded. "Use them as a counterpoint from offstage. That way—"

"We foreshadow her death. Yeah."

"But you've already written most of the lyrics," Duff said.

"Doesn't matter. I can use them somewhere else." This was power of ten. Duff groaned. "I guess it was too much to hope for to ever finish a show on time."

Edan cued up the second song. "Now this one."

After going through all the pre-recorded songs, he glanced at Selina to be sure she'd been taking notes.

"Got it all typed in," she said.

"I've got notes for—"

"Edan," Selina said. "You've been at this for an hour now. Could you introduce everyone to your friend?"

Rico was already squinting at Jasmine. "Jasmine Rochelle," he announced. "Yeah, saw you on NewsPort. You ain't so mean in person."

Jasmine laughed then glanced at Edan. "See my problem?"

"Edan Loffler's muse." Kath laughed with delight and the three musicians introduced themselves.

"Maybe we shouldn't be so friendly. Maybe we should be throwing her out," Rico remarked with a smile.

"Cursed you all the way through recording your requiem," Duff explained. "What was it he kept saying?"

"More anger. More anger," the other two chorused with mock sternness.

They welcomed Jasmine like a lost sister. The rest of the afternoon they spent reworking the entire opera. Edan asked her to play, but her eyes grew sad and she shook her head. At the end of the day Edan wondered what he could have accomplished by now if he'd had Jasmine by his side.

That evening the crew gathered in Selina and Edan's room and Jasmine entertained everyone with stories of her misadventures in the jungle. The worry she had come with faded away. Edan realized he hadn't thought what it had taken for her and her crew to get the VJX to people like Kevin. She made every misfortune into a joke, but it was clear her life had been full of challenges. Yet, despite heat, rain, insects and warriors she remained determined to protect her camp and her operation—to live among the trees. He couldn't understand how Mane had always seemed to pity her—treated her like a wounded child who needed his help. He'd wondered from the beginning why she always felt she needed to lean on Mane.

Selina squeezed in to sit beside him on the couch and took his hand in hers. "Amazing, isn't she?" she whispered.

"Mmm," he replied and put his arm around Selina.

Jasmine seemed to have forgotten why she was visiting, and for the next two days worked with Edan composing or with Selina tracking down the instruments they needed. The days were a blur of new sounds, new melodies, the expression of his heart and hers in telling the story of Carmina and Cartiffe, and of Jasmine's laughter. Her jungle stories tugged at his imagination—there was such a visually rich world there.

It was nine in the morning and Edan wanted to get an early start in the studio. He heard music as he approached the door—someone had beaten him to the instruments. His hand was at the door when something about the punctuation stopped him. Jasmine. They'd all tried to get her to play, but she'd refused. He opened the door a crack. She sat at the 'board lost in the emotion of the music. Edan leaned against the wall outside the door and listened. Over the next forty minutes he was joined by Duff, then Rico, then Kath. Duff raised an eyebrow in appreciation. "Yeah, mister," he said. "That's you five years ago."

Jasmine played her requiem, thundering the keys with anger until the whole piece disintegrated into discord. When he peeked in again she'd laid her head on her arms on the 'board, her shoulders shaking with sobs. He stood frozen with indecision—he'd never seen her cry. Finally he went in, crouched beside her and softly said, "Hey," just to let her know he was there.

"These past few days . . . this is so easy," she finally choked out. "What am I doing? Music would have been so easy."

He wanted to hold her, but he knew he only needed to touch her to be lost in those fierce eyes—lost so deeply not even Selina could save him. He smiled at her. "Should have been here three months ago when I blocked on lyrics two days before deadline."

She chuckled, more, he thought, because she needed to laugh than because he was being clever. She stared at the keys in front of her.

Edan wanted to tell her she had made a mistake. She belonged here. Together they could have turned the music world inside out.

Jasmine sighed. "I have to get back to work," she said. "I've spent the past few days daydreaming."

"Jasmine. You made the right choice."

She looked down and smiled. "Oh come on. My playing wasn't *that* bad."

"No, listen. When we work together we are power of ten. You're good at it but haven't made it yours. Your jungle stories." He shook his head. "Never seen you get such a glow on." What was he saying? "It's where you belong."

When she looked back up at him her eyes tried to shut out anything else he had to say on the matter.

"Told us a lot of stories about jungle life," he persisted. "What's really going on out there?"

Jasmine stared at the 'board for a long moment as if carefully weighing each word. "We've lost clients since my interview. Adrien had three researchers lined up who needed plants but they all backed out once Escalente had his say. Our rec sales are dropping off. The Green stuff isn't as popular anymore. Then there's Trina's fines. Fines all seem to come in denominations of tens of thousands of dollars. If we don't get legalized soon, I don't think we can keep going."

"Mane know?"

"He suspects. I think they all do. None of us is taking a salary. Everything we make is going to living expenses and to keep the operation going. It doesn't help that we've had to spend twenty thousand on surveillance equipment so we can avoid getting ourselves killed."

Yet she seemed determined to fight this battle on her own.

Jasmine stood. "But I can turn our image around and lobby for changes. I'm calling Martinez. With all the coaching you gave me, he'll wonder what hit him.

"Jasmine." He waited for her eyes to go earnest. "I may be able to help more than that. How about a benefit concert?"

"For the camp?"

"If the band doesn't take wages and I can get the stage crew to agree, we could clear over ten million dollars for you—for 'Jungle Haven.'"

"We could pay Trina's fines and her lawyer's fees. We could buy the last of Adrien's replacement equipment." She cocked her head at him. "But why?"

"Why should you have all the fun?" That didn't convince her. "I've seen what Lightning Madness does. Anyone who gets in the way of a cure is the criminal here. Music is the most important thing in my life, but it's not the only thing. Besides, I've already got an idea for the most fantastic set."

"'Kay, but you have to do 'The Longest Time' for me."

"Done . . . well, if I still have the notes somewhere."

*   *   *   *   *

Jasmine stayed the rest of the day, growing more pensive until she seemed entirely preoccupied. Her expression hardened into the same perpetually worried look she'd come with.

Edan clung to Selina as Jasmine said her goodbyes to the band. Then it was his turn to hug her. "Stay synced," he said. She smiled goodbye and was gone.

Jungle drums. The thought bounced into his head. "I have to call Chanel."

* * F O R T Y - F O U R * *

"Since our reports on Lightning Madness and Greens harvesting, opinion broadcasts all over the world have been swamped by demands from their audiences to provide more information about these issues. Today we begin a new series to answer this demand. Our new program, Pillage or Progress, will examine the issues of human exploitation of the preserves."

Edan stopped playing to give the broadcast his full attention.

"We kick off our series with an interview with Jasmine Rochelle who has brought these issues to the forefront through her harvesting operation. She and her crew want nothing less than to be allowed to harvest in the jungle preserves in South America."

Jasmine appeared on the screen, small and stiff against the green of the forest around her. The camera slowly zoomed in on her as the announcer continued.

"Welcome, Ms. Rochelle."

Jasmine relaxed a little to smile and say, "Thank you."

"We've talked about this before, but I know our viewers all want to know from you—why are you doing this? Why harvest the preserves?"

"No one else thought of it," she said. "Not of harvesting the way we do or of dealing with researchers directly rather than with Core Rats. And there was a need for VJX and other drugs."

Now some passion, Edan thought. Let them see your passion. This was the point Edan had pushed the hardest.

Jasmine looked down, nervous now. "At least I started for those reasons. Now we've found a way to live that is challenging and gives us a freedom you can't get in the city." She smiled. "We never know what new problems will come up each day. We're constantly testing ourselves to solve these new problems. We're trying to live in an ecosystem that's huge and overwhelming and beautiful," she said, as if realizing it just now. "That's why it's so important to change the laws—because people have to become part of the natural world again. Up to now it's been put it under glass or destroy it. Those aren't our only choices. We can become part of it."

Scarpulla smiled at her enthusiasm. "People have speculated that your real reasons have more to do with your criminal past. That you have no respect for the law and never will have."

Jasmine's mouth set into a grim line. "I'm not that person anymore."

Focus, Edan thought at her again. Focus on what you want to say, not what he wants to hear.

She took a breath before continuing. "If I were just a criminal, I wouldn't be here today trying to get the laws changed. My past is not an issue."

"What about your crew? How did you convince them to leave promising futures behind to join you in the jungle?"

"They wanted to be part of this."

"Is that what you promised them? That they'd be part of something important, a movement to—"

"No!" Jasmine turned fierce.

Edan could see the excitement in the announcer's eyes. Focus. Focus on the question, not the anger.

"Each member of my crew asked to join because they wanted to supply VJX and other medicines that would not be available if it weren't for us."

The anger seemed to drain from her with every word she spoke. "They also like the challenge of applying what they've learned to a totally new environment."

"How has the loss of Trina Josell affected your operation?"

"It's been power of zero without her," Jasmine replied, unsure only for a moment. "In the years before Irretrievable Loss was declared, a lot of evidence was gathered. Trina interpreted the research and set harvesting limits. We have to do all the recording ourselves now. We keep track of everything we take."

"What is it you want from EcoTech?" The interviewer had wisely given up on trying to fracture her.

"We're asking for special permits to keep harvesting for two years. Once we're legal, anyone can come in and observe the operation. If anyone can show we are doing harm, we'll stop after that two-year period. If not, then open the forest, let people in to see for themselves what all of us have sacrificed to create."

"President Escalante saw your operation and is opposed to it. How can you hope to make a case to get harvesting permits?"

"Escalante isn't an impartial judge of what we're doing. He's spent his career evicting people and making sure they don't get into the preserves. Besides, EcoTech makes all his decisions for him. Of course he's going to be against giving us permits."

The interview continued with questions about what life in the jungle was like. Even if Jasmine had suddenly become a dull interview because she couldn't be goaded into anger, what she'd been able to say in those five minutes had put her a huge distance ahead.

*   *   *   *   *

Edan didn't hide his surprise when he turned on his screen and saw Shelly VanDaal smiling at him.

"Mr. Loffler, I'm a fan of your work."

The concert promos had only gone out that morning. Had she seen them already?

"Thanks," he replied. "But that can't be why you're calling."

"No, it's not. I'm calling to warn you. You realize that what Jasmine Rochelle and her gang are doing is against the law?"

He shrugged.

"Mr. Loffler, I suggest you call your lawyer immediately. Perhaps a lawyer can convince you that holding a concert in support of an illegal act can get you and your entire crew arrested."

* * * * *

After half an hour with his lawyer, Edan called Selina. "Pull the promos back in," he said. "They have to be rewritten." He told her what VanDaal and the lawyer had said.

"Are we going to cancel?"

"No." He'd found a fabulous new world to explore and already had two songs written. "I can't be arrested for using the forest as a theme and where the money goes after the concert is no one's concern either. As long as I don't mention Jasmine or her camp, or harvesting Green, we'll be fine." But it wouldn't be the same. He'd imagined starting a public outcry in support of Green harvesting and if it were only him risking extinction, he'd still do it, but he had his crew to think of.

✶ ✶ F O R T Y - F I V E ✶ ✶

In front of the mirror, Edan set his elbows on the dressing room counter. He watched himself put his chin in his hands and closed his eyes. Two hours—in just two short hours the show would begin. The whole concert felt rushed. He took a few deep breaths and cleared his mind of worry. His preparations for the show had to be the only thing now.

He opened his eyes. A hooded man was reaching for him. Edan dropped to the floor and rolled. He heard someone set the lock on the door. Another hooded man cranked up the music. As Edan stood and turned, he was pinned against the first man's chest and the other was about to take a swing at him. Edan straightened his arms and dropped, but the hold couldn't be broken. He only succeeded in ducking the punch. He gave his captor's shin a vicious kick and escaped the loosened grasp. Someone was knocking at the door. Edan's answering yell was lost in the booming music. He backed up towards the mirror, then when the two were almost on him, he ducked and rolled and lunged for the door. His hand was on the handle but they pulled him back. The punch connected this time and sent him reeling, clutching his side. He had to get to the door. Twice he dodged being pinned and twice the other man blocked his escape. Then they had him again. The noise outside grew louder as the shorter man landed another punch.

The door splintered.

Edan was pulled out of the room into the backstage area. The stage crew stood transfixed. His rescuers backed out of the dressing room. The hooded men held guns. Where would these dogs get guns from? Rico and Max backed up further than they needed to and stood blocking a clear shot to Edan.

"Wait—" Edan said and moved to step aside. The guns were trained on him, then it seemed a dozen crew members tackled the men. Gunfire cracked through the air. Edan was pushed down. He could no longer see, but screams and more gunfire filled the air, then finally the sound of two men running. Edan struggled to get out from under Candy Nelson. She lay wide-eyed in shock, blood oozing from her shoulder. He wadded up her shirt and pressed down on the wound. He'd seen the technique work on knife wounds. He tried to convince her she would be fine as he held the red sodden fabric against her for what seemed like an hour before a woman in paramedic gear told him she would take over.

"Is anyone . . . um . . . " he stammered.

"Nobody is dead yet," she answered.

He stood, unsteady. Selina found him just as the stage manager did.

"Are you all right?" she asked.

"Could have been worse. They forgot I was a Core Rat."

The stage manager surveyed the damage. "I'll make the announcement," he said.

"No," Edan shook Selina off. "Technical difficulties—announce a delay, that's all."

Edan finally lost his balance and fell into the wall behind him. The stage manager rushed to his side.

"But you're—"

"Do you want me to do this show without you?"

"No, but—"

Edan looked to Selina. "Find out who needs replacing and do it." He struggled to stand again. The hand he'd put on his leg came up red. No one had noticed fresh blood against the black of his pants. "And find me a doctor. Guess I sorta got shot."

∗   ∗   ∗   ∗   ∗

Selina checked Edan's harness again. "Are you sure—"

"Stop fussing! I need you in the FX booth."

Selina frowned at him then turned and left.

His leg was stiff from both the swelling and the bandages. He fought against the numbing effect of the painkillers. He'd only taken half the dose—he needed a clear head more than he needed a painless leg.

Edan gave the signal and the rope carried him up . . . up the six stories to the top of the set. It was hard to believe that even the twenty-four-meter-high jungle they had created here was on the small side compared to the real thing.

The cries of jungle creatures came sporadically from the foliage, louder and more insistent until the audience began to hush and the lights came up to reveal the trees around him. Chainsaws roared and the animals were silenced. The lights grew dim again and bled out entirely.

Edan checked his harness connection. He'd agreed to some changes in the opening. At first he was to have climbed up, now he was to be lowered. The lights came up again and animals once again made themselves heard with grunts, and birds with voices that sounded like the plucking of strings on exotic instruments. He waved as he was lowered beneath the foliage that hid him before and the audience cheered as they saw him descend while a drum solo started. Chanel had helped him compose the drum piece and the beats grew louder the lower he came. As he landed, the drum beats faded into the music that slowly came up from behind him.

"Listen," he said in a stage whisper amplified by his microphone, then sang, "The forest sings our birth." He dropped the blue robe and instantly blended into the background, hidden by the forest greens he wore. He continued singing as the music came into full chorus. He climbed between verses and every time he was ready to start up again, he lifted his arms to reveal the bright red folds of fabric beneath his arms and the crowd cheered each time they spotted him again amongst the foliage.

"My forest sings of wonders," he continued.

He spent the next few songs letting the cloth and paper forest be his backdrop. He never made it as far as the upper platforms. He would have been too winded to sing.

At the end of the set he ran to the stage front. Blinded by the lights, he could feel the audience, excited, cheering, baffled because this wasn't his usual street opera. Edan took another bow and ran off stage where he promptly crumpled to the floor.

Two of the crew carried him to his dressing room, while Selina issued orders to the stage crew. Fluids were forced on him and then Selina was helping him into his next costume. He had fifteen minutes while drummers recreated ancient rhythms and dancers in fake feathers and furs performed acrobatics in the jungle.

His fans must be wondering if he'd gone insane. "Any word from the hospital?" he asked when his mind cleared.

Selina looked at him and he knew she wanted to tell him to stop, to go to the hospital himself . . . but she didn't and he loved her all the more for it.

"They are all going to be all right."

Five of his crew hurt after he'd agreed not to mention Jasmine, Lightning Madness or Green Harvesting. Someone had sent gun-dogs to stop the show.

Just as the drummers moved off stage, Edan bounded back on. The forest stood in darkness behind him and now a four-story holoprojection of him stood to his left. The band waited, spot-lit behind him.

"This is the first time you'll have heard this song," he said. "I wrote it because we all have someone in our lives who we want to protect from life's pain." A soft, sad melody drifted into the audience.

Won't you let me fight your demons,
    and do battle with your fears.

And he sang the words he'd written but saw Selina's face right to the end.

Each fight I fought, I could have won
    now you lie dying.
What has my fighting done?

The music continued, sad and slow, then Edan hung his head as the music died to the sound of cheers and applause. He raised his head and marched to the edge of the stage. "Are you weeping?"

They cheered more loudly at his signature line and he smiled.

"This next one is the first song I wrote that mattered. Synced me with my muse." He smiled for Jasmine as the music started, a strong anthem. It seemed a lifetime ago that he and Jasmine worked together to give the music the rough and angry edge it needed.

Will you stop for no one,
    your dreams are much too real?
Will you stop for everyone,
    obey them as you kneel?
Will you be the driven?
Will you be the scattered?
Will you be the chosen one,
    standing proud though battered?

It had been so long since he'd sung it for an audience, the words seemed to have a new power. As he sang, he listened and the audience disappeared. These were his words. Had he stopped believing them?

A battle hymn swelled with the next verse.

I found them out, the evils there,
  stood righteous to the bone.
I tore them all asunder,
I found myself alone.

The music softened.

So I followed those around me,
  was taken with their passion.
I followed and I stood with them,
  following the fashion.

The anthem began again.

Will you stop for no one,
  your dreams are much too real? . . .

He let the chorus go on without him. The audience filled in the familiar words and told him what to do. It was all about choice.

My vision faltered as we went,
  the horde stood in my way.
I cried for help but no one there
  could catch us as we strayed.
I could have been the driven one,
  lost sight of what was real.
I could have been the chosen one,
  but now in guilt I kneel.

The anthem faded into a sad hymn.

My children ask if I was there,
did I also stand in line?
Yes, I'm an old and broken man,
though it took the longest time.
I am an old and broken man,
though it took the longest time.

Edan bowed to the applause then walked to the front of the stage and looked up at the booth. "Give me the house," he said. Lights flooded the audience and the applause slowly faded. "I sang that song for Jasmine Rochelle," he announced. "She and her crew are working in heat, rain and insect swarms to bring us medicines like Veejix. They have had to battle EcoTech and Emerald Warriors to do it. People all over the world should be free to walk into a forest and say, this is ours. These forests belong to the people who gave up their land for the preserves, to the people who live in boxes in the cities because it's the only place they can find, to the people whose tax money paid for the research, paid for the warriors and the razor wire, to the people who need the medicines we can harvest there."

The audience started tentative applause that slowly swept the thirty thousand seats.

"You may have noticed a few effects didn't come off quite right tonight. Some of the sound mix was off. That's because we are missing a few friends who almost died because someone wanted that badly to stop this performance. They are in the hospital now. Alan Ross, stunt coordinator; Sheila Murdock, chief mixer; Nell Kosak, lights; Max Dermont, visuals; Candy Nelson, lights. Will you send them your best wishes?" he asked, his voice suddenly gone. The sound system had been disabled. Nevertheless, the audience cheered.

Edan concentrated on the first few rows. "What do we say to EcoTech? Let us in!" Stamp-stamp-clap, he started and a wave of chanting began at the stage and made its way back, replacing applause with a rhythmic demand. "Let us in."

Edan smiled. This was the right choice. Then darkness advanced on him as the lights over the audience went out until he stood in a shroud of black on the stage. The crowd kept chanting, thinking the darkness was part of the show. Lights flickered around him. Hands and familiar voices pulled him back. What had happened to the emergency lights? Then he was pulled into a stumbling run back-stage with them. He hesitated when the rhythm stopped and yelling began but insistent hands pulled him along. "Somebody get those lights on!" he shouted into the black.

Miguel stared transfixed at the blank screen. "There's still no sign of power," the announcer said. "And without lights it's impossible to tell why so many in the crowd are screaming. All the exits are still locked. Emergency lights should have come on long ago."

This was getting worse and worse. They should have just let Loffler be.

Simon came in.

"What happened here?" Miguel pointed to the screen. "I asked that Loffler be stopped, not shot at."

Simon shook his head, "That wasn't us. Shelly and I decided to use lawyers, not gunmen."

"Who was it?"

"I'd guess Green Splinter because they seem to be behind everything."

"How are they getting their information?"

"Watenabe's reports would—"

Movement on the screen made Miguel silence him.

"With the stadium lights operational now, everyone is anxious to find out what happened." Cameras panned ambulances and the police trying to control the exit of the crowds.

Loffler's concert had at least exposed his affiliation with Jasmine Rochelle. By having a benefit for her, he could be charged with supporting a criminal act.

"Edan Loffler and most of his crew seem to have been able to exit the stadium." The reporter walked over to a group of people huddled around someone as they watched the stadium empty. They parted as he approached to reveal Edan Loffler. He looked fractured but regained composure as the camera approached.

"Mr. Loffler, can you tell us how this happened?"

"Hard to figure. We were attacked before the show. Whoever was responsible probably managed to sneak backstage during the chaos of the shooting, then sabotaged the concert."

"So the blackout wasn't staged?"

Loffler winced. "The count so far is that sixteen people have been seriously hurt from when the panic started," he said softly. "My technicians stayed backstage to restore power, possibly while the attackers were still there. What do you think?" he asked, his voice never raised.

The reporter hesitated. "Who do you think is responsible?"

"So many groups have an interest in the preserves. EcoTech, Green Splinter, the EC. We may never know, but we can make sure it doesn't happen again."

"How?"

"The people's voice. Let the people decide if the preserves should be opened. Let them hear what Jasmine Rochelle has to say."

"There are rumors that this concert was initially conceived to be a benefit for her Jungle Haven."

Loffler smiled sheepishly. "I have to admit, that would have been my first choice, but I don't want to spend our fan's money on something illegal. The money we made today will open a new foundation for the Repatriation of the Rain Forest. In two weeks we will release the Jungle Haven discs. Proceeds from sales will go to the foundation."

"You said you were attacked before the show."

Fatigue settled on Loffler's face. A weak smile made him look entirely fractured. "That's all I have time for," he said, gave a small wave to the camera and turned. Friends on either side of him supported him as he sank and helped him walk away. The camera caught a patch of bright red blooming on his leg.

"Mr. Loffler, were you hurt?"

Several of Loffler's stage crew, pleasant but immovable, blocked the cameras.

Miguel didn't hear the rest.

"That crafty little bastard. I've seen romance vids with less melodrama. Get me Ortega." This had gone far enough. Rochelle and her gang were breaking the law and they had to be made examples of or the preserves would be overrun with people after today. Following the beacon, the Warriors could walk into camp and take everyone into custody.

"Miguel." Simon hadn't gotten up. "Be very careful what you decide. Maybe that crowd was cheering out of group frenzy, but I don't think either of us believe that. People want into the preserves. If you open them, the EC remains the guardian. If we fight this, we may loose more than the safety of the preserves."

"I won't be coerced by a bunch of educated Core Rats."

"They may be the least of your problems."

Miguel stared at him.

"I spoke to Watenabe today. She's been looking into the Green Splinter connection. They're responsible for Owen Lamberin's murder, of course, and destroying Dr. Lamberin's lab, but they don't have the human resources to have done the research needed. Watenabe is very close to proving EcoTech has been helping them."

"Why? They shouldn't need to resort to terrorism. They're protected by law."

"They're desperate to keep people out. Apparently, so desperate that the laws aren't enough."

Aberrations—maybe they were hiding aberrations. Could Jasmine have been right? If she was, the EC's dream really was hollow and if people found out, there would be no hope left. No way to recreate the world their great, great grandparents lost.

She had to be wrong.

He needed time—time for EcoTech to fix this. Because if EcoTech fell, the EC could follow.

"What is it?" Simon asked.

"Get me Ortega."

Simon waited, perhaps to be sure . . . then, with eyes that held more sadness than Miguel had ever seen in them, Simon left to call Ortega.

Simon reappeared. "Ortega is busy. It seems he received a tip about the location of some poachers."

"Get Shelly."

Ortega hadn't known Miguel took a beacon with him. But if he somehow knew now, it was a simple matter of tracing inventory. He had the security clearance to ask for the activation code.

"Hello, Miguel." Shelly was in the EcoTech jet.

"He's found Rochelle's camp, hasn't he?"

"What do you mean?"

"I'm going out there."

"Don't! They'll shoot anyone they see." Her concern melted into a guarded expression as soon as she said the words. They stared at each other for a moment, broken trust hanging heavy between them.

"I've got to save this," he finally said and broke the link.

If more people died, it would only make his position worse. His presence could very well ensure Rochelle and her gang were captured, not killed and that would end it.

"I've got to save this," he repeated to Simon this time who silently nodded, preoccupied with his own thoughts.

✴ ✴ F O R T Y - S E V E N ✴ ✴

"What is it?" Jasmine asked, shining the light into Mane's hand. The small metal disc reflected light back at her.

"A beacon," Mane replied.

"Escalente."

Levi leaned over Mane's shoulder for a look. "Bloody brilliant. We're dead."

Mane turned it over to expose a tiny switch.

"What if we destroy it?" Jasmine asked.

Mane shook his head. "Already transmitted our location, but just for a few seconds. Right now they're wondering if they even got into contact. They'll come here if they don't get a stronger signal from somewhere else."

The crew huddled around Mane in silence in the dimly lit shed.

"When the broadcast site was hit," Dustin said, "it took them twelve hours from picking up the signal to attack."

"That's only because they waited for daylight," Jasmine said. "They'll hit in the morning. That gives us four hours. We got any cameras to spare?" she asked Dustin.

"Yeah."

"Then let's go."

In minutes Jasmine and Dustin had mounted the bush buggy. They could have moved as quickly without it but this way they didn't exhaust themselves. Dustin held the flashlight over her shoulder while she drove. The jungle around them was black and formless, except for the small patch of it that was lit in front of them. It was as if they were standing still with the forest moving around them and bumping underneath them every so often. Once she got used to the motion, her thoughts went to Escalente. Eating and drinking with them, drumming with them—practically speechless with wonder when he came down from his climb. He had pretended to consider the compromises she offered just to come here and destroy everything.

$$* \quad * \quad * \quad * \quad *$$

Though it had been light outside for an hour, Jasmine and her crew sat in darkness underground in the cramped cave beneath the ruins lit only by the console screen.

"There it is again." Levi pointed to a corner of the screen. Jasmine and Dustin had taken the beacon as far as they could and set up a camera with microphone. A warrior walked into camera range, searched the ground for a moment, then held up the beacon.

"Found it," he said then looked around. "They must have moved on."

"This isn't it," said a vaguely familiar voice. Miguel Escalente walked into view. "This isn't where I dropped it. They live over a field of rubble large enough to have been a small city."

"Miraflores," an older man in uniform walked up to him. He looked like the Generals in the old war vids, more by the way he moved than because of what he wore. The General pointed to his pad. "We can be there in one hour."

Indra groaned and the rest of the crew stared at the screen in silence. Stark fear crept onto their faces. If only Escalente hadn't shown up they could have hidden through this raid like they'd hidden through the others. Escalente had declared war on them—on Jasmine's crew.

"They *can* make it here in one hour," Mane said but no one moved.

Jasmine blinked once then was with him. "We have to wipe all the consoles and bury anything we want to keep." She stood. The crew remained frozen. "One hour! That's all we've got!"

"They'll scorch it, won't they?" Dustin's eyes were wide. Like everyone, he was remembering Arri.

"No," she replied, not believing it. She looked around at the people who had come here with her. "No! They won't."

Indra shook off her daze and gestured towards Levi. "We'll get supplies down here."

"I'll purge the consoles," Mane said.

Jasmine glanced at Dustin. "And we need to adjust the security cameras."

*   *   *   *   *

Jasmine and her crew watched the screen in silence as the Warriors picked their way to the shed following Escalente's directions. Dustin was right. They'd torch it. Eventually they'd find everything and torch it.

Dustin and Jasmine had set the cameras to show as much of their camp as possible. Warriors disappeared and reappeared between rocks and trees though the trees didn't grow as closely spaced in the rubble as they did in the surrounding forest.

One of the Warriors went inside the shed and came out with a small bale of dried leaves that he shook out and scattered on the ground. Months of work had gone into gathering the harvest that had accumulated in the shed.

She wouldn't lose everything again.

"That's it." Jasmine stood, seething.

"What are you doing?" Indra asked.

"I'm going to stop them."

"They'll kill you," Dustin said.

"They are not going to destroy everything we built here. I won't allow it."

"I'm going with you," Mane stood beside her.

"No—"

"I stand beside you. That's never changed and it won't change today."

The rightness of that prevented any more protest, but his show of loyalty almost brought her to tears. She shook the emotion off and turned to the rest. "No matter what happens," Jasmine paused to survey their faces, "and I mean no matter what, stay here. They won't find you."

She waited for the Warriors to turn away from the direction of the secret cave then crawled into the light. Jasmine and Mane moved low between the boulders, hidden from sight until they were closer to the shed.

"Hey! You break it—you pay for it!"

Her words were greeted by gunfire and something struck her shirt as she dropped to the ground protected now by the boulders around her.

"You okay?" she asked Mane.

"Yeah, you?"

"They shot a hole through my shirt," she answered with disgust.

"Stand up!" Escalente shouted at them. "We will not shoot again. We don't want anyone hurt." Then he muttered at the gunmen. "I mean it. Capture, don't kill."

Jasmine got up and Mane stood beside her. Escalente and the armed Warrior picked their way towards them.

Jasmine glanced at the shed. A warrior shook out another bale of leaves.

"Stop it!" she yelled. "You want the whole world to watch you destroy kilos of Veejix?"

That caused some confusion. "Turn on NewsPort," she suggested. Dustin had started sending live feed from the security cameras as soon as the Warriors set the perimeter alarms off. It didn't matter now if the whole world knew where they were. Now the cameras were their only weapon.

As Escalente came into easy speaking distance, Jasmine tensed. His eyes locked onto hers with his final steps, fierce and dangerous.

"You are done here," he said.

"How many cameras?" the General asked.

Mane shrugged. "Two." There were five.

Jasmine found herself mesmerized by the anger in Escalente's eyes.

"Where's the rest of your gang?" the General continued.

"You won't find them," Mane answered. "They scattered into the jungle when we heard the alarms last night." He sighed. "It's so hard to get loyal help."

The General took a threatening step towards him, then stopped—the cameras doing their job.

Warriors had moved to either side of Jasmine and Mane, ready with restraints.

"No," Escalente said, probably thinking of all the people watching him. "We don't need those. We have a perimeter presence. They can't get out. We just need two guards."

The General seemed angry at his orders being contradicted but then, when Escalente couldn't see, a small, sly smile crossed his face. He shrugged and turned to his Warriors. "Get those bales ready to ship out."

A perimeter, he'd said. They had brought enough warriors to surround the entire rubble field.

Rain splattered onto leaves in the upper canopy and thunder rumbled in the distance. Escalente wandered off. Jasmine and Mane sat on the moss-cushioned boulders.

Mane's idea to set up camp here was a good one. Normally the Warriors had become so frustrated at trying to find a path through the boulders that they gave up. The Warriors now were becoming short-tempered. They stumbled every few steps trying to find more of the camp and attempting to reach the spots Escalente pointed out.

Escalente had the Warriors looking into the trees for their homes. The crew had dropped the cables so even if the Warriors found all four houses, it would take a while to get up to them. It was a good thing they had never shown Escalente the underground storage. At least the rest of the crew were safe.

A rain began and created the white noise of drops hitting leaves. The two guards were called away. Escalente moved out on his own, arrogant and unapologetic. As if he weren't about to evict her crew from their homes, as if he weren't responsible for Edan being hurt, for Trina's ordeal, for Arri's death, for her father's death. Her foot hit a rock and she stumbled, not realizing she had even gotten up. Mane stood right behind her. The cameras had some blind spots and the noise of the rain now made it more difficult to be heard. It had become a downpour. She could barely make out Escalente's blue shirt between the trees and the rain. She and Mane began to herd him into a blind spot. Thunder shook the forest. At one point Jasmine was certain the General had spotted her but he turned away and continued supervising the Warrior's ascent into her home. With the mental image of the General's thugs going through her things she moved faster.

"Hey!" Escalente finally called as he realized how close they had gotten to him. His call was drowned in the rain.

Out of camera range now, Jasmine pulled the knife from her boot. Escalente stood his ground. Mane was behind her and his calm washed over her. Jasmine wiped the rain out of her eyes.

"It was you," she said. "Somebody has been paying Green Splinter to take credit for their dirty work. Somebody with the same goals. Somebody who wanted my father dead."

"That wasn't me."

"Green Splinter is a scattered flock of fanatics. Their biggest trick is scaring people. They couldn't have stalled a police investigation. They couldn't have covered up Arri's cause of death."

"Maybe not, but it wasn't the EC."

"There *is* no one else."

"There's EcoTech."

"The EC would never give them that much power. Don't try to squirm out of this."

He glanced at the knife she held by her side and worry planted itself on his features. "Look, when we're finished here, my staff will listen to all your allegations. There may be enough evidence for an investigation."

"EC staff is going to investigate itself? You've gone extinction. You had Edan and his crew shot, locked thousands of people into a black room, destroyed Adrien's lab. You're not going to investigate—"

"That wasn't us."

"Shut up!" She took a step towards him, surprised that the rage that gave her power hadn't come. Fear flickered for a second on Escalente's face and the life bled out of Jasmine's arms. The knife dropped from her hand. She turned to Mane for an explanation for what was happening. Mane put a hand on her shoulder and stepped beside her to face Escalente. Jasmine struggled to decide what to do. The rain eased.

"You can't hide behind Green Splinter forever," Mane softly said. "Doesn't matter if some of it was EcoTech's idea, *you're* responsible."

Any fear Escalente had shown was replaced by anger for now he understood they wouldn't hurt him. "Hey!" he shouted again, his voice reverberating now that the rain had stopped. Jasmine ducked to retrieve her knife but before they could move away, one of the Warriors appeared, weapon ready.

"Keep them here," Escalente ordered, his voice a growl. "And give me your com set." He waited to catch Jasmine's eye and looking hard at her spoke into the radio. "Shoot out the cameras. There have to be at least five of them. Then torch it all. Every scrap of it."

"You crazy glitch." She took a step towards him. His hand flashed out and stuck her in the face—hard.

"Don't ever threaten me," Escalante spat at her. Then he turned to the Warriors restraining Mane. "She's got a knife."

The knife was wrenched from her hand as Jasmine stood staring at him.

Gunfire cracked and echoed through the trees.

"That's the first two," a voice crackled from the radio in Escalente's hand. This was it. She had gambled everything on Escalente caring more about his image than his desire to destroy the camp. She looked at Mane. After the cameras were gone, the Warriors would be free to act. They would destroy all evidence of what she had accomplished here then she and Mane would be next.

More gunfire. Escalente smiled at her. "That's three and four down." He chuckled and peered into the trees towards the shooting.

Jasmine whispered to Mane, "I won't be executed." He nodded. An instant later, he kicked out at the Warrior beside him. The man went down with a yelp but fired at them as they ran. By that time they were dodging boulders and running for clear ground with only a ring of warriors standing between them and freedom.

Mane stopped short and they both dropped. A pair of Warriors ahead searched for them and moved towards them from the left. Jasmine followed Mane towards the right, working his way to the edge of the boulders. They'd got by them but were spotted as they made for the trees. They were fired on and Jasmine froze with her hands out. Mane went down.

As soon as the warriors were near enough, Mane leapt up, grabbed the man's gun and swung him into the tree trunk. Jasmine tackled the warrior beside her, keeping him too busy to aim his gun until Mane grabbed him and hit him in the face.

Mane's arm was bleeding but it didn't slow him down. They grabbed the warriors' guns and ran a few steps when Mane was hit by gunfire so hard it knocked him off his feet. Blood bloomed on his chest.

At least six armed Warriors appeared around them and all Jasmine could do was drop the gun and stare at Mane. She took a step and a punch in the face knocked her to the ground.

"Mane," she called and got up. He didn't move. Another punch doubled her over, breathless and gasping for what seemed like forever.

Mane lay helpless.

She staggered up again. A strike to her leg sent pain shivering through her and she went down once more.

"That's enough!" someone said.

Jasmine struggled to stand, determined to make it to Mane. This time she was pulled up and held in a painful grip.

"Oh, my God," Escalente said as he saw Mane.

"It's not so clean when you actually hold someone's death in your hands, is it?" she hurled at him.

Escalente turned away, his expression impossible to read.

The man holding her twisted and she gasped at the pain in her arms.

"Don't you look away," she called to Escalente. "I want you watching when they do me."

"We are not going to execute you," Escalente said as if he actually meant it.

"Where have you been for the last hour?" she asked. "I saw Arri Deckert die. That's what Warriors are trained to do. If they're so compassionate, why aren't they helping him?"

His vision seemed to clear. "Get a medic. Get one *now!* You! Put some pressure on those wounds."

A whump sounded through the trees as a flamethrower was lit. It didn't matter now. Mane lay dying. She tried to believe Escalente; that they really would help Mane, that he hadn't followed her into the jungle to die.

"We found your crew," Escalente said, his voice flat.

"More deaths to add to your list."

He scowled at her then and shouted into his radio. "Nobody gets hurt!" But his voice was pitched high with panic. He was losing control of the Warriors. The General had smiled when Escalente refused to have her and Mane restrained. He had called the guards away and ignored Jasmine and Mane when they went after Escalente. He'd wanted them to try to escape or to attack Escalente. She and Mane had obliged him and done both. Without the cameras he could shoot all of them and claim they were trying to escape.

"Jas!" a voice called from another world. She looked around to see if anyone else heard it.

"Jas!" he called again.

"Over here," she answered still unsure if the voice was real.

"I'm coming," Adrien shouted back.

This time everyone looked in the direction of the voice. After a moment, Adrien hurried into view. He ignored the guns trained on him and took a step towards her.

"I'm fine but Mane . . . He's been shot." She nodded towards him.

"I'm a doctor," Adrien said with a voice that demanded to be let through, and he was.

Escalente stared wide-eyed at the woman who followed Adrien. She swung her camera over the scene. A NewsPort press tag hung from her neck. As she turned towards him, he regained his composure and spoke into the radio.

"Continue extinguishing fires," he said. "Oh, and let the camera-hand from NewsPort take any vids she requires," he added as warning.

Adrien instructed the Warriors beside Mane, then, still on one knee, turned to Escalente, "Hey!" he shouted. "Get a chopper with a cradle down here."

Escalente stared at him, not accustomed to taking orders.

"Now!" Adrien said before turning back to Mane. Jasmine couldn't see what he was doing.

Escalente ordered the chopper.

"How'd they get in here?" The general had found them. Escalente gave him a look that shut him up and set him to pacing.

After what seemed like an eternity, Adrien stood again and walked over to her. The Warrior holding her finally let go and she fell into Adrien. "How bad is it?" she asked as he steadied her.

"Not as bad as it looks. Missed the heart. Punctured the lung. He's lost a lot of blood. I've got him hooked up to the plasma I brought with me."

"How did you know to bring . . . to come here?"

"We've got friends in some very strange places."

"They found the crew."

"I know. They're all fine. Dustin told me where to find you."

"I should—"

"No, you don't need to do anything else. The rest of this is my fight."

Chopper blades fluttered above them and Adrien let her go only to catch her again when her legs wouldn't take her weight. "Stupid glitch almost broke my leg."

"There's your chopper," Escalente said. "Get her back in restraints."

"No," Adrien said. "She's coming with us."

"She's under arrest."

"That may be, but your dogs have done enough damage. She can't even walk. I'm taking them both to Bogota. You can arrest her there."

Escalente glared at him with the NewsPort camera looking on. "I'll do that," he replied.

The cradle came down through the trees and Mane was lifted and strapped in.

A harness for two came down once he was inside. Adrien helped Jasmine into it taking most of her weight. Just before they were lifted, Adrien swung around to face Escalente.

"You are a dead man," he said. "Maybe not today, but you won't survive what's happened here."

The harness was pulled up and they rode the cable through the trees. As they rose, Escalente and the warriors became hidden by foliage.

Once inside the chopper, Jasmine turned her attention to Mane. It was her first good look at him. Adrien peeled off what was left of Mane's blood-soaked shirt and checked again for other wounds.

She caught her breath at the pain in her leg as she sat beside him. With the adrenalin fading, she felt every bruise. Her left eye was so swollen now, she could barely see through it. She took Mane's hand.

"Hold on," she said. "We've still got a lot of work to do. And I can't do it without you."

His eyes opened and he looked at her for a moment, then whispered through the mask. "The crew."

"Everyone is safe, so is the camp." She looked up at Adrien. "How did that happen?"

"I got a tip that an attack was coming. I tried to call you but you'd shut down so I called NewsPort to see if they had heard anything. I convinced Martinez that this was worth sending a reporter out for. We headed to Bogota and figured you were in Columbia somewhere. Once you started broadcasting, we traced the signal."

He looked back at Mane. "You'll be fine, my friend," he said though Mane's eyes had closed again. "A collapsed lung is all. Just keep breathing."

"Is he still bleeding?"

"Internally, yes. We need to get him into surgery soon."

They both watched Mane's chest rise and fall. Adrien took his pulse again then squirmed forward.

"If you can make this thing go any faster, do it," he said. When he returned to his spot beside Mane, he eyed the almost empty bag of plasma. "It's bleeding through as fast as I can pump it in. Once that bag's empty, he'll go into shock."

The plasma bag emptied ten minutes before they landed. A dullness had crept over Jasmine as Adrien took charge and ordered the waiting medical team to get Mane on another unit of plasma, and, although every order he gave was relayed to Escalente for approval, every thing he asked for was provided.

The trip to the hospital was a blur until Mane was wrenched from Jasmine and she was left alone. After that, she just felt dead. Faceless people wheeled her to different rooms for different readings. A buzz of crisply dressed medical staff took fluids for testing, examined, poked and asked questions. Jasmine did as she was told, answered what was asked, saw very little and remembered even less, except the image of Mane, helpless and bloody.

None of what they had done together was worth losing him.

* * * * *

"Hey, Jas." The words drifted in and Jasmine struggled to waken. She sat up and Adrien smiled at her.

"He's going to be okay. They got the bleeding stopped in time," he said, then squinted at her. "Are you there?"

"He's going to be okay?" Her voice trembled. "Oh." And her whole body shook. She reached for Adrien and held him while she cried for no specific reason she could figure. It was a way she could react to what had happened, though what function this served, she didn't know.

And when no more tears came, Adrien held her until she exhausted herself from dry sobs.

She must look a mess. "Sorry, I don't know what happened."

"Relief," he said while bringing her some tissues. "How's the leg?"

Her leg? "I don't know. Um . . . I think somebody said it wasn't broken."

Adrien checked the temperature sleeve that enveloped her leg. Slow waves of alternating temperatures were supposed to take down the swelling. Hot—cold—hot—cold. It really didn't matter.

"They're treating you for deep bruising." He took a close look at her face. The hospital people had done something to take the swelling down around her eye.

Adrien sat in the chair and leaned back. "I'll try to get Mane transferred into your room," he said. And he would do it too. Adrien, who hated causing trouble, who always wanted to do what was expected, who had given the president orders and demanded they be carried out.

Somehow, tears welled again, but Jasmine smiled. "Did I hear you call Escalente a dead man?"

Adrien shrugged.

"On international broadcast?"

She shook her head. "If only Dad could have seen that."

Adrien grinned at the thought. "Yeah."

"Did Dad ever get arrested?"

"No. He left that to you," he said without sarcasm. "But I think he'd be proud of you for this one."

* * * * *

Jasmine started awake and immediately looked for Mane. He lay on his bed, still connected to a variety of machines. Adrien had been escorted back home. Not under arrest, but certainly under watch. True to his word, he'd been able to convince the hospital and the Emerald Warriors who guarded her that putting her and Mane in the same room would be less trouble for them all.

She stood on her good leg and reached for a crutch then hobbled over to Mane to be certain he was not in danger. If Adrien hadn't come with plasma . . . Tears flowed again. She placed a hand on Mane's, careful to avoid tubes and wires. She'd almost lost him but for a few centimeters . . . a sob caught in her throat. If Adrien hadn't come she might have lost them all. Five people could have lost their lives for her dream. If Adrien hadn't . . . she had to stop replaying it. She pulled a chair over so she could sit within reach of Mane and turned on the vid screen. She tuned in to a mystery vid and paid just enough attention to prevent her from thinking. Several hours later, the crime had been solved, and justice dispensed to the guilty. Jasmine continued to stare at the screen as NewsPort came on broadcasting again the details she was trying to forget. She didn't have the energy to turn it off.

"Now a re-broadcast of the return of three of Jasmine Rochelle's jungle crew."

Indra, Dustin and Levi emerged from a small plane. Then a closeup of Indra. "None of us is prepared to make a statement. Jasmine Rochelle is our spokesperson. I suggest you speak with her."

Jasmine had been as puzzled as the reporter by Indra's response.

"Jasmine Rochelle and Mane Silverstar are apparently still in a hospital in Bogota, but attempts to reach them have been unsuccessful."

That was it! Indra wanted to be sure the media didn't forget her and Mane. She wanted to be sure the media attention kept them safe. If Indra and the rest of the crew wouldn't talk, NewsPort would be looking for Jasmine. Jasmine started to cry again.

When her eyes cleared, NewsPort was doing another interview. Matt Scarpulla had found the missing researchers.

"When Trina Josell challenged us to investigate the old harvesting site, we did," said the older man in the jungle hat. "The camp and processing lab were burned so the only investigation we did there was to sample soil and ground water. We found traces of solvents in both but that can be attributed to the fire. We searched the wreckage and found the lab had been equipped with fermenters."

"What about the harvesting?" Scarpulla asked. "How much vegetation had been taken out?"

"Hardly anything, actually. We had to do a second sweep before we realized we weren't looking for trees cut down or stripped. We had to look for gaps in the epiphyte cover, bushes that looked pruned—that sort of thing."

Jasmine couldn't believe it. She kept checking her watch and sure enough, NewsPort was spending at least an hour on preserve harvesting. This wasn't just her fight any more.

"Oh . . . and we found bullets in the soil, which we thought was odd."

"Is it true you are applying for permission to study the new site, Jasmine Rochelle's 'Jungle Haven'?"

"Yes, and if we can have access to Trina Josell's records, that would make our work even more valuable. Edan Loffler's foundation has been very helpful with—"

Edan. He was involved, too. So many people were fighting for her dream now, but what did she really have left? Mane and her crew were safe and the camp wasn't destroyed, but they could never go back. The poaching charges alone could keep them tangled in the courts for months and if Escalente got his way, they'd all be in jail for the next few years. He seemed determined to keep people away from the preserves and to hide EC and EcoTech's dirty secrets. It would be a long fight for anyone to get harvesting permits now.

"Jashm . . . ?"

She almost fell getting up. "Mane?"

He smiled at her. It was the first time he'd woken with any clarity in his eyes. "What's new?"

"We're under arrest." She laughed, delighted.

"Nice cell." He drifted off again.

Jasmine held his hand and wept.

*   *   *   *   *

Despite the turbulence, Jasmine got up to stretch her legs and check on Mane. Several rows of seats had been removed from the small plane to make room for his cot. After two days in the hospital, Jasmine and Adrien could no longer convince either the doctors at Bogota or the Emerald Warriors that her injuries were serious enough to keep her hospitalized. They were sending Mane to a hospital back home. Going to jail didn't bother her nearly as much as the thought of leaving him. But then, back home Trina could get in to see him without breaking the terms of her release.

Security people were suddenly in a flutter. She checked her watch. They should be landing in minutes.

"Hey," she said softly and his eyes opened. "Trina's waiting at the hospital."

He grinned back at her.

"I'm so sorry I got you into this. I almost lost you."

"Hey, doll. You saved my life—you gave me a life I want to live."

Security people tugged at her.

"Soon," she said as Mane was wheeled into the waiting ambulance.

She was led through corridors and back ways she had never seen before. Her crutch slowed her down, but eventually she and her security swarm came to a public area. They entered into a crush of people. It took Jasmine a moment to notice they all focused on her. The security people pushed through the snarl of cameras and microphones, but when

Jasmine came to the top of the escalator, a sound stopped her cold. Applause. A sea of people looked up at her and cheered. One of her escorts tried to move her to the steps but Jasmine stood her ground, several microphones now pointed to her.

"Ms. Rochelle, do you have a statement?"

She didn't want to answer questions or make statements. She couldn't do this—not without Mane. But all those people had come to welcome her. Surely she owed them something.

She must have looked like a terrified child—that's how she felt. But then she smiled. She imagined that Mane stood behind her. She imagined his calm and his laughter. She could do this.

"Thanks for your welcome," Jasmine said and the crowd hushed. "We appreciate your support. My crew and I are being treated like criminals, but we haven't done any damage to the forest we've lived in for four years. Ask EcoTech why they won't let us in. Who are we saving the forests for, if not for us?" Her father's words, she realized. The security man tugged at her but she stood fast. The questions came like bullets and she plucked one after another out of the air.

"One of your crew was killed and another remains in hospital. Do you feel responsible?"

"No. It was the Emerald Warriors who shot anyone they saw. They are responsible. My whole crew had the watts to say we *can* do this, we *will* do this, we are *right* to do this."

The crowd applauded.

"That's enough," the security man beside her said and pushed her to the top step to be carried down. Jasmine and her swarm descended into the crowd amid their chanting. "Let us in," to the beat of stomp, stomp, clap. As she pushed through the crowd, Jasmine realized that last question should have enraged her.

Jasmine sleep-walked through the arrest procedures and was thankful when she finally sat alone in a cell. Adrien was trying to get in to see her, lawyers were calling—all she wanted was some peace.

She paced the tiny room, despite her crutch. The more she thought of the legal battle to come, the worse she felt. The EC was moving quickly. They wanted a fast trial and the maximum sentence. For poaching, that meant at least two years. For resisting arrest and assault—even more time.

She kicked the wall and savored the resulting pain in her foot. They should never have been found. The interview with NewsPort was done a full day's walk from camp, even after Martinez promised a secret line. Escalente and his bodyguard and all their things had been thoroughly searched. Still her camp had been found.

She dropped onto the cot. She and her crew had lost everything because she'd insisted on getting the word out. Because somehow that was supposed to help. She couldn't remember why or how.

Jasmine lay down and tried to picture her shelf of seed pods. She went through them one by one. No doubt they had all been destroyed with the rest of the contents of her home when the warriors ransacked the camp.

She wanted very badly to listen for hours to Edan's music, not the angry songs, the sad ones. The ones that let you weep, believing it was the music making you cry.

∗ ∗ F I F T Y ∗ ∗

Miguel smiled as the vids once again showed Jasmine Rochelle taken to jail. He'd done it. The whole jungle crew was finally behind bars, *and* that delinquent they called their leader who had threatened him. He remembered her fierce anger and narrowed his eyes with satisfaction. He would see to it that when the courts passed sentence, Jasmine Rochelle's crew would be jailed for years.

∗　∗　∗　∗　∗

"Accusations made by Dr. Lamberin that the mold bearing VJX is a genetic aberration created by EcoTech have shaken the Applied Ecology community. If EcoTech cannot recreate ecosystems without aberrations, are our dreams of rebuilding the earth dead? Dr. Samantha Reynolds joins us to discuss her theories that it is indeed an impossible dream."

"That's right, impossible. We can never go back to the ecosystems that were. When the EC was founded, the techniques proposed by EcoTech were still being developed. Even now they are in their infancy, but through EcoTech's work we've been able to understand how complex recreating an ecosystem is. It is a noble dream—the natural world exactly the way it used to be. But is that really what's needed? The ecosystems of the past may be forever lost, but they can be replaced and if they are nurtured, they will be just as successful and beautiful as what we've lost."

* * * * *

"It was decided today that charges against the jungle crew would be heard in EC court, not the South American courts. The jungle crew is expected to plead guilty to charges of poaching. A trial would merely decide sentencing. The jungle crew could face years in jail or hundreds of thousands of dollars in fines depending on directions received by the EC court judge. A short investigation will assess the damage caused to the preserves and will be considered during sentencing.

"This being the most publicized case of poaching since Robin Hood, EcoTech and the EC are expected to press for maximum penalties."

* * * * *

Miguel looked up as his office door chimed and Simon entered. He was frowning. Finally the jungle crew had been caught and Simon was frowning.

He sat and looked at Miguel. His whole body carried his sadness. "Watenabe finished her report. EcoTech is responsible for everything," he said.

"What?"

"Green Splinter may have taken the credit, but they weren't the only ones involved. First of all, Owen Lamberin's murder, paid for by EcoTech. The investigation and trial, sabotaged by EcoTech. Adrien Lamberin's lab destroyed by Green Splinter paid by EcoTech. The investigation of Arri Deckert's death, sabotaged by EcoTech. Our security people tried to stop Edan Loffler's concert, but the gun dogs and the tech who locked the doors were hired by EcoTech."

"Who has seen this report?"

"Watanabe and her team. The two of us." Simon studied him for a moment. "What do we do with it?"

"Nothing. I need time to distance the EC from EcoTech. And we need to put the jungle crew in jail before this information is made public. I won't risk releasing anything that will make these criminals more sympathetic."

Simon shook his head. "Talk to your ministers. They'll tell you public opinion no longer supports keeping preserves closed indefinitely. They'll also tell you the idea of harvesting permits is gaining popularity." He leaned forward on the couch. "This could win us the election. Expose EcoTech. Announce we're considering harvesting permits. Let research teams investigate allegations of genetic aberrations. You've got a chance to bend here. Cut EcoTech loose."

"I won't give in to a gang of young hot-heads with no respect for the law. I won't base decisions on whoever the media is making into heroes this week."

"If you don't bend, the EC will break."

"No. Keep this out of circulation until after the election. Don't even let it out to the ministers."

"You've built a reputation on honesty. How can you think suppressing this will help you?"

"I won't risk it. If the EC dies, there will be no one to carry on our work."

A flicker on the vid screen caught Miguel's attention. In the clip, Ortega's men methodically shot out a camera.

"If only we'd been able to take care of Rochelle's camp quietly, this wouldn't have turned into such a media frenzy."

"If it weren't for their cameras, would those young people have survived Ortega's raid?"

Probably not, Miguel thought.

Simon turned grim. "If Dr. Lamberin hadn't arrived with med supplies, that blond fellow would have died."

"How did he know to bring medical supplies and a camera? How did he even know to go there?"

Simon looked him in the eye and seemed to roll an answer over in his mind a few times. "I didn't think you'd be able to stop Ortega. I thought you could use some help."

"You? This could ruin us!"

"Haven't I always said that openness is an honest man's best strategy? How many elections has that strategy won you?"

"After the elections. We'll admit everything then. Then we'll have a whole term in office to explain ourselves and fix this."

Simon was silent.

"We have to survive," Miguel insisted. "At any cost, the EC has to survive or we lose everything we've all worked so hard for."

Simon, who had been his constant support through years of fighting his own party, looked positively un-anchored then and Miguel paused. "Where is your loyalty?" he asked softly.

With pained eyes Simon answered, "To the people who trust us to do what's right."

Not to Miguel, not to the EC. To the people who voted them in. Not to Miguel, who had struggled for two terms to cleanse the party making countless enemies along the way. Not to Miguel, whose first thought was always to keep the EC going to realize the dream that began generations ago, to prove that the Declaration of Irretrievable loss was wrong.

As Simon left, Miguel's anger bloomed. How could Simon not see that the EC was the key, that if they were lost, everything would be lost to the entrepreneurs and history would merely repeat itself.

* * * * *

"Demands for Edan Loffler's Jungle Haven disc have outstripped supply again this week. Money from sales continues to support the foundation for the Repatriation of the Rain Forests. Much of the money is being spent on lawyers at this point. In addition, the Repatriation foundation has expanded

its office and has become a strong voice for allowing research and harvesting in the preserves.

"This is good news for the jungle crew. Any fines that result from sentencing would easily be paid for through the foundation. There is speculation that this is the reason that the EC lawyers are pushing for jail time for all the jungle crew and Dr. Lamberin."

* * * * *

"We couldn't get either of them to comment, but ever since Edan Loffler's concert for Jasmine Rochelle, we've been looking into their relationship. Apparently they met when she was still a music student. They were very close for several years. Jasmine reportedly visited Edan at the King Edward Hotel just months before his concert. We can only guess what Selina Maravitch thinks of all this. Perhaps the poor woman is too worried about her brother to think much about Edan at the moment."

* * * * *

"With an election coming within months, the opposition is delighted by the support being shown for Adrien Lamberin and Jasmine Rochelle. With us is opposition leader Inge Mueller."

"Thank you. As we've all had a chance to witness through the bravery of Selina and Kevin Maravitch, Lightning Madness is a terrible disease. Withholding the cure because it can only be harvested from a preserve is absurd.

"Preliminary studies have shown that Jasmine Rochelle and her crew were able to harvest enough at her first site to be economically viable yet caused very little damage. Unfortunately, the records that were kept were burned in the fire, but surveys of the area show barely perceptible evidence of harvesting. When we are elected, we will ensure that trial research and harvesting permits are issued to ensure a continued source of VJX and other medicines."

*   *   *   *   *

*   *   *   *   *

"On today's episode of Pillage or Progress we present a retrospective of the events leading up to the capture of the jungle crew. Interviews from as long ago as two years will be shown with commentary from—"

"EcoTech has once again refused to grant either research or harvesting permits, stating that the preserves are still not stable enough to support human activity . . . "

Miguel finally had Shelly on the line.

"There's something I have to ask you," he said, all pleasantries put aside.

"What is it?" Her eyes grew wary.

"What is EcoTech's time line for opening the preserves? Not the press release version. I want the truth."

She smiled slightly. "We've talked about this before. Humans aren't ready to—"

"When will we be ready?"

"When we can be sure the new forests are stable enough for—"

"Or maybe when you've eradicated all the aberrations?"

She frowned at him.

"Isn't that what EcoTech is doing?"

"We wouldn't have gotten the contracts if we weren't capable of—"

"I want the truth!"

"That's what I've been telling you!"

"If I find out you've been lying to me about this I will take EcoTech apart myself."

"That wouldn't be wise."

He stared at her.

"We made you," she said. "The EC would be nowhere if you didn't have the rainforests to show off."

"And if you've failed the purity imperative, we're both out of work. The entire coalition's mandate is to recreate the globe the way it was— sixty-five percent natural areas, just the way they were. If we can't do that, we've failed."

"EcoTech will make it work. Stop worrying."

She didn't sound consoling, she sounded angry. He had called to give her a chance to . . . what? Apologize? Tell him the truth? Admit there had been more between them than a mutual cause? He read no warmth in her at all. Then he smiled. "I don't like being used," he said, and cut the transmission.

Jasmine was the last to be processed and released. She hadn't seen the crew for two weeks. She hesitated at the door and tried to prepare for the disappointment she knew they all felt. It wouldn't surprise her if they were angry as well. After all, it was her doing that they'd been arrested.

Jasmine stepped through the doorway. The station lobby looked more like a bar with people milling around in excitement. Adrien and Indra spotted her first.

"Woohoo!" Indra cried and began a round of applause. Then Adrien was hugging her and everyone else took turns after him. The crowd parted so Mane could be wheeled up to her grinning from his wheelchair. "Hey, Doll." He held out his arms and she piled into his lap.

"I missed you," she sighed into his chest, then looked up. "I missed all of you."

Trina helped her up and smiled. "We missed you, too."

Dustin hovered at Mane's side.

"Ms. Rochelle."

Jasmine turned to be caught on camera by a vid reporter.

"What does the future hold for the jungle crew now?"

"Not much. We've lost everything."

"But," Adrien said standing stood beside her. "We've accomplished a lot. We've opened people's eyes to new possibilities. It's inevitable now that the preserves will open."

Jasmine let him go on while she surveyed the happy faces around her. Why were they smiling? Maybe it was just easier than being angry.

Jasmine looked out at the backyard filled with her crew. Chanel had brought her drums over and was trying to teach them some new rhythms.

When the crew were first released, they scattered. Only Dustin and Mane, who were orphans by choice, had no place to go so they'd come to the house with Jasmine.

While the lawyers argued and the Repatriation Foundation lobbied, the crew had drifted back together. Trina was the first to come—mostly she missed Mane. Adrien moved out to give Mane and Trina his room. Chanel invited him to her place. Levi and Indra eventually felt left out and decided it was warm enough to take up residence on the back porch and happily hung their hammocks there.

Jasmine rubbed at the moist patch of skin under her tracer bracelet. They each had one. It was the only way the police had to ensure the jungle crew stayed where they were told.

Dustin handed her a mug of coffee and she smiled her thanks. She'd miss them all. Like the buzz of cicadas and the happy creaking of frogs, these people had become part of her life and she planned to savor every day they spent together.

* * * * *

"Polls show that support for EC has almost fallen below re-election numbers for the first time since the party was formed. Now that there is a real possibility that the Restoration will be elected to the coalition, Inge Mueller continues to focus her campaign on how her party will handle the transition. Many questions are on the minds of voters. If the opposition takes over, do we stop building preserves? Does regeneration stall? Who will ensure we keep rebuilding? We asked Inge Mueller to recap the position of the Restoration party."

"While our party has been working hard over the past forty-five years to keep the EC accountable to the voters, we are now ready to give up that role and form the next coalition."

"The charter of Coalition Integration gives you eight years to fold all of the EC's function into the existing government. Is that a reasonable timeline?"

"We've had many years to plan the assimilation. It's a testament to the sacrifices made by past generations that we are now able to govern without having a portion of the government whose sole purpose is the protection of our Earth. We are mature enough as a people to balance our needs with those of preservation. This is a very exciting time."

* * * * *

"Kevin Maravitch fell into a coma today. The young man who's become a part of almost every household in the world is not expected to regain consciousness. We speak with his sister, Selina."

"I am so very grateful for all of your best wishes. Kevin agreed to the death watch because, though it was too late for him, he wanted to publicize the research into VJX and he did that with your help. Thank you."

* * * * *

"Once again Dr. Adrien Lamberin insisted that when he called Miguel Escalente a dead man, he was referring to the man's political career and he never intended it as a threat to do him physical harm. Here again is the vid clip from . . . "

* * * * *

"Just weeks before the election, the opposition has released the summary of a series of investigations done into wrongdoing by EcoTech. We are assured that the report contains evidence that EcoTech is behind a murder, widescale cover-ups and the shooting of Edan Loffler. Here with the details is NewsPort's Matt Scarpulla."

"Those who have read the report are outraged that an environmental reconstruction company, entrusted with restoring our earth and having the support of a major political power, could be responsible for these criminal acts. I'll let you, our audience, judge for yourselves.

"First, the murder of Owen Lamberin, also known as the 'Raker.' Originally thought to have been murdered by Green Splinter, evidence now shows . . . "

* * * * *

"Again, Miguel Escalente has made public appearances with his aide, Simon Bonsorte, nowhere in sight. Insiders speculate that Simon Bonsorte has taken medical leave. The president's aide could not be reached for comment.

"The president continues to deny that he had any knowledge of wrongdoing by EcoTech. He also denies any knowledge of the report that alleges EcoTech's involvement in many criminal acts."

* * * * *

"Tonight on *Pillage or Progress* we discuss genetic aberrations and ask several genetic engineers if EcoTech could have done anything to prevent them.

"First of all Dr. Lou Fergusen joins us from Genetic Development. Dr. Fergusen, your company, Green Patch, has been around for a long time and it's rumored you bid against EcoTech for the restoration contracts."

"Yes. Even at that time, those of us in the business thought it unlikely anyone could meet the purity imperative. EcoTech was secretive about their methods and we just couldn't see how it could be done. They were able to convince the EC to hire them and have done some extraordinary work."

"Can the purity imperative be met with today's technology?"

"We can come closer but there will always be a possibility of new species being produced."

"EcoTech had always seemed like the only body capable of doing ecological restructuring."

"They have very good public relations people. There are a number of groups who have worked on maintaining the heritage vaults who have similar expertise. If you are asking, are we dependant on EcoTech to continue restoration, no—certainly not."

"Several groups have come forward and advocated that all aberrations be eradicated. Do you agree?"

"Not at all. These species have become part of the ecosystem and to remove them may unbalance the system and cause the loss of other species. We need to study how these organisms fit in."

∗   ∗   ∗   ∗   ∗

Jasmine lay on a blanket in the yard as the evening sky turned yellow. Levi carefully painted over the pencil sketch he'd made of the nasturtiums. He was taking advantage of the long summer days to do portraits of every plant in the garden.

A listlessness had settled over everyone. A month now and the lawyers still fought over the damage assessments and sentencing dates.

"Sue Nakimata just called," Trina said from the porch.

The lawyer.

"So, do we have a new sentencing date?" Jasmine asked, sitting up.

"No," Trina came out to sit on the bench across from Jasmine. Dustin and Mane followed her and Indra listened from her hammock on the porch.

"This doesn't make sense," Mane remarked. "When we were arrested, the EC couldn't get a sentencing date set fast enough. If Escalente wants us in jail so much, why is he waiting?"

"Something has changed," Jasmine stated then looked up. "I don't know what,"

"He's afraid," Indra called from the porch and came to sit on the step. "He's on the edge of losing this election. All the polls show his loyalty to EcoTech and wanting to jail us is hurting him. Public opinion wants to give us the harvesting permits."

"So why not just fine us and be done with it?"

"He knows that won't hurt us. Edan's foundation is big enough now to swallow any fines the courts hand out."

"After the election." It dawned on Jasmine as she remembered the fury in Escalente's eyes. "He'll do it after the election. For now he can pretend to be considering the polls, considering letting us off with a fine. Then, once he's re-elected, he puts us in jail." She asked Indra, "The Restoration has a chance to win?"

Indra shrugged. "According to the polls, Inge Mueller has almost caught right up. If she wins, she plans to open the preserves and is willing to start granting limited research and harvesting permits," Indra reminded them.

"If she wins," Indra continued, "she'll instruct the courts to consider public opinion in their sentencing. If she wins, we could very well be fined and sent on our way."

If she wins—the possibility hung in the air between them. Then Mane's voice rumbled through the silence. "We can rebuild. Remember that spot in Brazil we almost chose last time?"

"Hey, Jasmine," Indra said, "is NewsPort still calling you every day?"

Jasmine nodded.

"Then what are we waiting for? Let's help Mueller win this thing."

NewsPort wanted to interview Jasmine about her relationship with Edan, about her past in the core. Don't be afraid to insist on your own agenda, Edan had told her. If they want you on their vid screens, they'll take whatever you're willing to give them. Jasmine smiled. Perhaps she hadn't been able to hurt Escalente in the jungle—she could hurt him now. She stood and shook off the lethargy that had settled around her like a heavy blanket.

"I'll call Adrien and Chanel," she said. "Let's plan our strategy so we can get out of this pile of concrete and back where we belong."

The crew smiled back at her.

They could rebuild, Mane had said, and she let herself believe it.

✴ ✴ F I F T Y - T H R E E ✴ ✴

Carla Watanabe watched her husband say goodbye to his favorite chairs.

"Daniel," she scolded, "you'll see them again in just a few weeks."

He smiled and hugged her.

"I'm sorry," she whispered.

"Stop saying that. You know I'm proud of you."

And he was as relieved as she was to be going someplace where Green Splinter and EcoTech couldn't find them. Even with the house guarded and surveillance for the kids, Green Splinter had found and threatened Becka and Josh at school.

She kept telling herself it had been worth it. Her investigations had exposed EcoTech's connection to a number of crimes. Considering who she was working for, it surprised her that it was Simon who insisted she and her investigation team be protected. He would see to it that no one in the EC would be able to find her and her family.

She'd expected she and her team would be the ones accused of taking her report to the Opposition. That was a loose end she wished she had time to investigate. Who would have had the access required to find her report?

"Mom, can I take my Blaster 3000?" Josh called from his room.

"No. It's too big. Only what fits in one suitcase."

"Aw, Frass!"

"Watch your mouth," Carla and Daniel said together.

"Sorry, Mom."

Becka sat on the couch watching news vids, not because they interested her but because it was her way of refusing to pack.

NewsPort was interviewing Jasmine again. This time it was about her requests for harvesting permits.

"What do your friends think of Jasmine Rochelle?" Carla asked.

Becka shrugged. "She's power of ten," she said as if it were obvious.

"Why?"

"She had the watts to do the right thing even when they killed her friend. She helped cure Lightning Madness. And everybody figures she and Edan are secretly deep spliced only Selina is too upset about Kevin to notice but that's why Edan is making all this money for her—for Jasmine, I mean."

"You know she's a criminal."

"Why do you keep calling her that? She's not a criminal. She's the one who's been hurt by criminals. They killed her father and she couldn't get any help finding out who did it. Then they killed her friend and nobody was caught. And after all that, she still found a cure for Lightning Madness."

"That was her brother. She just harvests it."

"Well, it doesn't matter. She's power of ten."

If Becka and her friends found out that Jasmine Rochelle might have killed Martin Yit in cold blood for killing her father, their admiration for her would only grow. Eventually Jasmine could be made to pay for taking the law into her own hands, but in order to get there it was guaranteed there would be several years of media frenzy and public sympathy for Jasmine for doing what the police and the justice system couldn't.

Once it became clear that Yit was paid to kill Owen Lamberin, Carla hadn't been able to find the time to find out who killed Yit. She had her suspicions but, compared to the work of gathering evidence on EcoTech and Green Splinter, accusing Jasmine Rochelle of avenging her father's death seemed trivial. So her report to Simon only showed one question unanswered—who killed Martin Yit? And that's the way it would stay.

It had been the right decision. She didn't want her daughter taking a murderer as a role model.

"Come on," Carla said. "Stop pouting and get packed."

"This is so unfair! I have to leave all my friends because of some stupid investigation you did."

Daniel came over. "That's enough. We've discussed this all week. We're leaving."

At that, Becka got up and stomped into her room.

"I'm sorry," Carla whispered again.

"Hey," Daniel kissed her. "She'll adjust—we all will." His hands remained clasped behind her waist. "So tell me again how big this new workshop of mine is going to be."

She smiled. "The whole basement, just for you."

Jasmine stood in the wings, listening to the rally. The energy of the crowd unnerved her. This wasn't just another interview between her and one reporter.

" . . . Mane Silverstar, Dr. Adrien Lamberin, and Jasmine Rochelle!" Inge Mueller shouted to the crowd, Jasmine's cue. A throng of people clapped and cheered.

Jasmine put a hand out on either side. Adrien, on her left, placed a hand in hers and Mane on her right, did the same. With Adrien's passion for the work on one side and Mane's steady strength on the other, how could she falter? They walked onto the stage hand in hand, into the noise of hundreds of people cheering. Jasmine had been told not to wait for quiet so she gave Adrien and Mane's hands one more squeeze and let them go to take the podium.

"Hello—" she said, taken aback by the sound of her own voice amplified through the huge space of the meeting hall. "Thanks for your support," she said and smiled unseeing into the crowd.

"Just a few generations ago, we almost died as a species. Not because of a natural disaster or some fluke of a disease. Two out of every three of us died over fifty years of famine and disease we created ourselves. It seemed as though we had become so big a burden, so big a disappointment, that Gaia simply shrugged most of us off."

None of what Jasmine was saying was new but the throng in front of her was silent.

"As a species we ravaged this planet and nearly destroyed ourselves. Countries refused to be the first to cut emissions, conserve forests, stop population growth. So, because we were narrow-minded and greedy, we created deserts in Africa and South America, the oceans ran out of fish, we lost New York, Miami and the Caribbean to rising oceans, we drowned all our reefs and the farmlands of the river deltas. Our atmosphere became depleted of the ozone that had protected us since we crawled from the ooze, our immune systems crashed from UVB exposure, retroviruses spread over the globe and our antibiotics no longer worked. Four billion people died over fifty years.

"Then we did something extraordinary, something wonderful. We started to fix things. And not just the simple things. World governments got together. A plan was developed that would demand sacrifices from everyone. Those who wanted to farm were given more land. Those who didn't, moved off theirs. People gave up land to build preserves and industry gave up billions in profits to rebuild factories with reduced emissions. A million people made way for EcoTech to begin their work. These are the actions of a mature people. A people ready to walk out of the cities, into our new world and say, this is my home. I belong here and I can live here without doing harm."

Jasmine was interrupted by applause and cheers. Edan had coached her on what to do if this happened. She waited a moment then continued. "That's all we are asking for. Not just for the jungle crew, but for everyone—the chance to live where we belong. Thank you."

Applause rushed at her again and she turned to see Mane gape at her for a moment before applauding too. Adrien, who had grown up hearing their father make speeches, simply applauded along with everyone else. Jasmine smiled and turned back to the audience as the now familiar stomp, stomp, clap, "let us in," began. She dearly wished she'd never have to do this again.

*   *   *   *   *

"Miguel Escalente made a dramatic shift in position regarding EcoTech today. He now alleges the reports of wrongdoing are true. His previous denials were made to ensure the investigators could be adequately protected from EcoTech reprisals. A man who won his last three elections on a platform of integrity now hopes to do the same again. The polls show it's working. Support for the EC is on the upswing.

"Inge Mueller continues to question the EC about the details of the report and when the findings were actually known by the president. She also questions why it was so easy for EcoTech to suppress the truth for so long.

"Many feel this has now become a battle between Escalente and Jasmine Rochelle. She and her jungle crew seem to be taking to the campaign trail, although their travel is severely limited by the conditions of their release. They are, after all, still awaiting sentencing."

★ ★ F I F T Y - F I V E ★ ★

Hey Trina," Dustin called from the study. "Jimmy wants to know if you've seen this blue-bird in breeding plumage."

"What time is it down there?" Trina untangled herself from Mane and got up from the couch. "Shouldn't he be in bed by now? His time zone is two hours later than us."

Jimmy was a member of the research team going over Trina's notes. Why was he studying data rather than watching election results like everyone else?

The vids showed Escalente congratulating his people on their efforts as he strolled through a crowd of his supporters. He'd launched a scathing attack on EcoTech for their involvement in illegal acts. EcoTech was still blaming Green Splinter for the worst of the allegations.

Escalente still maintained, though, that the preserves weren't ready for free human access.

He'd made no move to ask for sentencing for the jungle crew before the election, though the EC attorneys had tried to curtail Jasmine's political activities. The judge had been adamant in his insistence that the terms of release could not be changed. When he asked about their readiness for sentencing, the lawyers claimed they still had research to do to assess the damage the jungle crew had caused. That action made it even more clear that if the EC won tonight, Jasmine and her crew were in for years in jail.

The vid reports switched to Edan and the Repatriation Foundation party. As always, he was in his element in front of the cameras. Selina stood beside him, a distant smile all the exuberance she could manage. Jasmine smiled at Edan's cunning. Selina stood beside him as an example of the consequences of not allowing harvesting.

Maybe that was unfair. Could Selina be to Edan what Mane and Adrien were to her?

The door entry chimed and Adrien came in.

"Hope you don't want your house back," Indra called.

Chanel came up beside him and kissed him on the cheek. Adrien grinned. "I may not need it back."

"Hey, wait. I don't see any beer," Mane said. "They're empty-handed. Throw them out!"

"Hey," Adrien protested. "Who called Escalente a dead man?"

"Boo," the rest yelled. Dustin and Mane rose to do the honors when Adrien reached outside the door and pulled in two beer boxes. "Now can I come into my own home?"

Soon everyone was settled and watched as NewsPort announcers filled time until the results from Alaska came in. Finally, thirty minutes before the Alaskan votes were tallied, NewsPort began reporting the global results in painful detail.

District after district, block after block, the EC was being defeated. Not in every district and not by much, but by enough. Just the North American Block to report, where the campaign had been fought the hardest, where the EC typically had most of its support, where the deciding vote could still be cast.

With the votes in from Alaska, EC lost North America by two percent. EC had lost the world by five percent.

For a moment, everyone stared at the screen in silence. All of them understood that these weren't just election results—the world had been forever changed this moment.

The console in the study chimed and Dustin got up.

"Ha!" Indra said. "We did it!"

The spell of silence broken, everyone was suddenly up and hugging each other.

"It's Edan," Dustin called and Jasmine got up to talk to him.

"That looks like quite a party," she said as Edan grinned back at her surrounded by cheering supporters.

"Congratulations," he said. "Let's hope they get the sentencing over with now so you can go home."

"This could never have happened without you."

"All I ask is that I can come visit when you're set up again."

"No problem."

Before he could reply, someone dragged him laughing into the crowd.

"Where is she?" People were calling from the living room. Jasmine emerged only to be swarmed by the Neon Club gang and their friends. And before Jasmine could comprehend what was happening, Luminous Flux had set up in the backyard, more food appeared, and drinks were being handed out. Indra and Chanel gave her a few sly smiles. They had planned this.

"I am so glad we won," Sally said, unwrapping plates at the improvised buffet. "Otherwise I would have had to eat all this by myself."

Then the drumming started. At the jungle camp they had drummed to soothe body and spirit, but today the drums were for dancing. Jasmine was pulled in to dance and finally gave herself up to the celebration.

* * F I F T Y - S I X * *

Jasmine took the familiar path through the trees and the rest of the chopper passengers followed her. She and the jungle crew walked in silence while Jimmy breathlessly explained the research his team had done so far. His enthusiasm was greeted with kind grunts and Jasmine was relieved when he gave up and let them listen to the familiar forest. Rain still dripped from leaves and frogs had started their songs of celebration of the rain.

Jasmine shifted her pack. She hadn't been sure what to bring. She'd have to take an inventory of equipment that had been saved, then ask for replacement funds. The Restoration government had agreed to buy any equipment her crew needed for the next two years in exchange for the promise not to harvest recs. The jungle crew had also agreed to help with setting guidelines for harvesting permits using Trina's research and her reporting system.

A toucan cawed above her and Jasmine looked up to see him as he flew off between the leaves. There was no doubt that EcoTech had created a wonder here. She hoped it wouldn't be too much longer before a successor was appointed. EcoTech had been ordered to open their research for scrutiny so their work could continue even though EcoTech itself had been ordered broken up and its executive arrested.

Before they reached the boulder field that was the camp, they came across the new bunkhouse. Three more enthusiastic young researchers swarmed Jasmine and her crew. They were overflowing with news about their findings and questions about harvesting practices.

Trina and Mane answered some of their questions. One of the researchers asked Levi about the drum he carried. Dustin and Indra fidgeted—they wanted to get home.

"Let's go," Mane whistled.

He grinned at the puzzled looks from the researchers. "Secret whistle language," he explained.

"What did you say?"

"Can't tell you," Mane whispered. "It's a secret."

"Let's go," Dustin whistled back and the jungle crew started the walk through the boulders.

Jasmine forgot everyone else once she saw her home still in its tree. She hurried to reach the cable newly hung below it. Jimmy caught up to her as she gazed up. He handed her a harness and stopped her before she clipped on.

"Um . . . ," he said. "The warriors left a real mess up there. I hope you don't mind, we straightened up a bit."

She sighed. The Jungle Haven had suddenly become public property, no longer her secret. It would take some getting used to. She smiled at him. "No. I appreciate it. Thanks."

She climbed with the sequence of motions that had become as natural as walking.

Her home was tidy with a few things out of place. The screens were stitched where they'd been torn and some of her seed pods, though carefully placed back on her shelf, were broken. She took off her pack and rummaged in the bottom pocket. She untangled her t-shirt from the spines of her father's purple murex shell and placed it on the shelf. Someone had found her flute and tucked it into the corner. She picked it up and weighed it in her hand. Jasmine opened the door and looked into the green, listening. The frogs, content with their earlier exuberance, had ceased their chirping but birds called out and cicadas sang.

She brought the flute to her lips and answered.

With no walls to contain the sound, the forest took the notes in. The music she made belonged here. Jasmine sat crosslegged in the doorway of her home and played while the forest listened.